D0492560

# Awakening

# AWAKENING

## Stevie Davies

PARTHIAN

Parthian
The Old Surgery
Napier Street
Cardigan
SA43 1ED

www.parthianbooks.com

First published in 2013
© Stevie Davies 2013
All Rights Reserved

ISBN 978-1-908946-98-0

Cover by www.theundercard.co.uk
Typeset by Elaine Sharples
Printed and bound by Gomer Press, Llandysul, Wales

Published with the financial support of the Welsh
Books Council.

British Library Cataloguing in Publication Data

A cataloguing record for this book is available from the
British Library.

For dear Rosalie

ἀστέρων πάντων ὁ κάλλιστος

*Friends firm. Enemies alarmed. Devil angry.*
*Sinners saved. Christ exalted. Self not well.*

Charles Haddon Spurgeon, letter (late 1850s)

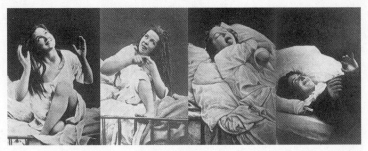

Female hysteric under hypnosis at Salpêtrière, 1876-80

*I am almost convinced (quite contrary to opinion I started*
*with [sic]) that species are not (it is like confessing a murder)*
*immutable.*

Charles Darwin, letter to Joseph Hooker (1844)

# Prelude

Anna sits back on her heels. The wilderness at the garden's end is her world, and the grassy mound's a world within this world. A tump in a field of tumps. Secret from Beatrice. A place where, if you look, you'll see things, both beautiful and terrible, that nobody else notices. Gorse and broom send up their heady scents and screen Anna from the house. From her pocket she extracts her finds from Old Sarum where the men were digging and they'd found, they informed Papa, a skeleton wearing leg-irons. A felon or a slave, or conversely a martyr or a heretic. His head had been cut off, and lay beside him. Anna did not see that. She saw the shackles, rusted and black. He may have died for Truth, said Papa. Or lies.

Once there was a cathedral at Sarum, Anna knew, but the monks weren't happy because the soldiers from the castle terrorised them. Also, it was draughty in the windy middle of Salisbury Plain and they liked their creature comforts, said Papa, being idol-worshipping Roman Catholics. So the cathedral moved to the banks of the Avon, where it stands now. Anna likes to think of a flying cathedral.

Anna's own finds are an amber bead and a leaf-shaped arrowhead. She levers up the turf of her mound and here's the earthenware pot she buried there. Opening it, Anna takes the amber bead and the leaf-shaped arrowhead, kisses them and places them in the pot with her other treasures, which she fingers one by one: the silver bell, the bone comb minus four teeth, the ox tooth, the green fragments of mosaic. You glean these bright fragments as you ramble, for the earth is planted with treasure like seeds: it works its way up to the chalky surface, the plough releases it or a badger's sett uncovers it. She pats the turf back into place over her hoard.

Everything settles down. Anna, cross-legged, observes the entanglement of life on her beautiful tump, the best in the world: insects flitting, plants quivering, ants clambering over grass blades. It's not still under the earth. Mama's in the earth, over the road in the churchyard, beneath another mound. There's life down there in the dead realm, a tumult of activity. Earthworms, beetles and moles enrich the soil, treasures light the blackness. And it's not still above the earth either. When you think all's quiet, there's violence. The blackbird died, Anna's blackbird with the yellow beak – the cat caught him, Anna's cat with the mint-green eyes. Maggots feasted on his gaping wound. Oh put that down, shrieked Beatrice; look what she's got hold of now – she's covered in filth; don't come near me; her brain is skewed; she's left-handed.

# Chapter 1

## 1860

Body to body in the one bed: this is how they've always slept, lying like spoons, back to front. Or face to face, mouths lax, sleep-drool slipping from the corners; opening eyes upon the other's opened eyes.

'The two of them ... like twins, so devoted to one another,' the Pentecost family agreed.

The motherless sisters would strive silently, wielding different weapons. Beatrice, who remembered a time before Anna, would start it. From the first she'd cherished the dream of sending the usurper back where she came from, especially once she heard it whispered that the baby had killed Mrs Pentecost. She banged Mama's murderer's forehead against a window clasp, accidentally on purpose, and the telltale sign remains to this day, a curved scar between Anna's eyebrows. Beatrice, wincing, smooths it with her fingertips. Other attacks have left further marks. Early in her life Anna mastered a knack of turning blue and toppling backwards, eyes wide but the pupils sliding upwards, mouth squared in a silent scream, not breathing.

'Speak to me, Annie!' Beatrice fell for it every time.

The innocent lamb was hushed and shushed, hauled high in the arms of love. The arms of their father the Baptist pastor were also in some sense the arms of Almighty God.

'I'm sure it was an accident,' everyone agreed. 'Dear Beatrice never tells lies. Do you, darling? Honest to a fault.'

And yet the closest tie Beatrice knows is to her younger sister. It's a bond of which she's all but unconscious when they're together but, sundered for more than a day, the root of their affection twinges; kinship all but biblical quickens. Ruth and Naomi, David and Jonathan. Don't leave me, Anna, never do, let us live and die together.

When Papa married for the second time, a half-brother Jocelyn killed a new mother; he was confided to the care of a wetnurse. As he grew, Joss attached himself to Nelly the maidservant. He'd trail her round like a puppy, a bunch of her woollen skirt in his fist. He'd be found kneeling at the sooty grate, his cherub face nearly as black as hers. Beatrice and Anna, recoiling from the soiled boy, had one another and saw no need to attach themselves to a dirty servant and a dirty servant's hanger-on, though Anna in course of time has grown close to the good-natured, unambitious Joss. Anna asks less of people.

Warily, the family recovered and Papa eventually married again.

The fire subsides in the grate; the last coals jostle; ashes flake down. Anna's pain shakes the walls of Sarum House at night and brings Beatrice's reprobate soul to heel.

She climbs into bed with Anna in the early hours: it's as homely and familiar as when they were youngsters dreaming one another's dreams, embroidering the dreams with Anna's stories in the morning. Anna wrote them down in tiny books fashioned from wallpaper scraps and flour bags. She sketched the characters they imagined, matchstick people running amok up and down the margins. But Anna did not write down the tales *correctly*: the matchstick folk would keep rebelling against their stories. They were never set to rights in a wholesome way at the end of their adventures, for the writer was nearly as unruly and anarchic as they were. They changed gender and acted inconsistently. In their lawless realm the wicked went unpunished, the good unrewarded. Beatrice was bitterly critical. She preferred order. Anna said it was not her fault. The daredevil people did what they liked and she couldn't control them.

Anna also kept a secret collection of papers sewn together and labelled in her minute writing 'Tump Book'. What's a tump? Beatrice asked. It's a little world, Anna said, smirking. My little world. Where is it then? Somewhere else, was all Anna would say. Beatrice pried into the mirror-written tump book a few times, deciphering it in the looking-glass. Very silly stuff and rather nasty: insects eating each other; flowers throttling other flowers. None of the creatures or plants did or said anything quaint.

In the twinkling of an eye the feuding, loving lasses have become twenty-eight and twenty-six. Both parents are in the earth, the mother long ago, Papa only last year. I feel as if God were dead, Anna confided, her face ashen; I can't feel Him there any more. At all. Papa seemed immortal. We all came and went but he was a rock. There's no sense in any of it. Although his God was so harsh, Papa was mild and tender.

Beatrice endlessly corrects Anna: there is sense, of course there is, but we can't yet discern it. Jocelyn does his best but cannot do for the young women what Papa did: stretch eagle wings over them and hold off Heaven and Hell. He was a roof against rain and against whatever else up there waits to fall on them, God Almighty's inscrutable justice louring down.

5

Beatrice, the heir, must take his place; hold out both arms, act father and mother. And now Anna threatens to die.

Inside the parental bed, Beatrice slips into Papa's dip, warms her cold hands between her legs before nestling at her sister's back, folding her petals round Anna's ribby thinness.

'Where does it hurt? Show me, darling.'

There are paroxysms of pain in Anna's belly; Beatrice's warm, calm fingers seek out the root of its billowing madness and soothe and bless it away. Perhaps in the past she has been tempted to welcome her sister's pain: it brought Anna to heel. Not now. Give me back my sister, on any terms. Slant rain drives against the pane. They snuggle close. As a child Anna would lisp, 'I hate doctorth, don't you, Beatrith?' Dr Quarles is an ass, up to now they've agreed on that, but he may have to be called in.

*

Eternal Wiltshire rain souses smocked labourers as they lead carthorses through the lane that bounds Beatrice Pentecost's two acres. They tip their hats, most of them. Some of the older men glare, the sullen remnant of the Swing riots thirty years back when rebels fired ricks, destroyed machines and their leaders went to the gallows or the colonies. The remnant bent to their lot, living in thatched cottages built of cob, rubbly chalk mixed with chaff, horsehair and water. When derelict, the cob houses vanish into the fields nearly as rapidly as they were built. The labourers and their multitudinous offspring have nothing to complain of, living to ripe ages on a diet of bread, bacon and skim milk, with apples and potatoes, and eggs perhaps on Sunday.

Chauntsey, with a population of two thousand, boasts seven Christian churches, as many as in Asia Minor at the turn of the century. Opposite the Baptist chapel stands the ancient parish church of St Osmund's, whose disdainful spire echoes the needle of Salisbury Cathedral on the skyline. There are Methodist and Congregationalist chapels – and the meeting house of the Plymouth Brethren. Though few in number, the Brethren make their presence felt: the elect pass by in black, as if in mourning for the crinolined persons mincing along the pavements. A mile out stands a Supralapsarian Chapel which teaches ... whatever does it teach? Beatrice is unsure. There are traces of atheism too in Chauntsey and a handful of freethinking or frankly atheistical tradesmen cluster around an infidel analytical chemist and an unfrocked minister who has taken what Papa called 'German Scissors' to the Scriptures.

Despite the busy activity of prayer meetings, Dorcas meetings and tea meetings, Beatrice senses that something has leaked away. Her childhood Jesus, who walked the potholed flint and chalk roads of Chauntsey barefoot, who jounced the children on his knee outside the school and carried his cross between the thatched houses of Butterfurlong Street, has withdrawn. Jesus was so real to the child that the hem of his garment had only just whisked away round the next corner. He might be that shepherd over there in Farmer Musselwhite's pastures, carrying a black lamb. The forge of Edwin Fribance, the blacksmith, was the site of his fiery glory. Now cabbage fields and pastures rolling to the grey horizon are spiritless matter, empty of his footprints.

Beatrice prays, down on her knees beside the bed where Anna lies in an early morning trance of light sleep under a dark hump of blankets, her hair caught up in a net. Long may my darling repose, enjoying dreams of health, Beatrice prays; bless her and pour out sunlight upon her. And may Sukey behave herself today and I be less tyrannical and vile-tempered when she irks me.

Only Joss can get Sukey to take her duties seriously, not

7

that the large, flabby fellow ever issues orders or reproaches. His genial presence is enough to encourage Sukey to use elbow-grease on the brass; at a wink from him she'll kneel to the scrubbing of the front steps, backside in the air, sleeves rolled up. What is Joss's secret? Whatever it is, Beatrice doesn't share his knack. Many a time she has come upon Sukey sprawled with her feet up, toasting herself at the kitchen range. Oh well, says Joss. We all need a rest. Her brother has always seemed happier in the stable or kitchen than amongst clerical guests. Beatrice has put it to Joss that this indulgence cannot be good for Sukey. It teaches her to live beyond her sphere. Spiritual equal she may be: who could dare to deny it? But social equal, of course not. A modern generation of girls turns up its nose at the distinctions God has set between higher and lower orders. And Sukey who, at her hiring, expressed a vague wish for salvation, remains profane.

I'll pray for her, Beatrice thinks. And be silent about her shortcomings. The liberties Sukey takes with Joss or that Joss takes with her: which?

And yet one cannot imagine harm in Joss. The word *eunuch* comes to mind and Beatrice recoils from it, ashamed. Is he, however, quite manly? There's something flaccid in him. Effeminate even. The way he prinks his moustaches. Beside Christian Ritter Joss looks plain feeble. But who wouldn't?

Up and bustling, Beatrice chivvies Sukey, but as usual does the lion's share of heavy work herself. She tries to be patient with the lumbering girl, who's moaning that she didn't get a good night's sleep at all; the blooming owl woke her up and besides her throat hurts. It really does. She can't swallow. Beatrice mixes her a warm drink of honey and camomile and hopes she'll feel better soon.

'And now shall we get on, Sukey?'

The Pentecosts organise hospitality on such a heroic scale that Sarum House might be a lodging house or mission station. Folk tramp in, folk traipse out, folk guzzle at their table, folk snore in the nine spare beds, turn and turn about, so that often there's no possibility of changing the sheets. Like it or lump it, Beatrice murmurs inwardly to ministers who arrive without warning, expecting hospitality. This is the house we were born in and will die in; Beatrice's inheritance. *My* house, *our* home, *your* hotel.

Pastor Elias and his man-of-all-work carry Anna downstairs: 'Where shall we put her?'

She's not a sack of potatoes, for goodness' sake! Settled on the sofa at the look-out window, Anna draws shallow breaths. In her gaze, rain and wind drive a blizzard of blossom over the garden. The fire mopes and spits as rain finds its way down the chimney. She's clutching a pile of papers tied with ribbon.

'Well, I'll be off then, ladies! Ta ta!'

'Already?'

Off prances the pastor over the road to tinkle on his piano before evening service. Dandruff speckles his dusty old jacket: Beatrice itches to spank it with a brush. If his wife were any kind of housewife, she'd spruce him up by turning the jacket for him outside in. The Welsh have no pride. The Eliases' house is a pigsty. The small Eliases are never still and rarely disciplined. Tom's and Jack's mop-heads bob at the window as they caper to their father's polkas. Little tykes. Whatever is wrong with the world has infiltrated God-fearing households. The older Elias children backchat not only the mother but the paterfamilias, whose word should be law. Doors slam; they snarl, feral. Old values are everywhere under siege. Chauntsey's poor no longer feign gratitude for their comparative good health but murmur and perhaps curse behind the backs of their betters. They snatch the charity from one's hands as if it were a right.

The knot that secures one's own contradictions is being unloosed: Beatrice, feeling this within herself, tries to grip the threads tight.

The back of Anna's head is infinitely touching, hair caught in a topknot, curls straying at the nape. Her dark, thick and usually glossy hair is greasy, really needs washing – and Beatrice will do that for her later. Anna will feel better then, her scalp will relax. Anna's neck is so thin. Like a swan's, Papa would say fondly: just look at her, our baby Annie will be the beauty of the family. Jealousy seared through Beatrice's veins. But now poor Anna is wasted. Perhaps because of my ill-wishing? The wonder is that such a stem can support the head at all. She wants Anna's luscious, headstrong beauty back.

Even if it does outshine her own mere handsomeness. For Beatrice will always enjoy the rank of elder sister, head of household. The suitors flock for her, not for Anna.

Hands on Anna's shoulders, Beatrice looks along Anna's eyeline. Between the chestnut and the end of the tumbledown stable and paddock, the Pentecosts' pet lambs adorably pass the Sabbath of their springtime. Do the creatures recognise they're orphans? Do they take their human benefactors for their mothers? Have they an inkling that we fatten them for the kill? For even pets must be translated into mutton. That's just how it is.

Sarum House and its grounds are what remain of generations of Pentecosts. Father and three mamas: their own, then Jocelyn's mother, sensible, devout Mary, and finally, surviving only long enough to present the family with a defective infant, the bride Father brought from his visit to Lübeck. Lore Ritter, two years Beatrice's junior, was a shock.

– Who is this pockmarked foreigner coming in my door claiming to be my new Mama?

Anna adored her. Beatrice tried and failed to ignore the fact that Lore made their father silly in his uxoriousness and melted her sister's heart. However did she do that? Beatrice disliked the tender way Papa and Lore climbed the stairs hand in hand at the end of the day. She recoiled from the likelihood that Sarum House would be taken over by a mob of children. And surely Papa would favour the males: without intending to, he would: only natural. Joss has somehow never quite counted. But Lore could well be breeding for twenty years. Instead she had time only to coach her stepdaughters in German – and Anna in the rudiments of Greek – and to sew ten lacy dresses and caps. Then she too was blown away like dandelion seed. Father and his three wives lie together in the turf of the chapel garden.

The only way Beatrice and Anna will be evicted from Sarum House is feet-first. As long as they possess these intimate spaces, these two acres, the great old trees and pasture, the Pentecost sisters will be secure. Papa, who left two houses and the farm with its tenant to Joss, willed the home and half his capital to his elder daughter. Safe, I am safe, she reminds herself.

The scullery's thick with steam; the window runs. Beatrice, a sweating scullion, heaves the wringer handle and grey water gushes from the sheets. She transfers the load to the mangle, extracting a pinch of jaded pleasure from completing the chore. No genteel woman has muscles like Beatrice's or hands roughened by labour: yet to her these signs are worthy of respect. An active and practical person, she's unashamed to work alongside the household's one servant. If only the servant worked half as hard as the mistress. But Beatrice was stung when Joss's friend Arthur Munby, visiting for the first time, took her for the maid-of-all-work and seemed confused when she drew herself up to her full height and introduced herself as Miss Pentecost.

Mr Munby is a gentleman and an enigma. What can Joss have in common with him? Just as bafflingly, how come Mr Munby condescends to know Joss? For he's an Anglican and a university man – and not a saved person. His wife Hannah only intensified the conundrum. Statuesque in her black London silks, mightily gloved and hatted and entirely silent, she sat to attention while the charming and loquacious Mr Munby held forth on the condition of the female working classes. Even in their gloves, Mrs Munby's hands were like shovels, Beatrice thought, still smarting. And her complexion! As if she'd been left out in wind and rain for a year. Mr Munby expatiated, with relish, on collier-lasses soot-black from head to foot; London dustwomen in their filth; crossing-sweepers and the flither-lasses of Filey who scale the cliffs to haul up baskets of bait – sitting on ledges way above the sea, shouting and whistling to the ships. A powerful woman in trousers in Wigan, he said, is considered less barbarous than a crinolined fine lady. Joss hung on his every word.

The rain dies down. Beatrice steps out to peg up sheets and, glancing back, sees with a qualm an invalid behind the pane. The heavy sheets billow like canvas sails. In the interior gloom, the sick woman, not yet twenty-seven, is a patch of shadow against the cushions. *Anyone* else she could bear to lose. But spare Anna. Beatrice offers the Almighty without a second thought Elias (not his wife though), Mrs Peck and all the Salisbury Pecks and Hatchers. Toss in the small Eliases. Beatrice can't abide children. They bring noise and care; they kill mothers. She's seen it too often to be intensely eager for marriage.

Don't think these things, don't. But how do you stop

yourself thinking the thing before it's thought? It's a test. Mortals cannot win. Calvinism is in the Pentecost blood. Jehovah decided everything aeons ago: when He created the world, He knew me in advance. He sees through me; His lidless eye penetrates to my heart and kidneys. You're open to the Almighty like a coroner's corpse on a slab, putrescent with sin. To Him we are like the jelly tadpoles wriggling round in the pond, transparent.

And Anna said the other night in a lull between pains, 'Have you ever thought, Beatrice, that if Almighty God were human, He'd be a criminal, we'd have to send Him to the penal colonies or … hang Him as a mass murderer? Look at the mess He's made.'

There's something that comes over Anna that makes one think the word *hysterical*. A word Beatrice prefers to *heretical*. If truth were known, they're both backsliding daughters. But only Anna seems to reckon this a virtue rather than a sin.

'Annie, we did execute him,' was all Beatrice said. She spoke in a tone of rueful triumph. 'We crucified our Saviour. You know we did. For loving us.'

'I didn't.'

'You did. The Jews killed him on behalf of the human race.'

'Not with my consent. I wasn't there. Anyway I meant God the Father, not the Son.'

'They are the same, dear. Think before you speak.'

'Well, that's what I do. Perhaps it's better not to think?'

'Or not to read all those unsettling books and journals.'

'Mirrie brings them. I like to discuss them with her.'

'When is Mrs Sala going off to the Continent?'

Anna's friends, Mr and Mrs Sala, are rich and cultured Unitarians from the north of England: to them Jesus Christ is not God, just a good man. Beatrice shudders at this atheistical rationalism. Something in Mrs Sala distresses one: a big-boned lady with a contralto voice, the light of a terrible, questioning sincerity in her pale eyes and no limit to her powers of speculation. She exerts an all but mesmeric influence over Anna. Indeed, it's not impossible that Mrs Sala practises the art of mesmerism. Her face plunges forward at you, staring with sympathetic intensity. Apparently there exists a phrenological cast of this formidable skull: Mrs Sala is said to have had her hair shaved off in order that its bumps could be measured.

Are all these bluestocking females such simpletons? Can they really imagine that the key to the human soul resides in the bumps of a skull?

First Lore, with her head-in-the-sky philosophical notions, and now Mrs Sala with her heresies have holed Anna like a colander full of doubts.

Hush now, hush: Father would have counselled that doubt is natural, a part of faith. And I was a better person, kinder, less caustic, Beatrice thinks, before I had to step into Papa's shoes. Tapering, buttoned, many-times-mended, Father's boots intimately remember him. His scent is trapped there, so their neighbour's labrador bitch told them, nose snuffling into leather innards. Beatrice is still giving away his belongings to the Baptist poor. Good folk with only one pair of boots apiece. Beatrice will not give to every pauper or pariah or Methodist or Irishman down on his luck. How would that further God's work? Following in Papa's footsteps, she dispenses charity, exhortations and pious tracts, reading aloud Mr Spurgeon's sermons to the sick, with a burning face because this is not easy for a woman to do. A husband would relieve her of such duties.

I have no likeness of you, Annie, Beatrice thinks with a shiver. We should have your photograph made or perhaps a miniature. Never mind the cost. There should be something left of your face. Beatrice kneels at the sofa, head on Anna's cushion; lavender fails to screen the unhealthy sourness on her sister's breath.

'Is Mr Elias still here?'

'No and good riddance. Wouldn't you think he could at least offer to pray with you or read to you, Annie?'

'Well, quite honestly, I can do without Elias reading to me. He gabbles.'

Anna's affliction is a stronghold from which she assails the values on which their house is built. Affliction should temper the soul, subduing us to acceptance of our lot. But I'm no better, Beatrice thinks. Principled master of herself though she likes to appear, hardly a day passes without internal rebellion; discontent races like port wine through her veins.

And part of it is that one gets a kind of nether view of the visiting clergy, in rather the way that Sukey is acquainted with the contents of the Pentecosts' chamber pots. Subtle and gentlemanly Mr Montagu is distinguished by his surprising avarice, for despite his wife's affluence, he's a skinflint. Mr Elias is known for his facile piano-tinkling; Mr Kyffin for nervous tics and the ginger tobacco stains on his teeth; Mr Anwyl for his capers and caprices. And all by their appetites; their guzzling enjoyment of Sarum House's hospitality.

Up to the elbows, Beatrice's hands are swallowed in the chilly insides of Tilly the Goose. Tilly's mate Hector continues to search for his mate in the pond, swimming in baffled circles. Sukey mixes herbs for stuffing, humming a folk tune, something pretty and profane. Beatrice wants to whistle and refrains. The side door opens: Mrs Elias – bonnetless, hair a muss of greying waves tumbling from its bun, a wide smile.

'You'll come tonight, won't you, dear, to the service?'

'Of course, Loveday. If Anna feels she can manage without me.'

'Oh Anna, dear heart, you can't miss this! You get so few treats, *cariad*.' Loveday Elias, seating herself beside the invalid's sofa, takes Anna's hand. Can't they push Anna across very gently in the wheeled chair? It's just over the road, no distance.

'Bowels,' mouths Beatrice. She shakes her head behind her sister's back. Anna's bowels close up or they loosen, without rhyme or reason. They are quite honestly hysterical bowels.

'Mr Elias warned me,' Anna sings out. 'Your countryman Mr Idris Jones of Bedwellty and his three ranting, canting sons! Oh no, please. I just couldn't bear it.'

Loveday takes no offence; never does. '*Dyna ni*. But you'll miss something *world-scale*. Mr Elias prevailed upon Mr Jones to preach tonight. The chapel will be packed out, if last week at Mickel Green is anything to go by. Weeping they were in the aisles. Stamping and crying out like Methodists. And indeed Wesleyans attended. Souls were touched.'

'*I'd* be weeping in the aisle if three youths with conkers on a string and round-button collars undertook to lecture me.'

'Well, *chwarae teg*, Anna, the Jones boys are all over seventeen and baptised,' Loveday says, smiling. She receives Anna's asperities with comfortable serenity. 'And – consider – they are getting older by the moment. I must admit that Mr Elias and I were sceptical. But, as I reminded him, how old was our Saviour when he lectured the elders in the Temple? Two years younger than Mr Spurgeon when he set out on his great work. And you know, we do need an Awakening! It's been too long.'

The Eliases often chat in Welsh together and with Mr Anwyl; there are so many Welshmen in Wiltshire that their homeland must be depopulated. Ministers in Wales don't have two pennies to rub together, so it's hardly surprising that sixty pounds a year in England is a magnet. Still, Beatrice is fond of Loveday; can't help warming to her scatterbrained sincerity. Loveday can be quiet at the heart of a storm: a storm she has herself awoken in the form of five little sinners she and Mr Elias have called into the world and permitted to thunder barefoot over the tilting wooden floors while the piano plays a mazurka and unused mops rattle in pails and they all fall into bed at night innocent of soap and water.

'Babes and sucklings have their place,' observes Anna. 'In cribs, on reins.'

*

And still you are smitten, Anna thinks, with the quivering expectation that Papa will appear up there in the high pulpit; he's been hiding, round some twist in time and space. The mind tricks itself into thinking that if it waits long enough, the beloved will come home and set us all to rights. He'll calm my tumults with a 'Peace, be still.' Oh, you are such a coward, Anna goads herself, forever on the run from reality. Your father will never come again. You'll never see his face on this side of the grave, any more than you'll see Lore's. Accept it. The arrow speeds into the soft tissue of her belly; it lodges there and the venom it carries spreads. Pain radiates, she'll faint, she perspires, she's unwholesome: what if Anna soils herself in front of the congregation? Better to make Jocelyn take her home while there's still time.

The chapel reeks of rotten lilies or is that Anna's own smell?

The doors close behind her. Folk crowd the back of the chapel and gallery. Leaving the wheeled chair at the door, Joss supports his invalid sister to her place. Seated between Beatrice and Loveday and catching her breath, Anna is penetrated by birdsong from beyond the arched pane of plain glass. A yellowhammer surely, calling 'A-little-bit-of-bread-and-no-cheese!' She'd like to be out there in the freedom of the open air. Joss with a small cough excuses himself and sidles off to sit amongst the servants. Anna hopes Beatrice will not notice and have her outing marred. She probably will. If there's something negative to see, Beatrice's eye will register it and darken. The dear fellow hasn't even been baptised: never quite got round to it.

Joss, who never came up to scratch, was an embarrassment to Papa but he always hoped for his son's improvement. Joss tried his best and Papa, a just and charitable man for all his hellfire Calvinist theology, acknowledged the boy's good heart while he lamented his flabby will. As for Anna, he indulged his younger daughter; denied her nothing and praised her even for ruffianly behaviour, which he called 'spirit'. Down on the dappled grass Jacob Pentecost cast himself to snort like a pony, bucking while she rode him under the apple trees, whipping his horsy flanks with a switch of twigs. His silver hair was a mane she pulled or stroked. Paternal displeasure, which Anna rarely felt, was the end of the world to her.

He was curiously innocent, she thinks. So interested in the antiquities at Sarum and Avebury, he never allowed questions of geological time to touch his faith. Never, that is, until the last couple of years. Every modern town, the suave Mr Montagu wryly remarked, should have a Village Darwin as its idiot, a Lesser Baboon, if one might so phrase it. He and Papa attended a lecture on the mutability of species by Mr Lee the analytical chemist. Mr Montagu was well pleased with his own contribution to the debate; he'd shot a whole quiverful of arrows into the soft belly of the undereducated fellow. They say one comes to look like one's dog or one's hobby horse: in the case of poor Mr Lee there's a speaking simian likeness, Mr Montagu observed.

Papa was quiet; he didn't throw stones. In our day, he muttered, shaking his head, it seems most naturalists are infidels. And poor Papa did not make a good death. But that was his illness.

Curious expectation murmurs round the chapel. The deacons, seated in a row facing the flock, swivel their heads as one. There's a sudden stillness, a rustle; the preacher slips through the partially open door – and is not Mr Idris Jones of Bedwellty but Mr Clifford of Praed Street in London.

Easy, all too easy, to fall headlong for a young man floating aloft in a shabby coat and the mercy of Christ Jesus in his eyes. So easy if you cared a fig about young men. Anna can't seem to melt feelings of friendship into passionate attraction to any of the eligible young ministers who visit Sarum House. She remains cool, comradely. John Clifford, introduced by Mr Elias in glowing terms, is a shy-looking soul in his twenties, pale hair beginning to recede. He looks as if he never ate cake; his face is all angles and points. At the same time he'd be glad to see you eating cake. Anna glances sidelong at Beatrice: she's taken up with the wrigglings of Tom and Jack Elias, who, managing to dodge their ma (and how willing Loveday is to be dodged), have nabbed a place at the outer end of the pew.

Yes, a lovely man, to whom Beatrice will surely be susceptible, having collected in her time reverend followers as a cat laps cream, turning from one to another in a whirl of bewilderment, finding that none could offer the thing (what is it?) that she craves. As one does crave, Anna thinks. Above them all towers Christian Ritter for whom – ever since she was a girl – Papa intended poor Beatrice.

What Anna herself desires, she cannot exactly fathom. An end to pain and physical weakness would be a start. Beyond that: some urgent scope denied to her. Action. Vocation. Rather than sitting here under the pastor's spell, Anna imagines *being* the pastor, up on a public stage, offering milk and honey from her lips, and bitter herbs too. To be the mouth rather than the ears.

Foot-binding. Mr Thoms brought home from the mission to China a pair of doll-sized slippers. He told of women mincing on crippled feet; they were considered more beautiful when deformed. Anna said, 'Oh yes, Mr Thoms, we have that here but less blatantly.' Beatrice kicked her under the table. Mr Thoms looked mildly puzzled. Silenced, Anna exploded inwardly: our tongues are bound, our brains are bound. Women are not fully awake; never have been. One is condemned for *thinking* – and thinking *aloud* – oh, heresy! This farce, this hypocrisy, this stupefaction! With every throb of rebellion, Anna finds transient relief from her spasms. The spirit of the Puritan Pentecosts scintillates in Anna's veins, hot as the brandy Mr Sala brings to relax her pain, as he puts it, and for a while it does.

Mirrie Sala, intellectual, freethinking, has somehow got away. Or rather she's got away with it. How did she do that? I don't believe I shall, Anna thinks. The worst thing about being ill is being unable to ride Spirit. Anna can hardly bear to meet her pony's melting eyes.

I'll get better. I'll ride again, she promises herself. I will write if I cannot speak.

She hears the word *slave* and pays attention. Mr Elias, introducing Mr Clifford, explains that Mr Idris Jones of Bedwellty, accompanied by the fruit of his loins, has taken ship for America. Not in search of lucre but in order to invite Mr Henry Ward Beecher to return to England. Beecher the anti-slavery preacher, charismatic, brilliant, stands at the centre of the tempest at present shaking that unhappy nation. America is moving inexorably, it seems, towards civil war. Baptists have a long and honourable record in the anti-slavery movement. Anna remembers Mr Knibb, their father's friend, describing the hell of slavery in Jamaica so that they all wept and, more to the point, opened their purses.

Mr Elias explains that a fortnight ago Idris Jones visited Aberystwyth, where a great Awakening has spread from America. There he dreamed of its advance into England. A Revival. The name of Mr Beecher occurred to him. Accordingly Mr Jones left for Boston on *The Petrel*.

'Shushie shushie, darling heart,' whispers Loveday to Jack, leaning across Anna and putting a finger to her lips. He takes no notice. Beatrice, red in the face, grips the squirmer's wrist and gives it a spiteful tug. Mouth squared up to bellow, Jack Elias takes her measure through his tears.

'You little *monster*,' Anna hears her sister whisper to the lad. 'Sit still.'

Jack's resistance collapses. He slumps into a doleful heap of boyhood; his nose runs green mucus; one tear trickles down his cheek. Tom hugs him up against his side and tickles his armpit with the free hand.

'Has he got earache, do you think?' Loveday whispers helplessly. 'He's usually such a cherub.'

Beatrice's face says: I consider you a true friend, Loveday Elias, but you're half an idiot when it comes to your children.

Loveday's face replies: I like you, Beatrice Pentecost; you are an excellent woman with sundry gifts, but maybe it will be wise for you and kinder to children not to marry.

Mr Clifford is on his feet. It's no secret, he tells them, the northern accent thick on his tongue, that from the age of eleven he was a factory worker in Beeston, a jacker-off in a lace factory earning half a crown a week. And there he learned much; it was a college education to him. Splicing the cotton off the bobbins to ensure an even thread, he worked sixteen hours a day, slave of the machines. His father was a Chartist and he too has been a Chartist.

And John Clifford would say that he worked there with Christ. Yes. Jesus Christ in person. 'You will perhaps wonder what I mean by that.'

He means his workfellows, the lace-makers, the suffering men, women and children of the northern factories, the so-called 'hands': and inasmuch as suffering was inflicted on these our Saviour's children, it was inflicted on our Saviour.

As the workmen came out on strike, so too did Jesus. What was Jesus but a workman with lathe and saw? A radical workman who wants for his workfellows homes, food and hospitals, decent working conditions and a fair wage: aye, and a vote for every man in this land. John Clifford has since studied law and moral philosophy, geology and palaeontology and oh so many ologies. At base he remains not just the jacker-off of lace but his mother's child. 'John,' Mrs Clifford said when he left for the Academy in Leicester to be trained for the ministry. 'Find out the teaching of Jesus, make yourself sure of that, then stick to it no matter what may come.'

'How simple,' Mr Clifford says. 'And how profound. Her voice still rings in my ears. The mother is the first educator of and minister to the child. In her gentleness, her humility, her grasp of the great simple Truth.'

Simple Truth in the person of Jack Emanuel Elias is chiefly under the pew, entangling himself with the Pentecost sisters' skirts as he tunnels through to the aisle. His plump, bonny face pops up open-mouthed, bobs down again; he rams his way past his dreamy mother and is gone.

Mr Clifford looks down at an urchin pointing up. 'Come on then, my little fellow. Up you come.'

Jack, hoisted up by the deacons, slips his right arm round the minister's neck and sucks the thumb of the left.

'We'll change our text to the Book of Isaiah: *And a little child shall lead them.*'

Soft laughter pulses round the congregation; Mr Elias swivels round to his wife with a happy shrug; curly-haired Mr Anwyl also turns, winks, raises an eyebrow and grins at Beatrice, who pretends not to see him. Anna observes a small smile twitch the side of her sister's mouth.

Restored to earth, Jack kneels on his father's lap and seems to reflect on recent events, his flight to the kindly skies and his safe descent. He worms a finger into his father's beard; half his face peeps round at the congregation. Hooking his chin over Mr Elias's shoulder, Jack topples into sleep.

Mr Clifford's social radicalism flings open the chapel's doors and windows. He raises the roof like an awning to allow Anna, all of them, to peer for miles. The congregation's eyes speed west towards the dying iron mines of Merthyr and its stinking slums, north to the sweat shops of Manchester, Leeds, Huddersfield and Sheffield. They see as angels see – but without the comforting immunity of angels.

Yes, this is the real thing, thinks Anna, this slaughterhouse of civilisation, policed by the birds of prey who rule us. These are the matters dearest Lore opened to Anna: the political meanings of the feeding of the five thousand, how the first should be last and the last first, how the leper begging at the gates would be fed and clothed and set in judgment over the rich. 'Revolution will come, Annie, for God will no longer tolerate these injustices.' Her father had been wounded on the barricades in Dresden in 1848, not so much fighting for democracy as standing for it, weaponless, a quietist. A quiet firebrand was Lore too, if such a thing can be said to exist. How I loved her, thinks Anna, and the pain shakes her again.

If Beatrice were to marry Lore's cousin, a mirror of their stepmother would be forever haunting Anna. But it would be an authoritarian likeness. Christian's a man who knows what he wants and will have it and can wait until he does. He terrifies Anna. It's not that she dislikes him: he forces you to like him. His great height gives him a ridiculous advantage – and even tall Anna is dwarfed. There's a glamour about him. Papa meant Christian for Beatrice. And now? Christian's letters arrive weekly from America. Anna does not ask to read them, for her sister's puzzled blush tells the story.

Mr Clifford makes other preachers, even the sublime Mr Spurgeon, look trite: they're constantly referring you to the umbilicus of your own salvation. She forgets her belly's gripings and clasps John Clifford's wing as he soars. Anna sees it all now.

Half the congregation reaches its hands deep into its pockets; the remainder, uneasy about the political message, values the spiritual fare at sixpence.

Introduced to Mr Clifford at the door, Anna squeezes his hand. If she were to fall in love with one of these flying visitors, she thinks, it must be one like this, for sincerity and righteous anger are lovable beyond beauty. I want to tell you about Lore, she thinks. I want to tell you that Lore taught me all this before I heard it anywhere else. And yet what in Lore was theory and idealism, Mr Clifford has lived. Anna suffers herself to be lowered into the wheeled chair and to drop below the general regard. Mr Clifford chats with her sister and Mr Anwyl; he will gladly sup with them, he says, and perhaps, if they have a bed for the night? The weak light greys around them, lending an ashy pallor to skin and hair, as though all those lingering on the chapel path between the grave mounds were ageing by the moment.

# Chapter 2

It's like having a rat in the cellar. You make sallies with a broom and lay down poison. You invoke the rat-catcher. But what woman can be thinking of her depravity and its antidote every minute of every day? Too busy. Meanwhile vermin down there stealthily multiply into a colony. Beatrice hides her streaks of lust and greed, cruelty and envy as best she might – but your sister sees through every veil with eyes of caustic.

Beatrice wishes daily for some outlet for her own turbulent spirit but submits to her lot: catching the blood from the slaughtered sow, testing the rennin in junket and blackleading the fireplace. Feeding her guests.

Knives clink on plates; the company consumes scraps for dinner, odds and ends of cold pork, potato, egg. 'Delicious! Miss Pentecost is a miracle worker!' Conversation flows. Beatrice, who was faintly alarmed at the preacher's political message, finds herself liking the unpretentious Mr Clifford and sees the point of him. He has a modest and kindly manner, a knack of listening, which, Heaven knows, not all the ministers she feeds at Sarum House share.

Mr Anwyl has not come.

A visitor of Mr Clifford's stature can hardly be expected to lie in another guest's sheets as the lesser ministerial fry cheerfully do. Where is Sukey when wanted? Would Joss help turn the heavy mattress? But Jocelyn and Mr Elias are moving off towards the smoking room to fill it with fug and spittle. Sukey follows with the pipes: Joss makes way for her, his arm stretched out like a courtier's, a soft smile on his rosy face. Tobacco rots the moral being, it's a scientific fact. Most male visitors reek of smoke. What's worse, their offspring also sin in this way. The race is degenerating. Beardless Charlie Kyffin from Salisbury, a virtual child, not only out-smokes them all but consumes beer under his father's very nose, and nothing is said.

Mr Anwyl will hardly come now.

John Clifford is explaining why, in his view, the church should not fear the new Biblical criticism that has come from Germany like a high wind. The more accurately we understand the Gospels, the clearer our faith will be. Why fear radicalism when our Jesus was himself a radical? Anna is expressing fervent agreement: but what does she know? Has she read Strauss and Feuerbach? Of course she hasn't. She takes the Salas' word for it.

The latch clinks. Beatrice's spirit bounds up and races to the magnet of Will; she wraps her arms around his neck and he lifts her clean off the ground, whirls her round, skirts belling out, and oh, be careful! we'll fall, put me down, you ruffian!

Of course she does nothing of the sort. Miss Pentecost sits still, feigning deafness. The hairs stand up on her neck; a tremor shakes her body. He's wiping his feet, exchanging a few pleasant words with Sukey, who loves him, they all love him, though most have reservations: somehow, pastor or no pastor,

'Mr Anwyl is Miss Pentecost's inferior.' That's what they say. He's the son of a labourer in some unpronounceable part of west Wales and it *tells*, every time he opens his mouth. His words tumble over themselves and stammer to a halt. Granted, our Saviour was the foster-child of a Nazareth carpenter but there the comparison ends. Sloppy manners, singsong accent – impoverished, overfamiliar, playful. Lackadaisical in his pastoral duties, by Papa's standards, Mr Anwyl is unequal in status, education and property. Yes, yes, we know all that.

None of this need matter. No, it's something to do with the honey of his attraction that rouses Beatrice as though she'd been bee-stung. It hurts.

Everything hurts. Her body rings with pleasurable pain. She withstands the throb at Will's approach, welcoming him coolly. She avoids his gaze. What choice has her suitor but to retaliate by seating himself beside Anna; bending his head to the younger sister, speaking with quiet attentiveness? There's a burst of laughter, as if he and Anna were sharing a private joke and the joke is Beatrice.

Anna's languid body on the sofa looks sensuous, sinuous – and though she has lost weight, the drapery of her dress expresses the curve of breast and hip. But Anna is not paying full attention to Mr Anwyl's blandishments, Beatrice sees: she has darkly lustrous eyes only for Mr Clifford, who is married already. And in any case, how could Anna marry? Her health would never stand it.

*

Mr Clifford has departed after his three-night stay. Anna's upstairs resting. And Will arrives, the Peck girls in tow and callow Mr Crisp, suitor to one or the other. They've walked across the fields from Fighelbourn, whipping one another with long grasses, playing tag and gathering spring flowers, which Will presents with a bow and a grin. The Peck girls chirrup and whirl, to show off the gowns their aunt has made from imperfect stock: the mass of the skirts trailing behind them, the front being flattened, and this, claims Rose, is how skirts are worn in *Paris* now, a big bustle at the back, see?

'My oh my. So that's what the Roman Catholics are wearing in Paris,' Beatrice manages not to say. The Whore of Babylon dresses flaunt the rumps of the two plump, sturdy girls; the hems have picked up cuckoo spit and burrs and must be sponged down. Beatrice takes in her hands the wilted celandines, periwinkles and buttercups Mr Anwyl and his fashionable disciples have brought.

Let's play parlour games! Yes, do let's!

Blowing the feather. First find the feather. Beatrice lets go of constraint. She races Will around the arbour walks. Here we are! Will snatches the feather; holds it out of reach and laughs into her face as she jumps. He puts the feather to his lips; tickles hers with it. Beatrice's mouth opens slightly, lax. Something in the depths of her secret body seems to be tickled too. Sensations ripple there. The cellar-rats all run together this way and that. Her gut knots. Beatrice steps back.

'Do you give in?'

No, Beatrice will never give in. She twists away and hurries back indoors.

Chairs are positioned in a circle. Sukey angles to join in the fun and has to be frozen out. Mr Anwyl explains the rules. No touching the feather; keep it in the air at all times. Once the feather touches you, you're out, starting … now.

John Crisp leaps up and puffs for all he's worth, whisking the feather out of reach of all players and chasing it round the room; he is sternly disqualified and ordered out of the circle. Players may lean. Like this. Mr Anwyl leans over Rose and sends the feather twirling up: Rose shoots Mr Crisp a look

28

that says: You're an inferior article, you booby, and I'm only putting up with you until someone better comes along, so there.

'What about "Poor Pussy"?'

The chairs are pushed back. The pastor of Fighelbourn Baptist Chapel falls on his knees within the ring, raises his paws and meows. Uproar. He slinks round the circle, glancing up at each young lady with predatory eyes. Rose Peck places her hand on his springy brown hair and buries it in his curls. Pussy smiles and snarls and pads on. As Will angles his furry head sidelong at Beatrice, querying, tantalising, she has a sense of someone ... over there, looking on, repelled.

The parlour door stands ajar: Beatrice rises. There's no one outside. She turns, leans on the door and views the scene through Papa's eyes. What have I let into my father's house? Behind Papa looms the man Papa intended – destined – for her. Mr Ritter, who so possessed her childhood as to deprive her of it; who fashioned her like a clay pot. She views the young folk – and Beatrice's no longer quite young self – romping like hectic children behind their parents' backs. The pastor of Fighelbourn crawls on hands and knees mewing 'Poor Pussy!' to gales of laughter.

Lily is down. Down where she belongs, the cat. Down in her bestiality, not too strong a word, it's in us all, the fangs and the claws and the heat that call the tom to the molly. They rub up against you in oestrus, they lick their genitals, yowl for days on end, they present their rears and spray out malodorous fluid. That's how they are, they are beasts, they cannot help it. He made them so and blessed them.

But we are the tarnished children of the Redeemer; immortal souls immersed in carnal slime. Beatrice is ashamed, and crimson. And the fact is that, if Miss Pentecost so much as clapped her hands, they'd all have to disperse: she holds the authority. Then what does she do but rush back into the delirium? Harmless pleasure is not forbidden, after all.

*

Anna frees her hair from its coils and lets it flop into waves all down her back. She shudders her nightgown on, uses the chamber pot, creeps into bed. Lying listlessly, she listens in to the muffled hilarity downstairs. She sips wine and teaspoonfuls of the jelly Mrs Quarles sent round. As long as Mrs Q does not send her husband, everyone is happy. The pain gradually abates, allowing her to think of Lore. Her dear face, scarred as it was by *variola*, held such an expression of benign intelligence that you thought of her as handsome. Well, Beatrice didn't, but I did. And this despite some spinal deformity that was also the result of smallpox. It thrust her head forward, giving Lore a questing look. Had she lived into old age, she'd have been a hunchback.

The painter of the miniature portrait in Anna's locket erased the pockmarks by painting Lore in black silhouette. There's something ghostly about the image: Anna looks at it rarely but likes to feel the warmed oval of metal against her throat.

Beatrice was jealous of Papa's adoration of Lore. She resented the closeness that grew up between Anna and their stepmother. When Papa took Beatrice off to London on church business, the two girls left behind explored their world together, making a collection of fossils and flints – scallops and ammonites and especially the egg-like flint fossils that country people call 'shepherds' crowns' or 'fairy loaves', pocketing them for luck and keeping them on their windowsills, to guard against evil spirits. Millions of years ago they were sea urchins, Lore said, creeping along the sea bottom – imagine that! And they died and their insides were eaten and the shells filled with silica jelly – and the sea became land and farmers ploughed them out of the chalk. It's abject nonsense to say that the world is only six thousand years old, Lore maintained: which simpleton believes that nowadays?

Picking up one of these little beauties from her bedside cabinet, Anna coddles it between her palms. She traces with her fingertip the stippling of the five-pointed star. They fell from heaven, say the old folk. No, they wandered the earth like us, she and Lore believed; they had their moment too.

Anna recorded all their expeditions. She removes the diary from her chest. A life without pen and paper would be unthinkable. Pen and paper immortalise your witness. How sad for the children of the labouring poor that, even if they're literate, they lack pencils or paper and must shape their letters with their fingers in sand trays, shake the sand and start again. Anna leafs through the diary to 1856, that golden year.

*Lore & I to Stone Henge. We picnicked on a fallen bluestone & rambled round discussing the origins of the place. A temple, said I. To the Goddess, said Lore. We found nine chalk balls & part of a green glass jar, L believes the jar is Roman – some Ancient Romans came on an outing and ate their picnic here too, she said, & left their litter. It lay there for one thousand six hundred years or so whereupon those explorers of genius Anna & Lore Pentecost came along with their picnic and cleared up after them. Next week we plan to visit Old Sarum where Papa & I saw the skeleton unearthed.*

*Dined with the Montagus. Lore spoke not a word. If her inner voice doesn't prompt her, she keeps her mouth shut. Papa tried to coax her – thinks she's bashful. Mrs Kyffin knows better, she considers L uncouth, she heard us whistling in the wilderness – said nothing, her eyebrows said it all. Papa asked me if I thought L might be a trifle deaf & did it run in the family? Christian is also someone who cannot always hear what is said to him.*

*Lulworth Cove. First time I have <u>ever</u> seen the sea! A sheet of shiningness.*

*Today we bathed. Biting cold – delicious, delirious! Lore was flung by her father into the Baltic at the age of 5. She is practically fearless. Today she showed me how to float, holding her hand under the small of my back. The women's bathing huts are sequestered & we can swim without concern. I wrote Beatrice & Joss a long letter & L wrote to Papa. My darling Lore is to have a baby – it is an intimate matter, L says, something a woman keeps to herself until she is ready to share it. She will tell Papa when we return. I woke in the night & placed my hand on her belly.*

Anna can only bear to read snatches. Her diary is a calf-bound book of Mama's in a brown paper jacket, stuffed with smaller leaves. Tiny, secret writing, cryptic as she can make it, writing backwards often: you can do this if you're left-handed. Think of the calf that made the binding, Lore would say; the creature many years ago butchered and eaten. Everything in this world makes me sad, she'd say, the next one will be better. It's a topic Anna sometimes muses on and can get no further than wondering at the slaughter the Almighty has unleashed on the Creation. She has qualms about questioning His ways but when it comes over her to do so, she's helpless to resist. Lore, who questioned everything and still believed, held it lawful to do so. The patriarch Jacob wrestled with an angel for three days, and threw him. If Jacob, why not Lore and Anna Pentecost?

You, Almighty Father, have <u>killed</u> my Mama and Mary and Lore and Papa, Anna challenges Him. I cannot accept that I shall never see their faces again in this world. Perhaps in another world but that scarcely comforts me. If You, God, had been <u>my</u> child, I could never have treated You in the way you treat us and just leave us to it.

She has wrestled the Almighty to the floor many times – just by thinking, by following a logical train of thought. How can it be helped? If her sister could see how far down the road to heresy Anna has wandered, she'd be appalled. There'd be retaliation. Mirrie and Baines Sala have crossed over: doubt has led to agnosticism. Humanism, Mirrie prefers to call it, emphasising her positive faith. She respects and honours the faith of others, though she cannot share it. Anna shrinks from taking that step: she could never be at home in a godless universe.

Opening her portable desk on her knee, Anna brings out her best pen; unscrews the cap on the inkwell and dips the nib. Her minute and costive script is meant to have a printed effect.

*Watching the dragonfly on the pond I was amazed at the sapphire & emerald colours of his wings, his darting speed. They land on the water & I recall noticing as a child – face almost on a level – that they actually stand on a skin or film or membrane. Their feet dimple this membrane. A membrane of water? Dr Browne, who we had before Quarles, once allowed us to look at a water drop thro his microscope – what wonder! It comes over me how I'd love to travel the world – or just visit St Ives with the Salas – but if that cannot be done, a woman could curl up as Hamlet said in a nutshell & call herself queen of infinite space.*

Laughter bursts from the parlour; there's a crash, a stampede – and everyone's streaming out into the garden. Anna looks down on the crowns of their heads as they bubble out of the door and float towards the summer house. Mr Crisp strolls in their wake and one sees he is in a sulk. Such a boor, snatching kisses from anything female with his little moist mouth – and you're hardly better, Gwilym Anwyl, she thinks as the fresh-faced minister of Fighelbourn chases the squealing

Peck girls into the arbour. Beatrice steps out in their wake, to stand, arms folded, in a dream, her head in its intricate maze of plaits a swirling blur through the pane's irregularity.

How burdened Beatrice is. Go on, my love, join in, Anna silently urges her sister: don't stand apart feeling lost. Just play. They hide their love from themselves and one another in frequent squabbles. She remembers Papa's final delirium; he cursed them all roundly and called for his wife. Which wife did he mean? Anna quailed before the rush of filth from his tongue. Where had such gutter language come from? It was as if Pastor Pentecost had stored up the leavings of all the sinners tended through his long and virtuous life. Cramming it in some cellar of the mind, he'd shut the door on that heaving mass of ordure, until it rushed out on his dying day, to spatter the stricken hearers.

His daughters flinched, shawls tight across their bosoms, cleaving together. Dr Quarles administered a terrific dose of laudanum and after that no one could rouse Jacob Pentecost in the mortal world.

Papa taught that our whole life is a preparation for those sacred moments of deathbed trial and witness. A dying Christian's a telescope trained on the other world. Looking over the wall, he sends back a message. Mr Montagu, penning the obituary, drew a decent veil over that harrowing scene. The *illness* spoke, he privately reassured Jacob Pentecost's seared children, not our beloved; the illness was the last throw of our envious Adversary.

But did that not mean that Papa would go to Hell? The final breaths are ultimate moments of truth. But perhaps in the closing second of his life, faith flickered in Papa: and, if so, God, whose grace welcomes the least sign from repentant sinners, would take Jacob Pentecost to his breast. Imagine arriving in Heaven and finding ... no Papa there waiting.

Mama, saved but bereft – or, worse, indifferent. Or Mama absent: not, for inconceivable reasons, one of the chosen. I've never seen her, Anna thinks: my birth killed her. I must see her. Only one tenth of the elect is female, according to some Calvinists. How could Heaven be Heaven without those one had loved? It would be an affront to all that's divine and human. 'Send me to Hell to comfort Papa and Mama,' Anna would plead. She has no wish to join the heartless angels who'd consented to be immunised to suffering and exempt from sympathy, just to save their skins.

God comes apart in one's hands like an old toy, when one searches into Him. The child stares aghast, holding the mess together.

The young folk are back indoors and playing hide-and-seek, to judge from the sounds. Half-dozing, Anna remembers that there's something in the wilderness she must find. Something spellbindingly lovely. Very secret. What was it? No idea.

Anna awakens to find Mr Anwyl in the room with his finger at his lips and his ear to the door. His sleeves are rolled up to the elbows; his collar's open. Will has beautiful arms and hands, slender and supple. He's always gesturing, so expressively. But his mouth is facile and perhaps the hands too. She thinks: Will's body would be all but hairless, epicene. Soft as a girl's. And perhaps Beattie will marry him after all, rather than Christian. Will's nakedness will lie in their father's sheets with Beatrice's pale body where Anna lies now, for she'll cede this chamber, with its spacious windows, green view and gracious morning light.

Feet thunder past the door towards the attic. Doors bang. Silence.

'Annie *fach*,' he whispers. 'May I come and sit with you for a little?'

The tiny see-through creatures on the surface of the pond

change shape to slip in every direction in search of their minuscule diet. Anna with her sharp eyesight has watched them pour themselves round their prey. Which victim could see them coming or fear these creatures' motives when they slide so subtly where the spirit takes them, absorbing whatever comes near? And before you know what's happening, you're being digested in the acids of the predator's stomach. You're being transformed into his substance. Mr Anwyl can hardly be in a room without sliding close to you. How would he be then as a brother-in-law? Sarum House would sing and dance on its foundations. How long before it rocked and trembled? For Beatrice would be as exacting as Will would be capricious. But fun and games there'd be in abundance.

And, Anna thinks, he'd be a blithely wonderful father. She can see him now, on all fours, playing horses and riders with a row of white-petticoated, tempestuous toddlers.

Gwilym Anwyl stands to gain Sarum House. Lock, stock and barrel. In possessing Beatrice, he'd enter into all our property. Me he would not possess, Anna thinks, but I would diminish to a poor relation. She understands why Beatrice holds off and plays one suitor against another.

'May I ask you something, Anna?'

She knows what's coming. He wants to pour out his heart. Wants to know about Christian and when this paragon is expected to visit and what was in the long letter he saw in Beatrice's hand last week. And oh, how much more eligible is the principled Christian Ritter than Mr Gwilym Anwyl. A *manly* Christian hero of the overseas cause. But who could advise Beatrice to accept Christian? He'd either kill her by taking her to foreign parts or arouse the anguish of long absences. And in all events, he'd flatten her.

'Ask away. I may not give you an answer, of course. Now, sit you down here.' She pats the bed. 'If we're going to whisper.'

36

'I always feel I can talk to you and you'll give me honest answers – a pinch of mustard or pepper if I need it.' And, yes, he knows he needs seasoning, in every sense, he acknowledges: too often he catches an unflattering reflection of himself in Anna's eyes. 'The thing is, I care about you very much. Do you mind my saying that, Anna?' His warm palm covers her hand; she withdraws it but his follows. 'As a friend. A sister. I came late to God and to my calling, comparatively. Not like the great Mr Spurgeon.'

'You're absolutely nothing like Mr Spurgeon, Will. I can't disagree with you there.'

'Exactly,' he agrees, chagrined.

And I like you the better for it, Anna refrains from saying, rescuing her hand and hiding it beneath the covers. That moon-faced boy-preacher is a star in the Baptist firmament. Spurgeon is characterised by endless loquacity, towering over the massed thousands of hero-worshippers at Exeter Hall and the Surrey Gardens Musical Hall. She can't stand it, not least because on the one occasion she attended, she wasn't only tempted: she fell. Anna melted with the rest, wept, cried *Selah!* and worshipped God's creature in his lofty pulpit. Never before had she been in the presence of such a multitude; the roaring murmur of mortals seeking salvation or entertainment, one was unsure which. Anna abandoned herself to the torrent of this man's tongue. Mesmerised by his operatic voice, her body relaxed. She might have been asleep but when she came round, she felt ... what was the word, *handled.*

Wasn't it like worshipping a loin of pork? That's how he struck her then, so well fed that his very being has congealed to a mass of marbled fat. No sense to the spell he wove with his angel's voice.

'What did you think of Mr Clifford's sermon, Anna? I saw

you were moved. Your eyes – they are, you know – what's the English word? – unearthly.'

'Don't *do* that, Will.'

'Don't do what?'

'Flatter. It's ugly and demeaning. And you're so bad at it. It might sound better in Welsh but – unearthly eyes! It's *un*flattering actually. You do it to everyone. How is the way you are with women and young girls fair to my sister?'

What she thinks is that Will *prostitutes* himself. It's a word considered sullying to a woman's lips. But the Pentecosts support the mission to the London prostitutes. These women are paupers, rejects, human souls preyed upon by vile males, respectable by day, beasts by night, the conduits of disease to their women and children. Will, you *prostitute* yourself, she thinks, staring silently as he flushes.

'If *she* would accept me, can you seriously imagine I'd ever look twice at another woman? Do you, Anna?' He has never acted dishonourably to a woman, Will swears. That's unfair. Well, perhaps he is a little susceptible. But he loves Beatrice with all his heart; he's devoted to Anna too, and if Beatrice won't have him, he has a good mind to ask their brother for Anna's hand, only he's sure she'd laugh at him.

'Yes, I would.' Oh very nice, to be always tagging along, second best. A bit like you, Mr Anwyl, never the first object of choice.

'You would prefer someone like Mr Clifford.'

'I admired Mr Clifford for more than his blue eyes.'

'I dreamed of you all in blue, Anna,' he says. 'Do you want to hear it?'

'No. But I'm sure you're going to tell me.'

'Forget-me-not blue. You wouldn't look at me; I was beneath you; you stared straight past me.'

'Sorry to have been so rude, Will, in *your* dream.'

They both laugh.

'What do you think it means though, Anna?'

'Blue is the colour of Heaven, Will, isn't it? – the Madonna's colour. So I am guessing you see me as a nun.'

The Madonna is a Papist idol; he wouldn't dream of the Madonna, he insists.

'Anyway,' she says gently. 'It was just a dream. Dreams can be very nonsensical.'

In her heart Anna recognises it as a dream of death, her death. He has seen his dead sister-in-law-to-be laid out for her funeral.

# Chapter 3

Two pairs of eyes, startled by the creak of the door, swivel towards Beatrice like a single guilty creature. Anna's face is unnaturally flushed; the bedclothes are rumpled. What's *he* doing on *her* bed? Beatrice speaks no word. Her black heart bounces into her throat. She stands with her back against the door, sucking in breath to let him past, face averted.

Her underlip recalls the sensation of the feather; her breast remembers brushing against this light man in the garden before the day curdled. Night after night I break my own sleep to join you, Anna, to soothe your suffering. Praying till my knees hurt. And I'm repaid by this ... what should one call it, canoodling? There is something that periodically unhinges Anna, hysterical damage to her integrity. It is situated in her disordered womb. But it's also a modern infection brought into their house by the Salas of Toplady. Beatrice has sometimes vowed to herself: they shall enter my house over my dead body. But what authority can she assert over a twenty-six-year-old sister?

Dr Quarles will have to be brought in, to apply a drastic,

dramatic remedy: a blister, a bleed, an enema, all of which Anna loathes and denounces as unscientific.

*

'So, Beatrice,' says Loveday Elias, seating her guests in the chilly parlour, which smells of damp, in front of a fire she's only just lit, of green, wet wood. 'What's all this a little birdie has been telling me – about you and a certain young man?'

'I wish you'd quash tattle like that as soon as you hear it, Loveday. It's odious. Please.'

Mrs Montagu, ever practical, offers to draw the fire. She holds a newspaper over it; the flame roars up behind the page, which is open at a picture of a slave sale in New Orleans, the males dressed in dandy suits and the females in calico, wearing forced smiles. A smoking hole appears; flame licks and Mrs Montagu scrambles the paper into a ball. 'Now then, there we are!' The fire is soon in a state to receive coals and be left.

What do Mr Anwyl's follies matter compared with the horror of godless cruelty practised in the slaving states of America? Providence, placing the newspaper in Mrs Montagu's hands, brings this to Beatrice's attention. She bows her head as her friends lament the heinous doings in the New World. How will it end? O my beloved Lord who shed his blood for my freedom, make me more patient and charitable. I could hardly be less so than I am now. Christian Ritter is on an anti-slavery speaking tour in the northern states: perhaps he's mentioned in the burnt newspaper. For God is not pointing in the direction of the deceitful Welshman, that much is clear. And if – when – Herr Ritter returns to ask for Beatrice's hand again, she ought to accept him. Mr Jones of Bedwellty with his sons is also in America and between them they may bring home that prince of liberation pastors, Henry Ward Beecher.

A fog of damp taints the air. The velvet mantel cloth, once purple, is so stained with moisture that its ball-fringe is discoloured into a kind of green. At least they have a fire. Leaning forward to the flames, Beatrice warms first her palms, then the backs of her hands; receives the steady heat on her face. She'd like to fall on her knees this very minute like a Methodist, and pray, racked with sobs, for a contrite heart.

Two small Eliases sidle in at the door. 'Look, Ma!' says Jack, holding up his hand. 'Fish scales!'

'Oh, you naughty Jack, whatever will your papa say?' Loveday feebly protests. 'What have I said about playing in the larder? Come here, let me wipe your hands.'

'No! They're *my* fish scales!'

'I hope you put the trout back where you found it! Did he?' Mrs Elias asks seven-year-old Patience, who shrugs.

'Come on then, young man,' Beatrice says. You see, I can be tender to children. 'You may sit on my knee, Jack, but only once Mama has wiped your hands and face.'

Jack shakes his head, tongue out, eyes shut, and won't stop. Instead, Patience dumps herself in Beatrice's lap. Slipping her arms round the child's middle, Beatrice feels the warm, strong body through the woollen dress. The body heat seems to declare the untamed willpower of the child, something almost indecent in a girl. There has always been a problem regarding the children of the saved: brought up within the fold, how can they be awoken to conversion? How can they be shocked from torpor or bored rebellion?

Jack shrieks, dives across and fights to get onto Beatrice's loaded lap. Mrs Montagu swoops the lad up and, advising Loveday to go and check on the whereabouts and condition of the trout he's been playing with, clamps the boy to herself. Jack gives in; sucks his grimy thumb. Patience swipes at her brother with her foot.

'Oh no you don't!' Beatrice slaps the child's knee. Not hard.
'You hit me, you – spinster!'

'I tapped your knee, Patience. Behave yourself if you wish
to sit with me, miss.'

'I don't want to sit with you, *Miss*.' Patience wriggles down.
'This is what your sour old face looks like.' She inserts fingers
in the corners of her mouth and pulls, wags her head, rolls
her eyes. 'Anyway my papa says you're an old maid past your
prime. He says you're thirty-seven if you're a day. *Miss*.'
Having dealt this blow, Patience whisks out of the door.

'Well!' Mrs Montagu whispers over the sleeping tot's head.
'What can one say? Sheer anarchy. 1848 all over again. Did
I tell you about poor dear Mr Kyffin?'

The minister of Florian Street Baptist Chapel in Salisbury
is a favourite with them all. But turmoil's brewing in his
chapel: accusations are being tossed around by Mr Prynne
and his family, of perfidy and embezzlement and 'something
worse'.

Beatrice, ruminating on her wrongs, cannot bring herself to
be interested. Thirty-seven? Of course I don't look thirty-
seven. I do look thirty-seven. My bloom has faded. Will floods
her head with longing and disappointment. He'll never
change. Admit it. I'll cut him out of my heart, Beatrice
decides, that's all there is for it; he is a tumour. Some of my
heart will adhere to the malignancy and that must be cut out
too, and the rest will bleed, but it will not go on forever.
There's no chloroform for the hurt Will's dealt me.

I shall be an old maid. I'll lose what looks I have. I'll be
alone. Anna will die. And leave me. Or she'll marry Will and
take him from me. How could you bear to do that, Annie?
Beatrice's eyes brim. But how could one be cross with Anna
or wish to deny her anything she desires? The love between
sisters is paramount. Mr Anwyl, you'll marry Anna over my

dead body. Not only because it would kill me to see the two of you climb the stairs at night but because you'd divide me from my sister.

They are called in to dinner. Jack, flushed and grizzling, is put to bed. Patience has gone fishing with Henry.

'Really, I shouldn't let her go off with the boys but what can you do?' asks Loveday. A faint smile licks her pouchy face. 'Are your girls so wilful, Mrs Montagu?'

'No *indeed*. My daughters are brought up strictly but kindly.'

Loveday, deaf to implied rebuke, placidly claims, 'Oh, so are mine. Now do sit you down, dears, I shan't be a moment.'

A fur of dust coats the dining room in a disgraceful mantle. The bold forefinger of Patience E. Elias has signed her name in dust on the mirror above the fire.

'Squalor,' whispers Mrs Montagu. 'Never seen the like. Is this how they do things in Wales? I suppose it is. Ah, here is luncheon.'

A very good luncheon, as it turns out. The Elias family is beloved, for all its defects of housekeeping; gifts of meat, fish, cakes and puddings pour in, chiefly in a cooked form Loveday can't ruin.

'What were you saying about dear Mr Kyffin?'

It seems that Florian Street is heading for a hurricane – either a secession or an expulsion. What it's all about is unclear. Mr Kyffin has been accused of sowing heretical doctrines but what's behind that? Something heinous is hinted at by Mr Prynne the shoemaker, a powerful deacon who has gathered a party against their pastor. Financial mismanagement, embezzling? An indelicacy? Suspicion of antinomianism – of placing the elect above the law? Mrs Montagu will get to the bottom of it, never fear: whatever it is, she will never believe ill of Mr Kyffin. Unless she's forced to.

Loveday appears anxious; her forkful of apple pie pauses on its way to her mouth. She's clearly pondering whether this might this happen to the Eliases? What if their flock decided to expel them? Why are Christ's people so quarrelsome?

Beatrice imagines the robe of Christ torn to shreds by his followers, dragging their wounded Saviour this way and that between them. Factious Baptists pierce his naked side with disputes as vicious as they are petty and self-righteous. They'll all quarrel one another out of Heaven, to the rejoicing of Papists and Congregationalists alike. But indeed all sects are at one another's throats. Cromwell and Milton had their hour. Then came the great Awakenings of the eighteenth century. What now? It's a new Dark Age. Beatrice's grandparents in their youth surely had the best of it. Baptisms in the Severn and the Avon; Russell Pentecost and William Carey taking ship together to convert Bengal.

The wave crested decades ago; now it falls and we fall with it. Only the nature of our punishment remains to be revealed.

*

Anna is harrowed and fascinated to read back fragments of her diary, as though a demon's pen had prised open the gaps in God's logic, inserting a steel nib, twisting it this way and that to see how much further the loophole can be forced. If – when – I die and the book gets into Beatrice's hands, she'll be shocked to her marrow. *Heathen, atheist.* But I am neither, Anna thinks. I am the girl who was baptised by Papa in the Avon. First the elder sister, then the younger, all in white, stepped down into the living water; they plunged beneath it, emerging as one day they will rise from the dead, as newborn creatures.

Grey weather: swans glided upstream, leading a fleet of cygnets. The willows, bent like penitents, trailed their boughs in the river. It seemed a day of dark mirrorings, the

45

congregation casting its drowned shadow in the water. A breathless drama of eternal moment was enacted. On the bank the sisters waited, arms round one another's waists, while their father addressed the flock.

Anna, the less pious, had first undergone conversion. Tree-climber, fishergirl, she had run wild from her earliest days. Then her chest budded; her hips rounded. Her own dirt began to obsess her – the grime beneath her fingernails; fur growing in her armpits and a triangle of pubic curls in the smelly place between her legs; the monthly flux of shameful blood and its attendant cramps. Fits of wild tears shook her: how could the Lord Jesus look compassionately on such a beast of the field? Beatrice remained flat as a pancake, innocent of monthly blood. Anna's fingers slid on slick flesh; earthquakes shook her little world as Beatrice slept – Beatrice the clean daughter, always spruce and neat. Anna slid into guilty dreams and unfocused animal desire.

One morning in her abjection, having done the unmentionable thing, lying panting, Anna opened her eyes and saw a hand.

Jesus's hand reached from above, through the bedroom ceiling. A spider on its high web trembled. The dawn chorus paused. It was a workman's hand, strong and able and callused, honest earth beneath the nails. First it pointed and Anna shrank, guiltily afraid. Then it turned and opened. The soiled girl reached up to the gentle carpenter. Simple as that.

'I think I have seen my Lord,' she told her family at breakfast.

Rejoicing. Kisses. Anna's testimony was received with attentive rapture. Then Beatrice piped up, 'Oh, so have I!' She hadn't, as far as Anna knew, but she understood why her sister couldn't be left behind and accepted what Papa said, that conversion can take place without commotion: it can come as a still, small voice, heard in the quiet of the night. They broke bread together as a family renewed.

'I was worse than Nebuchadnezzar,' Anna exclaimed proudly. 'On all fours. Now I am whiter than white.'

And Beatrice cried out, not to be outdone, 'Yes, and I was worse than King Ahab who walked in the sins of Jeroboam and was eaten by dogs.'

They were to be washed in the blood of the Lamb. Pussy willows and catkins powdered the boughs with pollen. The Avon and the Jordan were one river.

Beatrice, followed by Anna, descended into the scalding cold; they placed themselves in their father's hands, receiving his smile as their last earthly experience. As they rose, gasping, the same smile welcomed them into a new world and led them towards the shore. A rapture of rooks burst in the air high above; about them echoed the *halleluias* and *selahs* of the brothers and sisters of the church. Navvies trudging to the main road stopped to stare, sandwich boxes slung round their necks. Upriver a fisherman and his spaniel looked on. The universe wheeled around the Pentecost sisters, who for that white immortal moment stood at the hub of all being. Many hands hauled them to the bank. The very river-dirt on their soles seemed sacred as they took turns kneeling to wash one another's feet by a leaping fire.

Not even your wedding day could compare with the once-in-a-lifetime drama of baptism.

Faith remains but it has twisted under the impact of bereavements and a too eager intelligence. 'You are like me, *liebe* Anna,' said Lore. '*Konsequent*. What you think, you must also live. You can do no other.' But Anna on the verge of rebellion sees a high wall and balks at it. 'Prove me wrong, oh my loving Lord, prove me wrong,' she begs. Part of her scampers away like vermin cowering in the diminishing circle of corn with other pitiful prey while His reapers' scythes close in. Whimpering, whispering: 'I take it all back.'

Knocking at the door: Miriam and Baines Sala. Sukey trudges upstairs to see if Anna's well enough to receive them. Yes, and it's better they come now while her sister's out: Beatrice's mood since the Anwyl incident has been none too indulgent.

A face of glorious gentleness framed in a plain straw bonnet peers round the door. 'May I come in? Baines is with me – is that all right? Are you sure? We've brought you food for the soul. And some port wine, rather good; I thought I'd better sample it myself beforehand! How are you, *dearest* Anna?'

Mirrie removes her bonnet and cloak and hangs them on the back of her chair. Her husband hands over the packages of books Anna is greedy for, plus three bottles of port.

'George Eliot's *Adam Bede*. Something by Mill. *The* book by Mr Darwin. *Freedom Seeks Her* – a novel, let us know what you think of that. All hot off the press or at least warm. Here you are, love. There'll be something there to interest you.'

'Thank you, thank you. I don't generally read novels.' Beatrice, whose eye is everywhere, will not condone the reading of fiction, for what is it but fakery from beginning to end? But ... how old am I anyway? Anna asks herself. When we're a pair of codgers, shall I still be writing my diary under the bedclothes and pretending to read the pieties of Jeremy Taylor?

'Well, no, but keep them anyway, you never know. If one of *us* were to write a work of fiction, I'm sure you'd read that, wouldn't you?'

'Of course I would, Baines, of course. But have you?'

'Aha, who knows?'

'When you were a child, did you write behind your hand – like this?' Miriam cups her hand round an imaginary pen.

Anna thinks of candle flames that have to be protected against the draught. 'Oh yes, I still do – well, I keep a journal. A mess, rather. It's all in bits.'

'Writing is really quite magical, don't you find? A magic circle. Stories will fly away, if you let them out too soon – like a dream when you tell it. Anyway, a novel might be nonsense, who knows? Who wants to be found out and made a fool of or worse?'

'Nothing of yours is ever nonsense. Neither of you could ever be laughed at,' Anna says devoutly.

'Dear. I for one am sniggered at in the street every day for my droopy dress and my innocence of stays. But – Anna – one of these books is rather special. Please accept it with our love.'

Anna opens *Freedom Seeks Her* at the title page. The author is unknown to her, but then she has not kept up with modern literature: Calder North. Mirrie has written in her elegant hand: 'To Anna Pentecost, from her friends B. and M. Sala'.

'Well, there you are. I hope you like it. But anyway, never mind about that, how are you?'

'Better for seeing you, of course. And thank you, dear Mirrie, for these treasures. I go on much as before.'

'Can't we take you away to the seaside? You'd be so revived.' Mirrie sits down beside her, squeezing Anna's hand. 'A change is what you need. I get so mouldy if I don't get a change of air and scene.'

'Not possible, Mirrie,' Anna says simply. Mirrie has no idea of limitations. Having broken bounds herself, she seems to think anyone can do the same. 'Tell me about yourself.'

'Well, we had Barbara staying – such a lively time. Madame Bodichon, that is. And Miss Parkes. But now our friends have left for London – I waved their train off. We were like a hive of intellectual bees and we moped when they'd gone, didn't we, Baines? Baines never minds being the sole male.'

'Why would I?'

'Goodness me, plenty of men would simply hate it. Or like it for the wrong reasons.'

'If Mirrie's happy, I'm generally happy. Simple as that. Anyway, I had plenty to keep me busy.'

And something in the way the two incline to one another with that private, intimate look gives the clue. That's it! Baines has published a novel! Surely. There's always something mysterious about the Salas, a reticence that says, You don't quite know us – yet.

'Anyway, we're off to St Ives carrying zoological specimen jars. And then by paddle steamer from Ilfracombe to Tenby – where our geological hammers may come out.'

Anna can imagine her short-sighted friend bending over rock pools at high tide, skirts tucked up, *that* look on her face, intense, ardent. Baines has in mind to study and photograph a creature called *Anthea cereus*: a polyp. According to the great naturalist, Mr Gosse, she fixes herself on one foot and waves her tentacles like vicious little serpents. And Anthea has this secret hair, which, when touched, sends a harpoon full of poison to its prey, inflicting paralysis. And then her tentacles deliver the morsel to her mouth. Ingenious.

'But there's an odd twist. Parasite fish that are *immune* to the poison thrive all round Anthea and dine on what she misses. How do you think they have become immune?'

'But is Anthea an animal or a plant?' asks Anna.

'Good question. An animal that looks planty. She's mostly a stomach. And not really a she, of course! Some are male, some female, some hermaphroditic. We so wish you could come.'

*Male and female created He them*, Anna thinks. But everything, seen up close with or without a microscope turns out to be more slippery than you assumed. And she likes that, it piques her curiosity. It's as if her mind retains a particle of Lore which lights up in controversy. She yearns to join the Salas' expedition. To find some answers. Answers that might open further questions, as they should.

'Perhaps I could come, though?' Anna suggests, sitting up, arms round her knees, wondering how many changes of train it would take. The sea air would be reviving. It would be like going to Lulworth with Lore. 'Where will you be staying?'

'Come! Please! Come – we can't take no for an answer.'

'You know very well that is out of the question,' says Beatrice in the doorway. She has returned from the Eliases without being noticed. 'Mrs Sala – Mr Sala – excuse me for interrupting – but Anna's health is delicate. She needs to lead a very quiet and sedate and retired life. And I'm sure you will understand that too much excitement … it simply will not do. You will worsen her condition.'

*

'You are quite mistaken, Miss Pentecost. The last thing I should *ever* wish to do is to disturb a person's *faith*,' says Miriam Sala in her honeyed voice, before Beatrice all but thrusts them out of the door by walking straight at them. Mrs Sala's horse-face seems to have elongated in dismay. And what Beatrice reads in it is, I am going to be caught out and exposed. 'Faith I reverence, I do most truly. Faith is always a good.' Mrs Sala backs away over the threshold of the door, stumbles and has to be steadied by her husband. 'And truth – but I do not worship cold reason. For what is truth but truth of *feeling*? But, forgive me, your sister knows her own *mind*. She is no child or weakling to be protected against me – or against herself. Anna is an original.'

How dare this scarecrow presume to tell Beatrice Pentecost what her younger sister is or is not? And to dictate her sloppy, slipshod, slippery notions of 'truth'? Beatrice's eye, sweeping

Anna's sickchamber, has observed a new pile of heretical books, as well as three bottles of expensive port wine. And what if Anna goes to her Maker with that literary filth polluting her soul? All the good seed choked with tares?

'It's enough to *make* Anna ill,' the woman calls back. 'The constraint.'

The husband has the grace to shush her; his hand hovers under Mrs Sala's elbow, to coax her away. He stands no higher than Anna; a good inch lower than his wife, who in the wild disarray of her outdoor clothing takes up space enough for two. There's not half a man in Mr Sala, less manliness than in Mr Anwyl, which is saying a great deal. Few manly men are left. They're all away on missions to Jamaica and India like Mr Knibb, Mr Phillippo and Mr Wenger. They are in America with Herr Ritter. Baines Sala is an effeminate who hides behind his wife's petticoats.

Beatrice can tell by Mrs Sala's shaking shoulders that she is sobbing. Good: weep. And learn. Keep away; you are unwelcome in my house.

'When are you leaving for Switzerland, Mrs Sala?' Beatrice flings after her.

The woman halts in her tracks; turns; hesitates; retraces her steps. 'Miss Pentecost,' she says. Tears stand in her eyes; she has the grace to look ashamed. 'Pray forgive me. I have alarmed you and spoken impetuously – rudely – under your roof. I was once an iconoclast, looking for idols to destroy. But, believe me, I am not so now. I reverence the human Jesus and read the Gospels every day. I have a cast of Thorwaldsen's figure of Christ on my work desk. Your sister, she is … very special, very dear. I listen to her more than I speak, believe me.'

She holds out a grey-gloved hand.

Beatrice bows her head so as to appear not to see it. 'I don't think you realise how much Anna stands to lose. I don't mean her earthly life, Mrs Sala. I mean eternal life.'

There's no answer to this and Mrs Sala can summon none, for – statue or no statue – she is a secularist who denies Providence and the Divinity of Christ. Beatrice watches the pair walking away up the street, leaning inwards, arm in arm – the husband half-supporting the wife, the wren and the cuckoo. Perhaps that's the last she'll see of them.

When Beatrice looks in on Anna, her sister appears shrivelled. She droops against the pillows, dark circles under her swollen eyes, lids closed. But, oh no, you're not asleep. As a child, Beatrice would jump on Anna and dig her in the ribs when she took this passive strategy. The assault rarely worked. The submerged spirit dived deeper. Now the averted face says, dumbly, These people are my friends, my guests. And you I have not invited into my bedroom. Beatrice stands over her sister. What has Anna done with the books? They must be destroyed. Beatrice crouches: nothing but the chamber pot under the bed. *In* the bed perhaps? Beatrice's heart is pounding, her face is hot.

Experience teaches that Anna can keep up this brooding torpor for longer than Beatrice can maintain vigil. There's too much to do when you're mistress of the house. Beatrice sighs, slides off the bed and leaves to perform her round of duties. She will find the books.

Sukey lags into prayers, in a pet, in a pout. Her foot taps annoyingly. At 'Let us pray', the girl heaves a slouching sigh, folds her arms and has clearly kept her eyes wide open all the while, for when Beatrice chances to open hers, Sukey stares unblinking.

Immediately after prayers, the servant says, 'Excuse me, miss, I'm going to leave.'

No, please don't say so. Nothing holds Sukey in this bond.

She can desert her mistress at any time. She, the inferior, is free and I, the mistress, am dependent. You can't do this to me. I've been so good to you. However Beatrice says evenly, 'Oh. Why is that, Sukey? Have you not been happy with us? Is there something not to your liking?'

With that, Sukey pulls off her cap. Her sandy-red hair falls in crinkled waves down her back, brazen in the soft evening light. Beatrice gasps; takes a step back.

'It's all so dismal, miss.'

'In what way though, Sukey? What is dismal?'

'Everything. Except Mr Joss. *He*'s a good sort. But obviously he can't keep me company all the time. And otherwise there's no one else here but me.' Once unleashed, complaints become torrential. 'Where I was before there was plenty of servants, see, and we could have a laugh and a joke together. And another thing is, I hate going to chapel. All the praying and canting and Methody stuff … it's not what I'm used to and I don't want it stuffed down my throat.'

Beatrice, astounded, hears her voice come out in a squeaking protest: 'But we are not Methodists, Sukey, you know that. This is unhandsome.'

'Which it may be and I'm sorry. And more's the pity you aren't Methodists, at least there'd be a bit of singing and jollity.'

'So – you don't wish to meet your God at chapel?'

Sukey, standing to her full five foot two, says with some dignity, 'If I might say without offence, Miss, that's my own business – this is what I been taught anyhow – and private. I'll work out my notice, don't worry.'

Beatrice lowers her head. 'I think you should put your cap back on, Sukey. I've no idea why you took it off.'

'I don't know neither.' Making no move to replace it, Sukey flashes Beatrice a smirk. 'You can be more holy-like without me,' she says. She picks up a scrubbing brush; gives it a little toss in the air and flounces off to scour the pantry before departing for the night. Does it scrupulously. All is spick and span when she departs. She bangs the door behind her.

And so the house begins to totter on its foundations. Beatrice crosses the road for the prayer meeting, her heart troubled. Not least that the girl said she was alone in the house; there was no one there. I work alongside her. I share everything she does. Am I then no one?

# Chapter 4

June is wet. The butter won't churn. In the fields the shorn sheep huddle shivering in the unseasonable weather. Bread is sixpence halfpenny. The Salas have gone. Christian's departure from America is delayed. Will fails to visit. Joss is in a mortal sulk at Sukey's departure; he'd grown fond of her, he mutters when reproached for his attachment to an unsaved female servant. He won't know what to do without her jolly face to come home to. He lolls and lounges and takes too much wine: you smell it on his breath the following morning. Beatrice interviews unsuitable girls. Anna gradually sinks. Her bowels don't move. Beatrice is prey to a need to force-feed her sister like a goose.

The invalid shrieks, shrinks back, as her sister advances with a plate of lambs' tails fried in egg and breadcrumbs. 'Don't bring that muck anywhere near me; I can't stand the smell.' She twists round to bury her face in a cushion and her book dislodges, to lie splayed on the floor.

Beatrice fishes it up. Reading the word *Species*, she thinks the word *specious*. Anna snatches it back and buries it in the blankets.

'Yes, you can,' Beatrice says. 'Don't be silly.'

'Go away.'

'I won't go away until you've eaten three teaspoonsful. If you're well enough to make such a fuss, you're well enough to at least try to eat.'

'Take it away.'

Beatrice acquiesces. Nothing for it but to call in Dr Quarles. Placing on the table the delicacy she's taken trouble to cook, Beatrice stands at the kitchen window, draws several deep breaths and fits in a tense prayer for patience. She would be more merciful to her sister over the lambs' tails if Mr Anwyl had only been over to visit. Or if a letter had come from Christian. Back she goes, with half the quantity of food on the plate.

'Annie,' she begins. 'Dear Annie love – won't you try for me? Because it does hurt so to see you starve yourself.'

'I could try a little gin in hot water, Beattie. Or some of Baines's port you've hidden somewhere.'

Beatrice hastens to prepare the gin, whisking the food away. Amy, the new servant, reheats it and Beatrice brings it back with the gin. The infidel port is no longer in the house: Miss Pentecost has given it to three deserving and abstemious villagers for medicinal use. 'Three tiny spoonfuls first, darling.' She waits.

Anna's obstinacy sets rock-hard. 'I'm not a child to be harangued. I'll drink the gin. If you'd let me go to St Ives with my friends ... '

That childish whining tune again. Beatrice wonders, as her sister sips the gin and lemon, if Anna has made up her mind to follow their parents, brother and stepmothers to the mound in the churchyard and there abandon herself to final peace. To leave Beatrice alone in the world. Draughts gust between door and window; the sickly fire gutters. She hears Anna's unridden horse, Spirit, whinny in its stall. It will have to be sold. The books must be disposed of.

Beatrice darts the spoon forward; as Anna's mouth opens again, morsels enter her lips. She retches but swallows. Clamping her mouth, she turns her face away.

'Now, just two more,' says Beatrice.

Silence.

'I won't give up, Annie. I daren't give up.'

Silence.

Anna puts out her hand. At last. Beatrice brings the plate closer. Her sister, laughing and crying, grabs the rim and slings it across the room like a quoit. The plate smashes against the fireplace. 'Ha!'

Amy, taken on just this morning, is called in to clear the mess. 'How did that happen. Miss?' she asks.

Anna laughs again, unpleasantly. 'Ask her.' She stares at her sister without blinking. But Beatrice can see that her whole body quivers.

Hysteria, Beatrice thinks.

It's hysterical to talk to oneself in private, as Anna does. To hide smirking grins behind a hand when there's company. To keep books in your bed claiming they act as hot-water bottles. To hurl your lunch across the room like a child in a tantrum.

Beatrice comprehends the root of Anna's hysteria, of course she does. Its origin is her womb, whose vagrancy expresses itself in her bowels. These are unstable, contradictory even. For weeks at a time Anna will have loose motions; then everything will silt up. Dr Quarles explains that faecal matter undischarged from the belly exudes poisons which mount to the brain. Beatrice knows that the bowels could never have polluted the system if Miriam Sala hadn't introduced poison. Just as Indian sailors brought cholera to England, so Mrs Sala, that foreign body, has contaminated Anna, as Lore did before her.

Beatrice is the link between Anna and health; Anna and eternal life. But she allows her sister to win the current skirmish; backs off and marches straight over to Dr Quarles's house.

He's over in the twinkling of an eye. Quarles examines Anna thoroughly, lamenting that one cannot actually see into the intestines. Displaying none of the nervous agitation Beatrice would have predicted, the patient acts like an incredulous third party observing a South Sea islander from a distance.

The words 'enema' and 'blister' are spoken in private conference.

The moment Anna claps eyes on the soda-water bottle, she knows. She screams that it's violation, she won't, you mustn't, get out of her room. Beatrice shushes her, laying out the red rubber sheet on the bed. Anna, with more energy than she's shown for weeks, slips out of bed, grabs the rubber tube and flings it towards the fire. It lands on the rug; Beatrice rescues the apparatus, takes it to the wash bowl and rinses it thoroughly.

'Come on, Annie, this is silly. Don't be childish.'

As children they accepted without complaint the weekly enema to keep them regular. They understood the reasons for it. You could not go shopping or visiting or to Sunday School if you were likely to be caught short. The Pentecost children were treated with respect and felt little indignity in submitting to harmless turpentine and green soap dissolved in hot water. Jocelyn seemed actually to welcome and enjoy it. Beatrice did feel curious about that.

Anna won't. She fights. They scuffle silently.

'You're killing me, Beatrice.'

Beatrice sits down at the end of the sofa, places one hand on her sister's calf. She'll have to bring in a neighbour to help. 'Do you not believe in Dr Quarles?'

'I believe he *exists*. I *know* he's an ass.'

'Well, sweetheart, never mind; I'll leave you in peace for now.'

'What do you mean by *for now*?'

Anna is on to you like a shot. Beatrice prevaricates. 'I'll look in on you later. Shall I bring you a cup of tea? Or some hot milk and water? No?'

When Mrs Bunce arrives, there's another painful scene in Anna's sick room.

'There, there,' says Mrs Bunce, and flips Anna over onto her stomach like a fish. She's a large woman, nurse, midwife, layer-out. She wears a black hat and carries a black bag wherever she goes; the children call her a witch. There's little Mrs Bunce hasn't seen before. In goes the nozzle; Beatrice, taking a deep breath, presses it deep into Anna's anus. It has to be done, so do it efficiently, she tells herself – for Anna's sake. Her sister, who's given up struggling, lies bathed in tears and cold sweat. When it's all over, she will not look at Beatrice. She curls up in her bed, tears seeping into the pillow.

The bowel movement follows. Beatrice removes the chamber pot. As she washes her hands, she hears Quarles's man at the door, delivering the blister. She hardly has the heart to administer it; her throat chokes with unshed tears. But it must be done. She swallows some gin and feels ashamed, not at the actions she must perform but at her own rancorous absence of pity. Beatrice's goodness is tainted with something obscene – this endless assertion of predominance.

Gently, Beatrice draws back the blankets. Anna, compliant, has lost her fight; rolls onto her back, eyes shut. Beatrice raises her sister's nightgown. One – two – three. The wax blister with the hot boiled leaves is rolled onto the delicate skin of her abdomen. Swiftly, Beatrice pulls down the nightgown and kneels at Anna's bedside, holding her hand in both of hers. Tears leak from the corners of Anna's eyes at the searing pain. She seems to pass out; is whispering something, over and over.

'I'm so sorry,' Beatrice says, weeping too, without restraint. 'Please forgive me, Annie. I wish I could take the pain myself.'

Anna opens her eyes; nods. She understands that the treatment, by producing blisters on the outside of her body, will draw to the surface and drain the muck from the blisters whose presence Quarles suspects on her intestines. She lies trembling, bearing the biting pain that increases throughout the night.

At three she screams: 'Lore! Oh, come back. Help me, Lore.'

She talks to the dead. She's not Anna any more. She is abject pain; pain is all Anna is. Beatrice wonders whether to send out for laudanum. But wouldn't that begin the blockage problem again? And so she'd have to hurt Anna for her own good, all over again. She'd rather chew a mouthful of stinging nettles than add a mite to her misery.

# Chapter 5

*How beautiful are thy feet with shoes, O prince's daughter.*

Mr Kyffin, exchanging pulpits with Mr Anwyl, announces the text for his sermon: The Song of Solomon. Beatrice has arranged the invitation as a way of showing Mr Kyffin's persecutors at Florian Street the high regard in which Chauntsey holds its minister.

Their friend's manner is exalted. Mr Kyffin dispenses with notes, having placed his trust (so he explains) in the Spirit to speak through him, to pierce the hearts of Christ's stony-hearted people. For there will be an Awakening! A revival! It is coming! He gazes upwards. We see the signs throughout this lethargic, secular land. Who knows whence Revival will come: north, south, east or west? Perhaps from Wales? Or from Fighelbourn or Chauntsey?

There is a Boy, Mr Kyffin announces, a common boy of West Grimstead, chosen of the Lord, preaching at the Market Cross. Isaac Minety, the baker's son. Who has heard the boy speak? Not yet perhaps? You shall!

There is Mr Spurgeon in his London pulpit. Perhaps he is the coming man.

Maybe the man will issue from America, on board the *Petrel* with Mr Jones of Bedwellty. It is not impossible that Mr Idris Jones may himself be the man. This we do not know! As yet. But the high wind is coming.

'And do remember,' says Mr Kyffin in a more ordinary tone, 'when the glorious tempest of salvation shakes this nation, that it was your friend John who told you the news. But to my text! *How beautiful are thy feet, prince's daughter.*'

The Song of Solomon is a book at which Bibles regularly fall open but on which little is ever said. A chaste veil is drawn. But why, enquires the pastor, should we fear to read Christ's love song to his spouse the church? What should hold us back from contemplating the naked and the shod foot of the beloved? In all reverence.

Embarrassment seethes in the chapel. Shufflings, coughs.

Sensuous love, he says, is not a game.

No wonder poor Mrs Kyffin has cried off; no wonder Mr Prynne is up in arms, if this is Mr Kyffin's new theme.

'For what has John Milton, that great Puritan spirit, to say about nudity in *Paradise Lost*?' Mr Kyffin enquires. 'Does anyone here remember? What are clothes but *those troublesome disguises which we wear*? And what is excessive modesty but *dishonest shame*? Sensuous love is a sacred and mysterious *language*, spoken only in deep trust between bridegroom and bride in the sanctuary of their marriage bed.'

'I shall show you the bed!' he exclaims with a dramatic flourish. 'Here is the bed! Here it is!'

Silence in the pews. Consternation. Faces red as radishes. Beatrice's lower body within its drawers, shift, petticoats, corset, crinoline cage and skirts is aware of itself. Ladies sit rigid as conscious statues. They hold their breath. What next? Will there be a walkout? Will the respectable worshippers in the pews protest?

'In my hand! The Word itself! The Book is, so to speak, the bed of consummation.' John Kyffin holds his Bible aloft. 'Here it is. Love itself. The wooing tenderness of my blessed Jesus for my erring human soul. Pillows for my delinquent head! Quilts of love to warm me, even me, the unchaste bride!'

There's some relief and relaxation as the sermon moves to consideration of the pattern of shoe that might have been worn in the Holy Land by the prince's daughter.

'Let us say, sandals. The Lover looks down at the humblest portion of his beloved's person and praises its beauty. Sandals are closed (in order to remain attached to the foot) but also open to the air, most necessary in the torrid temperatures of the Holy Land. And is this base function something of which we should be ashamed to speak? My children, we walk through the dust – and of this dust we're fashioned – and to it we'll return. Let's consider also that this is where the *sole* meets the earth. Can we call to mind occasions when we have perceived the *soul* of man, woman or child *in the feet*?'

Mr Kyffin pauses.

Beatrice's thoughts swing about wildly as the pause for reflection lengthens. A nervous laugh has to be thrust down.

'Bring to mind,' the preacher exhorts them, 'the foot of love.'

It flashes through her: Jack Emanuel Elias at four months old in his crib under the apple tree. Anna in a blue summer dress snaring both his naked feet in her hands, kissing them till the baby shrieked with laughter. This is how it will be, Beatrice thought, when we are mothers.

But first we must have husbands. We must lose our virginity. Don't think that; why are you thinking it; why is the pastor arousing such thoughts, in the chapel of all places? Beatrice seeks to block out Mr Kyffin's words, his surely deranged words. She throws herself into prayer. But the thought of a wedding night, banished, creeps back.

The ram is brought by Farmer Hewison to tup the Pentecost ewes.

The dog mates with the howling bitch behind the sheds.

Coupled fox and vixen, caught in the tie, tear at the swollen root of their attachment, struggling for freedom.

Beatrice has nothing whatever to learn about the mechanics of mating, never having viewed it as unwholesome or shameful. But how the equivalent negotiation is transacted between human beings is unclear. Her body swirls disquietly. She can imagine a man gripping the tender instep of her foot in his hand, maternally: a strange and pleasurable thought. She can imagine a tempestuous bed brought to a hush, the sheets allowed to lie where they fell, lovers lying naked to one another in married trust. She cannot see the man's face. One must trust this person with one's life.

Afterwards the elders and deacons, as one body, flee Mr Kyffin, ignoring his outstretched hand. Mrs Mussell and her six daughters sidestep, nod and depart at the double, shoulders high, cheeks pink. Mrs Bunce the midwife chats amiably with Mr Kyffin, as does dear deaf Mr Turnbull who congratulates the preacher on an elevating sermon. Handsome Daniel Pittaway the gardener winks at Edwin Fribance the blacksmith, who preserves a grave countenance.

Mr Kyffin rides high on a windy afflatus. At supper in Sarum House, he refrains from enlightening the Pentecosts about the painful events at Florian Street. After the cheese platter, the afflatus wilts; he goes quiet and retires without taking a pipe with Jocelyn.

Beatrice recounts to her sister the gist of the sermon. 'Poor Mr Kyffin, he seems to have gone off on his own strange road.'

'Christianity is fissiparous,' says Anna. 'That's how it works, I'm afraid.'

'Whatever do you mean?'

'Worms in a garden. To grow, they have to break. They divide to reproduce. Protestants divide and subdivide until there's no union left, just thousands of sects all wriggling away to their own tune. Until in the end there are ten million churches of one person.'

'Honestly, Anna. What will you say next? Do you ever know what you are going to say before you say it?'

'No. Not always. Do you always?'

'Yes, Anna, on the whole yes, I think I do.'

'Poor you, Beattie, you are deprived of the spice of novelty.'

Beatrice, not for the first time, flinches from her sister's thinking-aloud; pretends to laugh it off. Anna is an odd mind out and really can't help it. Since you cannot gain complete control of her, you need to veil her anomalies from other people's sight. Sitting back, Beatrice contemplates her sister's melancholy but beautiful eyes, looking into the distance; she admires the lustrous darkness of Anna's hair, just washed, all brought forward over one shoulder. Her face is gaunt but Anna has rallied significantly since the medical treatment, indicating to Beatrice that Dr Quarles knew what he was talking about.

There's a pile of books sticking out from under the bed. Aha, you forgot to hide them! 'Fissiparous': Anna could not have dreamed that up on her own: Miriam Sala is somewhere behind that. 'Christianity is fissiparous! Worms in a garden!' Is that a sample of Anna's reflections when she's lying prostrate in her room all those tedious hours?

'But perhaps an Awakening would bring all the churches back together again, Annie. That, I am sure, is the idea. General Baptists would reunite with Strict and Particular Baptists, Congregationalists, all the different Wesleyans, Unitarians, Brethren, even the Anglicans, High and Low and

High-low. All of us would be one. So perhaps there is something in it and we should pray earnestly about it? This may be *the* moment.'

While Anna dozes on the couch after tea, Beatrice runs lightly upstairs and removes the offensive books. Without examining the titles or investigating their soiled contents, she conceals them in the cupboard under the stairs until evening. In the wilderness at the end of the garden, Beatrice lights the pyre. She tears out pages quire by quire. The fire licks, then rages. Kindling's all they're good for. Flakes of charred paper float up into the air but on a windless evening they don't travel far. The fire burns low and Beatrice stirs the ashes with a stick until every trace is extinguished. And she'll be watchful and do it again and again, should the need arise. Her heart is choking her throat with its drumming.

*

*Turdus philomelos*, Anna records in her diary, *the speckled song thrush has had her nest smashed. Five eggs, powder blue, 9 days old & near to hatching, stolen. This whole nesting arrangement was a mistake on her part. She should build nearer heaven for we down here are raptors. Never trust us. We do not trust one another or ourselves – & how wise we are in this regard. But our thrush too is an engine of death: an empty litter of snail shells marks her presence. She beats them against the post to extract the meat. & this she must do until the Almighty calls a halt to the slaughter.*

Anna will get up today. She's sick of sickness. Meeting her own sallow face in the mirror, she's shaken. 'Emaciated; not long for this world' are the words she reads in the sympathetic faces of visitors: they conceal what Lore would have called their *Schadenfreude*. Hens peck the runty chicken to death, after which deed they run about squawking with five minutes' relief. The healthy feed on the ill: that's a fact. It ensures that

67

the mad and bad survive. And then, generation by generation, they select and breed for madness. Outwit the mob or be devoured. Outwit Beatrice. But Anna was sad through and through to see her observations confirmed by Mr Darwin in one of the snatched books. The zoologists sorrow over the bloodbath of nature and are reluctant to acknowledge it. It has made Mr Darwin ill. But tell it he must. Tell it and be vilified. Speak and be mobbed by the beaks of the *cognoscenti*.

Mrs Bunce brought trout from the Avon for the invalid. The creatures lay on a slab, a mortuary company, their yellow eyes glazed. The fish cried out with Job: *Why did you create me, O my Maker, to be the food of vermin?* Their creaturely life spoke to Anna and harrowed her. All life is kin to all life. This would sound insane. 'But Anna, the creatures were given to us for our use.' And the smell. Even in her romping days, Anna Pentecost was never more than a light eater, a slight child. Too much to do, trees to climb, cartwheels waiting to be turned in the morning garden. 'You're a fairy,' said Papa. 'You eat the dew on the leaf. But I'm an elf, my lamb, a porridge-elf, so let me feed you this teaspoon of magic porridge made of oats soaked in rainbows.' Yes, she opened her beak then and accepted the delicacy. And throve.

Anna accepts a portion of fish, poached in milk, her sister hanging over her, staring at the fork as it travels to and from her mouth. Afterwards, seized with a violent headache, Anna suppresses the pain and agrees with Beatrice that Dr Quarles' remedy has done her good after all. Yes, she was wrong to object to the quacks and to make such a fuss about being *violated*. Anna smiles at Beatrice none too pleasantly, a sardonic rictus which Beatrice apparently chooses to accept as the real thing.

Anna manages to creep downstairs under her own steam and settles herself on the sofa. She considers her plan. It's to take up her bed and walk. But not too soon, so as to avoid a trip to London with Beatrice, who'll be meeting Christian Ritter at Regent's Park College. He's to lecture on slavery in America and about new horizons for the world ministry. The great Mr Spurgeon will attend.

Yesterday a long letter arrived from Christian, which Beatrice has not shared with Anna. Beatrice's colour is high and she spends a disproportionate amount of time trying on her best dresses and selecting hats for London.

'Oh I wish you could come with me, Annie. I dislike leaving you.'

'I'll be perfectly comfortable. And getting stronger every day, you can see that. Mrs Elias and Mrs Montagu will keep me company.'

'I don't like going without you, I don't *like* it.'

A little-girl look crosses the elder sister's face. What self-respecting woman wouldn't comprehend Beatrice's apprehension? Solitary in a railway coach, you're prey for any rogue who chooses to insult you. Together the Pentecosts are a match for anyone.

'You'll be well cared for,' Anna reassures her. For what if Beatrice becomes so nervous that she cancels her trip? 'I'll write every day. Joss will take you to the station.'

'Yes, but it's you I worry about.'

'Well, don't.'

'I've been unkind to you, Annie. Dearest, I'm just – so sorry.'

Anna stares. Her sister is rarely known to apologise; can only with difficulty concede that she may have been mistaken. A caress, a vase of anemones, a cake baked with cinnamon constitute her usual language of contrition. And, look, the penitent is already beginning to regret it. Beatrice has to be forgiven on her own terms.

What she mustn't know, for fear of reprisals, is that, no, Anna will never forgive her sister on any terms, ever. You're a one-woman Inquisition, thinks Anna. If there's an hysteric in the house, we know what her name is.

*That* evening, when the precious books were filched, Anna watched a plume of smoke rise in the wilderness. Next day she had Joss push her there in the wheeled chair. She examined the blackened circle of grass and plucked a few charred scraps of paper from a broom bush. They are now between the pages of her journal, like pressed black flowers of mourning. In that hour Beatrice passed beyond Anna's trust.

She'd only skimmed the first page of Baines's book. Well-written. A touch bombastic. A woman looking not wholly unlike Anna herself was sitting in a window. The townsfolk were all peering in the window and gossiping about her. But, Beatrice, books are immortal, she thinks. Publications can't be extinguished. How on earth can you have ignored the fact that replacements are always available? When you're away, she thinks, I can order the books. I have money of my own, you simpleton. The small allowance from her aunt Anna never spends: it mounts up, not enough to emancipate her but a nest egg. If you destroy the copies, I'll replace those. Obviously. But where to hide them?

'Annie, I've said I'm sorry,' Beatrice repeats, with slightly less conviction.

Anna smiles. 'Oh, well, never mind. I expect I provoked you. It's all in the past. Shall you not say goodbye to Mr Anwyl?'

Beatrice shrugs and flushes. 'Why should I?'

Mr Anwyl comes and goes, taking little notice of Beatrice, chatting instead with Anna, annoying Joss by bestowing attention on the Rubenesque servant, Amy Light, and any other female visitors to Sarum House below the age of forty.

Anna watches Will winding tendrils round women's hearts; observes Beatrice ignoring him; catches a sour whiff of mutual mortification, high as hung game on a hook.

*

On the verge of sleep you occasionally startle: you're falling. Suddenly you're wide awake. You've seen something dreadful. But what was it?

In the darkening garden after supper, Beatrice informs Will, 'I am going to London to see Christian Ritter.'

'Then I am done for,' Will says. 'You'll come back engaged. I shall have to turn to Anna.'

They stand in the shadow of the chestnut. Unseen lives settle in the branches above. Beatrice teeters off-balance and Will reaches out to steady her. He understands me, she thinks; in some way he intuits me: why is this not enough? His hand slides slowly across her breast, just above the stays. Through every layer of fabric, she feels the warmth of his palm nakedly; ripples spread, out and out.

Everything melts inside Beatrice. *How beautiful are thy feet with shoes, O prince's daughter. Those troublesome disguises which we wear?*

A cobweb stretches between twigs in the shrubbery; by day you're blind to its filaments but moonlight picks out the web's complications. Will opens his arms to Beatrice; then with his fingertips on her shoulders, he draws her closer. He lets out a faltering sigh. She cannot allow it; does allow it. A tear sparks in Beatrice's eye for she has no one, her parents are dead, it's dark, they're buried over the road, her father died cursing, her sister is mentally and mortally ill, she herself is going away, faith burns low.

Beatrice observes Will Anwyl's mouth come down, come close … receives it, no, not on her mouth but the corner of her eye which at the last moment closes. A planet swims towards another planet, horizon-filling. She discerns each lash and the crook of his eyebrow as he kisses the tear away; feels the soft push of lips on her eyelid, a sensation that persists like eucalyptus oil when he has drawn back.

She runs. A barn owl's out hunting and she catches his territorial call. Reaching the candle-lit interior, Beatrice glances back and sees no one, for the dark beneath the chestnut is impenetrable. Amy lollops about the kitchen, a lump of a girl, heavy-footed. Joss is sitting with his feet raised against the fender, chair balanced on its back legs, eating a scone loaded with blackcurrant jam. She rushes past them.

I am compromised, Beatrice thinks. This phrase chimes throughout the evening, as she superintends this, arranges that, says good night to Jocelyn and Mr Elias smoking a pipe in the stinking snuggery. On the stairs she pauses and covers her left breast with her hand; it remembers.

But nobody saw. Pleasure licks out from her hardened nipple along a network of nerves. Shakily, Beatrice undresses, turning from the mirror, catching a side view of a woman's face like a cat's, sleek, well-fed, slyly knowing. She lets down her hair and takes the brush to it till it crackles. In her imagination, Will has wound her hair around his fist and is drawing her head back on the pillow. *But if they cannot contain, let them marry*. Will's wide open eye is approaching her eye, forcing it to blink and close. *For it is better to marry than to burn*. Picking up the candle, Beatrice bends forward; the hair singes; a whiff of burning is on the air. She pinches the charred tress and some falls away into her hand; she hurries to her bed and blows out the flame.

Nobody saw. It can be denied. The intimate touch. The kiss. But either Beatrice cannot now marry Mr Anwyl, ever, or, having permitted indelicacy, she *must* marry him. And if she does not, surely Anna will.

# Chapter 6

'It has all come to a *climax* at Florian Street,' Mrs Elias, bonnet strings hardly loosened, loses no time in informing Anna. Clearly she'd rather have told Miss Pentecost but in her absence the younger sister will have to do. 'Mr Kyffin has *resigned*. Prynne and the Prynneites were accuser, judge and jury. Odious fellow! At the best of times he seems to have a bad smell under his nose. Rising in a prayer meeting to beg the Almighty to forgive Mr Kyffin's *heinous* offences! Mind you, Mr Kyffin does seem to be behaving strangely. The young Kyffins are distraught. I am distraught, come to that. Do you happen to have any port wine, Anna?'

'No, we did have some. But it was unholy apparently. Beatrice gave it away. A little brandy and sugar?'

'Oh, thank you. What are you reading, Anna?'

'*A book of sermons*, Loveday.' Anna locks the volume away in her portable desk. The parcel has just arrived, with the new copy of *Adam Bede*.

The poor Kyffins: the disgrace will mark them for life. Mean tongues will wag through every church and chapel in Wiltshire.

Anna promises herself to visit tomorrow to offer Antigone what comfort she can. She's now mistress of Sarum House, and how it invigorates her. The costiveness in her bowels has eased. Anna has been eating peaches till the juice runs down her chin. And what one feels for books is also appetite. A good book, said Milton, is the precious lifeblood of a master spirit. Yes, Anna thinks, but to me it's a peach, succulent and delicious. She has written to her friends in St Ives.

'But what worries me,' says Loveday Elias, sipping the hot brandy gratefully, 'is where is all this going? What can be done when a minister of the Baptist Church turns Methodist?'

'Turns *Methodist*?'

'So I hear. Though whether Wesleyan, Free Methodist, Primitive Methodist or whatever else, is not known. Mr Kyffin is not himself. Quite frankly, his sermon here was – indelicate – don't you agree? Naked bodies! In front of ladies and children.'

'Well, in all fairness, naked *feet* only,' Anna puts in. 'And not even naked: wearing sandals. From what my sister told me. I was not present.'

'Oh neither was I, dear; I accompanied Mr Elias to Salisbury to hear Mr Anwyl, as you know.'

'So neither of us is in a position to judge.'

'But from what I'm reliably informed … *well*. Especially when we consider our young people, who face numerous temptations in this day and age. Mr Elias has remonstrated with Mr Kyffin, in a tactful way of course. He has put to him that our true enemy is the spirit of secularism. We worry that all ministry will be tarred with the same brush.'

'Oh, I don't honestly think Mr Elias need worry, Loveday.'

Such an insipid speaker as Mr Elias leaves only the faintest impression upon listeners' minds. You know you've sat through a sermon but what it was all about, who can say?

Mild tosh, like tasteless soup. No pepper. Anna wonders at Loveday's indignation. Generally the soul of tolerance, Loveday has struck up against the outermost limits of her blandness. 'About the nakedness, Loveday. I don't think Mr Kyffin was saying what you've heard. It was all allegorical.'

'Allegory, fiddle-de-dee. As Mr Spurgeon says, go to the Gospels. Call a spade a spade. Allegory is Popery.'

\*

The boy-preacher of West Grimstead is a puny, tow-haired lad, his skin ingrained with the flour of his parents' trade, lending him an albino appearance. The heckling schoolboys and apprentices massing outside the public house seem to trouble neither him nor the village lads he has gathered as disciples. The youngest, scarcely more than an infant, is dressed in the girlish skirts of infancy. This dribbling child, whose name is Harry, is much invoked by the young prophet as one of the helpless babes in whose welfare Jesus is supremely interested. Isaiah Minety has trained his followers to shout 'Halleluia!' and 'Selah!' at a gesture from himself.

Anna, accompanying Mr Anwyl to West Grimstead to examine the callow revivalist, is surprised at her companion's enthusiasm. Will wonders if placid Wiltshire might be roused to the mass conversions seen in his homeland. Not since John Wesley's field meetings, camps and love feasts has the county seen a spiritual kindling, and if an Awakening could be harnessed to the Baptist denomination, they could be harvesting souls by the hundred.

'Harry here will be first in Heaven,' Isaiah Minety proclaims during a pause in the apprentices' braying.

'Not too soon, we hope,' Anna can't help exclaiming.

'No, Miss, but if our Saviour decides to take Harry unto himself, he'll be sitting in Jesus's lap or standing between his kindly knees. Won't you, Harry?'

'Yuss,' the cherub agrees, taking his thumb from his mouth and slipping it straight back in. Mucous hangs from his nose and he coughs round his thumb. Looking at the sea of faces, Harry takes refuge behind Isaiah.

'Praise the Lord!' call the disciples.

'Kindly Knees! Kindly Knees!' bellow the apprentices.

'I call upon you all,' cries the boy-preacher. 'To become as little children ...'

'How come it's allowed?' asks an onlooker, who's told that the constable has on several previous occasions dispersed the rabble. The vicar has remonstrated with Mr and Mrs Minety; the boy has been taken before the magistrate and warned. He is incorrigible.

'For unless ye become as little Harry, ye shall not enter the Kingdom of Heaven.'

'Sheer blasphemy. And look at the urchin, crossing his legs, he'll wet himself in a minute.'

'Wet yerself! Wet yerself!' bawl the apprentices. 'Go on, Holy Moses, wet yerself!'

It's now that the young prophet makes a tactical error. 'Yes, my friends. But I *shall* wet myself. I acknowledge it! I shall wet myself before the Mercy Seat!'

Pandemonium. Ironic apprentices are holding themselves between their legs and hopping in circles.

'Baptism by total immersion is what I mean – dipping!'

'Duck him! Duck the rat!' The apprentices bolt with their victim toward the Avon as the heavy-footed constable arrives from Mill Street. Mr Anwyl follows the crowd, to return with a saturated and shivering Isaiah. Anna hears Will telling the child that, whereas he himself is a minister of the Baptist church, Isaiah is just a lad.

'Yes, Mister, but a child of God.'

'I hope we are all that.'

'I am chosen, Mr Anwyl, I am picked out of the rubbish. I know I am.'

'But how do you know, dear, that's the question? And why do you call people rubbish?'

'The Spirit tells me.'

'You can't read, can you, Isaiah?'

'I can so!'

'Well, I don't think you can. You've truanted from school. Learn your letters and study the Word – sedulously – and then consider where the Spirit leads you.'

'There may not be time for all that,' the child objects. 'Who knows how long we've got left in the mortal world? Sometimes there are extraordinary Dispersatans.' He lifts his right hand, looking up soulfully at Mr Anwyl in a spirit of brotherly correction. 'I often wish I was in China, India or Africa, that I might preach, preach, preach all day long. It would be sweet to die preaching.'

Anna, amused, waits quietly while the martyr is delivered to the care of his parents. Isaiah has done her good: no pain all morning after a breakfast of new-laid eggs. Fresh energy licks along her veins.

And when she wants to laugh aloud, she'll have her laugh out. Tuck her skirts up and climb a tree. Stay up into the early hours.

Travelling home, Will angles for information about Beatrice and her visit to the capital. Anna reads the play of emotions in his face. Will is all too legible. But how deep is the root of his attachment to Anna's sister? How long till the Fighelbourn congregation begins to murmur against its pastor's frivolities? And yet this is a man who'll sit long at a bedside, hearing the repetitions of senility with good humour. She's seen him playing on the common with the small boys after Sunday School, a flour bag on his head. Shouldn't warm-hearted humour count for something in the great tally?

The two of them are like brother and sister. Anna feels easier with Will because of his feet of clay. Look, mine are clayey too. With him she doesn't have to be forever watching herself in case her oddities escape, like urchins truanting from school. There's something about a man pocked with an acne of visible blemishes that reassures a common sinner.

The arrangements are all made; Beatrice has not been informed. Anna will pack her bags and on Saturday she'll board the St Ives train. Many hours later, doubtless more dead than alive, she'll step out into the salty Cornish air and be greeted by Mirrie and Baines. Anna tries to contain her excitement; her heart thrums as they pass the familiar woods and fields, thatched cottages, cabbage fields and farm labourers. A pauper woman carrying a baby in a shawl, followed by barefoot children, tramps the verge. A flock of sheep from Butterfurlong Farm blocks the road. Anna's ordinary world: farewell to it. Tomorrow is reserved for a visit to poor Mrs Kyffin. And then. Freedom.

At Sarum House Will, alighting, reaches to help Anna out. She steps down; he does not release her hand.

'What is it?' she asks.

'Oh … nothing. You. Your eyes. What's going on? What do you have in mind?'

'Come in and have tea.'

A weighty letter from Beatrice arrives as Will leaves. Anna sees his eyes fasten forlornly on the handwriting. He hasn't heard from her in London and has no expectation of doing so.

*

'How is dear Beatrice?' asks Mrs Kyffin, hollow-cheeked. She has always been a plump, bustling body, happy with her world, fond of millinery, kind to children, proud of her immaculate home. The close-fitted waist of her bell-shaped blue-black dress hangs limply to her figure, for not only has she lost weight but she has clearly abandoned tight-lacing. The wedding ring is loose on her finger.

'She's enjoying London very much, thank you.'

'And yourself, Anna? We've been most concerned for your health. Beatrice tells us your *nerves* ... she worries about you so.'

'I'm much restored. Out and about, as you see. But how are you, dear Mrs Kyffin?'

'Quite well; I'm quite well. I don't complain.'

'You never do, I know.'

'Oh, but Anna, yes I do. Too often I have grumbled, when my life was cushioned and everything was done for my comfort. And now comes the tempest. But,' she reminds herself, 'I do not complain.'

Antigone prowls the room, as if searching for something mislaid; she cannot think what. She touches each of the ornaments on the mantelpiece, picks them up, frowns. The attractive parlour, with its large-leaved plants in their polished urns, seems to have flown asunder and nothing adds up. The ornate walnut clock ticks morosely. All but one of the children being out, the house is hollow. 'Now comes the storm, my dear, and I must bow before it.'

'Whatever can be done for you? What have these poisonous Prynnes ...?'

'You must faithfully promise never to vilify the dear Prynnes.'

The *dear* Prynnes? That's hard to swallow. The shoemaker and his family, frugal, upright and severe of countenance, deacons of the church for three generations, have always impressed Anna with their appetite for mastery. Prynne prides himself on speaking his mind 'in all charity' and 'under correction'. A canny and philanthropic businessman, he has a finger in every pie and is forever licking it in public, a mirthless smile on his lean face.

'I can see what you're feeling, Anna. But it won't do. I fully believe that the Prynnes have acted as they have solely out of Christian love.'

Mrs Kyffin allows herself to sit down with her guest. She talks in a rapid whisper, twisting a sodden handkerchief between her fingers. Her husband is accused of embezzlement of church funds as well as of heretical doctrine, causing faction and ignoring the elders and deacons – and 'something else, something not to be spoken'. And now he proposes to convert to Methodism. She whispers the word.

'But how is Mr Kyffin taking his trouble?'

'If I raise the matter, he quits the room. He has *resigned*. Just like that. What would my father say? But luckily Papa is dead and cannot see what his daughter has come to.'

Tears seep from Antigone's red eyes; she doesn't bother to wipe them away. Beside her on the sofa is a green sateen cushion embroidered in gold silk with the motto 'Here rest, weary traveller'. Shame upon them, Anna thinks, for causing this shame. For shame can kill. Anna chafes Mrs Kyffin's hand.

'I envy you your Christian spirit, Antigone, I really do,' she says. 'And yet …'

'It's my one consolation, Anna. Don't attack it.' Antigone sits up and blows her nose; tucks the handkerchief away in a pocket. 'Promise me you won't.'

'Of course not. Not for the world.'

'I enjoy a deep sense of the divine presence, Anna, in this hour of travail. But – let me offer you a cup of coffee and some gingerbread Ellen has made.' She rings for the maid. Tea arrives and so does Mr Kyffin, bluff and hearty as ever, glad to see them, asking after Beatrice and Jocelyn. Anna squeezes his hand, which he withdraws as if scalded. He takes a step back onto the tail of the cat.

Mr Kyffin regrets that he cannot stop for tea, murmurs an apology; his face works; he digs his hands in his pockets and vanishes into the study.

'Come and see my Ellen before you go.' Mrs Kyffin leads the way to the parlour where all this while Ellen Kyffin has been amusing herself. It's a lovely room, set aside for sewing and the children's study, with a globe, cottage piano and table, lit by a central conical gasolier. It has always been Mrs Kyffin's project to educate not only her sons but her daughters so that, if necessary, they can earn their own bread as teachers or governesses. All are sent away to school and in the holidays coached at home. This must cost a great deal of money, Anna thinks. Wherever has that money come from?

The youngest Kyffin, kneeling back on her heels, gravely assesses the visitor. 'Would you like to come and look at my dolls' house with me, Miss Anna?'

Nine-year-old Ellen's careful fingers reach into a dolls' house, whose miniature people live a wholly superintended life. Anna peers into a parlour papered in a miniature version of the frondy swirls that curve their way up the walls of the Kyffins' parlour. A nursery, with a thumb-sized crib, is decorated with an alphabetical design. Toy people sit at mathematical intervals round a table.

'It's wonderful. A perfectly ordered world.'

'Did you ever have a dolls' house, Miss Anna?'

'No – but I had a little place in the garden where I used to go that was my own little world. Not as well organised.' Anna is intrigued to recall the mound or hillock where she'd play her secret games. Now whereabouts exactly was that? 'And you've been reading too while your mama and I were busy talking. What have you been reading, Ellen?'

'I am reading *Pilgrim's Progress*.'

'She is a child of grace. Aren't you, angel?'

'I hope so, Mama.'

The shadow of a dark wing flits across Mrs Kyffin's face. A child so biddable may not be long for this world. The one your heart treasures is the one God is likely to envy you. The white ewe lamb, if it survives, is the daughter destined to stay and comfort her Mama and Papa in their old age. This was the destiny wordlessly assigned to Anna by her family, from which their deaths released her.

'You cannot know what a consolation Ellen is to me. What with Charlie smoking. He owns five pipes. And shouting at his father.'

'I shall never shout at my Papa, Mama,' says Ellen in her singsong voice. She looks up devotedly into her mother's eyes. 'Or at you. Or at anyone at all.'

'I know you will not, angel. It is not in you to do so.'

'And Charlie's a good boy really, Mama. He doesn't mean to vex you.'

Ellen turns to Anna with an expression of anxious triumph. Filial Christian obedience enables her to conciliate and to a degree control the Kyffin household: at least her corner of it. As Anna leaves, mother and daughter close the door gently on their visitor, returning to their fragile sanctuary.

The carriage to Chauntsey jolts on. Something has disagreed with Anna. She tastes a sourness in the throat; sweetness rising in the mouth, a desire to open the carriage window and spit. Oh no, I can't be ill again. Just now that I'm ready to live. There's nothing you can do for people.

They pass through Alderbury and Fighelbourn. Not far now. But how slowly the horses creep. They're passing the Hanging Meadow where there was once a temporary gallows. Huge crowds, she overheard Papa telling Mr Elias, came out to see the girl hang – and she took so long to die, for women get only a short drop. Infanticide was her crime. She was an ignorant girl, an illiterate pauper. Is this a Christian country? Mrs Elias asked. Or are we barbarians? We must speak, she said, speak out.

There's so little a woman can do. You keep silent because you walk on the mute, the distaff, side of the road, muffled in shawls and bonnets. No excuse. A woman has a voice. She should raise it. Throne, pulpit, magistrate's bench: if these fail, a woman should speak out if she sees injustice or cruelty. But, Anna thinks, so far I have said very little.

# Chapter 7

'The Christian name of the young lady beside me,' announces Christian Ritter, with a theatrical gesture, 'is Miss Jewel Randolph.'

On the platform of Regent's Park Baptist College, she glances up at him with shy eyes; lowers them again. Miss Randolph's hair is flaxen, her face pale. She wears a pale blue crinoline. Gloved hands clasped at her waist, she stands before a college packed with ministers and their wives. All eyes are on Christian, who seems to Beatrice astonishingly changed, flamboyant in a flowing cloak. He has grown his blond curls to his shoulders and flourishes a wide-brimmed slouch hat. His great height displays itself to towering effect. Clean-shaven among the mighty beards on the platform, he suggests – disconcertingly – something of the showman, resembling nothing so much as the familiar engraved portrait of the great but controversial Mr Beecher.

'Miss Randolph,' explains Christian, 'was the third lot to be sold at auction by Mr Henry Ward Beecher at Plymouth Church, New York.'

Gasps.

'You heard me correctly. This Christian child was sold. Mr Beecher's congregation donated thousands of dollars that she might be free.'

The splendid auditorium is silent. There's a single unspoken question: are they now selling white women in the slave markets of America?

Christian has always commanded perfect English: he and Lore had been taught by a classically educated English tutor in Lübeck. Now Christian's accent has taken on a slight American brogue. Isn't he somehow making an exhibition of this young lady? And yet, *and yet,* Beatrice reminds herself, if slavery is not a spectacle of outrage, what is? How else are we to know, really know, what goes on in the world? Wilfully obtuse, we require theatre. And I must enquire and know, and see my bleeding Saviour in the flesh. As He appears to me in this girl.

'How old are you, dear heart?' Christian bends to Jewel, who whispers a reply behind her gloved hand. 'Miss Jewel's exact age is uncertain. Perhaps fifteen. She has been sold by her father, a Virginia physician. Let me repeat: *sold* by her *father*. The Plymouth Church in New York bought Jewel's freedom. I repeat, the legendary Mr Beecher's church *bought* Jewel's freedom. This *father* traded Jewel's mother and sisters downriver to cover his debts. Are there words to express the depravity of this *father*? Tell the good people the names of your sisters, if you will.'

So that is why she is blonde and fair: a white father and a dark-skinned mother.

'My sisters are Amethyst, Ruby, Emerald and Pearl. My mother is named Mary.'

'And do you know, darling, where they are?'

She shakes her head.

'Miss Jewel's paternal grandmother, a worthy evangelical lady, intervened on her behalf. Jewel was sent north to be bought by Mr Beecher's church. And sold she was! And free she is! Redeemed in every sense! Show these good people your freedom-ring, dear.'

Jewel raises her hand: a plain gold ring, contributed by a wealthy member of Mr Beecher's congregation, sparkles on her little finger. Men as well as women shed tears and cover their eyes in silent prayer. Collection plates go round for the cause.

Afterwards, when Christian forces a path to Beatrice through the crowd, she can hardly speak for trembling. He bends to her, the suitor who was tutor and mentor, uncle and friend.

'My *dear* Beatrice. At last. And thank you for coming. For your letters. They have meant everything to me.'

Her hands are in his and his face is above her face. It's where it has been since she was ten: a sun looming above her small planet. The power of him over her. *His banner over me was love*. From the first Mr Ritter wooed her with passion suited to a lover, addressed to a child. Seating her on his knee, gently jouncing her up and down. 'Ride a cock horse to Banbury Cross.' Papa didn't object, though Mrs Montagu took it upon herself to counsel that Christian suspend such fondlings. Something in Beatrice objected, loathed it, found no voice to express her cringing distaste. She was found sticking pins in a portrait of Christian muttering, 'Beattie hates! Beattie loathes!' In his long absences, she daydreamed about him, writing letters brimming with devout affection. He educated her to be his wife while waiting patiently, impatiently, for her to reach the age of consent. Which she desired and abhorred. *Set me as a seal upon thine heart*. Once grown up, Beatrice gathered herself together; found ingenious ways to prevaricate.

Christian's fame burnishes his charisma. He smiles down into her eyes, only to be swept away, for the great Charles Haddon Spurgeon has made his entrance. He is, in himself, a one-man Revival. Ministers, students, newspapermen, missionaries' wives flock around Mr Spurgeon, Miss Randolph and Mr Ritter, putting questions while the guests drink tea. Ladies encircle Christian, who seems more interested in the newspaper reporters. And he's hers, isn't he? Beatrice has the sense that her life is on the point of changing, and for the better.

'Miss Pentecost! Glad I am to see you.' The white-haired little man pumping her hand is Idris Jones of Bedwellty. 'Am I right that congratulations are in order? You and – Herr Ritter – ?'

'Not that I'm aware, Mr Jones.' Beatrice invokes a formula she regularly deploys to parry insinuations about her other suitor, Mr Anwyl. Mr Jones passes on to his great theme of Revival, which must come from Wales, for Mr Beecher cannot be spared from his great American work. Already at Aberystwyth and Ynys Môn the fires are lit and the saints kindled.

'I trust you're right, Mr Jones. But shouldn't we return to our places?'

Beatrice steals glimpses of Christian on the platform, the freed slave girl having retired to rest. Dr Angus, principal of the college, thoughtfully stroking with white fingers his considerable beard, is seated next to the guest of honour.

Mr Spurgeon rises.

Already the great hall of the college is spellbound – if puzzled. For he seems to be criticising the great Beecher.

Mr Beecher is a man of prodigious gifts but he is not a Calvinist. No!

Mr Beecher is not a gospel preacher. No!

But on the subject of slavery, Mr Beecher is categorically right! Yes!

Mr Spurgeon, plump and snub, is transfigured into a seraph before Beatrice's eyes. What produces this magnetism, she can hardly tell. But who does not surrender to Mr Spurgeon's spell? You're not your own but the seraph's. Fast-paced oratory; jests where you least expect them; rustic anecdotes and soaring rhapsodies. Spurgeon's voice reaches with perfect clarity the scarlet and golden ceiling of the college; carries into the intimate self its honey and sage, the sweet and the bitter.

'I thank my Maker; England is a free country! Aye or nay?'

A roar from the audience: 'Aye!'

'No slaves here in the home of liberty. Aye or nay?'

'Aye!'

'Ah. You say so. Perhaps, my friends, perhaps. But only the Christian is truly free. All hail, thou breaker of fetters! Glorious Jesus! Ah! that moment when first my bondage passed away!'

The Atlantic Ocean is a duckpond, Mr Spurgeon holds. What happens over there involves ourselves. The globe has shrunk. Beatrice sees in her mind's eye a network of connections between Wiltshire and the whole world. She can no more huddle in her petty concerns than she can ignore the existence of the railway and telegraph. Jewel Randolph has crossed the ocean to make a claim upon Beatrice Pentecost. She must answer it.

But as for marrying Christian – what kind of life would that be for a woman? Following him from country to country, perhaps ill, bearing child after child amongst strangers, Beatrice would have to wrench herself up by the roots, to live and die far from Sarum House and Anna. And Will. Dorothy Carey, wife of the first missionary in Mudnabati, lost her mind, burying her children, a screaming harpy, accusing her husband of whoremongering, having to be locked up.

After Mr Spurgeon's ministry she stands on the steps in the dark, gusty air, Mr Montagu at her elbow.

'A word of warning, my dear.'

'Warning?'

'I'm afraid it concerns – my dear, don't take this badly – some friends of yours. At a meeting of the joint missionary societies in Manchester I heard the unfortunate – I might say, disreputable – story of a Manchester family named Sala.'

'No, really, they are not *my* friends.'

'But I understand they visit?'

Miriam Sala. It all comes out: a sordid tale of illicit relationships, as Beatrice has always suspected. This is what Unitarianism is: a net to catch a falling Christian. A net made of string, through which men crash and continue to fall eternally. Mr Montagu has placed in Beatrice's hands a weapon. And a vindication. The book-burning has begun to trouble her conscience. It should not.

Anna must be told, directly Beatrice is home. In the end, Anna will not forsake the fold. She must and will detach herself from this contaminating friendship – spinning in the vortex of 'Mrs' Sala. Beatrice stows the morsels of information to be tasted later. I knew, she thinks, I knew all along. It's like a smell. She thanks Mr Montagu, in a level voice, for informing her. Distasteful as it is to deliver the message of the Salas' infamy, it must be done.

'And I understand,' says Mr Montagu, glancing at his gold fob, 'that congratulations are at last in order ...'

'Oh, no, Mr Montagu, nothing has been ...'

'But let me be the first to know, my dear. Your dear father had set his heart on this union ...'

The news has gone before the event, with the resonance of prophecy.

Perhaps Beatrice can marry Christian but without accompanying him on his travels. If he agreed to let her stay at Sarum House, himself coming and going, she would not wholly forfeit the independence she cherishes. One might live as a husbandless married woman, neither fish nor fowl.

It would mean a final goodbye to Mr Anwyl. Though the excitement of London has driven Will from her mind, Beatrice now thinks, distinctly, and for the first time unambiguously: I do love him. Not just the sight and sound of him, not only the touch of him but, God help me, the very scent and smell of him. She shivers. His shirt: ironing it at the last minute for a service. Damp steamed off the fabric. Some intimate essence of Will came with it. She'd never have enough of it. Nobody was about. Beatrice raised the warmed cotton to her face and breathed Will in. Stood there inhaling the scent of the private place where the arm joins the side.

Beatrice's face burns. I'm like the bitch in oestrus whose fishy stink calls all the dogs for five miles around, she thinks. The bitch that will rub her belly against the fence, other dogs, a man's leg, anything.

There is attraction in Christian. Of course there is. His height and bearing carry a quiet command. He has thick fair hair, a pale complexion. There's none of the sweetly treacherous yearning she suffers for Will.

If God has called Beatrice to be Frau Ritter, she cannot, dare not, refuse. Her vocation would be to stand as yoke-fellow and soulmate to one of the most eminent pioneering Baptists of their era. Besides, he's already family. But how could the two Ritter cousins have been so different? The qualities that have made Christian a powerful preacher of the Gospel showed in Lore Ritter as flighty, opinionated egotism. Beatrice remembers Papa's love for Lore and that late, lost child. And how, after her death, the babe, Magdalena, lay in its crib for seven long months, yellow-skinned, eyes wide but inert, head swollen with encephalitis. A monster scarcely feeding or moving. Dr Quarles offered no hope, but hope was fabricated by the elderly father and Magdalena's aunt.

When the baby died, Anna was inconsolable. She declared she'd throw herself in Lore's grave and be buried alive. That would make her happy, she said. The only thing that would ever make her happy again. Hush, don't let Papa hear you being hysterical, Anna. You cannot rebel against God's dispensations. Hush now. It's for the best. Consider: the baby is with God. Magdalena was not a fully human being in any case, her brain being no more than a cauliflower. Dr Quarles told Beatrice so; said the sooner it died, the better. Suicide is a mortal sin; I know you don't mean it, Beatrice told Anna. Anna slit her own arm from wrist to elbow. It hurts, it hurts so much to remember Anna's urge to quit the world. For what would Beatrice do without Anna?

In Mr Leek's boarding house in Paddington, Beatrice toasts her hands at the fire. Outside horses and carts go by; men shout. The stridor is indescribable: London seems to want to funnel in through the window. Muslin is nailed over the pane to keep out smuts; the corpses of bluebottles rot there in dust. Beatrice's skirts, heavy with mud from the sordid streets, steam on the fender. Once they're dry, she brushes off the worst of the grime; feels more herself, spruce and kempt. She settles to write Anna a long letter. Gradually the world composes itself around a busy, competent Beatrice; this happened, then that happened. Everything is in its proper place. She will tell Anna face-to-face about the Salas, gently, carefully, and comfort her. The fire, taking heart, rustles in the grate.

'A letter for you, Miss Pentecost.' Mr Leek hands over a long screed from Anna. She breaks the seal eagerly.

*& I visited Mrs Kyffin, the poor lady is greatly afflicted. I believe Mr Kyffin is broken. & what other news do I have for you? Mr Anwyl arrived with Rose & Lily Peck. Remarkably silly girls & becoming sillier by the day, each convinced she is the apple of his eye. (All in their imagination). They have learned by heart a dozen words of French, which they name an accomplishment & their latest affectation is to speak English words with a French accent – their notion of a Gallic accent at any rate. As for me, I feel so much better, I'm riding Spirit every day – & am well enough certainly for a weekend excursion.*

Rose and Lily Peck. One on either arm of their pet minister. In Regent's Park there's a monkey house. Will has dwindled into a mechanical monkey somersaulting a bar: you wind it up and it answers to its own invariable set of inane compulsions. One day it will wind down and who will care?

\*

And there he is with his portmanteau, on the platform at Salisbury Station: 'Well, what a coincidence, Miss Anna.'

'What are you doing here? Have you come to wave me off?'

'No indeed. For I too happen to find myself travelling to St Ives!'

As the train rounds the long curve from Chauntsey towards the chalky downs with their gentle, maternal contours, there's a moment when, looking back, you glimpse the grounds of Sarum House: a section of the wilderness area, her childhood haunt. Anna stands and cranes. Amongst those high grasses with plumes of purple, there's something planted ... something lost ... whatever was it now?

'What are you looking for?'

'A ... tump,' she says.

'A what?'

'Oh, I'm not sure. The word just came. I like to look at the house from the train. I always do it – it feels like jumping out of yourself and looking back at your world.'

'*Cae twmpyn*,' Will says. 'The field of tumps. Out there.'

He means the rounded contours of the downs, mint-green in the milky sunlight, where the ancient people buried their dead. He seems to understand when she tells him of her passion for the barrows and stone circles and henges everywhere in her shire; and of the rambles with Papa, returning home laden with treasures: shepherds' crowns, flint knives, tesserae. Nothing of what was unearthed disturbed the serenity of Papa's faith in those days.

Bless him, Will is so kind and funny and considerate on the long train journey, handing Anna in and out of carriages, superintending luggage and laying out the picnic on his lap. He'll be mother, Will announces: 'Now, which sandwich would you care to start with, dear heart?' A passenger, amused by the young man's fondness, refers to Anna as 'your good lady'. Anna makes no objection. 'Hold still, *cariad*': Will snares a smut in the bud of her eye on the corner of his handkerchief. Entering into the spirit of his game, she relaxes into Will's surprising presence, having foolishly overlooked the extent to which the journey south would tax her powers.

Anna scarcely bothers to ask herself what her sister would make of this escapade. A reckless craving for flight, for life, sweeps her on. Yes, it's my turn now. Anna will never forget reaching under the bed, to find the precious works replaced by pious tracts. She laughed aloud with dark incredulity.

Will's portmanteau contains, he tells Anna, Bishop Morgan's Bible – his childhood Bible in Welsh, plus one change of linen, for he'll return by the next train, overnighting at Exeter. He chats in Welsh with a passenger from Bangor. Anna glimpses in Will a different man, easy and confident.

More gentlemanly, if that's the word. It comes to her that he exists amongst the English in cumbrous translation. 'Teach me a few words of your beautiful tongue,' she asks when the passenger disembarks.

Alighting at St Ives, Anna breathes in salty, blue air; tastes the tang of it. Mirrie and Baines are on the platform in sun hats, waiting to welcome her.

'I am present solely as Miss Anna Pentecost's porter, waiter and dogsbody,' says Will. The freethinking Salas don't faze him: he's a minister without obtrusive theology or strictures. A man, Anna thinks, before he's a minister. Mirrie and Baines won't hear of their guest's turning straight round and going back.

'You came all this way!' says Mirrie. 'And brought my darling safely to me. You must stay at least the one night, Will. No – we insist.'

Mirrie, in this bohemian setting, seems more youthful, less burdened. You've come out into the light somehow, Anna thinks, and can be yourself. But, strangely, it's Lore who surfaces in her mind. Ahead on the steep main street a young woman in a tawny shawl, fair hair all down her back, has a look somehow of Lore. When Anna comes abreast, of course the girl's nothing like her, not really: a tanned fishergirl of thirteen or so. Before they reach their cottage, Anna has seen another phantom Lore, climbing some steps to the gentry houses on the cliff.

'Is something troubling you, Anna?' Will asks. 'Is it because I foisted myself on you? Are you concerned at my staying the night? I can easily go back.'

'Why on earth shouldn't you stay? How is this different from Sarum House? You're always staying over.'

In the fisherman's cottage perched high in the village, low ceilings and doorways force you to stoop. The floor slants like a ship in a high sea: drop any object and it rolls westwards over salt-eaten floorboards. The walls are simply whitewashed and there's no clutter of ornaments or small items of furniture, none of the modern conveniences they are accustomed to – neither wringer, mangle nor copper. No servant. Miriam declined the offer of a little girl from the workhouse as a general servant.

Mirrie's appearance is distinctly odd: she adapts her clothes to serve for a life of practical activity. After all, in sultry weather, why should women be trussed up like sacks of potatoes? She pads around the house in bare feet, her opulent form shown candidly beneath light fabric. Anna kicks off her own shoes. Why not? While Mirrie makes a feint at cooking, Baines cleans. Not much of either, when it comes to it. Either they order in a mackerel supper or rely on bread and cheese, salad and apples. To Anna everything tastes delicious, especially the conversation, and she's hungry all the time. Anything may be broached; thoughts extemporised. Nothing is censored or assumed. You have the tonic feeling of being listened to.

Getting ready for bed – the women are to share while Baines sleeps with Will – Anna watches Miriam take the brush to her thick, pale brown hair.

'Let me.' She takes the cool weight of it in her hand. 'Your hair is lovely.'

'It will do,' Mirrie shrugs. 'But it's nothing compared with yours. So dark, so shining. Darkly shining. You are fearfully beautiful, Anna, I suppose you know that. And I am ... not.'

'Don't say that. We don't know how we appear to others. People love you. You are – I can't find the words – but – properly alive, Mirrie. Very few of us are.'

There's a pause. Is Miriam looking to be told she's beautiful too? Physically she just isn't. And she's so sensitive that she'd detect and resent a fib. Mirrie meets Anna's eyes in the mirror and asks, 'Anna, did you read *Freedom Seeks Her*?'

'I couldn't, Mirrie. It was ... lost. And I tried to replace it, along with the others, but the edition is all sold, apparently, and they're waiting for the new one.'

'How, lost? All of them were lost?'

Anna blushes deeply. It seems treacherous to Beatrice and degrading to yourself to admit that your sister censors your reading. Anna can hardly admit that she's left her new books packaged up in the disused coal hole in the cellar. 'All your books – went. I've replaced them of course, except *Freedom Seeks Her*. Please say nothing more about it.'

'But I will replace the copies now. Of course. You must know, Anna, money is the last thing I have to worry about.' Mirrie fetches a copy of *Freedom Seeks Her* from her box and places it on Anna's side of the bed. 'Oh and by the way, Anna, I like your Mr Anwyl so very much. Such a freshness and warmth.'

Mirrie is soon asleep; Anna can't drop off. She opens Baines's novel.

*Can darkness shine? You wondered when you saw the lustre of her black hair in the sun, burning in some lights blue in its depths. But you wondered more when you heard her speak. Miss Cartwright was thought by some headstrong, by others original, and by all a dangerous presence in the town.*

Can darkness shine?

Is that really me, Anna asks herself, a version of me, in Baines's book? Mirrie said, 'Your hair – darkly shining.' Was that a quotation? Anna leafs forward, skimming for the story. It's nothing like her own life but possibly something like Miriam Sala's: a wealthy and idealistic young gentlewoman has an impetuous tongue, a freethinking intellect and an impulse to ardent actions which offend her kith and kin. Miss

Cartwright is a great maker of well-meaning mistakes who donates a vast sum to an ill-run orphanage and marries a philanthropist who looks like Baines Sala. *Freedom Seeks Her* is written with rueful irony, long, sinuous sentences and a godlike commentator.

Baines has fused herself and Miriam in a composite figure. Or rather he has clothed his wife in Anna's body and whether to feel flattered or queasy, Anna cannot decide.

After that there's no sleep, though Anna cannot continue to read for long. At dawn she rises before anyone else is awake; takes some bread and cheese and lets herself out. Here you can come and go as the spirit takes you and nobody asks why or where. And perhaps I'll never go home, she thinks, to the reins and halter, but find some cottage of my own and read and study and write.

Flocks of waders scurry in and out of a chalk-turquoise sea. The beach in the early light is primrose yellow. From the quay Anna climbs towards the ancient fort of Pendinas, or The Island as the Cornish call it, although an isthmus links it to the mainland. In the harbour fishermen haul in their catch, calling to one another; and a drowned fleet shifts and slides beneath the boats on the glassy water. Their voices liquefy into the shush-hush of the waves; Anna can hear her own footsteps and the rustle of her dress. She's suspended in a dream of light and space, on an edge where earth, sky and sea meet.

The turf of the promontory is pitted with puffin burrows and strewn with their droppings. From Pendinas she looks across the immense sheet of bright water. Dolphins break the surface once, twice, and are gone. Smoke rises from a steam boat. A cormorant dips down, emerging with a silvery fish. With a swift motion, he turns it in his beak and swallows it head first.

Yes, I'll start to be myself now. At long last.

# Chapter 8

Yes, she has said yes.

Apparently. For he sat her squarely on his knee, as though this – in the deserted college chamber – was the most natural thing in the world. He would not allow her to rise until she agreed to marry him. The intimacy of it appalled Beatrice, the outrage. Through layers of petticoat she was aware of the man's legs, his trousers, the intimate parts of him. And if someone should come in! But he knew, Christian said, with quiet certainty, that their union was God's will. '*Allerliebste* Beatrice, I have loved you now for seventeen years. During all that time I've never been drawn to any woman but yourself. I have never polluted my imagination with the thought of another. To me that would have been an adultery. I asked your dear Papa's permission to marry you when you were twelve years old.'

'Ten, I was ten. Or eleven.'

'Twelve. Nearly thirteen. And Mr Pentecost, whom I revered, readily gave it. In my heart you are already my wife, for God has predestined you to be my helpmeet in this world … and all it needs is for you to say the words.'

'It wasn't fair,' she broke out.

'What wasn't fair, dear heart?'

'You took my – childhood. I was a child.' She recalled the jouncing on his knee. She was a big girl, with a blue ribbon in her hair, wearing her Sabbath silk dress. Calling out with high-pitched excitement and distress in his iron arms.

'Not so. I was the soul of rectitude. Your dear father was ever watchful. I expressly stood back and waited. But I knew you would consent – as you have.'

And, according to Christian Beatrice has somehow spoken the words. She cannot go back on them. But when? It must have been in the strange moment when her struggle to break away from his tight arms turned into a kind of silken collapse into the safety of his lap, his breast. Dwarfed there, she settled against him, while saying that, no, this must not be; they must pray; she could not consent.

'You are right. Of course we must pray together.'

Immediately Christian released her. Beatrice rose, hot-faced, smoothing her skirts, feeling her hair with her fingertips in case the roll with its black satin ribbon had fallen askew. Her heart thumped around in her ribcage. She tottered and he steadied her; conducted her, so it seemed, down onto her knees, next to him, facing the window. He knelt beside her. Grey light fell through the pane onto the two figures as he prayed aloud for a blessing on their partnership on earth and in heaven. Kneeling there at his side, motionless beneath the changeless light, Beatrice opened her eyes and felt that she and he had turned to stone, condemned to kneel together like alabaster funerary figures of spouses in Salisbury Cathedral.

And when they rose from prayer, it seemed that Beatrice Pentecost and Christian Ritter did so as engaged people. And *soon*, the wedding must be *soon*, the bridegroom-to-be urged, holding her hand, looking down with earnest rapture. Not only because he has waited so many years but also because he may be called upon, within a month or so, to return to New York to aid Mr Beecher.

'But … the arrangements, Christian. Where are we to live?' Doubtless one should consider the lilies of the field which neither toil nor spin but are cared for by their Heavenly Father. Considerations of trousseau and the preparation of a house must seem unworthy in the eyes of Beatrice's husband-to-be. Often when she was a child Christian had corrected her concern for a pretty ribbon or some other frippery. He always did this in a sad, gentle way. What would Jesus think of the ribbon? he'd wonder. Did Mary and Martha wear ribbons? What was the opinion of the contrite Mary Magdalene concerning ribbons? But the fallen world is the real world, Beatrice tells herself: it's where we live. There are practicalities to be sorted out, social decencies to be observed. Wedding guests, the wedding breakfast. The matter of a settlement of her property on herself, the importance of which was always emphasised by Papa.

'*Liebling*, cannot we do things simply? I don't expect you to accompany me on all my travels, you know that. Your home as it stands is perfect for us. Your own mission may be in Chauntsey, for women have missions as well as men. My wants, in externals, are few. And our dear Anna, of course, will remain in her father's home. How happy Lore would be, if only she could know.'

But when did I consent?

Beatrice, letting down her hair before the mirror in her dingy room at Mr Leek's lodging house, scowls at her candlelit reflection. She hardly knows herself, transitional between states. Hotel doors close; pipes gurgle; the footsteps of two clerks sharing the room above Beatrice's creak as they traipse to and fro. Fragmentary messages arrive from other and cryptic worlds. At what moment did I utter the words that will make me, in a month's time, Frau Beatrice Ritter? She speaks the name aloud, a name of dignity and worth, aristocratic-sounding. The hairbrush in her hand staggers in mid-stroke; her lips quiver. And whether excitement or dismay is uppermost, Beatrice cannot say.

Oh Anna, if only you were here. Anna would listen with sympathy, in the light of her compendious knowledge of her sister. For she knows me through and through, Beatrice thinks, both the best and worst of me, the dark corners where I hide even from myself. And Anna would mediate if necessary. There may still be a chance to retract, before the month gets underway.

But if Christian is right and this is God's will for us, what can I do but let the insignificant drop of me pour into the ocean of him? God has judged Beatrice along the way but she has sidestepped His chidings. Now is the time of reckoning. Since earliest childhood Beatrice has read providences in everyday events – but with a wanton eye, making it up as she goes along. Only Beatrice knows the grubby secrets of her own hard heart; her need to predominate; her lip-religion, her pretence of heart-religion. The Almighty has never been deceived. For a quarter of a century He has observed Miss Pentecost punishing her younger sister for being born. And now God brings the elder to heel. He has taken over. He has spoken for her. Beatrice's Master has delivered her to a kind earthly master. Isn't there some relief in that?

*

Mr Spurgeon himself takes their hands and holds them for a moment. 'Ah,' he exclaims, looking bright-eyed from one to the other, 'So you two dear souls are called to this high and honourable estate of marriage. I recommend it! Heartily! For *whoso findeth a wife findeth a good thing and obtaineth favour of the Lord!* For five years Susannah and I have been bone of one another's bone, have we not, Wifey? Our engagement was sealed with a gift from my wife to myself. Would you like to tell them what it was, my dear?'

'I gave you a complete set of John Calvin's *Commentaries*, did I not, my love?' replies Susannah Spurgeon. She's a trim, upright figure, with pale, intense and rather anxious eyes, neatly and expensively clad in grey silk. The mother of twin boys. The companion of Greatness. 'For, you see, Miss Pentecost, my darling had led me to the cross of Christ for the peace and pardon my weary soul was seeking. I trust that is well said, husband?' She appeals to her spouse with her dignified head tilted in appeal.

'Very well said, my own.'

'You know,' Susannah goes on, as her husband moves away to speak to others, 'I hold firm views on matrimony. Mr Spurgeon urges me to publish them in a pamphlet. I maintain that one ought not to choose a wife blighted by hereditary disease. Should disease come, well and good. But we have no right to tamper with the health of subsequent generations, do you not agree, Miss Pentecost? And, again – quaint though this may sound – avoid choosing your wife on a holiday or at a pleasant party. Surprise her by dropping in during the week: catch her in her workaday clothes.'

Respectfully as Beatrice receives these precepts, privately she cannot help but hope that Christian will not address her as 'Wifey' when they marry. He receives Mrs Spurgeon's effusions with courteous gravity. From the corner of her eye Beatrice observes Mr Spurgeon over by a gigantic tea urn as he posts a succession of small cakes into his mouth, addressing himself betweenwhiles to Miss Randolph. In the same circle stands Mr Montagu, who will shortly join the hands of Herr Ritter and Miss Pentecost.

The ghostly Anna who lodges in Beatrice's head reassures her: Dear, you can change your mind. There is still time.

Beatrice's husband-to-be has enquired of Mrs Spurgeon whether she has matrimonial advice for ladies as well as for gentlemen.

'Oh certainly. As I see it, a *smoking,* idle fellow may leave off his bad habits for as long as his new toy amuses him – but, depend upon it, he'll soon revert. It comes down to this: only marry another converted one. Or fear a blighted hearth.'

To Beatrice's eye Mrs Spurgeon looks less than well, her face thin and gaunt. Does her husband's well-known partiality for cigars disturb her? Is Mrs Spurgeon happy with her lot, seeing her husband besieged by infatuated thousands? How can one see beyond the façade of married love to gauge the intimate truth of human beings? The front door closes upon the private world. The married parties remove shawls and overcoats. They let slip their guarded courtesies. And they never tell. No one tells. Only the servants who empty our slops and view our intimate linen see and whisper. Husband and wife are dumb. When Miss Beatrice Pentecost becomes Mrs Christian Ritter, she will not be free to confide, even to Anna, the secrets of her life. A married woman is alone in the world.

But no. What is she thinking of? As Mrs Spurgeon moves away, Beatrice looks up at Christian with a small smile: 'I hope you will not prove a smoking, idle one, Christian.'

'I shall earnestly try not to. But even so, my dear, you must keep a close watch on me at all times. I am so happy, Beatrice. I shall do all in my power to ensure that you never regret your choice. With your agreement I shall draft some precepts for our conduct, from which we must never deviate.'

*

Autumn has descended on Wiltshire. The fields are waterlogged, cattle having retreated to higher ground. From the streaming train window Beatrice watches labourers wade through floodwater to drive them back to shelter. The locomotive pauses. Through greenish light she sees a drowned sheep, bloated, just below the embankment. Her betrothed looks up from his book and smiles into Beatrice's eyes. 'My love,' he mouths and a fellow passenger peers swiftly from one to the other.

Beatrice, surveying this landscape of deliquescence, worries about her own sheep. In this unseasonably protracted downpour, foot rot is a very real danger. She needs to get a good price for them. There's some relief in returning to the banal practicalities of her daily world; her habits of control and her dignity as head of the family. But is this to be her world now? For I am his, and this is my life. Anna, I am to be *married*. The die is cast. Beatrice sees that this was always the plan and that, however she struggled in God's web, the more strongly the silken filaments netted her.

As the train inches towards Salisbury, thoughts of Will Anwyl haunt her. He loves me. I truly think he does. He'll be bereft. But for how long? Beatrice glances over at Christian deep in his book. She reverences him; looks up to him as she never has to Will. Even so, I never did say yes, she thinks. I never spoke the words. They were assumed. I went with it. You have forced me. God has forced me.

\*

The carriage awaits them, sent by Joss. Only three quarters of an hour and Beatrice will be snug at home with Anna. There's so much to tell and ask. Rain souses down and the ford in spate is almost impassable. They stick fast; under the lash of the whip, the horses' labouring haunches haul them clear. Beatrice sits hand in gloved hand with her husband-to-be. Chauntsey: One Furlong. Nearly home.

At the market cross a crowd, some with umbrellas, most

without, surrounds a dark figure waving his arms. It's Mr Kyffin.

Stepping down, Beatrice and Christian join them. The minister is expounding calculations of the end of the world. The sums appear complicated and he's obliged to move between the more abstruse verses of the Book of Revelation and a notebook in which the calculations, noted in blue ink, have bled into one another. Mr Kyffin flounders, appealing to his Maker to help him decipher the columns of figures. For never since the Flood has there been such a deluge in Wiltshire and this in itself, he feels, may be part of that mysterious system of signs with which Heaven guides and tests men of faith.

The Open Plymouth Brethren are out in force and there are even a few Exclusive Brethren, breaking their rule of separation from the cholera of sin that infects their neighbours, for they imminently expect the Lord's coming.

Mr Kyffin gives up on the apocalyptic mathematics; he'll have to repeat his calculations from scratch, he confesses, and stuffs the soggy notebook in his overcoat pocket. For perhaps this rain should be read as a criticism from on high: his sums may be wrong. It's God's way of putting Mr Kyffin to his abacus again.

'He leads his chosen out of error! And here is a chosen Boy – come and speak, Isaiah!'

The boy – isn't it the baker's boy from Grimstead? – comes complete with disciples, who break into song but what they're singing Beatrice can't make out in the gusty rain. Incredulous, she turns to Christian, only to discover that he is listening respectfully.

The baker's boy stands in an attitude of prayer. When he speaks, Beatrice is surprised by the music of his as yet unbroken voice; hardly less pure than those of the choristers in Salisbury Cathedral, where she has sometimes worshipped in a spirit of critical tolerance. Proof against stained glass, marble bishops, the Luciferian pride of funerary memorials, she has been reduced to tears by those angel voices. She notes the confidence of Isaiah's gestures. Mr Kyffin gazes down at him with respect.

'Never weep for Harry!' pleads Isaiah.

'Who's Harry?' asks a voice from the crowd.

'Harry Fribance, the blacksmith's son of Grimstead. Our dear little brother, now departed to his Father. For Harry was a saint. Elect before the world. He was two years and eight months old in this vale of tears. And when the profane Punch and Judy show came to West Grimstead he cried and covered his eyes so as not to see the wickedness of this bad Mr Punch.'

'Here's your rope To hang the Pope And a penn'orth of cheese to choke him,' bellow the boys.

'Harry's with his Father. Where perhaps according to Brother Kyffin, them of us as be chosen'll be snugly lodged by winter. Playing with Harry in the snow and he not coughing.' He pauses for this to sink in. 'Never coughing more. Knowing that Rome is doomed, Harry has gone easy to his grave, not but what we don't miss him.'

'He comes! He comes!' Mr Kyffin, pointing to the west, face ashen, convulsing with fear or ecstasy, takes three steps, reels and falls.

Dr Quarles pushes through the crowd: Mr Kyffin is suffering an epileptic seizure, he says. 'For goodness' sake, let me through to treat the patient. Everyone go home.'

Mr Kyffin, dead to the world, is carried into Beatrice's carriage and thence to Sarum House, where he remembers nothing but a sense that all this has happened before, in some other universe.

'Oh dear me.' He labours to sit up on the sofa. 'I fear I have bitten my tongue. But I have seen a great light. There are pins and needles in my arm, Miss Pentecost.'

'Quietly now, dear Mr Kyffin,' counsels Beatrice. 'You had a nasty fall. Amy shall bring you some brandy and you'll soon be restored. Dr Quarles has promised to come and ease you by letting blood. This gentleman I think you will remember? Herr Ritter?'

'I don't think I have had the honour,' says Mr Kyffin. 'Are you a postman?'

'Well, in a certain sense, dear sir, perhaps I am a messenger. I am come from America,' says Christian. 'Where there's a great Awakening, such as I think you are expecting.'

'You're an American? You don't sound …'

'Not an American by birth, no. I have just been visiting New York, Mr Kyffin.'

'And where is your homeland?'

Christian, about to complicate things by mentioning Germany, is illuminated: 'I am a citizen of *your* country, my friend. A citizen, I praise my Jesus, of Heaven.'

Mr Kyffin sighs. 'Then I must confess to you that the Lord has bruised me but I have faith in him, for has he not promised, *A bruised reed he will not break, and a smouldering wick he will not snuff out*. And I am smouldering. Yet radiant. Miss Pentecost, am I welcome in your house? Mrs Kyffin has shut her door upon me.'

Amy has grand fires blazing in the drawing room. Copperware and brassware shine like mirrors. Beatrice's father's clock in its glass cover ticks its reassuring pulse beat and tings the quarter hour and all around Beatrice is her father's presence, right down to … yes, they are in the bureau drawer … his spectacles and tiepin. Thank heaven she's home. Her wet gloves and shawl are off; her feet are cosy in their worn slippers.

'But where's my sister, Amy?'

'Oh, she is not back yet, Miss.'

'Back from where?'

'From Cornwall, Miss. She left a couple of days after you did. I'm sure she wrote to you to say.'

'Ah. Of course. Do we have her address?'

Beatrice studies the address, written in her sister's backward-sloping handwriting: c/o Mrs Sala, '*Gwenily*', St Ives, Cornwall.

*

Round the dining table, Mr and Mrs Elias join Christian, Beatrice and Joss for a six o'clock dinner, to discuss what's to be done for their friend. He lies on a spare bed sleepless or roams the bedroom conversing with God. He has drunk tea but refused food, saying that he could no more eat than Elijah when the land of Israel was cursed with famine.

'I'm the last one to judge, and hurt me it does to suggest it,' Loveday says, 'but I do believe he is deranged. That's what I've been telling Mr Elias.'

'You have, my love. But let us think the best.'

'Which is more than Josiah Kyffin's afflicted wife has done,' Loveday fires back. 'She has shut the door on the man. She can stand no more. Nor, in my view, should she.'

'And yet we are taught, my love,' says Mr Elias equably, taking a sip of wine, 'that the husband is the head of his wife.'

'Not when the husband is *gorffwyll*, Mr Elias.'

'But who shall judge when a husband is mad? I trust you will not go calling me mad, Mrs Elias, and sending for Mr Croft to remove me to the Lunatic Asylum.'

'Only if you try my patience extremely. But seriously, Beatrice, Dr Quarles is right; our friend requires treatment and restraint. For his own good.'

'Although I'm bound to point out,' says Mr Elias. 'That this is what a High Anglican like Dr Quarles *would* say of a dissenting visionary.'

Beatrice, preoccupied with Anna's absence, cannot attend to the conversation. Her sister has absconded, cunningly waiting until her back was turned. Anna has associated herself with Mrs Sala, adulteress and infidel. Somehow this desertion seems of a piece with Mr Kyffin's running amok. It's the age we live in, Beatrice thinks. Certainties spin like tops whipped by manic children.

Dessert is served – Brown Betty, baked by Amy with new apples and stale breadcrumbs – and the room is fragrant with cinnamon. There's a knock at the back door. Beatrice leaps to her feet for it's Will, she knows it is. She'll go herself, she tells Amy.

It's only Charlie Kyffin, soaked to the skin and spattered with mud. 'I heard Papa was here.'

Mr Kyffin sits in the drawing room with Charlie holding his hand and calling him darling Dad. A more tenderly filial boy there never was, despite his taste for tobacco and alcohol. Mr Elias seated at the piano plays 'The Moonlight Sonata', *Andante sostenuto*. He smiles across at Mr Kyffin and sways his head at him, as if to say, 'Here we are, my friend; it's not so bad, is it?' Mr Kyffin appears less electrocuted by the minute but how old he looks, drained and spent, though he's only in his early forties.

'Won't you come home with me tomorrow, Papa?' Charlie asks gently.

'I cannot.'

'But why, Papa?'

The father seems to grope for words. He looks round vacantly; leans forwards to study his own shoes. Charlie lays his hand on his back, to remind him he's still here. The fire susurrates in the grate. Finally Mr Kyffin manages, 'I bear the stigma.'

'Papa, Mama didn't mean to turn you out. She has been …
greatly tested. She has needed rest and I have suggested to
her that she should go for a water cure.'

'I know I'm a burden.' Childish tears trickle down Mr
Kyffin's face. 'And Prynne has stabbed me in the back. But
this is irrelevant. I say no, Charlie.'

'Well, in that case, Papa, at least come and enjoy a pipe
with us in the smoking room?'

The sufferer's face lights up. 'What a good idea.'

But this, Beatrice fears, is what triggered the aberration in
the first place. Burning tobacco is transformed in the lungs of
weak men to poison. The golden fibres that smell so fragrant
in the leather pouch besmirch and rot the soul. Thus the men
of their sect – Mr Spurgeon not excepted – abuse themselves.
If Mr Kyffin could bring himself to renounce tobacco, he
might yet be cured. At an All Night of Prayer last year in
Alderbury, thirteen pipes, several tobacco pouches and two
snuff boxes were handed in by penitents, amid scenes of
sobbing and quaking. Beatrice, though unimpressed by such
wild performances, was struck by the practical results.

Her husband-to-be startles her by rising with the men to
leave for the smoking room. And his look tells her, 'Do not be
hasty to judge our Saviour's children.'

Later she hears music and laughter. Mr Elias is playing his
fiddle, an Irish melody. Listening at the door, Beatrice peeps
through the gap at the men in their retreat. Short
Meerschaums and long clay pipes protrude from bearded
mouths. There's an air of relaxation rarely witnessed in mixed
company. Joss is telling tales of his boyhood. Charlie reminds
his father of a seaside holiday in Brighton. Later she hears
Christian talking about America: the tide of liberation that's
carrying the abolitionist north by storm into revival after
revival. In America, he says, there's less talk amongst

advanced people of sin and guilt; more talk of holiness and love. All men may be saved. This is the doctrine of Mr Beecher, whom he reverences, notwithstanding the aspersions cast on the great man as a loose liver and idol of the masses.

Beatrice gazes through the fog at her radical husband-to-be, who, though he has lit a pipe, does not appear to be smoking it. He cradles the bowl in one hand on his knee, occasionally raising it towards his lips, which it never touches. In a year's time perhaps Beatrice will have been brought to assent to these shocking doctrines of allowable tobacco and universal salvation: it will all seem a matter of course. She will have passed from the hands of her Calvinist father into those of her Arminian husband.

Mr Kyffin sits and smiles at everything and everyone. Perhaps he has glimpsed a new light and is once more travelling from star to star.

Mrs Bunce, bearing gossip, is announced. In the unlit drawing room, amid a parliament of black umbrellas opened to dry, she informs Beatrice that Anna Pentecost was seen by her husband's uncle departing from Salisbury Station in the company of a certain reprehensible young minister of Fighelbourn.

# Chapter 9

The passengers, having vomited their way across the Bristol Channel from Ilfracombe, await their connection at Swansea Station with three hours to spare. On the paddle steamer *Velindra*, an expansive Welsh doctor travelling home from his annual Devon holiday assured them that copper fumes had a beneficial effect on the lungs; Swansea metal workers and their families were happily in receipt of 'the beneficent kind of arsenic'. Oddly enough, he observed, cattle die of the fumes and a bed of rhubarb will turn brown as dried tobacco but men are seldom adversely affected.

When she sees and smells the thick yellow masses of cloud belched from the shafts of the smelting furnaces, Anna knows it's a lie. Or rather, it's a lie the doctor believes. Hills of slag tower around the town; the ground is barren and black. What Anna will remember of Swansea is the foetid stink and the warrior queen.

Fumes flood the station; everyone coughs, swathing mouth and nose with cloth. Metal clangs on metal; a pig waddles across the platform and the Sala party huddles on a bench while a female voice shrieks in the station forecourt. Anna, approaching Will's homeland in expectation of poetry, has been reading the Salas' copy of the translated *Mabinogion*, thinking: I was right, it's very simple, Will cannot be known in England. He's a foreigner there as surely as any Russian. She must be sure to explain this to Beatrice.

Close to retching in the fog, Anna closes her eyes. They open upon the grandest woman Anna has ever seen. The warrior queen stands poised at the platform edge, balancing a pitcher on the crown of her flat hat. Six foot tall or more, she peers up the line, her woollen shawl, doubled and thrown back over one shoulder, falling behind in graceful folds. A companion, scarcely less majestic, stands smiling as she looks back at the row developing in the station.

'Who are they?' Anna asks a local passenger.

'Cocklewomen. Picturesque, are they not? They dig for cockles in the bay and sell them at the market. Oh – watch out – here we go!'

A porter scuttles onto the platform, pursued by a cocklewoman. She picks him up bodily and slams the puny fellow down on to the track below, where he sprawls on his face groaning. Wiping her palms on her skirts, the cocklewoman straightens her shawl and looks round. You don't have to understand Welsh to know she's asking whether anyone else would care for a taste of the same?

Miriam, notebook on knee, hungrily observant, is scribbling pencilled notes. She's recording the episode in her journal perhaps. Anna is also conscious of hoarding the scene for her diary. Anna recalls Mr Munby and his notebook – how he flicked the pages over, revealing sketches of working women in trousers, coal-black from head to foot. There was a strange, quivering eagerness in his manner: something of relish in the way he described the dignity of brawny female arms and massive hands – his own being milky-white. What was in those other photographs he showed to Joss?

It's a relief to pick up your skirts and board the train, quitting the squalor of this industrial sink where thousands have to live, if you can call it living – those typhoid-stricken, pauperised multitudes of the coal and iron valleys. It's the world Mr Clifford brought before Anna's imagination, but to breathe its air is another thing. You cower and want to run.

The train speeds beside silver stretches of water, past Llanelli Vale, Ferryside and the ruined castle of Llanstephan. At Tenby there's a carriage ride – twelve on top and half a dozen inside, through lanes rich with foxglove and honeysuckle. At every village the population turns out to watch them pass, the women in their dark blue petticoats and tall black hats. Anna gasps at her first view of the harbour, cliffs and pristine yellow sands. White bathing machines are lined up on the shore. And she's back at Lulworth with Lore in a darkly glittering ecstasy that's only not forbidden because nobody imagines its existence. Cemented into the walls of the party's lodgings are great whelk shells, bleached white by sun and rain.

By the time they arrive, the cocklewomen episode has turned into an anecdote. Mirrie's friends are intrigued. This is what happens, they say, when you go too far with working women. Push down on the dough as you will, the yeast will rise. We shall grow a head taller in the next generation – and do not spit upon a woman then; she will toss you down on the line. Once the cocklewomen are literate, we shall have revolution.

'I hope not though,' Mirrie protests. Her long, lugubrious face is earnest. 'Joking aside. I don't want us to grow fangs and claws. Let's hope education and reform will do the job.'

'My brother's friend,' Anna chips in, 'said he'd once seen

an apple-woman sitting on a stool beside her cart, reading the *Life of Garibaldi*.'

Anna has never before shared the company of educated, radical ladies. Questioning everything is their norm. She should feel at home. She doesn't, except for the chance to be with Mirrie. Barbara Bodichon, with her red-gold hair and her resolute intelligence, is an artist who burns for women's higher education, votes, professional status. Matilda – 'Max' – Hays, a sculptress, smokes and affects a man's coat; lets it be known that she rides a horse astride. Max has translated the scandalous French novelist George Sand into English.

But where am I in all this? Anna wonders. Dowdy and provincial, she lacks education, style and background. Style here is expressed not in the following of fashion but in the cut of your clothes and an air of confidence. These are wealthy, cultured, eloquent people whose bohemianism rides on the back of privilege. Their accents mark out Anna's Wiltshire burr – the soft chalk of her Rs. And yet they acknowledge her as an equal, enquiring about her home and sister.

It's feels like a disloyalty to speak of Beatrice in this company. Imagine Beatrice visiting, steeling herself to hand out pious tracts – understanding little, fearing everything. She'd find so many books to burn; the conflagration would be visible from Ilfracombe.

'My dear sister is in London at present, visiting Regent's Park College – the Baptist college. She's there in part to meet our family friend, Christian Ritter.'

'I know that name. Ritter – wasn't he the author of *Die Pflichten des Christentums*, The Duties of Christianity?'

'That was Christian's father, Barbara. And his cousin was married to my father. She died in childbirth.'

'But how *fascinating* and how sad. Walther Ritter was, if I remember, a Christian Socialist, is that how one would describe him? – do I have the right man? We have several of his works at home.'

Anna tells them a little about life at Sarum House and describes the visit of Mr Clifford, assuming that this name will speak to their political idealism, as it does. But the more Anna invokes John Clifford and his collectivist social gospel, the more she's aware of falsifying her picture of Sarum House, skewing it into a haven of liberalism. How poorly their library and her mind are stocked. Devotional literature and dusty theology. But it won't always be like this, Anna promises herself. I'll accumulate books and stop hiding them. I'll face her out. Joss will help me. I'll carve out a territory.

Wearing wideawake hats and old jackets with sundry pockets, their skirts cut or pinned several inches above the ankle, the women talk their way down to the sea. The endless high-powered discussion is exhausting. It never pauses. I'm a provincial, Anna thinks. And yet she treasures the experience. There are zoological riches in the perforated caverns of St Catherine's Island, a limestone rock, the nearside of which is high and dry at low tide. While Anna carries a landing-net and a chisel, Mirrie has a leather case slung across her shoulder, freighted with hammer, oysterknife and paperknife, in quest of specimens for Baines to photograph. The others carry foot-pans, pie-dishes, soup bowls and vases as if preparing to set up house. Two other parties of ladies are making their way across the sands, similarly equipped.

Dropping behind, Anna and Mirrie saunter arm in arm, glad of a quiet interlude. There's something Mirrie wants to say, Anna can feel it.

A man with a hammer and chisel and a lad with a muslin net are zoologising amongst the rock pools.

'The great naturalist, Mr Gosse,' Miriam says. 'I venerate

him – despite the unreason of *Omphalos*. Shall I introduce you? And his utterly angelic little boy.'

Edmund is a beloved fellow-labourer, so his father remarks with a tender smile, fondling his son's nut-brown head, in the vineyard of Truth.

'What have you discovered today, Edmund?' Mirrie asks the serious child. She crouches down to speak to him, easy and tender with the child in a way Anna could never have imagined.

'Well, miss, earlier we found red-noses in the cave. Poor little things. They live in holes in the rock and stick their red noses out like knobs – when we come along they shoot off back into their burrows. And we go after them.'

'And no man knows,' adds the father, 'how this jelly-soft creature digs out holes in hard limestone. Does he secrete acid? Does he rub-a-dub-dub with his tiny foot? Edmund and I are on Mr Red-Nose's trail, depend upon it. And now we're collecting *Sagitta*, a very tricky little chap. Although he resembles a fish, he's a mollusc in disguise.'

Mr Gosse ruefully hopes that the current appetite for sea-science will not altogether strip these fashionable watering places of marine life. 'So many crinolined collectors,' he says, shaking his head. 'Such an influx of tradesmen selling specimens. Naturally I do not mean yourself. Mr Sala is a respected student of science. But already the caverns here are not what they were. I should hate to see Tenby and its caves robbed of Actiniae. It's like a plague of locusts. But, *mea maxima culpa*, have I not called the masses here, with my writings and aquarium?'

'Your boy is a credit to you, Mr Gosse,' says Mirrie. She looks at the child hungrily as if yearning to hug and kiss him.

As Miriam and Anna take their leave, Mr Gosse is edifying his son by a comparison of the scythe jaws of the *Sagitta bipunctata* with the torture implements used by the Papal Inquisition against the Protestants of Belgium.

'Mr Gosse is an eminent member of the Plymouth Brethren,' Miriam tells Anna. 'His zoological work is truly wonderful. And yet he clings to an old system that is dying in front of everyone's eyes.'

'But Miriam, *I* cling too.' Anna has stopped in her tracks, one hand on Miriam's arm. She can't help saying it; the words escape the more compulsively for the doubts that have beset her. Gripping Mirrie's arm harder than she intends, she swings her round, face to face. The wet sands stretch away, tobacco-brown, to the distant sea. Gulls stand still on the gale. 'I cling to the cross of Jesus. I cling. Whatever forces act to sweep me away, I cling on tight. Nothing – absolutely nothing and nobody – even myself – will persuade me to let go.'

Perhaps it's the first time Mirrie has encountered the stubborn force of Anna Pentecost, so familiar to Beatrice. A second's recoil is followed by swift adjustment. Miriam takes Anna's straight gaze: 'Oh but, my dear Anna, I cling too. To the *human* Jesus. Whatever would I be without him?'

'But for me that's not enough, Mirrie. He is also God.'

'Yes. Yes, I understand. And he is all I know of God. I was brought up in a narrow neighbourhood amongst ignorant bigots. Sects who were always going for one another's jugular vein. Unitarianism freed me from this zealotry – for bigotry is not what the Gospels teach. They teach humanity. We are not so far apart, dear Anna. Are we?'

'Aren't we?'

The red-noses are so soft, Anna thinks, and yet they are able to eat into rock. Are you feeding on me, Mirrie? And passing on what you've digested from me to Baines, who writes it and whatever else you collect into his novels?

Everything in solution with yourself. She thinks of *Freedom Seeks Her*. The story of a woman whose qualities are far above her peers and wants what's best for the world, flouting the laws of her society. An innocent transgressor. She'll have to pay for her anomalies.

The two of them, Miriam and Baines, are like an enormous intellectual stomach, she thinks, converting what they glean from their world into the substance of themselves. They can't help it. They're always hungry for reality. Just as I am myself: that's why I'm carping at them. Suddenly the beach seems flooded with lady naturalists, bending for live molluscs and empty shells, minerals, seaweed, stripping it bare.

*

Anna steals in through the back door. There's no one at home, a rare thing at Sarum House. Good: she can catch her breath.

Light slants through the tall windows; it edges the dark curtains of the morning room with scarlet and calls out swirling green patterns from the carpet's obscurities. The faintly dank, always welcome smell of an ancient house, in which generations have followed in one another's footsteps, lightly entering and lightly quitting a common space.

The fire has been banked up and guarded. Anna takes off bonnet and gloves; removes the fender and crouches to enjoy the warmth. She finds plum cake in the pantry and pours sherry to wash it down. Then she prowls the house, looking into each room: several visitors, all male, all rather tidy compared with her messy brother. Standing at her own window, Anna takes in the gentle tumult of the wind in the trees. Already the leaves are beginning to turn. Ewes browse the grass; the geese swim on the pond in a moody gaggle. Everything's just as it should be and always was. In her sister's room, Anna pours water into the ewer and splashes her face; pats it dry with Beatrice's towel, breathing in her scent. Perhaps it can all be forgiven. Would that be so impossible? One craves affection. Your sister is your sister. She collapses on Beatrice's bed; rolls over and lays her head on her pillow.

Hearing the front door open, Anna charges downstairs; hurls herself into her sister's arms.

'Where have you been? Oh, *Annie*, I've been so worried about you, so terribly concerned. Are you ill?'

'No, of course not. I wrote to you, Beattie, at Mr Leek's. From St Ives and then from Tenby. Surely you got the letters?'

'Anna, I've been back here for a whole week.'

'Oh no, that's the limit. I'm so sorry. Leek should have forwarded them. Well, anyway we're both here now. Oh, it's Joss – hallo. How are you, Amy? And – it's Christian. You're back.'

'*Liebe* Anna. I hope I did not alarm you. We have spoken of you so often. And I am a blissfully married man. Well, almost.'

'Oh ... yes. How lovely. *Ich gratuliere*. And who ...?'

'Goodness me, Anna. Can you not guess?'

Christian has removed his cloak with a flourish. His presence seems to fill the room; he stands rhetorically as if about to address them all, sofa and mantelpiece and the watercolour portraits of Papa and Mama at either side of the chimney. Christian's resemblance to Lore is fading with time, yes, it's going. And then Anna realises.

'Oh no!' is all that she manages to squeak. 'Not Beatrice?'

'*Anna!*'

'Sorry. Just ... I'm overwhelmed, that's all. I'd no idea. Well, of course, I *did*.'

'She's unwell. Sit down, Anna,' says Beatrice, bitterly hurt. I must be careful, Anna thinks, not to arouse her resentment. We need to live in harmony from now on, if I'm to have my

120

freedom and come and go as I wish. Anna cannot help but shiver as once she did peering through a partly open door at Christian jouncing her sister on his knee, a child, her cheeks hot and red, wrinkling her nose, her hands caught up at her chin like a mouse. His too large hand stroked the place between her shoulder blades. His face buried itself for a moment in her ringlets, breathing in her scent. There were others in the room, a ring of ladies, all, it seemed, in thrall to the glorious young man, all leaning forward, going *Aah* ... as if it were the sweetest thing in the world. It was not sweet. It is not sweet now.

My cousin is always hungry and thirsty; he wants to swallow the world, said Lore, for its own good. He needs to suck blood.

There's nothing to be done. It's too late now to explain to Beatrice her new and favourable view of Will Anwyl. Anna stands up; smiles; shakes her brother-in-law-to-be by the hand, asking about his work, his travels, the happy couple's plans. All the while the walls are closing in and Sarum House takes on the staleness of a sick-room, in which one has suffered whooping cough, dreaded ghosts and feared the touchy Deity who was incensed when you asked for extra plum cake. Whereas in Cornwall she expanded, now Anna shrinks.

Do not, whatever you do, relinquish your territory, Anna warns herself. But the parlour narrows further. She can't stand it. Anna brushes past Beatrice, a rigid smile on her face. In the kitchen Amy's chopping carrots and a kettle's boiling on the range, before which a stray tabby basks. Leaving by the back door, Anna strides down the garden, telling herself to be calm, all will be well. Unhappiness is just a habit.

Beatrice isn't far behind. 'For goodness' sake, Anna, what on earth are you doing? What an exhibition of yourself you've made. Come back in, you'll catch cold.'

'Cold will have to catch me first.'

'What on earth have you been doing?'

'What have *you* been doing, I could ask you the same thing.'

Beatrice takes a step backwards through the mulch of fallen leaves. 'I would have told you if I'd known where you were. And, oh, what a shock when I got home and learned that you ...'

'Told me what?'

'About my engagement.'

'But what about Mr Anwyl?'

'Anna, I could never marry him now. Never.'

'Why not?'

'Because *you* will have to marry him.'

'I beg your pardon?'

'Anna, how can you be such a baby? How can you not realise what you've done – running off with him like that. Did you not for one moment think what the consequences of that would be?'

'Of what?'

'Running away with your sister's ...'

'Sister's what?'

Beatrice turns away. Whispers, 'Love.' She seems overwhelmed by her own acknowledgment; holds her face between both palms.

'But if Will is that ... how can you think of marrying anyone else?'

They're both hot and red-faced – ready to rake their claws down one another's cheeks as in distant girlhood when briars were readily blamed for wounds. And the wounds, generally on the face of the younger, would represent a victory for Anna, especially if she picked the scars until they oozed pus and bore the stigmata with the appearance of uncomplaining patience – which produced fury in the belly of the aggressor and seduced her to renew her attack. All this is remembered here at the end of the garden where cultivated lawns give way to wilderness, glorious with poppies and cornflowers in the summer and where brambles yield a heavy harvest of blackberries that persist into early November.

And there's something here, the precious objects she collected and buried. Anna scans around. Now, which was her mound? I buried them for my mother, she thinks. For Mama in the other world, the other life. The tumps, like waves in a green sea, look alike; none of them seems to call. I need to dowse for it, she thinks. I need divining rods.

'What are you looking at, Anna? For goodness' sake. I can't marry him now, can I? – I couldn't, how could I?' Beatrice hisses. Her fine new London gown is saturated in the long grass. 'He's soiled. Like you. Only you are worse. Anna, *what* is the matter with you? Have you gone out of your mind? You ran away together. You were witnessed. At the station. On the train. You and Mr Anwyl. I was told.'

'But what were you told, Beatrice? That Mr Anwyl was concerned for my health and insisted on coming to take care of me?'

'Holding hands. I was told. That he was ...' – Beatrice turns her face away, her tears overflow, she speaks small – 'rubbing the palm of your hand with his thumb.'

'What?'

'With his thumb,' Beatrice repeats, ridiculously, despairingly, as if the whole issue turned upon this one observation. 'Like this.' She mimes with her own hands. 'Stroking. Fondling. Secretly. The inside of your hand. The whole of Chauntsey and Fighelbourn is talking about you and him. How can you show your face?'

'I just wonder,' Anna says evenly, although her face flames, because she remembers, yes, she does remember now and had no objection then to this tenderly playful gesture, to which she ought to have objected. And it must have been the elderly man in the carriage on the first leg of the journey who took silent note as she and Will jested and bantered and were taken for man and wife. Anna felt as if she were flying above her own head with the thrill of holiday. 'I just wonder how anyone could have seen a person's *thumb* doing *secret* things in the *palm* of someone else's hand? Does it sound likely to you, Beatrice? Quite honestly?'

Beatrice shakes her head. She sees the point but her closed face says that it makes no odds what actually happened. What signifies is that Anna Pentecost has exposed herself, her family and her denomination to reproach.

'And then,' Beatrice goes on. 'To cap it all. You went off with Miriam Sala, so-called, and her ... paramour. Behind my back. Atheists. You could hardly wait to get me out of the house – scheming with this creature. You do know, do you, that they are not legally married.'

'They *are* married, Beatrice.'

'I was told they were not. On good authority. Mr Montagu is not a gossip or a liar.'

'How does that old busybody know anyway? They are *married*.'

'Not legally married. Ask your friend where and when they were married.'

'It's tattle. You should be ashamed.'

Beatrice says, 'She denies Christ! That woman is rotten with sin. She has seduced you – yes, Anna, yes, she has – she's a blasphemer. She will never enter my house again. Not if she comes crawling to the door and begs.'

'Oh, very Christian of you,' Anna sneers. 'Oh yes, I like that.'

'And, Anna, this is my house. I shall never allow atheists and fornicators under my roof.'

'Your house for another three weeks apparently.' Anna no longer guards what she's saying. She just wants to hurt her sister. The words of Barbara and Bessie echo in her memory. They were discussing the campaign to amend the marriage laws. And Mirrie was very silent. A married woman owns nothing under the law. It's a crying shame, everyone agreed. 'In three weeks apparently you'll be handing your property over to another person. Sarum House becomes your *husband*'s – to whom you're lying in your soul, for you cannot love him. And you become your husband's property, bag and baggage. And any children you have are his. And the clothes on your back are his. And you'll be pretending to love him while you're thinking only of Will. You'll be taking Pastor Will Anwyl into your marriage bed. You'll be committing adultery yourself, Beatrice. Every single night of your life. So don't judge. Just don't. And the only way you'll get away from Christian will be through death. And, no, I'm *not* marrying Will Anwyl. Why the *hell* should I? I don't want to marry any man and I shan't. And I don't care if my friends are married or not, I don't care. I'm sorry for you, Beatrice Pentecost – I shall possess my own soul but you'll have nothing.'

*

Beatrice didn't push her sister or strike her; she knows she didn't. Anna caught the toe of her boot in the roots and crashed into the nettles. I didn't hurt her. I went to help her up and she refused to let me touch her. I crouched down; she rolled over and sat up, her cheek and her left hand and wrist red with nettle stings. She shoved my hand away as I offered dock leaves to cool the smart, saying that there was one thing I could do for her: disappear. Stop *violating* her.

The same old tune. Every time Anna doesn't get what she wants, she's being bullied and hectored and picked on. Beatrice makes her way, shaking, past the chestnut tree, the ewes, the topiary garden and the midden. Smoke from neighbours' bonfires drifts in the air. She pulls down her cuffs, straightens her bodice, breathes deep. The piano sounds from the parlour and singing voices murmur.

*Nearer my God to thee, nearer to thee.*

In the parlour they're grouped round the piano. Mr Elias nods and smiles as Beatrice slips in to join her fiancé. Reading signs of trouble in her face, Christian raises his arm. She slides in under her future husband's wing, as she'll be able to do all her life. Anna is beyond all reason. At last the wilful younger sister has crossed the line. That is clear.

The hymn concludes. Anna is heard to let herself in at the back door and to climb the stairs to her room. Later Beatrice taps on her sister's door. No response. Afraid to enter, Beatrice stands irresolute, her knuckles raised ready to knock again.

*Violate* was the word that stung, an arrow in her heart.

It's hard to bear the particle of truth in her sister's wild reproaches. *Not your house.* Of course it's Anna's house, just as surely as it's Beatrice's. The shadow of their father darkens over the elder daughter, there in the dim corridor. Papa would never have sanctioned a threat to thrust the beloved younger from her home. Gently he would have remonstrated with Anna, expressed his chagrin and disappointment. He'd have padded off to his study to pray for her. Subdued to Papa's love, Anna would presently have followed him in and freely laid her contrition before him. The door would have closed behind the two. Nothing was unforgivable.

So I will pray, Beatrice thinks. Right here and now. Down on her knees she drops, outside Anna's room, skirts belling around her.

Joss scarcely turns a hair at finding her there. Pulling a humorous face, he steps round his sister, fondling her head.

126

When he knocks, clearing his throat, he's asked to come in. The door's unlatched and through the gap Beatrice can see Anna, lounging on the bed, hold out her hand to her brother, asking in a perfectly normal voice whether Joss made sure to put his linen in the laundry basket. Have he and Mr Elias taken round the petition against tithes? How many signatures has he obtained? Beatrice thinks: she's punishing me. Well, let her.

'Goodness, Annie what have you done to your face?' she hears.

'Fell in some nettles.'

'How on earth did you do that? The rash must itch like crazy. Let me put some Calamine on it for you. Have you got some? Do you want Old Quarlie?'

'Dear God, no. On the shelf – yes, there.'

Shifting position, prior to rising to her feet, Beatrice gets a different view of her sister: Anna has chopped off her long, lustrous hair. It hangs in clumps round her face. Joss anoints Anna with lotion so that half her face is white.

'What a clown you look. Poor old Annie. Always in the wars. Shall I do the other half of your face so that your two halves match?'

Anna laughs. 'No, I shan't come down tonight, Joss. Can you ask Amy to bring me up a tray of tea? I'm not ill, I'm tired; I just want to rest.'

Joss bends and whispers to Anna, who shakes her head, categorically.

That was about me, Beatrice thinks. He's asking if she wants to see me. Or if I hurt her. Since when did they discuss me? Perhaps the two of them have always whispered behind her back, blamed the elder sister, humoured her, down all the years. Two of them against one of her. Beatrice rises, removes herself. You never know people, even or especially your kith and kin. Descending the stairs, she wonders how it came about that her half-brother and her sister understand one another so well, in that commonplace, low-key way. The two of them have rarely argued in their lives, accepting one another's vagaries.

Later, as Amy prepares lamb chops for frying and Beatrice slices carrots, Beatrice considers Miriam Sala, wondering about the identity of her legal husband. What is her real surname?

Has the woman abandoned children along the way?

The Montagus will know. Or be in a position to find out. She stands looking down at her cold hand with the knife in it. The joints are reddened, the pads of the fingers callused; a scatter of brown flecks, the seeds of age-marks that will bloom within a decade, defaces the backs of her hands. They're the hands of a menial. Leaving the vegetables to Amy, she finds a lemon to squeeze over her skin, to whiten it for her wedding day. This must be repeated daily. So much to do. A trousseau to be assembled – and Christian hasn't the least idea of the scope of the work to be done in preparation. Men don't. Chemises, nightgowns and drawers; petticoats, combinations. The bridal gown, a travelling dress, a walking dress, silk dress ... drugget, bedlinen. Beatrice's mind is packed to the rafters with objects that must be purchased. An immense outlay: can't be helped.

One is, lacking either a father or a serviceable brother, one's own daughter, holding the purse strings to defray the cost of giving oneself away. These are the last moments of an era. The natural order will reassert itself and what a relief it will be to hand over responsibilities to her husband. Certainly it will. Though I do have an appetite for mastery, she reminds herself. No doubt about that. Anna's hysterical remarks about marriage appal her. Chattel? Never. A Christian husband guarantees his wife's rights under God.

And anyway, Joss must make a settlement on her.

Now, for the wedding dress, violet grenadine perhaps, fine silk and cotton weave, that can be adapted and worn for best on future occasions. Last month there was a beautiful swatch in Miss Eliot's haberdashery: but will it still be there in sufficient quantity? White with faint violet stripes. Everything must be bought to last. And what else? Flowers of course, chrysanthemums, love-in-a-mist: the garden will furnish those. The wedding breakfast.

Then (she almost forgot) there is the question of the bridesmaid's dress.

And, oh, the bridesmaid with her cropped, scandalous hair.

# Chapter 10

Anna sits where she has lapsed, listless in the tedious mayhem. Sarum House is in uproar, with two strong West Grimstead lasses helping to clean from top to bottom. Joss whistles, self-elected inspector of their work, urging them to take a little break for they must be tired, while Amy stamps around the house in a filthy temper. Doors slam. One brawny girl beats carpets in the garden as if whipping malefactors. If Beatrice had her way, Anna herself would be grasped by the scruff of the neck and scrubbed with a hog's bristle brush until she'd shed her dirty epidermis. Then they could dispose of her skin and hang her laundered bones out to dry.

Though the sickness has abated, its aftermath leaves her feeble. Anna consents to be measured for a dress. Agrees with everything Beatrice says; her sister is her usual brightly practical self except that she never looks Anna in the eye.

Anna awoke this morning, thinking: Beatrice is death.

How could she have allowed herself to slump into the old angry torpor? No word comes from Mirrie, presumably lingering in Tenby. Or Beatrice has intercepted the letters.

Anna imagines the Salas, freed from visitors, walking barefoot over ribbed sand, all in all to one another, enjoying the intimacy of one another's company by the fireside or bent over rock pools. Far away. What is the truth about the charge Mr Montagu has brought against her friend? How could one stoop to ask her? I never can, Anna thinks. Mirrie will flinch back into herself like a sea anemone. That will be it.

Better by far, in any case, to continue to believe in your friend. What right has Anna to judge, whatever Miriam has done? Her friend will be a pariah, pointed at in the streets. Respectable folk will avert their heads. A patch of soreness remains at the knowledge that Mirrie may not have trusted Anna with the truth.

And Lore has dwindled to the dimensions of that wasp on the sill waving feeble feet as it perishes. Perhaps, Anna thinks, it's healthier to release Lore. Maybe her grieving ghost is detained here by my calls and cannot die. Can't you die, darling? How can I help you die? I'll look away, occupying my mind by studying the place in the wallpaper where the sheets are out of true and the rosebuds misalign with their stalks. When the wallpaperers introduce a tiny error, it multiplies to infinity. But beneath that paper lie layer upon layer of old paint, old wallpaper, plaster, lime wash, timber and at the centre the unseen irregularities of the mediaeval wattle and daub, a lattice of hazel glued together with clay and dung and straw.

Where is Lore now? Nowhere; she's layered into the wall. She's nobody: a name without a body. It's impossible to grasp; the whole matter of her death comes apart in your hands. But Lore believed in the god of the imagination, to create and unify and integrate. How disappointed in Anna she'd be, if she could see her abjection.

If only I could have one conversation with her, Anna thinks:

just half an hour. Not for the first time, Anna considers the Spiritualists.

'I hope you'll be recovered for the wedding, dear,' says Mrs Elias. Her daughter lolls on a stool at Anna's dressing table, opening bottles without a by-your-leave, sniffing the contents, trying out Anna's comb and brush. Loveday sits Anna up and plumps her pillows, mentioning Dr Quarles, who previously did Anna such good with his regime.

Anna replies stonily, 'He will come in here over my dead body, Loveday, and I mean that literally. And no other quack either.'

'Oh well, you know best,' Loveday says comfortably. 'You can always change your mind. It's such a pity, dear, that you cannot enjoy the *bustle* of preparations. It's so jolly and exciting – everyone is charmed with Mr Ritter, even those of us who might have preferred dear Beatrice to marry elsewhere.'

Christian has departed on a fortnight's speaking tour, shepherding Miss Randolph through the south-western shires. He has trained her to tell her story to congregations in her own voice. Some Dissenters have vehemently objected to Mr Beecher's 'slave auctions', with which Christian is associated. 'Vulgar American showmanship' is repudiated by critics as 'yet another form of mass entertainment demeaning causes dear to the Nonconformist heart'. Letters arrive daily for Beatrice, sometimes twice daily; the Epistles, Anna thinks, of St Christian. Will keeps away from Sarum House.

'May I try on your dress, Miss Anna?' Patience asks, as soon as her mother's out of the door.

'No, you may not.'

'Why not?'

'It's not public property.'

Anna shoots the little rat a poisonous look. Two shrewd

hazel eyes return it. Patience wears an air of malign irony, altogether beyond her eleven years. Intelligent, Anna thinks, but warped. Two apple-breasts are just forcing Patience's pinafore out and soon she'll be encased in stays. Not long left for *you* to scamper around like a hoyden climbing trees and swimming in the river with your brothers. You'll soon be hobbled, Anna thinks, like the rest of us. Gelded, even, for women are gelded. Give us all the runaround while you can. Indeed this may be Patience's final summer of freedom – and already it's September.

The girl has the skirt of Anna's dress between finger and thumb. 'Oh go *on*. Why not?'

'The dress has to be kept nice, Patience. And, in case you hadn't noticed, you're too small. And anyway, because I say so.'

'So?'

'Go and give your mother a hand.'

'What with?'

'Whatever she's doing. Quite honestly, I don't want you.'

Patience perches on Anna's bed. 'You are *putting it on*. Everyone knows.'

'Putting what on?'

'There's nothing wrong with you. You're just pretending to *languish*. That's what everyone says. Because you're in *disgrace*, you're trying to avoid trouble. Me and Jack saw you coming back from wherever you went with Mr Anwyl. You were skipping down the path! Your legs work perfectly well. And anyway you're *hysterical*. Your sister says so. *It's a mental malady*. Dr Quarles is going to come and see if they should put you away. When you least expect it.'

Anna keeps her composure; she grins and folds her arms. At last someone's playing into her hands. She says to the little rat, 'Oh, that's very interesting, Patience. Yes, do try on the dress. Why not? You can fold up the hem.'

The adversary is wrong-footed. After all, Patience is just a child and has no arsenal to match Anna's. She'd meant to give Miss Anna Pentecost a vicious poke in the ribs; to make her flesh creep. Anna's amusement wrong-foots her and, pausing for thought, she elects to seize her advantage while it's offered.

Off come Patience's disreputable pinafore and frock, down to her grubby calico chemise, which hangs to her knees. There's a smell of young sweat from unwashed armpits. She dives into the mass of material of the bridesmaid's dress, struggling her neck into the collar. Yes, go on, split the thing, thinks Anna: I hate it anyway. What is it but a shroud?

'Well,' says Anna. 'What – a – sight.' The unsupported crinoline trails in a wide circle on the floor.

'It looks *stupid*,' pronounces the pouting wearer.

'That's for sure.'

They both laugh. Patience staggers round in paroxysms of giggling. Back in her own clothes, she dumps the gown back on the chest, where it lies prostrate as a jilted bride.

'So when's Dr Quarles coming for me, Patience?' asks Anna.

'After the wedding. With Mr Thimbleby and Mr Ivor from the asylum. If I was you, I'd run away. Have you got any cake though, Miss Anna? Can I go and ask for some cake for you and I eat it?'

'Yes, all right. Just a minute though, Patience. You're not making this up, are you?'

'Would I?'

Probably not, Anna calculates. The whole thing has an internal logic of its own; it's unlikely to be a child's fancy. And the little rat has a habit of skulking at doors: Anna has seen her. But she doesn't seriously think Beatrice would fulfil the threat to certify her: she could never live with herself. Anna's sister has thought the unthinkable because she's hurt; ringing with pain.

'I saw your friend yesterday,' adds Anna's informant. 'Mrs Sala. The Sinner of the Unforgivable Sin, Ma says people are calling her. She and her so-called husband came back to Toplady's.'

'Oh – when?'

'On Friday. Ma says people are loitering outside their gates hoping to cut them dead. Mrs Sala will be shunned by all decent people as a godless harlot and a Jezebel. But she never comes out so nobody can ignore her.'

*

'I really do think, Beatrice,' says Loveday complacently, 'that dear Patience is growing up at last in a womanly sort of way and will be a credit to us.'

And indeed when the child comes downstairs to request tea and cake for Miss Anna, she shows such considerate sweetness that both women are beguiled. Patience waits quietly for a tray to be produced, offering to carry it up herself: she and Miss Anna are having such a nice chat. She asks nothing for herself. Beatrice cuts two handsome hunks of walnut cake and pours lemonade for the prodigal.

'Well!' exclaims Beatrice as the door closes behind the child. 'Is she sickening for something?'

'Ah, but a little angel she can be, didn't I always say? I shouldn't be at all surprised if this were to prove the first sign of conversion, Beatrice.'

Loveday has been a staunch friend, assuring Beatrice that she has made the right choice of suitor, persuading her to censure the bad influences on Anna rather than Anna herself. Mr Anwyl is one, Mrs Sala another. Loveday has begged Mr Elias to rebuke Mr Anwyl in a spirit of brotherly correction and to preach a sermon on the moral emergency: a sermon such as Mr Elias has never delivered, that will drive transgressors from Chauntsey or bring them to their knees.

Naturally Mr Elias proves slippery as a tadpole. He prevaricates until Loveday is ready to write the sermon and preach it herself.

When Beatrice taps on her sister's door, she finds an empty bed and an open window. The tray stands on the cabinet, both plates giving the impression of having been licked clean. With a shawl over her nightgown, Anna is reclining on her sofa, her Bible open on her lap. She seems engrossed; looks up and smiles.

And Beatrice smiles.

Something so natural and simple could not be forced. It flashes between them by accident or grace.

'Dear, won't you catch cold with the window open?' Beatrice asks gently.

'I needed the fresh air. The atmosphere in here seemed so stale.'

'But shall I close it now?'

'By all means, do.'

Beatrice looks out at the grey day, the saturated beeches turning copper, scatterings of tarnished leaves on the lawns and shiny conkers beneath the chestnut.

'Autumn's upon us. Where did the year go? What are you reading, Anna?'

'The Gospel according to St Luke. I felt it spoke to my condition.' Anna begins to read aloud. *'I will arise and go to my father and will say unto him, Father, I have sinned before heaven and before thee, and am no more worthy to be called thy son.'*

From memory, Beatrice continues, *'But when he was yet a great way off, his father saw him, and had compassion, and ran, and fell on his neck, and kissed him.'*

No call to say more. To humiliate her penitent sister would be mean and a goad to Anna's contrary spirit. Beatrice remembers the conversation between the father and the prodigal's self-righteous brother, which doesn't reflect well on the latter. The brother stomps out in a pet, refusing to join in the celebration. I've always behaved myself and you never killed a fatted goat for me. No, but this brother of yours was dead and is alive; what was lost is found. Kissing her sister's cool cheek and collecting the tray, Beatrice leaves softly. The relief is physical: a weight lifts from Beatrice's chest. She hums her way down the stairs. Someone's at the door, a man, she can hear the low murmur of his voice.

'Miss,' says Amy. 'It's Mr Anwyl. He won't come in. He just wanted to leave these for you.'

It's an armful of amaranthus, with its drooping scarlet tassels – love-lies-bleeding. 'Throw them away,' she begins to say but somehow the words come out in a jumble and Amy, with a questioning look, goes for a vase. And surely these horrors are meant for Anna, not for herself. But, no, the servant assures her from the scullery, he insisted on Miss Pentecost.

What kind of a minister is he? And is Mr Elias much better? Loveday is not wrong, though she spoke casually: when shallow men abandon their vocation, a woman is bound to testify. Not in the spirit of the shrill London bluestockings claiming the suffrage, degrees, property and marriage rights. A woman can only ever rank as a substitute or stand-in. But stand she must, where a husband, father or brother is absent or indolent. I must speak, Beatrice thinks. God forbid that my tongue should be cravenly dumb. Packing a basket of fruit, she gathers a handful of tracts. It's time to bear witness; to demonstrate to Chauntsey not who she is but *whose* she is – the life's companion of Herr Ritter who serves a Master not of this world.

All the while Beatrice hopes to bump into Will. In the most natural way possible.

Seven houses open their doors to Beatrice. Tracts are accepted meekly; pears and apples more sincerely. At other homes, curtains twitch as householders hunker out of sight of the window. At Mrs Moran's lodging house, a red-haired ruffian opens the door, stinking of gin, and bawls, amongst other filth, 'Holy Jaysus!' Taking aim, he ejects a gob of spittle onto her skirt. The door slams in her face. Seizing the knocker, Beatrice raps again; jumps back. These Irish Catholics, dregs as they may be, need her more than anyone in Chauntsey. The door is opened by another fellow, toothless and lined, less pugnacious.

'Good morning, sir. I've brought you some fruit – I hope you like fruit? – and some good news.'

'Oh aye?'

Mrs Moran's daughter, Theresa, a plump lass of sixteen, appears behind him. No shoes.

'How would you like some pears, Theresa, from our tree at Sarum House? I wondered if you'd care to hear a very remarkable story? – and I've brought a message just for you.'

The girl scoops pears into her apron and sinks her teeth in the flesh of one, chewing as she speaks: 'Ta, miss. But I only like stories about love or murder.'

'Well, as it happens, the story I have brought you has to do with both love *and* murder. Both those stories meet in the Cross of Jesus Christ.'

'Na, don't bother. Ta, though.'

'But accept a tract, Theresa. Do.'

'There's no one here as reads.'

'I can read,' says the Irishman. 'Give it here. We'll find a use for it.' He accepts a copy of *The Holy Life and Joyful Death of John Watkins, Chimney Sweep*. Beatrice tries not to see him winking at the girl as the door closes.

She turns and there is Will, who has been run running wild

in Beatrice's mind ever since she last saw him. In the market square he's feeding his chestnut mare a carrot, the palm of his hand nuzzled by the creature's soft nose; with his free hand, he pats the mare's neck. His expressive hands. He's murmuring to the animal, too quietly for Beatrice to make out the words. He hasn't seen her. She returns home.

And though she must counsel him to marry her sister, she also thinks: at heart he's mine, he'll always be mine, and he knows it.

*

The façade of Toplady's curves in a pale arc, shining with glass. In the stained-glass windows you read the story of Persephone in jewel colours: the maiden gathers flowers, whose tendrils undulate with the curves of her form; the dark god of the underworld reaches to gather her; her mother Demeter tears her robe in grief, cursing the planet with barrenness.

Toplady's, more villa than house, is amongst the most modern in Wiltshire. It stands on a gentle rise. At the back, kempt lawns slope down to the river, where Baines keeps a boat tied to the jetty. A cedar of Lebanon masks the bay windows, providing a screen from the road; its lowest branches trail like a skirt. Anna is nearer to quitting Sarum House than she has ever been. There's no future for her there. What life will there be for Anna with Lore's dictatorial cousin as head of the house; Beatrice forever at her heels sniffing for heresy? Trying to force her to marry Will. As good as saying, You're tainted, you're a disciple of the atheist Mrs Sala. Beatrice will not need to commit her to Mr Ivor's asylum; Sarum will be madhouse enough. Would Mirrie refuse her sanctuary?

Anna pauses at the gate: there's a carriage in the driveway, implying visitors. Her heart sinks: there's been no word from the Salas for so long. But Miriam has always said, 'Don't stand on ceremony, Anna: you're the first of my friends.'

In the dining room a visitor is already waiting. An austere lady in her late twenties, dressed for walking, she stands with a bag in her hand, gazing at a portrait of Miriam. *The* portrait. Mirrie has never permitted her husband to photograph her. Madame Bodichon's oil painting is an exception and anyone who knows Mirrie sees why, although its subject is anything but graceful or pretty. The face looms at the viewer, as if plunging through the frame. Mirrie's large mouth and heavy jaw are not softened: ah, but the eyes, the expression! As the visitor turns to address her – reluctantly, Anna feels – it's as if there are three people in the room.

'My goddess!' breathes the visitor, astonishingly. Anna at first mistakes this for a greeting and chokes down a laugh. The visitor returns to the portrait. This will be one of Mirrie's adorers: several idealistic young women, as Baines has laughingly mentioned, are moths to his wife's flame. Anna has never bumped into one before. There's a whole tribe of us, thinks Anna, discomfited.

'Anna Pentecost.' Anna extends her gloved hand to the disciple, a lean person wearing round steel spectacles which she pushes up with a forefinger.

'Eleanor Jackson. My darling is hard-pressed today. She's so bothered by noodles without the faintest notion of how precious her time is – how is she to do her great work if people will come and pester?'

Having flung this dart, Miss Jackson returns to the portrait, perhaps dreaming that she has said enough to send Anna creeping away.

'I think Mrs Sala has spoken of you.'

'Oh! Has she?' Miss Jackson wheels round, angular features lit by hope and fear. 'I'm glad she speaks of me.' She cannot bring herself to ask what the Adored has said. 'Have you read it?' she asks.

'Excuse me, read what?'

'Well – of course, her great novel! *Freedom Seeks Her.*'

'I knew Mr Sala had published a novel – but – '

'Good gracious no, it is *Mrs* Sala's work – I can proclaim it now that the pseudonym has been breached. Poor Baines is a mere copyist, a dabbler in photography. He could never *create.*'

Anna is crestfallen: Miriam guards her secrets. But don't we all? Most of my life is lived underground, thinks Anna. Perhaps Mirrie was trying to tell me and I was just too obtuse, when she quoted, 'Can darkness shine?' It flashes through Anna's mind that she'll have to reread the whole book in the light of a woman's authorship; this woman who appropriated Anna's form and face like a dress from a rail and robed herself in them. Miss Jackson is guilty of a smirk. She explains that their friend is the talk of literary London, a shock to Miriam, who'd wished to preserve her anonymity.

'Of the novel's greatness I have no doubt. I have whole passages by heart. It has been an open secret amongst her *inner circle* for some time.'

When Baines enters, Miss Jackson is on him like a mob at the shrine of a saint. She has brought along the cream silk nightgown, she says, from the women's cooperative; she trusts Mrs Sala will be pleased to have it.

'My dear Eleanor, how thoughtful – but my wife is far from well.' Baines stands in the doorway, blocking the visitors' path.

Miss Jackson is not to be discouraged.

'One of her headaches? A tooth? How dreadful for the darling. Now, all I ask is to sit with her – as quietly as a church mouse. She'll not know I'm there. My whole desire in *life* is to sit at her feet and kiss the hem of her garment.'

'I'm unsure how much use that would be to her,' Baines says mildly. He refrains from catching Anna's incredulous eye. 'In the normal way I'd be happy for you to kiss her slippers as much as you liked – or rather, as much as *she* liked, though a little of that goes a long way, I'd have thought – but this is not the time.'

Narrowing her body, Miss Jackson sidles past him. Anna stays where she is.

Mirrie's face is swollen and blotched. She's reclining in the curve of the bay, feet raised on a footstool. Anna, through two door frames, watches the obsequious handmaiden approach, holding out a swatch of material. Sinking to her knees, Eleanor clasps her idol's feet, kissing them repeatedly. Aeneas the labrador rises from the hearth rug to sniff at her.

'For heaven's sake, Eleanor, get up, do,' says Miriam, irritably. 'Think of your dignity.'

'I love you too much for dignity.'

'I can see you only for five minutes, Eleanor,' adds Miriam. 'And pray do not fawn.'

Miss Jackson names conditions: she'll accept the five-minute rule if she may sit or kneel at Mrs Sala's feet. Why encourage this abjection, Anna wonders? Perhaps somehow or other Mirrie needs us all round her, odd people standing a bit outside the pale. At last the disciple is got out of the room, not without shooting quiverfuls of annihilating arrows from her eyes at the favoured Anna.

'There's no harm in her at all,' says Baines. 'In fact Eleanor is a good, practical sort of person – she organises a women's cooperative. She's taken a weekend house in Salisbury. Miriam is her sole folly. We see her most weekends floating around at the gates, watching for us.'

'Miss Jackson says she can never love a man,' says Mirrie.

That sticks at a curious angle in Anna's mind. She twists the fingers of her gloves between her hands.

'I know what you're thinking,' Mirrie says. 'But isn't all love a good thing, Anna?'

'Well, no. Not really. Unrequited love is not good, or love that destroys. Or slavish love. Quite a few categories really.' *She says she can never love a man.* 'Has something happened, Mirrie, to distress you?'

'Come and sit with me – dear Anna. There are things I've kept from you. This I can no longer do. I am a published author, a novelist. Perhaps you had guessed this? An author rather than an authoress – that at least is what I aspired to be. But the secret is betrayed. And with it the *legal* irregularity of our marriage has become public knowledge. I shall be a pariah. You will be called upon to shun me. Only the Eleanors of this world will remain faithful.'

'How can you say that? No, Mirrie. Truly, I never shall.'

'You may be forced to.'

'Not ever. How can you even think so?'

'Bitter experience.'

'But not of me – not bitter experience of me.'

'I've always thought myself exceptional. But we all struggle in the same web. You cannot visit me and keep your reputation, Anna. That's just how it is. I am a woman writing under a man's name; I have been unmasked; stripped naked to public view. And in any case, Baines and I cannot continue to live in England.' She announces this briskly, with decision. 'We've been driven from our own country.'

'But where shall you go?'

'What does it matter? Weimar, perhaps. Paris. I shall miss you. And yet in some ways I'm glad to leave.'

Anna seems to see her friend across a room that has expanded to a continent of space. Nothing Mirrie can do will restore her to society's acceptance. Her parents and brothers have disowned her. 'And, Anna, I was a filial child. I meant to be a loyal wife. I was prepared for self-sacrifice but ... there are limits. And I've always nourished ambition. I married a gentleman with whom, as it turned out, I had nothing in common. I met Baines. He was the first man in my life to see and value my gift.'

Miriam has no wish to allege anything against her kin. With hindsight, she sees that there were opportunities before her engagement to recognise her intended's narrow, fastidious character and its incompatibility with her own: she fooled herself. Marrying him against the judgment of her family, she went on to leave him against their judgment. Miriam has carried her family's reputation into the gutter. They have all but one aunt repudiated her. She no longer has a family.

Anna glances from Miriam to Baines, leaning forward to listen, nod, sympathise. Yes, you're devoted to her now but how will you be in ten years' time? What if you desert her? Mirrie must have asked herself this a thousand times. It occurs to Anna that, having attained celebrity as an author, even if it takes the form of notoriety, Mirrie is at least equipped to support herself, should the worst come to the worst.

And were there children of this marriage? Miriam doesn't say. It's impossible to ask. Should Anna ask to accompany the Salas to Weimar or Paris?

But I have no sufficient private means, she thinks, being dependent on my sister. If I joined them, Mirrie and her husband, all in all to one another, would welcome, then tolerate, then suffer my presence – just another hanger-on like Eleanor Jackson. *She can never love a man.* Anna would begin to bore them. And then again the thought of abandoning Wiltshire is a fearful prospect: tearing up her roots, forfeiting the only home she has ever known.

'But, Anna dearest, let us ring for tea. I have not asked after you at all.'

As they talk, a draught crosses the room. The fire roars in the chimney, keeping its heat to itself. The cedar thrashes, rattling the panes. It will take no time at all for me to go mad, if I stay or if I go, Anna thinks. Either way I'll be alone.

If I called, who would answer?

All the while at the back of her mind, there's the recognition, *She says she can never love a man*. If this is also true of herself, Anna lives in a world of greater aberration than anything guessed by those around her. The best she can hope for is to hide her anomaly. At Sarum House she lives amongst the partially blind. Or in disguise, behind a thick veil.

'Oh, I'm well, thank you, Miriam. No tea – really. I should be returning home.'

The bells of St Osmund's toll as Anna walks the river path. A doomy, lachrymose message. Crossing the footbridge, she views a cluster of black-clad mourners outside the Anglican church, awaiting the hearse. *Conform, conform*, the bell insists. The coffin is removed from the hearse. The black plumes of the horses shake in the wind; leaves are lashed from the graveyard's ancient beeches. Anna recognises the family: the Tourneys, Wiltshire gentry, High Churchmen, formerly recusants, latterly Tractarians. The aisle is paved with their ancestral tombstones; the walls boast their monuments and inscriptions. The Quarles tombs too. The minister arrives, robed in pomp of alb, stole, chasuble, whatnot – and a phalanx of blond choristers in blue cassocks. A bearer carrying a cross. They file into the church; the doors close behind them.

Circling crows call: *Conform, conform*. Generations ago the Pentecosts took the momentous step into nonconformity; a dissidence not subdued by persecution. It held to its Christ with heroic quietism and still demands from its daughters not less than everything. The door of the Baptist chapel stands open. Anna steps in. The plain whitewashed interior is drenched in light, as if transparent to the day. Nobody about. Nothing to distract the eye. Anna kneels in the family pew. She listens. My beloved, are you still there?

The soughing of wind in the overarching copper beech: *Come home, come home.*

# Chapter 11

When she sees him, when she does not, Will is physically present, distressing Beatrice's nerves as if he brushed against her or breathed on her face. Performing all the necessary chores and the extra tasks in readiness for the wedding, Beatrice is shiveringly aroused.

He has said, turning away, 'You've killed me, Beatrice. You know very well I've never seriously loved any woman but you.'

And she said, 'Seriously? Do you even know the meaning of the word? You've flirted with the whole of Chauntsey. You have compromised Anna. You're honour bound to marry my sister now. If there's any scrap of honour in you, Will.'

'Why on earth do you say that?'

'You know perfectly well. Running away with her. You've made her into an object of scandal.'

'Run away! That's ridiculous. I love Anna. I love her because she's your sister. And therefore my sister.'

'There's no point in trying to woo me back. None. Just accept it, Mr Anwyl.'

Beatrice sees him walking in the garden alone, then later arm in arm with Anna. They vanish into the wilderness. Beatrice's ribcage squeezes her heart with the most intense pain she's ever known. But I can get you back from her any moment I like. Thirteen days is a period composed of tens of thousands of such moments. At any time I can stop the clock; the whole process can be brought to a standstill.

Three days pass in the blink of an eye: Mr Anwyl calls with news of Mr Kyffin. He relates it over lunch, directing his gaze at everyone in turn excepting Beatrice. The Florian Street congregation is in turmoil: nearly half have voted against the Prynne clique to invite Mr Kyffin back as their pastor, epilepsy or no epilepsy, heresy or no heresy. Mr Prynne and the deacons have initiated the procedure to expel the rebels. Charlie Kyffin, burning with rage, felt moved to rise and testify against Mr Prynne's malice and ambition. When Mr Prynne ordered him out, Charlie sat down and gripped the rail: Prynne would have to remove him by force 'from my father's chapel'. Mr Prynne and five irate deacons marched out themselves, leaving the chapel in uproar.

'What does Mr Kyffin say?' asks Joss.

'Not a word. He's understood to be awaiting a leading from the Lord.'

'And dear Mrs Kyffin?'

'I saw her yesterday. She is considering a hydropathic treatment.'

'For herself or for her husband?'

'That wasn't clear. Her Christian spirit up till now has been perfect, forgiving every persecutor. *Chwarae teg*, I think the candle's burning rather low; she's weary of it all. I have prayed with her and I shall go again. Dear Ellen is a great support to her mother. At her tender age, she's all but running the household. And – it's rather disquieting – the child has taken on a certain authority: the mother quite defers to her.'

Beatrice allows herself to look into Will's face. His calm, thoughtful voice affects her strangely. She has always looked down on him as a second-rate Christian, accusing him in her heart of lack of spiritual calibre. How fair has she been? Will has taken Beatrice at her word and given up on her. That's clear. And perhaps she herself brought out the worst in him.

'That's well done, Will,' says Anna, quietly.

Her sister's gentle tone pierces Beatrice. This last week Anna has spoken little. She has constantly had her head in a book. The Bible, as far as Beatrice could make out. Beatrice sees her visiting the chapel. And this is good: it should be a source of reassurance, a sign that her sister is healthily back in the fold. True, Anna eats little. But she tries everything on her plate and makes sure to thank Beatrice for her efforts on her behalf. She's sewing a hat for Beatrice's honeymoon journey; tries on her bridesmaid's dress and stands for the alterations, with a willing if rigid smile.

After luncheon, Will and Anna seat themselves at either side of the fire in the parlour. They do not talk. Yes, they do. They're speaking with their eyes.

Eight days before Beatrice's wedding: she awakens with a start, dreaming that she's giving birth. A boy-child's turnip skull rams aside the wincing tissues. It ploughs forward but then fixes fast. She cannot shift the man-child, however she strains. When Tibby died having given birth to one dead kitten, Beatrice dissected the dear body and found two further kittens, one putrescing in the birth canal, the other intact in the womb but lifeless. Opening the maternal body, she came face to face with death. This dream-birth threatens to kill her; she must expel it. In a cold sweat Beatrice begins to surface and detects her mistake. The child has grown into her own membranes and become a vital organ of her own body. It will not be ejected except by destroying the matrix of life. She'll have to live with the growth like a tumour, humping it obscenely around with her.

The double dream taints the day. Beatrice checks herself for blood. No blood. She calculates. How mortifying if she should bleed on the wedding night. This appears more than likely. Christian is fastidiously clean; one would not care to bring female mess and smells into his bed.

Throughout his young manhood, he kept himself pure for her. What if she lets him down?

An explosion of laughter, out of nowhere. And the Pentecosts are romping all round the house. Back to their old selves, up and down the stairs, hide-and-seek, blind man's buff. The last soft sand sifts through the hourglass with the appearance of a whirlpool. Surely time is speeding up? Or going back? Charlie Kyffin, Joss, Rose and Lily Peck, Mr Anwyl, Beatrice and Anna are all ten years old again. Piggy in the middle, Mr Anwyl leaps up to catch a flying cushion that jangles the chandelier.

Beatrice crashes upstairs and hides in her bedroom. In burst the others: 'Found you!' They look round in wonderment at acres of crinoline, violet, cream, yellow and scarlet, frills and lace and ribbons not yet attached to any garment. 'Oh that is so very Parisian, Miss Pentecost!' Rose and Lily marvel over the wedding dress with its flattened front and the drama of its billowing back portions. *Mais* it's so *belle!* The Peck girls address one another in pidgin French, the sacred language of fashion. Lifting the wedding gown by its shoulders, they hold it between them before the long mirror, a headless third party at whose reflection they gaze with critical reverence.

'You're going to look a picture, Miss Pentecost,' says Rose. 'I wish I were getting married.'

'You will, I'm sure.'

'But I want to marry *now*. Not in years and years.'

'But then it would be all over, wouldn't it, Rose,' says Lily. 'You'd have nothing left to look forward to.'

'That's true.'

'Well, there is the marriage itself,' Joss points out. 'The new life and all that.' A life Joss has never seen fit to embark on.

'Well, I suppose so. But that's the porridge, not the honey.'

The Peck girls study Beatrice with compassion. 'Old,' their looks say. 'Almost past it. You have a sprinkle of grey hairs, showing at the back where you couldn't reach to tweezer them out. We take note of it whenever you turn. Your skin is nothing like peaches and cream. It sags. But never mind.' Beatrice passes her hand over her hair. Turning away, she glances out at the autumn garden. Wasps have devoured the sugars in the windfall pears, leaving behind brown shrivelled corpses and a smell between ferment and decay.

When the doorbell rings, there's much smoothing of garments.

'Mr Ivor and Mr Thimbleby, Miss Pentecost,' calls Amy from halfway up the stairs. 'Where'll I put them?'

Why must the girl stand yelling? Why can't she introduce visitors decently? Beatrice hopes they haven't heard the infantile games going on in Sarum House. She descends sedately and, opening the parlour door, sees Mr Thimbleby advancing with his hand held out – and her sister retreating, face white as flour. What's the matter with her now?

Anna's hand goes up to her throat; she cringes. Half her face is lit by a strip of sunlight that makes her look one-eyed: an eye widened in terror. Is Anna about to be ill again? More hysterics? She is, isn't she? Can't you control yourself for five minutes? There's too much to do, too much to think about: and shouldn't Beatrice be the centre of attention in this prelude to her wedding?

Anna takes a further step backwards. She's now standing against the shadowy crimson of the curtains.

'Joss,' she hisses to her brother. *'Don't let them.'*

'Don't let them what, dear?'

Beatrice ignores Anna's little drama; greets the visitors. Thimbleby, eminent Congregationalist that he is, has turned his family home into a retreat for genteel female lunatics, run on modern, humanitarian lines: there are no barred windows, locked doors or physical restraints, just sustaining food, warm clothes, an intimate family home. So benign is the regime that Thimbleby can allow the best-behaved to mingle with his young family.

'Have I alarmed your dear sister?' he whispers.

'She's not quite herself today.'

Mr Thimbleby apologises for intruding at such an important time. Two inmates absconded in the night. May he and Mr Ivor look round for them in Miss Pentecost's grounds?

It has happened before, several times, and on one occasion a poor creature broke into the scullery of Sarum House and raided the pantry, going off with cherry tart and cheese. The Pentecost sisters sorrowed for her and hoped that the good food comforted the lost soul. Mr Thimbleby's inmates are rarely violent. They inflict wounds on themselves rather than on others, burning or cutting their own arms or faces. As Anna did when Lore died. They cannot be allowed access to matches or knives. Two by two, the least deranged are led through Chauntsey to Morning Service on the Sabbath. Beatrice, having shown the two men into the garden, returns to stand at the window; her sister has sunk down on a chair.

'Poor creatures,' Beatrice says. 'The temperature was below freezing in the night. What is it, Anna? I'm sure they're harmless. Oh look, he's found them.'

'It's true, then ... it wasn't a ... pretext.' Anna heaves a trembling sigh.

'Whatever do you mean?'

'I thought you might have – invited them.'

'Whyever would I do that?'

The women have fashioned a nest for themselves in a pile of straw and sacks, packing a quantity of it round them for warmth. They allow themselves to be shepherded down the lawn by Mr Ivor and Mr Thimbleby. Neither makes the least fuss. Perhaps it's a relief to have been found. Perhaps they only wished to taste the air of freedom. In the chill of the night they must have huddled to one another, fearful of the vast sky and the constellations. They hold hands, a woman in middle age and one somewhat younger, like mother and daughter, dressed in the same Quakerish grey; there's nothing to distinguish them from normal folk.

Afterwards Beatrice watches her sister examine the lunatics' nest; observing the shape left by the two bodies clasped in one another's arms. Anna seems calm. Can she have imagined that Mr Thimbleby had come for *her?*

Five days remain and Mr Ritter is expected early tomorrow. The final preparations are hectic. The wedding breakfast has been ordered: salmon and perch, beef and pork, poultry, mince pies and cake, jellies. The trousseau is complete and can be admired by visitors. Beatrice rests her aching feet and, with the kind of pleasure the tongue takes in probing a rotten tooth that's temporarily quiescent, insists on sketching Anna with Mr Anwyl. She positions Anna on a dining chair, with Will just behind her, as if for a photograph. Beatrice laughs with affected gaiety; the models remain glum, like a morose married pair after a tiff, the most recent of many, to which they'll return after the session.

Will catches Beatrice on the stairs. She pulls away. He follows her into her room without permission. He snares her wrist. She wants him to. She wrenches away. There'll be a scorch mark where Will has ringed her wrist. She rubs it. Look what you've done. It's a trophy.

'Please think again, Beatrice,' he says. 'It can all be called off. Nothing is lost.'

'I can't, Gwilym, I can't. And please don't ...'

Round and round they wrangle. Someone passes by the door and pauses. Beatrice thinks of Papa. His spirit can rest now that she's settled for the suitor he appointed. Chaos has reigned since his death but in a few days order will be restored. Somehow this propels her towards Will, as if someone had shoved her in the small of the back.

Will's goodbye kisses taste of his tears and remain on her face, an invisible coating. Salt and saliva. She cannot bring herself to wash them off but cries them away into her pillow.

Four days before his wedding, the bridegroom, whose tour has resulted in scores of conversions, as if these were the days of the Wesleys and George Whitefield, hands Amy his elegant cloak and hat and says that, heretical as it may be to say so, he has no need to die to be in heaven. Then he collapses into a chair, exhausted, as well he might be. A writer in the *Baptist Times*, comparing Christian's preaching style with that of his great mentor, Henry Ward Beecher, has described Pastor Ritter in action – sawing his arms in the air, howling sarcasms, discharging rockets of poetry, his cloak flying around like that of a Byronic hero.

Later the household sleeps. The fire ebbs in the grate but the room remains baskingly warm. As Beatrice rests her side against Christian, it's so quiet that she hears the boards creak as the house settles. Fatigued, she half-drowses.

'Are you sure, now, dearest? Quite certain? Has the Father sanctified our path? It would be no dishonour to change your mind even at this last moment. The door is open.' He folds his arms more strongly round her. 'It is right to tell you that

I have spoken to Mr Anwyl.'

Beatrice struggles to rise. 'Why? What have you said, Christian?'

'Now don't be alarmed, *Liebling*. I have always known that you have a special place in your heart for Mr Anwyl. And he for you. But Mr Anwyl himself explained that this was only a light-hearted friendship on both sides. His heart is given elsewhere.'

Crucifying thought. Beatrice cannot master herself. Fast breathing; racing heart. It was none of Christian's business to go checking up on her. No hope remains in the world, none, after her absurd tit-for-tat trifling with Will's affections. A few small motions of her tongue would release Beatrice from this marriage to a man respected but not, or not yet, adored – feared rather, with a childhood shrinking. The man who places you on his knee: fear him. *Beattie hates*; *Beattie loathes*.

'Mr Anwyl is bound in honour to my sister, Christian. And she to him. I hope and trust he'll do the right thing. He is a fallible man.'

'We are all that.'

'Yes, but – please, Christian – Mr Anwyl is not – chosen by Providence for me. I've always sensed this and now I know it – so may we close the subject?'

But can such a blemished creature really be a suitable husband for *Anna*? Beatrice has passed him on like the hand-me-downs of childhood, with their ingrained stains. Should one encourage Anna to bind herself for life to Will's invincible shallowness? – Anna, whose physical and mental frailty makes childbirth a threat to her balance, perhaps to her life. Beatrice, summoning courage, has questioned Dr Quarles about this. But the physician rules emphatically otherwise. He has spoken to a Salisbury colleague specialising in those delicate complaints peculiar to females. The two physicians will call and – he promises – tactfully reassure the Pentecost sisters.

*

Accordingly, three days before the marriage, Drs Quarles and Palfrey appear.

'Celibacy,' remarks Dr Palfrey, no country physician but a gentleman of the world in a magenta silk waistcoat, 'is, to be blunt, an unnatural condition. I speak as a medical man, Miss Pentecost and Miss Anna, a man of science.' He takes a sip of coffee; replaces the cup on the saucer with finicking care and allows his broaching of this delicate theme to sink in. Everything about Dr Palfrey from fob watch to shoe-leather looks suave and costly. 'I shall go so far as to say that celibacy is inherently damaging. Irrespective of gender. What's bad for the gander is bad for the goose.'

Anna observes Dr Palfrey's ginger whiskers and considers what it might be like to have such a moustache, or any moustache at all. To sprout hair under your nose and prune and preen it before a mirror in the morning; to raise your hand in idle moments to twiddle its extremities.

'And this is so, dear ladies, if one may put it thus, both biologically and theologically. Better, as the Apostle says, to marry than to burn.'

I am not burning, thinks Anna. Except with wrath. You unctuous old goat. Go away.

'Now the organs of Woman,' Dr Palfrey continues, as if to the lowest form in the school, 'are liable to distension by blood. Causing cramps, black moods, uncontrollable urges, so much so that the age of female puberty is known as the age of *miniature insanity*. Blockages are readily treated within marriage by the *beneficent* action of a *husband*'s attentions. Yet more curative will be the advent of what we might call *a glorious little creature*. But in the meantime, it would be as

156

well, dear Miss Pentecost and Miss Anna, that you drink one or two glasses of good claret a day. Unless of course you practise Temperance?'

'Oh no,' says Beatrice. 'Well, we are temperate, of course. In its true sense. But we have not espoused the Temperance Movement. We allow ourselves medicinal alcohol. From time to time. What I really wanted to know, Dr Palfrey, is whether bearing children would be dangerous, should one be in less than perfect health?'

Anna wishes she could swallow the good claret now, this instant. *You* didn't by any chance invite these quacks, Beatrice, did you, without telling me? She knows that look on her sister's face: eyes wide and innocent, lips tensely pursed. Anna has slept little since the shock of Mr Thimbleby's arrival. The prophecy of Patience Elias has been ringing in her ears: 'Mr Thimbleby is coming for you.' Why didn't she run away with Miriam and Baines while she had the chance? That day, sick with terror, she backed into the corner and beckoned Joss to her, Joss who would *never* so betray Anna. Gentle Joss. And he'll be here when the Ritters have left on their honeymoon. But would he fight off Ivor and Thimbleby if they came for her? She doesn't think so. And he seems so preoccupied these days: it's always Munby this and Munby that. And jaunts to London 'on business'. Joss seems to exist in a bubble of private euphoria. In a crisis Joss would shake his head; he'd feebly remonstrate and passively surrender, in awe of Beatrice's relentless willpower. He'd retreat to the kitchen and, taking the cat on his knee, would turn his plump palms to and from the range.

Thimbleby and Ivor didn't come for me, Anna reminds herself. They had other quarry. But how do I know that the second part of the prophecy isn't true: 'They'll come for you after the wedding is all over?' How can one be sure that

Quarles with his shining moon-face, so greasily genial, isn't preparing the ground even now, as he sits at their hearth, knees crossed, polishing with his palm the carved knob of his stick? When he smiles, his small china-blue eyes nearly disappear.

What punitive enemas has Quarles in store; what cups to catch her blood? Seldom has Anna felt so alone.

The fop Palfrey takes up the theme of the health benefits of matrimony for young ladies. One of his lady patients, he confides, was despaired of. Let us call her Jane. Prey to bouts of mania and so-called advanced views as a result of monthly irregularities, this lady would roll around on the hearthrug screaming. At times Jane was happy and gentle, at others wild and frantic, especially with her papa and her fiancé. The latter was an unassuming gentleman, whom – out of the blue – Jane attacked. She charged at him, with a view to pushing him out of the window. With preternatural strength. A diminutive person, standing hardly higher than one's elbow, her onslaughts on her nearest and dearest were murderous. Against his family's advice, the young gentleman insisted on proceeding with the wedding, from which day Jane was completely cured. She is now the mother of eight charming sons.

Yes, the net has snared the moth. She is displayed under glass, an entomological pin through her breast.

Anna adjusts her mask; sits with a listening inclination of the head and downcast eyes, nodding occasionally. I am more intelligent than these people. Than anyone in this room. I can outwit every last one of them. She constrains herself to think saintly thoughts, twisting them on vicious brambles of irony. Anna not only refrains from glowering but offers the visitors an expression like that of a Madonna. She manages not to seize the poker and smash it down on Quarles's bald dome.

*

Christian absents himself, staying with the Montagus until the wedding day. Sarum House is awash with visitors, all bearing gifts – of inkstands, pebble bracelets, worked chair covers, cut-glass dishes. Twenty of Chauntsey's saved poor sit round the Pentecost table tucking into plates of bread pudding, tarts, scones with jam and cream, washed down with gallons of tea. Beatrice, nerves twanging, catches Amy muttering to herself about the revolting table manners of yokels. Beatrice reproves her: 'Yokels we shall all be in the New Jerusalem, Amy, don't you agree? I wonder what our Master will think of our table manners then?' She fails to catch Amy's spluttered reply. The servant's back is turned; her shoulders are shaking. Joss is – for goodness' sake – helping Amy by piling plates on the draining board, his shoulders also shaking.

*

Dressed in her glory, Beatrice stands in the drawing room, the focus of all eyes, her head and shoulders covered in their grandmother's intricate white lace veil. All is white or cream, from her shoes to her gown of highly worked muslin. She seems to tower above herself, gazing down from a great height. Anna, her bridesmaid, stands silently beside her, in white grenadine with pink trimming and sash, wearing a veil of pink tulle.

It is time. Joss offers his brotherly arm.

The weather has been unseasonably cold and an overnight frost has not melted; puddles are black with ice. Under the gunmetal sky, a snake of carpets, a causeway patchworked out of different shades of red, links Sarum House with the chapel. Slow, mincing steps must be taken: the causeway slides on the treachery of ice. Anna shuffles along behind. Before the chapel gate, Beatrice turns and opens her arms. Everything pauses; a mist of breath hangs suspended in the air. You are my sister, Beatrice thinks. What else matters? We are made out of one another. Everyone watches, waiting for time to flow on.

What are the words? Finding none, Beatrice cranes forward to kiss her sister, the dry veil dividing mouth from mouth.

As the procession enters the chapel, *he* is in her eye. His eclipsing presence is all Beatrice registers as she and Joss walk up the aisle through the rustling murmurs of smiling guests.

Oh thank God. You're here. Otherwise it would have been unbearable.

She draws abreast. Her eye snags on the lashes of his eyes. In that expressive moment, nothing of his emotion is closed to Beatrice. They are naked to one another, as they will never again be in this mortal world. She flushes deeply and feels heat suffuse throat and breast. His look delays her and she twists in its hold, locked between Will and Joss, who, unconscious of a hitch, is carrying her forward. She feels the bridesmaid tread on the hem of her gown and start back. Will's eye is a burr with hooks. Walking the fields around Chauntsey burrs snag on the soft stuff of your skirt and, when you pull them off, a patch of gauze strips away. An expensive dress is ruined. It hurts to snatch back her gaze. In a rush, abashed, Beatrice feels a ripped rag of her most intimate self stick to the body of Will.

The bridegroom inclines his head fractionally. Mr Montagu's smile is a beacon that lights the whole chapel. I call upon these persons here present to witness ... the bridegroom smiles out of the corner of his eye, high above her ... the gravity of my error.

It is done. Tonight they will be one flesh. Hymeneal blood will soak Beatrice's pristine nightdress and the sheet; after which sacrifice the couple will pray and sleep.

# Chapter 12

Talk is all of the newly-weds on their bridal journey, until Mr Kyffin changes the subject. He arrests the tea-drinkers' attention by remarking, 'You know, my dears, I have lately been preoccupied with that cryptic promise in the Book of Isaiah. That Kings shall be thy nursing fathers and queens thy nursing mothers. Have you ever wondered about this mysterious verse and what the Prophet intended by it?'

Teacups hover over saucers. Heads are faintly shaken. Morose Mr Anwyl, plagued by a heavy cold, explodes in a sneeze and shows no desire for theological debate. He sneezes again and the line of ladies seated within range of the spray of droplets leans sideways like grasses in a high wind.

'No? No? None of you?'

Mrs Kyffin, lately reconciled to her husband through the mediation of their devoted son Charlie, whispers, 'Not now, dear.' It's no good. It has never been any good. Once a verse of the Scriptures has kindled his mind, the pastor burns to pass on the inspiration. Mrs Kyffin gives a little cough behind her hand. Mr Anwyl, red-eyed, sneezes again tremendously, this time into a handkerchief.

'Shouldn't you be in bed, Will?' asks Anna. It's Will's first visit since the wedding, after which they were both laid up. 'You're welcome to a bed. There's one made up. Amy can take up a warming pan. You can't possibly get home in this snow.'

Will, sunk in misery, shakes his head and shivers. He mumbles, 'Can't stay. Reputation.'

'Don't be ridiculous. You're going to bed and that's that. There's a fire in one of the rooms – just needs a bit of coaxing.'

'No, can't stay. Couldn't bear it anyway.'

'Don't be lugubrious. I'll get you something to drink.'

Will sits crouched over the fire, as though he'd like to creep into it and be raked out next morning with the cinders. Anna throws on another log. She goes off to fetch warm brandy and when she returns, Mr Kyffin is discussing the enigma of male lactation in the Old Testament and how the nursing father is a type of Christ. And the milk from the Divine's breast is more delicious and nourishing than either cow's or goat's milk, or, if one may mention a delicate topic, than the milk the human babe imbibes at his mother's breast. For why should it be beyond the Creator to fashion a father able to suckle his beloved children? The shed blood of Jesus is a kind of milk for babes. And after all, it is a fact that males are equipped with nipples.

The Father, who has created nothing in vain, would never have invented anything without a purpose. Mr Kyffin has heard it maintained by Mr Lee the analytical chemist that the male chest is the relic of an antecedent species, hermaphroditic or all-female. Of course this contradicts the Book of Genesis and therefore cannot be the case, as he has informed Mr Lee.

Mrs Kyffin squirms sideways to appeal to her daughter with mute eyes and burning face. Ellen stares from the window at the black and white trees, as if envying the hungry birds in their branches. Mr Anwyl tosses back the brandy at one go and sighs while Mr Kyffin gives his mind to the remainder of Isaiah's abstruse verse, which holds that the nursing fathers shall lick up the dust of the earth.

'I think I'll lie down after all,' mumbles Will. 'If it's no trouble, Anna.'

He leans on her arm as they mount the stairs; he's been weeping on and off ever since Beatrice left, he confides. And now he's caught this rotten cold.

'Well, the cold will wean you off the weeping, won't it? It's a godsend. Come on, brace up. You've the Advent sermons to give. I'll bring you an extra quilt. You'll be right as rain in no time.'

When Anna returns, Mr Kyffin has moved to a fresh topic. Mrs Kyffin has shrunk to half a lady.

'I have news for you all. I've already confided this to the remnant of my congregation at Florian Street – the *justified* remnant, I should say. The saints who stood their ground against the forces of Hell and Prynne. And now I shall share it with you, dear friends.'

Isaiah Minety, on a low stool at Mr Kyffin's side, has brought in a stray kitten which he's trying to feed with portions of a doughnut, oblivious to the fleas running across the yellowish-white fur between eyes and nose. The kitten will soon be dead, Anna sees, drained of blood by its massive infestation. She stoops, kneels and takes the mangy creature onto her own lap. Holding the head in one palm, she pinches between finger and thumb the most obvious of the fleas; dabs the eyes with a wet cloth to release them from a glue of pus. The skull's so frail: one could crush it in one's fist. The puny neck is slack.

'My dears,' Mr Kyffin confides. 'I have been given reason to believe that I shall never die! I am *immortal*.'

He sits back in his chair, shyly, as if concerned for the effect his enviable revelation will have on his audience.

The kitten quivers and gives up the ghost in Anna's hands.

In the quiet that succeeds Mr Kyffin's announcement, she bundles the creature in a cloth and gets to her feet. Isaiah, more childlike than she has ever seen him, overflows with tears. Recently his disciples have deserted him, after visits by the magistrate to their parents, threatening fines. The followers have been soundly thrashed and put to bed without pudding. Promises have been extracted from them, with savage penalties attached.

Isaiah follows Anna into the garden where he places the corpse in a small crate. No point in trying to dig a grave in this freeze.

The boy lifts up his voice and prays to the Great Father of All to take the innocent kitten into his lap and to nurse it with Harry. By and by it seems that Harry is also being prayed to. Harry is asked to exert his influence with the Almighty, like the child saints of the Roman church. Anna huddles her cloak around her and surveys the chequerboard of the land under snow. The wilderness rears forward through the trees, foreshortened. Round the chestnut run prints of famishing birds. She cannot be sorry for the kitten, its spent life delivered from evil.

But what is one to think of the creatures' suffering? The magnitude of it can hardly be conceived or imagined. All mortals have been stretched on a common rack of pain, terminating in a common oblivion. In Salisbury Cathedral there's a carving on the base of a pillar, a trinity of reptiles added by the recent restorers: a pig-faced gryphon cannibalising a fellow reptile, while its own long tail is being chewed by a third. Why did the restorers insinuate this group so unobtrusively low to the ground, like a telltale secret? She studies the kitten through the slats of the crate: here is a crucifixion by fleas, lives also God-given, and presumably themselves also capable of pain. The cold world throbs in a common agony. What is to be said about this; how can it be condoned?

Anna must write this down. It's time to go through the metal box, where she's kept her writings since childhood. I'll collect and arrange them, she thinks, and continue to develop my thoughts on paper. She can freely do this now that Beatrice is away.

Taking Isaiah's hand, Anna returns to the parlour where Mr Kyffin is acquainting the company with his recalculation of the coming End in the light of new information, partly visionary, partly founded on rational observation and millennial computation. Opening the Word at hazard and, taking as his point of departure Luther's publication of the German Scriptures in the autumn of 1521, Mr Kyffin has amended the date of his Master's Second Coming to 'not later than 1881'.

There's a maximum of twenty years to wait. It will pass in a twinkling. Much to be done in that time. Vigilance must become second nature. For what if the Lord came knocking at the door to find us engaged in 'animal functions', if one might so phrase it?

'How are you, my boy?' he breaks off to ask Isaiah, fondling his hair. 'How is Kitty?'

'Miss Anna and I have put her in a box. Mr Kyffin, has Kitty gone to glory? Shall I see her at the End?'

'Without a shadow of a doubt, darling. Lapping a saucer of delicious cream. And all the cats that ever were will be mewing around the Throne of Grace.' His eyes beam. Human kindness can remain when reason goes, Anna thinks.

'And what about birds? The birds she ate? And the worms the birds ate?'

'Well now.' Mr Kyffin ponders seriously. 'Do you think such regeneration is beyond the Almighty, who made the cosmos with his own hands, dear boy? He put us together once – he can surely repair us. Worms too, I've no doubt. And worms of course are a lesson to us, for, cut one in half and both halves regenerate. All life, all, without exception will be saved. Nature's a book and when we turn the page, does the previous page cease to exist? Of course not! And then again, take the Bible. This masterwork that I hold in my hand has been formed from calf hide and linen made from flax. The great bookbinder will restore it to its constituent elements. All creatures will be restored, you see, dear, everything will run back from destruction. Yes, spiders and the flies they have consumed. And the … whatever flies eat.'

Ellen Kyffin shivers. 'Don't, Papa. Please.'

'Love is our imperative though, my dear, even for low and dirty creatures. Is it not?'

'Yes, Papa, I'm sure. But they're still low and dirty. I'm thinking we should start for home, so that you can have your lie-down. And Mama is looking tired.'

'Oh, do you think so, dear? Are you tired, Antigone?'

'Perhaps, just a little.'

'Mama, let me put your cup down. The tea is cold.'

Antigone Kyffin can hardly be said to have been present, here or anywhere else. She makes shift to gather herself together in obedience to her daughter's plan, but one glove has been mislaid; her shawl slides down one shoulder as soon as it's hoisted on the other. Ellen's capable hands rearrange her like a giant doll.

'There you are, Mama, you're all nice and ready.'

As acting head of household, the child treads a tenuous line between authority and deference. Half of Ellen basks in her predominance; the other has been deserted by parents who've dwindled into errant children. She superintends the donning of coats. The mother submits calmly but her father, one arm in his sleeve, cannot seem to engage the other, circling at each attempt, murmuring to himself as he rotates darkly in a vortex of insane speculation.

Anna waves them off, returning with relief to the warmth. She has the house to herself, with only Amy working quietly in the scullery. Opening her portable desk on her lap, Anna takes out her journal and seats herself before the roaring log fire, feet on the hearth. Your front roasts while your back freezes. She pulls the hood of her mother's mantle over her head. Heat and peace steal through mind and body; her fibres relax and by and by Anna begins to luxuriate in a mood of tender melancholy. The feel of the kitten's small skull in her palm brought to mind Magdalena. The dark angel comes and guides her pen on the page.

*Had Magdalena lived, my life would have been so very different. I'd have lived a mother's life. Beatrice was happy to leave the care of our half-sister to me. It relieved her of the pressure of my grief & the child's monstrosity.*

*Mrs Bunce knew of women able to suckle babies without having borne a child. I'd been trying to feed Magdalena with drops of boiled milk and sugar on my fingertips. 'You can do better than that, Miss Anna. Put her to the breast. She'll get comfort from it & I've known grandmothers able to suckle orphans for if the breast is there, the baby will pull, can't help itself, & milk will come in sooner or later, if you want it to.'*

*The volume of Magdalena's head increased daily & the bones of the skull could not close, they were levered apart, the fontanelles bulged. The ass Q. said there was no brain in the cavity, only water. Nothing there, nothing human. & indeed she looked like some strange aquatic specimen. Her eyes were always lowered – never looked at you. Everyone thought: Poor creature wd be better off dead with her mother. I bathed, cleaned & cared for her, walked her up & down over my shoulder – kept her in my bed at night – offered my breast & she seemed to like the living softness; sometimes tongued the nipple, lapping like a kitten. The tenderest saddest feeling in the world. There was nothing in me for you. Dry as a bone.*

*Still I felt you were not absent Magdalena but asleep & dreaming. You went into convulsions & the ass Q. stopped his bleedings & cuppings for he said the end was near. He went on his holidays and young Dr Brimelow from Bourton was his locum. He said, Bless her, of course the dear little soul knows you're there – keep Magdalena warm and cuddle her – everything you're doing is the best that can be done.*

*You & I at the edge of the world – together – hanging – but sent to comfort each other, if any comfort was to be found.*

*Once Q. had given up, Magdalena seemed – in her passive way – to rally. Whose miracle was it – God's or Nature's? – when a bluish-white pearl of milk dropped from my nipple onto yr tongue? You opened your little beak. Again. Another. Indescribable sensation of grace, as the milk came in. How I cried. You never cried; it didn't occur to you. You were too busy, darling, with your dream.*

Knocking at the door. Nuisance. Send them away, do. Amy tramps through to answer the knock, grumbling under her breath, wiping floury hands on her apron.

'It's the doctor, miss, him and another one. Am I to show them in? They said you were expecting them.'

In the heat of the fire Anna has lapsed into a reverie she's in no hurry to quit: while she's writing, Lore and Magdalena are very present. She has noticed before that the pain melts into ink when you write. The misery of bereavement dissolves into melancholy. One is quiet; there is a balance.

'Tell them I'm busy, Amy.'

But the two men are here, without a by-your-leave, one at either side of Anna. She glances irritably from one to the other; closes the clasp on her desk and turns the key; starts to rise. Dr Quarles, smiling affably, rests one large palm on her shoulder.

'Pray do not trouble yourself to get up, dear Miss Anna. We shall, if we may, warm our hands at the fire and have a quiet chat. How are you feeling?'

'I am perfectly well. I didn't send for you, Dr Quarles. I'm not sure why ...?'

'Miss Pentecost – I beg pardon, *Mrs Ritter* as we should now call her – asked us to look in during her absence. She expressed some concern about your health.'

'But there's nothing wrong with me, Dr Quarles. As you see. And in fact, I'm very busy. With household accounts. So – if you –'

The word *hysteria* is spoken.

It is denied.

It is reaffirmed, with insolent courtesy. Another word is added: *neurasthenia*. The dilemma of the female psyche is mentioned. For anxiety, turbulence, abdominal pain, sleeplessness, irritability, nervousness, aberrant behaviour all stem from the congestion of the female organs. It's a common problem and easy to treat.

'How dare you? I am not hysterical! Get out of my house, you pair of vultures!'

Aha! This is what they had apprehended: this wild and uncontrolled burst of expletives. Anna's up on her feet, half-crouching. When she dodges out of reach, one of them stations himself at the door.

'Let me out!'

The medical men observe her with rueful gravity. 'Do not

distress yourself,' says Dr Quarles. 'My colleague and I are here to help you.'

At Wilton, trout basking at the surface of the Wylye can be tickled by a skilled hand, scarcely discomposing the clear chalk-stream water; the creature below hangs still among tendrils of waterweeds. From hidden aquifers the river arises, fed by rainwaters, pulsing past flourmills, through water meadows where the cattle drink their fill. In girlhood, Anna, wearing pinafore and buttoned boots, would crouch on the green bank, skirts tucked up, where salmon, minnow, loach and lamprey crammed the water. Perch and chubb sleeked by. The intent girl knew them all.

Anna convulses like prey that's all one spasming muscle leaping clear of the stream. Into full view. She's on the verge of falling into *their* hands. No. She resumes her seat and removes the cowl of her mother's cloak. Anna sits cunningly demure, back rigid. She smooths her skirts. You're frightened me. I do not know why you are here, she tells them in her quiet contralto. You should not come into my house like this, scaring me.

They've ambushed Anna. She has not been intelligent. What does a woman have to defend her except her intelligence? Anna schools herself. She parries every lunge of Quarles's foil.

We are the followers of Hippocrates. We have sworn a sacred oath, never to injure, always to heal. You can trust us. We would never harm a hair of your head.

'No, of course you would not, Dr Quarles,' says Anna, picking up a piece of embroidery. 'I know that. Of course I do.' She disappears beneath the surface again; its stillness puzzles the beholder's eye. Deep breaths. Her panic ebbs. She offers tea and macaroons; talks to them of macaroons, how success or failure is bound up with how stiffly you beat the egg whites. A properly feminine preoccupation.

Avicenna, it seems, the respected Arab doctor, had much to say about the malady of hysteria. So Dr Palfrey observes. Avicenna was an ancient philosopher-physician. An Arab, as a matter of fact. Has Miss Anna heard of Avicenna? No? Not many ladies have. The Arabs, who have since declined, were once foremost in scientific discovery. Avicenna was in so many respects a modern, and it's curious to reflect that the nineteenth century, the age of Science, has in some aspects scarcely caught up with his wisdom. Dr Quarles agrees, polishing the head of his stick, that there's nothing new under the sun. He gets to his feet and turns his back to the fire, speaking ruminatively, his hands under his tailcoats which he whisks up and down.

Anna keeps silent. She pricks her finger through the linen.

What happens next seems a bedlam without beginning or end. A swooping, a scuffle, a swift bodily removal. Conducted up the stairs, feet almost off the ground. Yelling to Amy for help. Bedroom door shut, bolt thrown. No fire in here. The cold shocks her splayed legs. Red male faces looming low over her prostration issue caressive words as they handle her, for her own good.

Relax, that's the way. Now, if I ...? How's that? Let go, for you've been suffering far too much for too long, poor young lady – and there's nothing whatever you can do to succour yourself. We are Christian gentlemen, professional men. We know what we're about. It is a man's job, a doctor's or a husband's job, Avicenna said so – but no, no, of *course* we are not going to break your hymen, good gracious no, there-there, do not be the slightest bit afraid.

Anna is covered with a sheet and they reach beneath it.

Manual stimulation will ease the blood blockage.

We are not looking at you. Your maidenly modesty is safe. A medical procedure. Virginity intact. Be assured. Of that. We know. How to. Find. The little – place by. Touch … alone.

She snarls; bites the hand of Palfrey hard. It stinks of tobacco.

But he finds the place with his left hand. Will. Bring. Her. To hysterical paroxysm. If it is the last. Thing he does.

And he does. At least he thinks he has.

There now. That's the way, lie back. You'll feel better directly. The *hystera*, do you see, is where it all begins. The womb. We have released the blood flow. When you are married, your husband can take over from us. You must under no circumstances try to do this for yourself. It's a purely medical business. In the past, pelvic massage was administered to sufferers by midwives but such females lack technical knowledge. Dr Palfrey is, in point of fact, devising a small machine for this purpose.

Oh, and one more thing: vigorous exercise on horseback will also help address the disorder.

They wash their white hands at Anna's basin and dry them carefully on her towel. They fit their fingers into supple leather gloves, which they button at the wrists.

*

All is bustle at Sarum House. Christmas approaches and the dear old goose must be throttled. Anna exists behind glass. Like a specimen. People come up and peer through; she pretends to acknowledge them. Her face is blank. She glides about on casters, a clockwork woman. The goose: will you do it, Joss?

Anna's brother finds himself about to depart on a vague but urgent errand. He states this while grooming his moustache in the mirror; twirling the oiled tips between finger and thumb, twisting his head to judge the effect of his tweakery.

'Why not employ Elias's man to kill the geese?' he suggests. 'Isn't the pig-sticker available? I'm sure he'll do us a goose for sixpence.'

'Amy and I will have to manage ourselves.'

Anna has never before been faced with such tasks. Beatrice, who killed her first hen at the age of eleven, took it in her stride; just came in a trifle pale and quiet. Anna, flinching and fascinated, stared at her sister's hands as she scrubbed the death from them. Well, said Beatrice in her grown-up way, I notice you don't say no to eating it. Anyway, nobody would dream of asking *you* to do an important job, Anna, *you* are not practical and resourceful; Papa would never ask you; you're just a little *pet*, a useless animal, that's all you are.

Before dawn, Anna walks out into the snowy garden and suspends a rope from a joist in the shed. She tugs on it to ensure it will hold. It's dark in there and darker in the goose pen. The geese are stirring. Anna, speaking softly, stoops to gather Henrietta into her arms, making sure to capture the wings. She clasps the living creature tight to her body: the weighty, solid bulk of her. Anna talks to the creature in a friendly voice; masters the throb of her own heartbeat so that Henrietta's heart won't sense danger. The animals know; they intuit everything. She strokes the glimmering white feathers. Shush, shush, all well, Henrietta my beautiful, this won't take long. A few moments and the light will be out; you won't know; you'll have soared away with the wild geese. Or folded your wings and settled for the night.

Is there room for Henrietta in Heaven? Is there room for Anna?

The loop snares her head. Anna embraces the skull in her palm; the feathers and the oil the goose secretes to insulate her from water; the bone around the brain. We're friends, are we not, my darling? We've known one another a long while. Amy slips a smaller loop over Henrietta's legs, between the first knuckle and the web. Grasping the bird's strong body and holding it near her hip with freezing hands, Anna thrusts her own body back and down, gives at the knees, feels the rope tighten, feels Henrietta's head cleanly part from the neck; no going back; the spinal cord snaps; it is finished;, the creature is dead.

Whereupon powerful wings begin to beat, they thrash at Anna. Henrietta, garrotted, is stone dead; her wings are alive and raging.

'Leave it hanging now, miss, I should,' Amy advises. 'Give it a wide berth. That's the way. Just the nerves, see. Stand back now.'

The bird gyrates on the line; white wings spasm.

'Good. That'll stop the blood from pooling in the carcase. Are you hurt, miss?'

'A bit winded.' Anna bends double. The dead wing has caught her such a blow that she feels some vessel or organ has burst inside herself. She reels and retches but nothing comes up.

'Go back in, miss. I can manage fine. She's a fat un for sure.'

'No, I'm all right.'

Amy releases the body from the crossbar. She drops it, thud, on a plank and begins to yank out fistfuls of feathers. She cuts Henrietta from the base of the neck to between the feet, removing whatever internal organs she can find. The guts steam briefly where she drops them. Cheerfully whistling, Amy wipes the body cavity.

I shall never die, so Mr Kyffin proclaimed.

We are followers of Avicenna, insisted Dr Quarles.

Was Avicenna a Christian?

Animals are our kin, wrote Mr Darwin.

Our Beloved became man and died for us, taught Pastor Pentecost. On the bloody Cross.

Amy lugs the meat back into the house. Bloodspots alongside her boot-prints pit the crust of snow. Anna follows slowly, grateful for the icy air that cools her forehead, and postpones the sick ache she knows will split her skull when she enters the fug of the kitchen. The animals sheltered in the barns, body to body, are hushed. Henrietta's mate Hereward has taken refuge in sleep, standing on one leg, the other retracted against his body for warmth. If one could take him now and kill him in his sleep, he'd never encounter his own mortality.

A wing of smoke-grey cloud stretches above the dawning sun; Anna watches the wing catch fire and burn in a rapture of light. Crepuscular rays beam into the blue, fingers of a bodiless hand. The crust creaks beneath her boots. Nothing can either ripen or decay in such cold. Chill comes sneaking into coat cuffs and collars; intrudes beneath petticoats. Anna feels exposed to insult and abuse. Anyone may open her door now. Any professional gentleman is free to rifle round her intimate spaces. Beatrice has taken away with her all the locks and all the keys.

Where to turn for safety? The vast machine of the world goes throbbing on according to its own laws, darkly obscure, godforsaken.

Which leaves what? No pieties, Anna thinks, only the decencies: to live as kindly as one is able, in the expectation that there's no life beyond this life. No divine plan. No heaven or hell. No safety because we are reliant on madmen and liars for protection. Women, she has heard, can be picked up in the streets near army garrisons and inspected for venereal disease: anyone so arrested is deemed a common prostitute and kept in a Lock Hospital until cured. In case we infect our masters with our pollution and our hysteria. Who will cure our keepers? A woman had better disguise her sanity and keep her own truth hidden in her breast. Better be cunning as a serpent.

175

A plan begins to suggest itself. The only way out.

Anna's saturated skirt's a dead weight in her hands; her muscles burn as she wrings it out and drapes it on the fender. Outside dense snow begins again; Anna will stay close to the fire for the rest of the day. And sew; yes, she will sew. And be seasonally merry in a composed, sensible way. The skirt steams. The luscious scent of roasting goose fat percolates through the house and mingles with strong coffee.

Anna dips a cinnamon biscuit in coffee and sucks the liquid warmth into her mouth. It can be done. It's the choice of the least of evils.

*

Locked in her bedroom, Anna has excused herself from entertaining company by dedicating her energies to the construction of fancy presents for her nearest and dearest. A treat-factory: no peeking! In this way she can be secure against ambush. But Quarles is ill, Amy says as she delivers a breakfast tray: a hacking cough keeps him from his rounds and his cook reckons he's a right old gawpus of a patient, thinks he's dying and gives Mrs Quarles no end of fuss with his complaints. Oh, what a shame, Anna says, thinking: *for Mrs Quarles*. As Christmas Day nears, Anna allows herself to emerge. Keeping close to her brother, she visits the chapel poor with gifts of food and money.

Yet again there's no room at the inn. Mary undergoes her annual birth pangs and readies herself to deliver the usual promising boy. Ox and ass admire. Carol singers of five denominations tramp the slushy streets of Chauntsey and are rewarded with figs, dates and farthings. Despite herself, Anna is moved; her own trustful childhood visits her, lightly tapping on the heart's door.

Anna greets her guests on Christmas Day dressed in her grey silk gown, with a brilliant red sash around the waist; her hair, gathered into a clasp at the crown of her head, falls in a shine of dark curls down her back. Transformed from Miss Anna into Miss Pentecost, acting head of household, Anna holds herself composed and erect. On her guard. The word *hysteria* will never again occur to any observer. The table groans with good things. Anna has manufactured winter logs for the dinner table: logs containing sugared almond bonbons wrapped in twists of bright paper, on which she has drawn individual Christmas pictures. For Joss a hearty Saint Nicholas sucking a Meerschaum pipe. For Mr Elias an angel with a trumpet. For Jack and Tom Elias, a jolly Santa with the head of a plum pudding. In each log there's a fragment of verse of Anna's own composition, together with a motto and a riddle.

Grace is said. Joss carves the goose. The fire roars. Candles flicker on the mantelpiece, hung with nuts, sweets and tiny bags of fruit. Mistletoe hangs over the door. There's a hubbub of conversation. Everything is as it should be.

'To absent friends!' Glasses clink. 'Merry Christmas to Herr and Frau Ritter! *Fröhliche Weihnachten* to them!'

There's a lull before the plum pudding. Anna gives permission for all to open their Christmas logs.

'Oh how charming! Anna, you have been a busy bee! What clever fingers you have!'

Anna smiles round cordially. 'I enjoyed making them for you.'

Mr Anwyl's sermon this morning was rather fine. For one thing, it was short. His words were suffused with a searching sadness as he reflected upon the loneliness of the Christ child in his cold crib, under the shadow, even in his innocence, of the tragic Cross to come. Only thirty-three years would be granted God's son on this earth. Our joy must always be shot through with pain and loss. This is what it is to be human.

'Whatever's this?' Will holds between finger and thumb a miniature scroll tied with a thread of yellow embroidery silk.

Anna has painted the page with a margin of gold leaf.

'Well, it's a riddle,' Anna smiles with her eyes. 'Aren't you supposed to be rather good at riddles, Will? Anyway it's specially for you. Can you guess it? There's a prize for guessing.'

Sliding off the thread, he unrolls the message and reads the words, 'I. WILL.' He studies them with a frowning smile; glances sidelong at Anna. Reaching for the carafe of wine, she brings the neck of the bottle to the lip of his glass, then hers.

'Now then, what do you call a collection of Baptist ministers?' Mr Elias wonders. He's shaking his log to see if it holds any further treats. 'A convocation of eagles. An exaltation of larks. So – a … what?… *fraternity* of Baptists?'

'An unction? A squabble? A derision? A cackle? '

'A *glory* of Baptists, surely,' says Mr Elias.

The plum pudding advances, burning blue and green. Amy's face, behind the platter, is visited by a fugitive blue light. Joss bounds to help her, inclines towards her and whispers. Jack Elias, pounding a spoon on the table, hurrahs. The eaters, having previously assured one another they couldn't manage one more thing, fetch deep breaths. There might just be room for a morsel. In the candlelight, Will's eyes are bright with charmed surprise. He gazes at Anna, who neither blushes nor drops her gaze. It's her only real chance of safety. Her silk gown spills liquid light in its folds as she breathes.

'Yes, Anna, I will. I *will*. Truly I will. But – *cariad* – will you?' whispers her neighbour, head bowed close to hers, lifting her hand from her lap, turning it over between both of his, lacing his fingers with hers but gently, ready to disentangle them if he senses a rebuff. 'Can you be serious? It's not a joke or a game?'

'The most serious and solemn thing in the whole world. I will, Will, if you will. After all, what else is left to us? And we suit one another down to the ground for we both have feet of clay.'

# Chapter 13

Why, Beatrice wonders, does the memory of a stuck pig arise in her mind? Old Bertha as a piglet was a pet to the Pentecosts, trotting round behind them – so droll – like a puppy. And she farrowed year by year, rows of blind mouths rooting at her teats. Never squeamish, Beatrice had always unsentimentally trusted the pig-sticker to despatch his duties with merciful effectiveness. Bertha was different, screaming like a baby as the blood pooled into a bowl, betrayal in her eyes.

Defloration is a performance Beatrice seems to observe from above, hovering somewhere near the ceiling. How can this coupling be thought of as creating *one flesh?* The prodding of her husband's member against the hymen; the scramble of slick fingers that come to aid penetration and thrill her with a moment's surprising pleasure, before they force a passage and the pleasure dies. The rubbing to and fro; the rasp of the bridegroom's breathing; a stifled grunt; his uncoupling from her, letting in a chill to her hurt tissues; the trickling moisture between her legs.

She has never felt as single.

And ashamed: Christian waited all those years for *this?*

But her husband is not insensitive to her wincing shock. When the work is done, Christian fends off sleep, clasping her head against his chest, lullabying her with fond words. By and by, warmth engulfs Beatrice; she dips into dreams of that other man with whom she might have shared a marriage bed, save that Herr Ritter caught her on his knee and claimed her.

When Beatrice awakens, her husband is gone. The first day of their honeymoon – a working honeymoon, beginning here in Leominster – has begun. His nightshirt's folded on his pillow; his comb bisects his brush on the dressing table. Sitting up carefully, Beatrice pushes off the heavy covers, twisting round to see that blood soils nightgown and sheet. What to do about such shameful stains, in a strange house? The place between her legs is raw; her lips and cheeks are chafed by Christian's bristles. A stuck pig. Her breasts tingle, not pleasantly. Beatrice rises, washes and dresses. Brushing her hair and tying it up with a violet ribbon, she strips the bed, folding the sheets so as to hide the stains.

'It will get better,' he promised. 'It will hurt less and less. Soon our relations will give you pleasure, darling, I hope. For now, yours is the sacrifice to our love.'

Beatrice hesitates on the stairs, hearing the murmur of conversation. The married ones will be knowing; the unmarried curious. Pondering the bloodied sheet, the maid will smirk. But I am Mrs Beatrice Ritter, she thinks, bracing herself. Miss Pentecost is extinct. I've put on the new woman and put off the old. For years Beatrice has been an ageing maiden in quest of a playfellow, flirting with suitors, enjoying an increasingly sterile sense of mastery, conscious of slow blight spreading through her being. Smiling with teeth that are growing discoloured.

Godly and familial love embraces Mrs Ritter as she enters the warm kitchen where her hosts sit informally round a deal table with a splendid fire. Her husband gives Beatrice his seat, brushing her hand tenderly in passing. Martha and Tabitha Jones, the servants of the house, staunch Baptists, are treated as near-equals by their employers and take their places at table with the rest. Talk is all of Awakening. Sparks are kindling the villages and market towns of mid-Wales and the Marches. Liverpool is on fire. Christian is spoken of as a leading light. Beatrice, breakfasting on kedgeree and hot spiced rolls, listens as Christian speaks of his time in Jamaica as a very young man with the great anti-slavery pastor, Mr Knibb; the present war in America; his hero and, he likes to feel, his friend, Henry Ward Beecher.

How could she not choose such a towering spirit over the jester?

I shall learn to love you, Christian, Beatrice thinks as the train rides through the snowy countryside towards the mediaeval town of Shrewsbury, with its centuries of Baptist witness. I don't love you yet. But I'm learning. A plume of smoke rides beside the train; the coach's rhythm lulls her tension. She's impressed by Christian's ministry. Her husband often speaks three times a day, without notes, for an hour together. He can make each auditor feel that the message is just for himself or herself, especially, apparently, *herself*, for ladies and young girls cluster round him effusively after a service. It's a novelty for Beatrice to have nothing to do but attend on her husband, hear him preach, fondly brush his coat and cede responsibilities.

They have the carriage to themselves and sit either side of the window. Christian's eyes are closed; his lips move soundlessly. She knows he's praying. She closes hers; prays too, that they may be one. God comes close to Beatrice in the green Marches as the train throbs its gentle way between the hills. She welcomes Him as a guest long absent. How can He bear to take up residence in such a filthy tabernacle as her heart?

Sitting with bowed head, Beatrice asks pardon for the cold formality of her worship in the past months; the vanity of her witness. For bringing the image of Will Anwyl into the sanctuary of her marriage. He is still here. The Spirit cleaves to her in forgiveness. It reminds her that the woman taken in adultery was freely and fully pardoned. But Beatrice and her husband are one. And that one *should* be Mr Ritter. To attain her womanly fulfilment, Beatrice must allow herself to dissolve into him and nestle there in the region of his heart.

God's responses to Beatrice's prayers are not always comfortable or welcome. Opening her eyes, she looks out to where – over in the west – the Black Mountains, flanks white with snow, conceal the deeper Wales of Mr Anwyl's childhood.

The train passes the Long Mynd and the rolling Shropshire Hills. With a sigh, Christian opens his eyes. Reaching out a book, he flicks through the pages; glances over at his wife with a loving smile. Sometimes she thinks he overhears her thoughts. Last night he read aloud from the Song of Solomon. Longingly. *A garden enclosed is my sister, my spouse. A spring shut up, a fountain sealed.* She flinched from the intuition that Christian was expressing a sense that she holds something back. But what is it? How do you know how to yield the surrender a man craves? The crude animality of their coupling still dismays her. The intimacies of marriage are a subject about which she has never spoken to a soul, not even to her sister.

Poor Anna – all that pain and sickness and hysteria. Thank goodness Dr Quarles has promised to keep an eye on her. For Anna would never voluntarily call him in, despite or because of the fact that he has intimate and long-standing experience of her quirks and maladies. When Anna lost her reason and attacked herself after Lore's death, he sewed up her arm. Beatrice has said to Dr Quarles: even if Anna resists, please persevere. Well, she thinks, I'll soon be home and Anna and I can start afresh.

A bearded, rough-looking fellow with drink on his breath embarks at Ludlow. He looks from one to the other, assessing the relationship; winks at Beatrice. She removes her left glove and lays her hand, with the wedding ring, on her knee. By the time they reach Shrewsbury, Christian has initiated the conversion of this bibulous cobbler from Wem.

*

At last! She scampers across the road. Sarum House – back at last – oh, thank heaven. Beatrice slides on slush, clutches at the gate to save herself and is in the garden, on her own land, where everything is precisely as it should be. Islands of grey slush persist in a sea of dank greenery. She relishes the long perspective of lawn, labyrinth, vegetable plot, chestnut tree, stable and outbuildings, the wilderness. Windows are bright rectangles of yellow light in the dim afternoon. Beatrice peeps into the drawing room, where figures encircle the hearth, as if they'd not moved since the moment the Ritters left. My family, my home, my world. She's through the door: a scent of nutmeg hits her. Boots kicked off, she's haring on stockinged feet through the house into the parlour.

'It's me! I'm home!'

Mr Elias moves seamlessly from a Scottish song into the wedding march.

'Oh! Beatrice! You never said. Why didn't you tell us you were coming? Where's Christian?'

'*My husband* – is just sorting out the luggage. Go out and help your brother-in-law, Joss, would you?' She's in her sister's arms, laughing, weeping. What a relief to have the honeymoon behind her! 'How are you? Did you miss me? Oh, Anna, let me look at you – you look, goodness, you do look so well.'

Christian arrives, to clapping and handshakes. How are you? What is your news? There's a huge fuss. Amy brings Beatrice's red velvet slippers, worn to the shape of her feet; her hands are chafed. Anna goes for mulled wine; the fire's banked up. Are you warm, are you cosy? The queen is back in her court and the court adjusts to receive her.

A commotion at the door. And here he is. Oh, at last. Mr Anwyl, pausing briefly, comes forward with his hand held out; no, his arms.

Beatrice leaps to her feet, elated, taken by surprise. Her husband's head swivels in mid-phrase. He sees all. Christian will always see all. Even so, Beatrice cannot be daunted by proprieties. The heart has its impulses and doubtless she'll repent afterwards and can obtain forgiveness – which is thinking like a Papist but ... oh, my darling Will. His hand reaches out.

To Anna. Who takes it in both of hers, her eyes brilliant. We have something to tell you. Our secret. We waited until you came home. It wouldn't have been right to make an announcement without Mr and Mrs Ritter. And now that they are home, not one more minute can we wait. We're engaged to be married! Yes, really. Thank you, we're so happy.

And there's a ring! Would you like to see, everybody? They show the ring. It belonged to Will's mother. A cheap circle of tin alloy, scored and worn. A metal of mortal softness.

And perfect.

'Anna would not hear of a gold ring, would you, *cariad?*'

'No, categorically not. This remembers the person Will loved most in the world. I'm in the best company on earth, the very best.'

'And I bless you for saying that, dearest Anna. *Dw i'n dy garu di, ti'n werth y byd.*'

'And I'm learning Welsh, to speak to my husband in his mother tongue. *Dw i eisiau siarad Cymraeg.*'

Christian comes forward with hearty congratulations; the rest follow. How Anna shines. Everything about her seems to catch the ebbing light as afternoon turns to evening. Beatrice is awed by her dark eyes, with beads of candle flame at the centre; her glorious hair, parted in the middle, sleek to the head and pinned at her nape so that it no longer appears cropped. Anna's cameo brooch glows at the collar of a charcoal grey silk dress Beatrice has never seen before. The cheap ring that belonged to Will's mother winks on her finger: the ring promised to Beatrice, had she deigned to receive it. But Will never showed it to her. And, being invisible, the ring accrued a legendary aura. This cheap thing was the most precious token Will owned in a life that began in pauperdom. This was what Beatrice had been challenged to earn. She failed.

Not once does Will meet her eyes. Even when he accepts her handshake and congratulations, the exchange is brief and correct. The room spins. Pain twists in Beatrice's side like the stitch that used to hobble her when she tried to race the village children down Primrose Lane. The rabble galloped past, jeering. She sinks into a chair. It will pass in a minute, this illegitimate pang. For I have no right to it, she thinks. It's adulterous. Her husband is cordially telling his brother-in-law-to-be, 'I cannot say how pleased I am. Congratulations to you both.' Nobody seems to notice Beatrice's qualm. Thank goodness. Give me a moment to command myself. And after all, this arrangement is what I ordained.

He looks so happy. But he can't be! Beatrice's soul stamps its foot. He's only a hand-me-down, Anna. He must have settled for you as a way to stay close to me or in a spirit of retaliation. You're second best; always have been, always will be.

'Beatrice – dear – you are glad for me?' Anna asks in a measured voice.

Those pearls at Anna's ears are their mother's, given by their father to Lore and removed when Anna laid out the corpse. Beatrice took them from her sister's hands, replacing them in their box, the box being hidden in the bowels of a chest. In this chest they used to climb as children, crouching in the musty velvets and linens of an earlier generation.

Beatrice's eyes swim with tears. She cannot speak. I shall – oh, no – disgrace myself, she thinks, and focuses on the delicate place between Anna's ear lobe and her throat, where the pearl gleams. She's aware of the high cheek bones in her sister's heart-shaped face that has come out of the shadow and blazed at them all. You've taken my place.

'Very happy. As long as you are. But – you never said, Anna. And there are things to discuss. Such as' – she whispers – 'income.'

'Oh, I did discuss that – with Joss, don't worry. But it was your idea, wasn't it? Everything changed once you were gone, as it was bound to do – or rather it clarified. I knew I must marry – marry Mr Anwyl, as you wished. When it came down to it, I had no choice.'

'It wasn't like that, Anna, I didn't wish –It was your conduct. I didn't mean you to –'

'You made it happen. As sure as eggs is eggs. And thank you for that, Beatrice.'

There's no way into Anna any more. Her face is closed. Don't leave me, Anna, don't leave me alone.

The room is full of spies. Darting looks, pretending to keep conversation light and open.

Anna says, sympathetically, 'But you're looking pale, dear. Are you unwell?'

'Oh, I'm always well. But, yes, the journey – it has been – fatiguing. I think I might go upstairs to rest … there's nobody in my – in our – room, is there?'

'Oh no, dear, I've moved out of it and kept it ready for you both. Is there anything you'd like? Something to eat or drink?'

'No … well, is there port or anything? No, I don't need help. Anna, *don't*. Just let me *be*,' Beatrice snaps, mortified tears brimming. A cold sweat has broken out on her brow. 'I'm all *right*, don't fuss. Put some lemon in the port.'

There's a moment's silence in the drawing room. Now at last Will brings himself to look Mrs Ritter in the eyes. He casts on her a deep, chastening, unsmiling gaze.

What do you mean by looking at me like that?

And of course the bridegroom's antennae have caught and interpreted the look. Irritation spikes up in Beatrice. Why can't he leave her alone? But no, Christian hastens to support his wife out of the room and up the stairs, like an overtired child being put to bed for its own good. Lifting her bodily (against her will), he lays her gently down on the bed. He removes her slippers.

'Never mind, *Liebchen*. It is better that we all get over this moment,' Christian covers his wife with the quilt; brings a flannel from the washbasin and lays it over her forehead. 'Better now? All is well, you know.'

'Much better, darling, thank you. Sorry for snapping. I do need a rest. It's all the emotion. Is she bringing some port? Will you bring it instead? And then do go back down and have tea, Christian. Apologise for me, please.'

He remains seated beside her on the bed, his hand on the mound of bedclothes over Beatrice's hip. She would feel it pressing down through a thousand quilts. Christian's expression looks gravely sermonical, like Papa's after some small act of childish naughtiness. Beatrice can't have this condescension. In her own house. She's not some giddy girl who can't keep her emotions under control.

'Please go downstairs, Christian. I need to sleep, I really do. I'll be right as rain if you will just allow me to *rest*.'

'Well, I will in a moment. I just want to say –'

'No, please *don't* say.'

'But you don't know what I was about to say, my love.'

'Don't say anything. I'm too *tired* for it, why do you have to make speeches when you know I can't stand it?' The tears rise. Beatrice's face burns. Shame drives out affection. Her lip trembles. 'I won't listen to your preaching!' she insists petulantly.

He gives a little cough, embarrassed for his wife. 'I am not preaching now, dear. Or am I? Maybe I am. I don't mean to. But I'm going to say it all the same. Are you listening, Beatrice?' He bends his head, looking towards the twilit rectangle of the window. 'Love is always the greatest good. Always and everywhere. So writes Paul in his Epistle to the Corinthians and Amen to that, say I. Don't you?'

She nods, biting her lip.

'So it follows that we cannot regret the giving and receiving of love. Your love for others – *listen* – your love for those who have shared your affections is not something I could ever resent. I feel your heartbreak as if it were my own. I do. But think about it – for surely it will prove a strength to you. I loved you as a child. Do you think I didn't learn everything there was to know about Beatrice Pentecost in those years? Even when you stamped your foot as a little heathen of ten years old, I smiled. You cannot disappoint me. I know it all.'

'That's horrible – don't say that, just don't, I *hate* it.' There was something not right about it, she sees that clearly. Lawful but not right. He has taken advantage. And the child he wooed has never died because it has never grown up. Thief! You stole my childhood! The blood rushes up to her face and the child in her slams out of the room.

'That pains me, Beatrice, it offends me. Mine was never a transgressive love. It was the purest affection a man can know. You were and are part of myself; I'm not myself without you. I love you the more for having loved the child you were. Was I not respectful, did I not consult your Papa at every turn? Did I not guide you? Did I ever coerce you?'

Beatrice says nothing; she averts her head and scowls. Why did you fix on me? I was a plump, banal child, very plain. What caused you to elect me for your angelic attention? For you did resemble an angel in those days: golden hair, willowy, lacking only wings. Why did you go for me rather than Anna the Beautiful? *Beattie hates*, *Beattie loathes*.

'I don't know what we're doing here, Christian. Or why you're lecturing me on love. Unless you're alluding to Mr Anwyl – is that it? Yes, I was fond of Mr Anwyl once – but that was calf-love. Nothing more. You can dismiss the whole subject from your mind. Don't look at me like that, Christian, just please don't.'

'Like what, my dear? What do I look like?' He allows himself an edge of exasperation, qualifying it with a smile. 'I'll try not to look like it.'

She does not say, 'Like your cousin', like Lore Ritter with that straight gaze, playing ice-blue stare-you-out over the breakfast bacon. Viewing you ironically through thick round spectacles from her pockmarked face. The Ritters are idealists with the light of God in their eyes: what they believe, they will live out. Not only in spirit but to the letter, if it kills them. Or you.

'Give me a clue. What face am I making?'

'Oh leave it, for goodness' sake! – Sorry. I'm talking nonsense.'

'Dearest, you are. You're in a thoroughly agitated state and I'm annoying you when all you need is rest. Should I send your sister up to keep you company?'

She shakes her head. Christian goes to kiss her; she pulls back. Patting his wife's shoulder, Beatrice's long-suffering husband rises from the bed and leaves, closing the door behind him considerately, as if on an invalid. Beatrice quails. He's the kind of man who always puts one in the wrong. How can he be so accepting of her love for Will? A normal man would feel pangs of jealousy but high-minded Christian Ritter could never be seen to stoop so low.

No, you'll punish me in another way altogether, won't you? A most invidious way. You are saying to yourself, My wife is hysterical; I'll have to humour her when she will not bear correction.

*

The walls that secure her are dove-grey, a peaceful colour, especially when early morning sunlight opens phantom windows of reflected light, windows that slide imperceptibly round the room. Observing this process, Beatrice's eyes become fascinated by blemishes and stains, areas where paint has flaked. The chamber, known since childhood, slept in by generations of Pentecosts, is a mass of effacements and half-obscured traces. The phantom windows reflect wind-blown branches outside; the swoop of a blackbird past the pane.

Beatrice lies in a magic box, the interior of a camera. Christian has left to instruct the students of Bristol Baptist College on the institution of slavery before travelling to Devon and Cornwall, collecting for the cause. Beatrice veils her willingness to relinquish her husband, showing and indeed feeling a proper tenderness and regret.

Time dawdles. Between bouts of fainting and nausea, Beatrice ponders the irregularities of the paintwork around the bed. Horsehairs from the painter's brush have dried into the building's fabric: you cannot tease them out with a fingernail. The forgotten workman's brush shed not only these filaments but also something of himself. His straight lines were not straight. The brush wandered as he drew it across layers of old paint and wallpaper. Somewhere between the layers there'll be traces of a mural the sisters had secured permission to execute, once it was decided that the walls must be repainted. If Beatrice's nail picks just – here – the lineaments of a family portrait will be revealed, with the overarching forms of Papa and Mama Pentecost. Mama was dead by then of course but Beatrice could draw her from memory, reinstating her mother, abolishing Mama's successor.

She longs to release that picture; to step through that door into an earlier world.

Upstairs and downstairs Amy and Anna tread on soft feet, so as not to disturb the invalid. 'Indisposed,' they tell all and sundry. Dr Quarles has calculated a date for the happy event. He hopes he will not be away in the Forest of Marmora, that sportsman's paradise in Morocco, where one shoots the bald-headed Abyssinian ibis and also the Great Bustard – so different from the European bustard, sadly extinct in England. If he is away, Dr Quarles promises that Dr Palfrey will attend – a most able physician as Mrs Ritter is aware. And a nurse should be engaged. Milk is what he prescribes for Mrs Ritter, and especially cream. This thought makes Beatrice retch. Oh, and by the by, Quarles adds as he departs, it was a pleasure to be of professional help to Miss Anna in Mrs Ritter's absence. The doctor presents his account for Anna's treatment by himself and Dr Palfrey: two guineas. He sees no need to pay further visits, however; the patient's balance has been adjusted and marriage will do the rest.

In the mornings Beatrice works secretly to liberate the mural. She has begun to uncover the graphite likeness of Papa's wrist and hand. During the afternoons, her biliousness lifts and she's carried downstairs. A change of view will do her good, they all agree, though Beatrice is reluctant to quit her chrysalis. No choice: she has ceded authority and must recline where Anna used to lie, on the old sofa looking out of the window. Anna lays a bunch of lavender on the little table beside her.

'Thank you, dear. That's so thoughtful.' Beatrice puts it up to her face, drinking the scent, which masks the traces of cooking smells and cat.

'Does it smell nice?'

'Lovely. Ethereal and clean. It smells of ... the old chest, doesn't it? Mama's chest. We used to climb inside.'

It was a little world of itself, an antechamber. Light sneaked in through cracks between the mahogany boards. The chest was monumental. Nobody knew how it had been dragged into the house in the last century; nothing would budge it. You and your furiously giggling sister felt safe amongst your grandmother's gowns, taking care not to damage the christening robes and a wedding veil a century old. More than once Joss had to raise the heavy lid to let them out.

'We did.' Anna perches on the edge of the sofa and the tension between them, despite a certain remoteness in her sister, seems to Beatrice to have slackened. 'How delicious it was, the scent. But what can I get you? Do you have a yen for coal?'

'For coal?'

'To eat it. Lore wanted to eat coal, don't you remember, when she was expecting Magdalena? I could never leave her alone in the parlour with the coal scuttle without worrying.'

'I don't remember that. No.'

There's a pause. I too may die in childbirth, Beatrice thinks. I may bear an encephalitic child. Was it sensitive to mention the monster Lore left us? Are you trying to frighten me? She pulls herself together.

'How's your trousseau coming along? I can easily sew for you, Anna, I'd like to. My fingers aren't ill, after all.'

'I don't need new clothes. I don't really need anything.'

'Well no, but you must do things properly.'

'Oh, I'd rather *not*.'

Beatrice takes time to mull this over. Anna would prefer not to do things properly? She'd rather do them improperly? That would be Anna all over. Beatrice decides that wisdom lies in not questioning this. And besides, in her dreamy languor, she can't be bothered. Let someone else worry about household business. Beatrice spends her mornings drowsing behind closed green curtains, tasting an unfamiliar lassitude; in truth, the nausea has subsided. Christian's letters float down into her halcyon calm, daily. She savours the postman's knock; allows herself to miss Christian, deliciously. His flamboyant gothic handwriting dashes headlong across the page, full of vivid descriptions, salted with humour and expressions of affection. Single again, but without the stigma of spinsterhood, Beatrice allows Christian to enter a space of the dreaming imagination, previously inhabited by Will. After all, this is how her married life will be, for Christian will be away more often than he's present. And perhaps there's a charm in that.

No sign of Anna's betrothed. Where is he? Beatrice doesn't like to ask. Too hurt and mortified. Let him go. Presumably Anna (always second best, bear that in mind) meets him in the mornings when Beatrice is upstairs, lying becalmed alongside the other world, where another hand has come to light – Mama's left hand, reaching out towards ... perhaps, myself. Loveday arrives bearing jellies; Mr Elias comes to play and sing Beethoven. *An die ferne Geliebte*. The music, so personal and confessional, as Mr Elias says, brings a rain of tears. Is God in the melting and the tears? In this supine condition, she can accept and forgive everyone, even her own unsavoury self.

After a while Beatrice comes to feel that she can accept Mr Anwyl as a brother.

'You and Will are welcome to live here, dear, for as long as you wish,' she tells Anna. 'That goes without saying. Perhaps I should have mentioned this before. I took it for granted, I suppose. After all, it's your home too.'

'It's a strange word, home, isn't it, though?'

'The least strange word in the world, I'd have thought.'

'One takes *home* for granted. It's always there. And then suddenly it isn't.'

'But it is! Of course it is. Whatever can you mean?'

'Home's where you feel safe. I stopped feeling safe here some time ago, as a matter of fact. If you want to know.'

'Of course you're safe. Whatever do you mean? Who should harm you?'

'It's a pity I didn't take up residence in Mama's chest while you were away, that's all.'

'What do you mean?'

'Do you remember how you used to flay my face with stinging nettles?'

'Annie! No! I would never ... you must have imagined it.'

'Oh yes, that's right, *I* dreamed it. And how you'd run in to Papa saying Joss had done it! Joss would never hurt a fly! They *knew,* you know, all the time they *knew* it was you.'

Tears rise into Beatrice's eyes. 'Anna, I truly don't remember anything like that. But if I did – hurt you that way – I was a child, we were children – I know I could be nasty; I've more than my share of original sin. Please forgive me.' Beatrice's chest is tight: she puts up her hand to it. Breathe now, breathe for the baby. She does remember struggles between herself and Anna, generally in the wilderness at the bottom of the garden. But Anna gave as good as she got.

Did she? For Annie was the younger. Slight and small. And sly.

'Yes and on one occasion my cheek flared up, my eye closed, and then you were in a panic; you were running round looking for dock leaves going, Oh, Anna what have you done to yourself? Anyway, what does it matter? What's done is done and can't be undone.'

Beatrice has to swallow hard. Is her sister about to unearth some catastrophic secret that will alter life forever? Anna sits at the fireside with her hands on her knees: strong, capable hands, whereas Beatrice's hands are beginning to look pale and dainty. Anna's squirming about as if she can't get comfortable. Did something bad happen while she was away? Beatrice catches the echo of a cryptic message that has not been spoken. Something to do with betrayal.

'Anyway,' Anna goes on, getting to her feet. 'Will and I are discussing whether to live in Fighelbourn. After all, his congregation may object if its pastor formally takes up residence here rather than living amongst them as he's always done and ought to do.'

'But, dear, you couldn't go and live in his present spartan lodgings and manage on £60 a year, could you?'

'I wouldn't mind.'

'One room, and nothing to call your own? There's no rent-free house attached to the pastorate. It's the poorest in the county. Certainly there'll not be enough to support a wife – not to mention all the calls upon a minister of the Gospel, who after all has a status to uphold and social responsibilities. And ... dear, if you have children?'

No answer.

Anna slopes off into the kitchen to roll pastry with Amy. What's all this about? Something has driven the younger sister up from her couch to take the reins of her life in her own hands.

Ah, but if not now, then later Anna will come begging, cap in hand. She'll never endure the heartbroken life of a rural minister's wife, the strain of pinching and saving, of having to do the family washing, sewing, housework, with not a soul to help, ending each day weary and sobbing. The Anwyls will never be able to afford a servant. And Anna is hardly the world's best housewife: look at the flour she's managing to transfer to her arms and hair. At present the whole thing's a novelty but Anna will never last.

Will cannot even afford to buy books for himself. And books are the bread of life to Anna. Books on shelves, books in her chest amongst her dresses, books under her bed, *in* her bed even, in those days when the Salas fed Anna all the latest perversions and perversities. I had to confiscate the worst of them, Beatrice remembers: is that what this is all about? Has Gwilym Anwyl the least idea what goes on in his fiancée's mind? What in heaven's name is her wayward sister doing marrying a Baptist minister at all? Let alone a minister innocent of the Higher Criticism who has never had to confront those who question the account of the Creation in the Book of Genesis. What does Will know of the German Scissors? A man without formal training whose first language is Welsh; a jester and ladies' man and a stammerer whose English is no better than adequate.

You're in a delicate condition, Beatrice counsels herself: show Anna how much you rely on her for support. She'll not leave your side. Lapsing back on the couch, Beatrice slips down, down, into a welcome torpor as the fire shifts in the grate. Drowses. When Anna returns with a tray of tea, Beatrice jolts awake.

'Did she actually eat it?' she asks, yawning. 'That's quite grotesque.'

'Can you manage a slice of toast with this? Who eat what?' Anna begins to pour the tea; she has brought in a toasting fork, with bread and butter.

'Lore. Coal. You said she craved coal.'

'Oh, well … she told me she licked a piece. I saw it on her tongue. I doubt if she actually swallowed much.'

'Poor Lore,' says Beatrice. 'Oh *dear*.' A sigh slips out. A moment of startled grace. She has seldom spoken kindly of their stepmother to her sister. Never, really, spoken at all. Who wants to plunge her hand in fire, even for a moment?

A sister should.

There are times when you see into a soul. Quite nakedly. The core of a person is revealed, terrible as the pink, nude heart of a field mouse Dr Quarles exposed in vivisection. When Lore died, Beatrice recoiled from Anna's wound, afraid not least of the godlessness her sister's anguish implied. Not just absence of belief but apostate hatred of God. Anna cut her own arm from wrist to elbow and the scar's still there. She threw herself on the grave, shrieking, 'I'm jealous of the worms that have her! I want to be where they are!' Beatrice shrank, embarrassed, from Anna's extremity. She became preachy; counselled patience. Lore was better off with God, she said, than here below.

This was true, one devoutly hoped (and doubted), but was it for me to criticise Anna's grief? And Papa's, come to that. He locked himself in his study and scarcely ate or slept. And in the end he was to make a bad death.

'You loved her,' stammers Beatrice. 'And she loved you. Perhaps I was jealous. Forgive me. Love is always a good thing, isn't it? That's what Christian keeps reminding me. He said I was too liable to neglect this and I think it's true. I hope he'll make me a bit wiser and better, Anna – I'll try, I really will.'

Anna's face is twisted and ugly. She murmurs something. Don't touch my pain, she seems to be saying; it's my love's sole surviving child. Once I let it go, Lore and Magdalena and the last remnant of my faith will be dead at last. Beatrice sees that. But how can you live with that degree and quality of pain? Opening the wound again and again, probing it.

What was the hymn they used to hear the Methodists singing, from the chapel in West Grimstead?

*O blessed Side-hole's cavity – I want to spend my life in thee –*

Beatrice and Anna wrinkled up their noses at the thought of taking up residence in a bloody, stinking, pus-filled hole. Even the sacred wound of the Saviour. The girls would block their ears and run from the obscenity.

*Yes, yes, I will forever sit – There where thy blessed Side was split.*

Something carnal there, almost Papist in its prurience; a violation of good taste.

'Could I ask you something, Beatrice?'

'Anything.'

'What did you say to Quarles before you left?'

'Why, dear?'

'I just want to know. What did you ask him to do?'

'Well, just to keep an eye on you.'

'And the other quack – Palfrey?'

'I didn't see him after they came and spoke to us about marriage and so on.'

'I see.'

'Why, Anna, what happened?'

Anna has rapidly collected herself. 'Nothing I want to talk about. They are animals,' she says. 'You weren't to know.'

Weren't to know what?

Beatrice watches Anna inspect the singed side of the toast and turn the other to the flames.

'Do you know what they're doing to women in Southampton?' Anna asks.

'What do you mean?'

'*Habeas corpus* suspended. Only for women. We are back to the Dark Ages. The Contagious Diseases Act. Any woman can be arrested by the police and examined for venereal disease. Anyone. I could be, you could be. If you refuse to comply, you could be held indefinitely. That's the kind of thing doctors are allowed to do, Beatrice.'

'Why are you telling me this, Anna?' If true it is monstrous. But surely in this day and age it cannot be true.

'Oh – I thought you'd want to know. Someone very brave will have to get up and oppose it. Very brave indeed. Because these are things we are not permitted to talk about. Like so much else.'

Spreading butter and honey on the toast, Anna leaves Beatrice to eat and drink her fill. She goes off to the kitchen, wiping her hands on her apron. Beatrice is aware of a weave of voices behind closed doors; scourings of pots and pans in the scullery; Mr Elias's gruff man at the door with a consignment of coal. Something unspeakable has been mooted. Beatrice floats swiftly away from the perilous region into which the Pentecosts have ventured together.

# Chapter 14

A rape? Was I raped? Anna asks herself. Is that what I should say, if I could speak about this to anyone? Which I cannot; how could I expose myself in that way? What could I accuse them of? There are no words for what has been done to Anna, none at all – and if there were, she'd never bring herself to speak them. Since Quarles and Palfrey's visit, she has lost the sense of herself. If she looks within, she glimpses someone answering her description but cloaked and hooded, a woman forever turning away at the end of a dim corridor, at vanishing point.

In Fighelbourn there's a deaf-mute boy, the blacksmith's apprentice. The lad gets on with his work, communicating by signs, but the face is a blank. He's never seen to smile.

Was it rape though? Or was it simply medical treatment?

'Oh never fear, Miss Anna, you are still *virgo intacta*.'

This the bridegroom will be able to determine on a night which slides perpetually nearer.

'Plato tells us – erroneously as it happens and yet we divine in the fable an allegorical relevance – that the uterus is a wandering organ. It is not fixed. It becomes dessicated and detaches. When in the course of its wandering the dessicated organ reaches a woman's chest, it maddens her. This is the derivation of the term hysteria. My dear lady, it is the commonest of female maladies. You should not feel ashamed. There are remedies.'

Anna wrenches her mind from the horror as she settles in her pew. Joss, sensitive enough to catch vibrations of his sister's moods but not to interpret them, reaches across to squeeze her hand. The congregation has begun to gather early at Florian Street for Mr Kyffin's return to the depleted and contrite flock. This will be a shining moment of justification for him.

Anna feigns prayer until the throbbing in her chest slows. The wandering womb sinks back into its approved place. Skirts swish and subside as ladies take their pews; umbrellas generate rivulets in the aisle. Mrs Kyffin's daughter leads her to a pew. Leaning forward, Anna touches her friend's shoulder and smiles encouragement, reassuring her that she's among friends, in a safe place. The Montagus are present, and the Eliases. The deacons file through, depleted in number. A majority of the leading tradesmen – draper, banker, baker – seceded with Mr Prynne.

Glancing sideways, Anna registers the fact that Joss's hand and Amy's are nearly touching. No, they are actually touching, surely? Or if not, their little fingers are separated by a hair's breadth. His on his right thigh, hers on her left knee.

Mr Lascelles has put up the hymns for the day and Psalm 118. *O give thanks unto the Lord, for He is good.*

Anna bookmarks the first hymn; then she finds the psalm. Mr Kyffin has entered his pulpit. *Halleluja!* His congregation welcomes him home with penitent joy. It awaits admonition.

The pastor looks down upon his flock with a grave, shy smile, right hand raised in a gesture of blessing.

'I have come home to you,' he says in quiet, shaken voice.

The congregation's faces wear an expression of stricken fellow feeling. But what outlandish doctrine will Mr Kyffin have brought home with him, Anna wonders. The pastor has been snatched up into a cyclone of theological rotation and it is not clear that, restored to the earth, his visionary intuitions will have returned to the fold.

'The ways of Zion have mourned,' he tells them. 'And doubtless I have been to blame. Who is more accountable than the shepherd? The flock has been divided. But your pastor is not here to crow over his enemies; I acknowledge no enemies. I have precious announcements to make! A Revival! The last great Awakening. Before He comes! And now let us sing Psalm number 118. *This is the Lord's doing and it is wonderful in our eyes!*'

Anna lifts up her voice with the rest: she well understands why Mr Kyffin has chosen this psalm. It speaks of the greatest of Christian paradoxes: the lower we fall, the higher we rise.

'*The Lord is on my side*,' she sings. '*Thou hast thrust sore at me that I might fall: but the Lord helped me.*'

And perhaps too the Lord she has half-abandoned will help Anna. Is it so unthinkable? The chapel is beautiful to her: its whiteness, its simple lines, broken only by the sequence of gilt scrolls near the ceiling, painted with gold lettering reading FAITH HOPE CHARITY. It would be hard to quit this world of the spirit, her home since earliest days.

*The stone which the builders refused Is become the head stone of the corner.*

And perhaps there's no one in the chapel untouched by the thought of a second chance. No, a thousandth chance. The flock has settled into the psalm; a measure of peace and order has been restored.

The vestry door opens. Mr Prynne enters. Mr Swales. Those Florian Street deacons and members who had revolted against Mr Kyffin. All their womenfolk in black. Nine young Prynnes with scrubbed necks and red faces, aged from nineteen to three, in descending order.

Swales makes his way to the hymn board, reaches into his coat pocket and substitutes Psalm 119 for Psalm 118. The singing wavers. Mr Kyffin, after the first startlement, waves on his singers and welcomes the arrivals, gesturing to empty pews and smiling hospitably.

What's happening Anna at first fails to grasp. The Prynnites, standing in a block down the aisle, begin to holler out the alternative psalm, *Blessed are the undefiled*. Number 119 is a psalm of devastating length, much loathed by children, for it runs to 176 verses. The Prynnites sing slowly in a foghorn boom. Bedlam. With the advantage of ambush, the late-comers threaten to outpsalm the Kyffinites. Psalm 118 terminates while the Prynnites have only reached Verse 9 of theirs: *How can a young person stay on the path of purity?*

Mr Kyffin is at a loss. Up leaps Mr Elias and starts the Kyffinites on Number 120. *Deliver my soul, O Lord, from lying lips, and from a deceitful tongue. What shall be done unto thee, thou false tongue?*

He stands beneath the pulpit to conduct, his tenor voice audible above the rest, conducting the loyal flock.

Faint and weak, Antigone is supported out of the chapel. Red-haired Charlie Kyffin has to be restrained from laying violent hands on Mr Prynne. Assisting the fainting Antigone out, Anna turns and the last she sees of Mr Kyffin alive on this earth is of a man staggering as if shot and Charlie thrusting Mr Prynne out of the way as he rushes up the steps to his father.

\*

'It's a form of parricide,' Mrs Elias says. 'What if all our people should rise against their pastors and sing psalms against them? It goes too far, the democratic spirit in our free churches. How is dear Antigone, Anna?'

'Very ill, I'm afraid. You know, Mr Kyffin truly believed that he was one of the favoured saints who'd never taste death. He expected to be caught up in a whirlwind with the rest of the justified, to meet Christ in the air.'

'But did he know he was dying?'

'I'm afraid he did and it was a bitter disappointment. He felt betrayed.'

'Oh *dear.*'

Anna goes back upstairs to Antigone, who keeps to her bed and does nothing but weep. Her husband, who was in debt, has left her destitute and she will soon be forced to vacate the house for another minister's family.

'I'll pour us a drink,' Anna tells her. 'You are to drink it. You mustn't have it on an empty stomach though so I've brought some cake.'

'Must I?'

'You must. It's medicinal.'

'Where is Ellen, Anna? I need her.'

'I sent her over to her cousins.'

'But I depend on her so. Don't send her away. What shall I do?' Antigone's tears begin to flow again. 'I rely on her.'

'Yes, but you mustn't. She's a child. It's too much. Charlie can support you.'

'Charlie can't stop crying.'

'He will have his cry out, darling, and then he'll be ready for the world again.'

'He's a child too, though.'

'No, dear, Charlie's a man. But Ellen is a child.'

'What will become of us? What shall I do? I'm alone in the world.'

'You're not alone, Antigone. The first thing to do is to eat and drink.'

'I cannot.'

'Well, try.'

As she drinks, Antigone repeats the story of her husband's deathbed. Cheerful nearly to the last, John Kyffin assured everyone that God would not let him die. The children were brought in and requested to kneel in prayer, to welcome the coming Saviour. Nothing. The dying man lapsed into sleep. The family scrambled up from its knees and rubbed them. Every time the door opened, Mr Kyffin awoke expecting an angel visitor and every time was disappointed.

'He did not make a good death. So where is he now?'

'In Paradise. A good death, whatever's that? My poor father did not make a good death. God is not so petty as to judge us *in extremis*. His own son cried out in despair on the cross.'

'My sister Sophia is coming from Bradford on Avon,' says Antigone. 'To look after me.'

'That's good, dear. A comfort to you.'

'Not really,' Antigone whispers. 'I'll be a poor relation, of small account in Sophia's house, with none of my lovely things around me. We must sell everything. Not that I care about my china and linen any longer.' She gestures round the room. 'My possessions became worthless when all this started. But when did it start? I've no idea. Where is he, Anna? Do you know?'

'At peace,' Anna says. 'Mr Kyffin is at peace. That's what we need to remind ourselves.'

'They called him a drunkard. He was not a drunkard. We both found that brandy on occasion would calm our nerves. But inebriated? Never. I will not say that Mr Prynne is a wicked liar – who am I to judge? – but this was a wicked lie! Oh, but Anna, I'm forgetting my manners. When is the wedding?' asks Antigone with a jolt. She remembers that the world goes on and that there'll be marrying and giving in marriage. 'Do try to ensure that your husband – for the life of a minister is enormously *taxing*, Anna, and many die in harness, they *crumble* in the pulpit – as witness my dear late husband – they go off with heart attacks and strokes, often in their prime – I do not mean to alarm you, I'm sure your betrothed is of hardy Welsh stock and he feeds himself well; I've noticed how congenial he is in company and how he enjoys his food and drink, that will be a comfort to you – what was I saying? Yes, whatever you do, Anna, guard Mr Anwyl against *obsession* – try to cajole him from too dedicated a study of St John's Revelation, this is what I wanted to say. Even dear Mrs Spurgeon confesses that she keeps a close eye on Mr Spurgeon whenever he seems apocalyptically inclined.'

*

Nobody at Sarum House is up and about except Amy who, yawning her way into the parlour with a hod of coals, greets Anna with vague surprise as she passes through. Anna puts her finger to her lips: *Shush, don't let's wake anyone.* Amy grins, nods. There can't be much that goes on in the Pentecost house that Amy doesn't turn over in her mind while scrubbing and scouring.

The dew's on the grass: the rising sun makes prisms in water-beads hanging from every branch. Appetite for a ride is a thirst that must be slaked. Wearing thick woollen breeches beneath her skirts and a close-fitting jacket, Anna is proof against the chill in the air. She leads Spirit out of the dim stable and saddles up. No one's around to help her mount, so, hoisting her skirts, she uses a pile of timber as a mounting block; flounders as Spirit wheels round in protest; struggles to swing her right leg around the pommel and fit the other beneath the leaping-horn. When Anna's foot finds the stirrup, Spirit steadies to her will.

One day she'll do as Max Hays did in Tenby: ride astride. Max was a tiny creature, fey and boy-like, cutting a caper with everything she did, making a joke of her transgressions. But when the womanly Anna rides astride, she'll need courage. Perhaps when I'm married, she thinks. One good thing about Will is that he's pliable, he'll let her do as she wishes.

The pony's hooves leave a dark trail in the grass. As Anna glances back the way they've come, she spots – surely – Joss sitting in the bay of the parlour window. The back of his head. Whatever's Joss doing up at this time? Amy will be laying the fire in there. Was he seated there silently as she rushed through? Slug-a-bed Joss, so slow to rouse in the morning? *Taugenichts*, Lore called him fondly: *Good-for-nothing*, in jest, for there was no harm in Joss, Lore insisted, none in the world, he was more innocent than anyone in this house. Perhaps Joss couldn't sleep.

Something tugs at Anna's mind. To do with Joss. Still waters.

So long since she rode. Walking Spirit out into the lane, past farm workers with cart horses, Anna moves to a canter so as not to get shaken to death by the trot in the side-saddle. She presses into the saddle; the body doesn't forget its knowledge. An elegant rider Anna always used to be, and fearless. Too fearless, Papa used to say: 'You'll come a cropper.' Of course she was thrown several times but Anna would remount immediately, keeping the telltale bruises to herself. She could not forfeit the pleasure of it, the freedom, the sensuous contact with the creature.

She enjoys the bulk of Spirit's body against her thighs, swaying and circling in the canter – the intimate contact between one life and another, the rider's mastery. There's always the element of risk, for full skirts can so easily entangle with the pommel and break the backs of riders.

On the downs Anna gives Spirit his head and is quickly gasping for breath, muscles burning as she holds her seat. But there's a moment when you pass through exhaustion to what lies on the far side of effort – a sensation of gliding, or stasis even. It's as if she and Spirit weren't moving: no, they are still and the green world races past. They flow and an early morning shadow flows alongside, stretching half a mile.

Anna dismounts at the Endless Pit, the opening of a deep hole in the chalk. The gentle, rolling landscape of the Chase contains ancient earthworks and barrows and tumps encircled by ditches. This is the mouth of the underworld, said Lore: an opening into our mother the earth, a sacred country. Does it disquiet you, Anna, she asked, to think that we are always treading on the heads of the dead? They picked up a bone pin at the Endless Pit and several flint tools. The land shelves beneath Anna's feet so steeply that she feels off balance, as if the hole were sucking her down. She lays her cheek against Spirit's shoulder, taking in the scent of sweat and leather as he crops grass. Years ago the mare Lore rode sickened and died but Spirit has plenty of life in him yet.

It has to be enough, living in the here and now. Let Lore go, she tells herself. She'll drag you down into the underworld. The places that remember her are reminders of absence. She had your soul and you gave it willingly but take it back now. It seems a brutal thought and Anna's tempted to feel guilty. Why would I be angry with Lore? But I am. It rears up in her while the pony bends peacefully to the grass.

I was angry with you for abandoning me.

The dying: there comes a moment when their eyes become remote. You're crouching beside them, loving them, you'd do anything for them: they just turn their backs. I've had enough of you now. I'm going off duty and I'm not coming back. You'll not see me again after this. The moment when Lore turned her eyes to the wall, away from Anna and Magdalena, has gnawed at Anna ever since, for she read in that gesture a capitulation. Gratefully, Lore laid down the burden of consciousness. She sighed deeply, it seemed with relief, putting out from shore, as if to say, I'm done with you now, I couldn't care less, stop bothering me with your distress and demands.

One of the last things Lore said was, 'I am going into the friendly dark.'

Up to that moment she'd been nervous of the dark. There must always be candles, even when she slept, a wasteful expense. A room with no candles she could not enter.

A flock of birds dithers this way and that on the skyline as if collecting its thoughts, skittering in an ellipse, a spiral. Anna takes from the saddlebag an apple for herself and one for Spirit. The pony's tongue rasps against palm and wrist and Anna shivers deliciously.

Mourning must have … not quite an end, but a completion.

Then there's Will. Anna, yes, loves him. Didn't I always? It's in some ways an uncomplicated affection. For years she's been the one he came to when Beatrice repulsed him, knowing that the younger sister wouldn't salve the wound with lies but speak an astringent truth. Since their engagement, they've walked and talked with an easy intimacy that may grow into something deeper. I can bend him to my will, Anna thinks. But only if I can shake myself free. And if he's free of his obsession with Beatrice.

Goodbye to you, Lore. I'm going to seal you up in the Endless Pit.

I'll mourn the loss of my mourning, Anna acknowledges.

Even so, no more of it. I'm young, with all my life ahead of me.

All the while she knows that Lore will fight to keep her. The Lore in her mind, a creature that hangs on blindly with hooks and suckers, will not give up. Anna heaves herself up onto Spirit's back; keeps to a walking pace for she's weary and already has a premonition of tomorrow's aching muscles. She'll be hobbling around like an old woman. Worth it, though. Their shadow has shrunk. Even without the tampering by Quarles, she would have felt trepidation. How to love Will as a husband when it's as a brother that she's always seen him?

Can I love a man? In *that* way? Max couldn't; Eleanor can't.

# Chapter 15

Will must be seen as a brother now. He comes and goes in nearly his old easy way and once more makes Sarum House his second home. His first home perhaps, for the Fighelbourn lodgings are cramped and drab. Although nothing has been said, there's a greater ease and kindness between the two of them. They've resumed something of their old jesting banter, in a minor key. And yes, Beatrice's heart quakes frequently, as now, observing the two of them walking in the garden, Will's arm in Anna's, their heads inclining to one another. She knows how it feels to link arms with Will and feel his hand on yours, stroking it as you walk. Accept it she must. Make the best of it. For she wants the Anwyls to live here with her; they must be courted. They bend to the orphaned lambs, Will's palm on Anna's shoulder.

Twisting his head, he looks back to the house: does he sense that she watches him?

Beatrice turns to her husband; smiles.

'They are happy, aren't they?' she says, voice steady, face unclouded.

'I'm sure they are. But not as happy as the two of us. Except that I am so often away. I'm sorry about that, dear. Especially now, when you're unwell.'

'I am well though, Christian. Flourishing. Truly. And, you know, I'm a minister's daughter. I understand the priorities.'

'Our Saviour helps and supports you. He is with you while I cannot be.'

'Of course He is.'

But her well-being has little to do with her faith. For all the while Beatrice knows that Christian's absences are a condition of her happiness. Not that she wills him to be gone. When he's due to leave she dissolves in tears, clinging to his hand as he leaves their bed in the dawn light. Then she awaits the letters. Beatrice has fallen in love with Christian less through his attentions to her than through his letters, his marvellous letters. His handsome Germanic script, with its frequent enigmas, keeps her guessing. Some words seem at first indecipherable. Others she construes wrongly, as it turns out, and the mistakes somehow colour the correct interpretation even after the riddle is solved.

Beatrice has learned better how to receive her husband's passion. Happily the act does not go on for long. He is courteous and kind and thanks her afterwards. Is he disappointed, to have waited all these years to mate with what she sometimes tells herself must seem a log? If so, he doesn't betray his disappointment. Now that the baby is inside her, he holds back. That's the best of it. She enjoys the caressive intimacies he offers.

In Christian's absence she's once more her own master. No sooner is Mrs Ritter's husband out of the door than Miss Pentecost rises from her grave. Sickness and inertia lift. Beatrice awakens, bored with the meaningless patterns on the bedroom wall, the dull view from the window. She bounds downstairs, to gobble bacon, egg and sausage, with fresh bread spread with lashings of butter. Never has food smelt or tasted so good. Grease all round her mouth, Beatrice sops up spilt yolk with a crust, to her sister's astonishment.

Then she waits to throw it up. And doesn't. Beatrice puts on flesh; her hair grows lustrous and her face, rounding out, becomes bonny. In the mirror she sees a glowing woman in a state of surprised euphoria; the years have fallen away.

Anna and Will must live at Sarum House. Everything will be done to ensure this; nothing to endanger it.

Poor Mr Kyffin's funeral is held in pelting rain at the chapel at Fighelbourn, since Prynne and the Prynnites have locked the Kyffinite congregation out of Florian Street. Mr Prynne has personally crossed their names off the membership list. While this tumult continues unabated, the dead man has to be buried. Mr Montagu, conducting the service, contributes the briefest of brief obituaries to the *Baptist Journal*: 'The Revd John M. C. Kyffin, late pastor of Florian Street, Salisbury, died in the forty-seventh year of his age. He laboured for the good of his flock. Well loved and loving.'

Mrs Kyffin writes from Bradford on Avon that she cannot help but feel injured by this brevity. Other ministers are accorded three pages honouring their godly works. Was Mr Kyffin unworthy of more than thirty-two words? But she reminds herself that Love is all the law and the prophets. Antigone enjoys the company of her young nieces. Most of the time. Her room looks over the vegetable garden. Her closest companion is a kitten. Her daughter Ellen is at school in Kensington, training to be a governess. Charlie is studying to become an analytical chemist, apprenticed to Mr Lee, the freethinking disciple of Mr Darwin. But Antigone assures herself that her son's mind will remain untainted by these errors. Charlie's face flames with eczema and he refers to

Prynne as an assassin, alluding approvingly to Jael's hammer in the Book of Judges, the lady who drove a nail into the infidel's skull.

Beatrice sits with her knitting in her lap while the others discuss the situation. She's constructing dainty boots for her little boy. Will his feet really be so small? She's sure it's a boy she's carrying. She smiles gently, without needing to assert herself. Anna is also knitting for Baby, and so is Mrs Elias, though the logic of Loveday's garment is cryptic: it's a sweet little jacket, she says, as they will shortly see. The fingers of young Patience Elias have contributed something to its grubby asymmetries.

And now, while they're discussing the coming Awakening, the miracle occurs.

To no one but Beatrice, seated there by the open window, a friendly company on one side and birdsong on the other. There's a faint flutter in her womb. A creature with softest wings, a being made of light called forth from the darkness, makes itself known. The needles fall from her hands. She sits upright, listening. *And the Spirit of God moved upon the waters*.

Life acquaints Beatrice with its presence. Life speaks to her, confiding, 'Wait, I am coming. Only for you.' She listens again. No. Now there's nothing. No movement at all and perhaps she imagined it, though she doesn't think so.

'What date is the happy day, Anna?' asks their guest, Mr Idris Jones of Bedwellty. Two of his sons sit at the table demolishing a seed cake. They have strange coxcomb-like hairstyles and address one another in Welsh. The middle son is busy with a revival on the island of Ynys Môn. Their talk, in so far as it can be construed, is all of bringing the Welsh Revival over the border. To Liverpool, home of thousands of Welsh chapel-goers, to Shrewsbury, to Ludlow and the border towns, Welsh evangelists will carry the sacred coals. All England will be alight, then Scotland, then the Reformed Churches of France.

With God's help, the continent of Europe will fall to the new Puritanism. This is the day, the happy day. The Spirit has no limits. Swiss missionaries will convert Russia and Turkey.

And it comes again. The mothy fluttering. Today, thinks Beatrice. Today is the happy day.

She beams, straight into the eyes of Will Anwyl – who colours up, disconcerted, and is caught on a hook Beatrice had no intention of baiting. The smile was not designed for him or for anyone in the room, come to that. But Will is smitten. Well, let him wonder. Let them all get on with their business in their petty antechamber to life. For everything Beatrice has ever desired is here within the compass of her own person.

Quickening. Awakening.

# Chapter 16

The Holy Spirit landed first in Wales, from America.

This is how Mr Jones of Bedwellty phrases it to the Chauntsey congregation. Beatrice, absorbed in the wonder of her own ripening, attends with only half an ear. Mr Jones is proud, he tells them, to be the bearer of this news – modestly proud – or in truth not proud at all, humble rather – for Christ's is the glory. The elders of the Cymric churches have seen revival at least fifteen times in the past century, most recently in South Wales during the cholera epidemic of '49. When the Welsh leaders heard of the new American Awakening, they prayed: 'Quicken us again, Lord, here in Wales!' One hundred thousand spectacular conversions have been achieved in his homeland at the last count.

Mr Jones has left dear Mr Anwyl and his bride in Aberystwyth. Fishing, he says, I left Mr and Mrs Anwyl fishing! They are fishers of men. Even now they are walking by the seaside netting fishermen and sailors. This doesn't sound much like Anna to Beatrice. Granted that marriage does incalculable things to the soul, she'll wait and see before applauding.

Change is coming, Mr Jones says. Be ready, Wiltshire! At Frongoch Lead Mine miners sank to their knees at six in the morning and rose at two in the afternoon: no lead was extracted that day. At Trefeca College the young ministers-to-be sang all night, repeating one hymn over and over. These radiantly touched pioneer spirits, Mr Jones has no doubt, will bring their spark, their *hwyl*, to English altars. And thence to India, Africa, China, the world.

Mr Jones moves on from Chauntsey and preaches outside the locked door of Florian Street Church to Mr Kyffin's congregation and several local reporters. Beatrice and Joss perch on the wall to participate. She can see little from here but she can hear. From within comes the sound of the Prynnites, bawling their way through the Baptist Hymnal. Mr Jones is more than equal to this. He enjoys preaching in the open air. Nearer to Him, he says, gesturing towards the cloudless sky. The congregation swells until the churchyard cannot hold them all. They spill onto pavements and climb trees. And now the graves and pavements and trees are singing: not only Baptists and Congregationalists but Wesleyans, Unitarians, Calvinistic Methodists, evangelical Anglicans.

In his sermon, Mr Jones describes Mr Gwilym Anwyl's visit to his home village and the surrounding hills, taking his bride, together with Isaiah Minety. The boy speaks to the Welsh of his friend and pastor John Kyffin, now with God, and how Mr Kyffin had been a bruised reed but never a broken one, how it had been given to this saintly man to foresee the Revival, and lastly Isaiah tells of Little Harry, who died of a cough and saw angels. And how Harry dreamed that he went out into the fields with a butterfly net and caught, not butterflies, but winged spirits.

Mr Jones has seen the effect of the child-preacher's powers with his own eyes; otherwise he'd hardly have credited it.

Isaiah's hearers become prophets; folk begin to sing, weep, pray as the Spirit takes them. The boy has latterly grown quiet as the result of a sore throat.

And this, says Mr Jones of Bedwellty to the hundreds outside Florian Street, will be coming to Wiltshire. Let us prepare our hearts to receive the seed. And let usurpers tremble.

*

'There it is, *cariad*. There!'

They're in mountainous country miles out of Aberystwyth. At first she sees nothing but rough pasture, stunted trees, a couple of huts. Her husband leads Anna to the broken door of the nearer hut and tramples a path through nettles, striking them back with a stick. Inside is a single room with a dirt floor and a collapsed chimney. One small window. A stench. Here all the washing, cooking, baking, weaving was done; here her husband's parents and six children lived and slept, their few possessions tucked into corners; from the rafters hung dried fish, salted meat and bacon. The walls are black with soot and birds have nested in the chimney. Here Will was born; here he saw his pauper *Tad* die of consumption; here his *Mam* gave up the ghost two years later of the same disease, followed by three of Will's five brothers and sisters. And then the pastor took Will under his wing.

'Mr Owen's cottage was no palace,' Will says, as they come out. 'There it is, adjoining the chapel. More like a shack than a house – it's used as a stable now. It had a few pieces of furniture, a couple of chairs and a bed supported by stone slabs. The roof was so low that Mr Owen could barely stand upright. A big man he was, mind – and looked a bit of a brute if you didn't know him. But to me, Annie, it was a rich and lovely place. Always plenty to eat and drink – no whippings – always a good fire in the grate – and books. Mr Owen taught me English. Mrs Owen was a second mother. She had no children of her own. I owe them everything. If only I could introduce you to them.'

Anna puts her hand in her husband's as they circle the chapel to the graveyard. Chauntsey has never really comprehended Will, she sees that. His frivolity and flirting are in part an adaptation to a foreign culture. Here he's respected for his genial warmth. Not that he won't revert when they return home: how can he not? – unless whatever happiness he can find in Anna can persuade him that he belongs. In Aberystwyth Anna is 'the Englishwoman', the *Saesnes.*

The Owens' tombstone has not been allowed to moss over. Whoever attends to it has left daffodils in a clay pot. The Welsh inscription Anna cannot construe for herself. She stands back as Will kneels. The song of building birds cascades around them.

Back in Aberystwyth Will preaches at Bethesda Baptist Chapel. Anna understands scarcely a word except that *Duw* is God, *Gwaredwr* is Saviour, *cariad,* love. She feasts her eyes on her husband's beauty. Her marriage has been a success beyond Anna's expectations. Yes, I love you, Will. *Dw i'n dy garu di.* She never expected to. Not in this way. In that love are coiled complexities she cannot begin to untwist. There's a sense of what her sister has forfeited; the sharp pangs that must have pierced Beatrice when she relinquished Will. And the compassion sparked by this awareness also triggers possessiveness. He's mine. Not yours. I shall have him.

When Anna sees Will's beautiful hands, gesturing as he speaks of *Duw* and *Gwaredwr* and *cariad*, she thinks of their intimate times, close and warm, his hands that seemed so surprisingly to know her from the start. And did Will wonder when they first lay down naked together that she was at home in her body and understood its capacity for pleasure? Did he ask himself whether she was a virgin? Anna couldn't tell. It was all done in silence. The only sound was the faltering and quickening of their breathings. She melted. She opened softly to receive him, aching for him to slip into her. There was scarcely any pain. And he knew how to give her pleasure. Knew it all apparently. How? Wasn't he a virgin then? Or did men just know? Or was it that he himself loves to be touched tenderly and for that reason understands a woman's desire? Anna proved her virginity by bleeding. But very little.

She's beyond the reach of Quarles, that's for sure. The memory that has branded Anna fades, leaving hardened scar tissue.

Out in the moonlight the Anwyls walk where the stars are so close to the hills that they hang like lanterns. The silence is unqualified until they catch a murmur which at first Anna takes for the rushing of a brook. The Anwyls stand still, listening. Presently she sees a light and hears music.

Men and women holding torches sing their way along the glimmering path. All her life Anna will see this procession, hear this music, the Lord's people walking the mountains from village to village, turning the Welsh hills into a Bible landscape. There's a Presence, she too feels it in her infidel heart. It is real, then? Our Jesus walked this earth before us? He really did. He was here just moments before us. He remains over there somewhere, just out of sight, and these folk are going to meet him. As Anna and her husband stand to one side of the bridle path, every passing face reveals itself in a flare of torchlight, each ordinary, peerless person, as if about to depart this earth for the other world.

At least two hundred pass by.

As the last singers move away, the Anwyls join the end of the procession. Will's singing. Anna looks back: inky darkness. There's nothing behind them except cold night. In the early hours of the morning, getting ready for bed, Will translates for her. She learns that the hymns that struck her so forcibly were written by a farmer's daughter of Dolwar Fach. Ann Griffiths died in childbirth at twenty-nine, half a century back. But to us Ann's still alive, Will says. And I hope she will be so to you. He and Anna kneel to pray.

Impossible to sleep. It's not that Anna was unmoved, there on the mountain path. She was. Nobody could have withstood – Miriam Sala herself would scarcely have withstood – the emotional power of that night walk. Mirrie would have acknowledged it as a human gesture of love and bonding. Its euphoria swept through Anna, a rising wave. The wave crested and overflowed; and again; and again. She was drenched in emotion. And that's the trouble. Throughout their stay in Wales, she has silently recoiled from displays of unmediated emotion. The charisma of the leader; the delirium of the led. This would never do at Chauntsey. The torrential crying of fifty children at Fishguard had to be heard to be believed. The prophetic David Morgan, after an hour of fiery preaching, would descend from the pulpit to harass the ungodly, eye to eye. An ancient woman vaulted a pew in her ecstasy, and a converted sailor at the *Tabernacl*, Aberystwyth, called on God to save his wife Betty whereupon she entered the church crying, 'Lord have mercy on me, the biggest sinner in Trefechan!'

*Hysteria*. What else can you call it? A word she abominates but Anna has been brought up in a strict household: the religion of the heart was, yes, paramount, but piety at home is sober and reflective.

'You're not asleep, are you, *cariad?*' Will whispers.

'No. Can't you either?' Anna turns and snuggles into his arms. She can't see his eyes as his back's turned away from the dim beginnings of light piercing the threadbare curtains.

'I was deep asleep; I was dreaming.'

'What about, love?'

'I'm not sure … anyway. It will have been about you. That's for sure.'

He doesn't want to tell me, she thinks. He remembers perfectly well. About Beatrice presumably. Beatrice is in our bed. She shares in everything we do. How strange this is, that they are accompanied wherever they go by Anna's sister, Will's first love, even into the Holy of Holies. That was the bargain, she reminds herself. I always knew that was how it would be. Will and I are each other's second best. But we do love one another. And sometimes I love him beyond reason, which is an infection I have perhaps caught from Beatrice.

Will sits on the edge of the bed in his nightshirt, elbows on his knees, fingertips massaging his temples and forehead. She kneels behind him, her head on his shoulder, arms loosely clasped around his body. His skin is nearly as soft as Lore's.

'I wanted to ask you,' Will says. 'Tell me the honest truth, now. You will, won't you?' He turns, takes Anna's hands, kisses her hair, his fingers meeting in the small of her back. 'Promise.'

'I do tell you the truth, love, always,' she lies. 'I try to. If I know it.'

There's a whole world in her breast that Anna doesn't acknowledge and Will cannot glimpse. And the same is true of Will and, surely, everybody. Is he going to ask, at last, about earlier loves? Should she tell him about Lore? Are there things he needs to unburden?

'How do you like this country, Annie? My *gwlad*, my *bro*. Do you think you'd be happy here?'

'Oh, I do like it, *cariad*.'

'But?'

'Oh. I don't know.'

'You'd soon learn the language, *bach*. You know you would; you're so clever. I've already taught you words for every part of your lovely self. Haven't I?'

Don't ask me, don't ask. For, no, she wouldn't like to stay here at all. It's so far from civilisation. Anna tries to say that she loves it here for Will's sake and because it's his home, of course she does. The people have been so kind and the landscape awes her. And now Will reveals that he has received an invitation to serve as minister of the chapel at Goginan.

'We'd be poor. But would we mind that so very much? We'd have to make do and mend. It is not what you're used to. But if I have a call ...'

'But do you have a call, Will?'

A pause. Part of him surely hankers after the comparative prosperity he enjoyed in Wiltshire and perhaps after those he loves there.

Eventually Will says, 'I must pray more and see what the Saviour has to say to me. What I felt was ... it may be ... *better* for us two, my Annie, in the long run, to build ourselves a home here. Do it from scratch. Just the two of us. And will you also pray, my darling?'

Into Anna's mind leaps the text, *If thine eye offend thee, pluck it out*. His eye does offend him and he's doing his resolute best to remedy this by breaking free of ties to his wife's sister and the relatively luxurious Pentecost way of life. If Anna looked into her husband's eye now, she'd spy a miniature of her sister in the darkness of his pupil. He's trying to blink it off. Honourably. Will is tacitly giving Anna the best possible chance. And a choice. Most husbands would not. You go where he goes. Your plain duty.

This is the moment when Anna ought to say, 'We will do whatever you wish, husband.' She does not.

No secular books in English here and no library. Nobody to

talk to. Questioning scepticism is anathema to these good people. She *cannot* read the Bible all day long.

Anna walks out alone along a high ridge, which drops away at either side to valleys scooped out in some past age by some inconceivable force.

The vastness of time and space reduces you. The world pitches and sways under the stress of your vertigo. The mountains are waves, the valleys their green troughs. She stumbles and peers down at where her boots are treading.

I am walking over a sea floor.

Shells have weathered out from the limestone: mussels and winkles, ammonites too. Anna remembers the meeting with Mr Gosse and how Miriam's friends talked of the war of species over millennia; their slippery mutations. Mirrie referred to Mr Darwin's theory not as conjecture or speculation but as matter of fact. Anna recalls a pillar of Purbeck marble in Salisbury Cathedral, which, if you look closely, teems with the fossils of tiny snails. They are suspended there like a coded message in the architecture of the glorious edifice: we are here to bear witness to the flaw at the centre of your design. Anna hunkers down to examine the path: one of the shells has weathered out so completely that she has only to tease it with a fingertip for it to drop like a hazelnut from its cup. It comes away cleanly and she closes her palm round it. The questions she has suppressed since marriage swarm upon her, a black host of excitable heresies, Anna's spiritual children.

*

Occasionally Luke opens his dark blue eyes but without gaining consciousness. The lids close. This was his mother's crib and cradled his grandfather before that. Two centuries ago it was hollowed from an oak trunk and one sees the whorls and indentations, the build-up of varnish and polish until its blackened veneer is a mirror. The rockers at the base are worn smooth.

An easy baby, that's what everyone says. A sound sleeper, a jolly smiler, a strong feeder. He rarely cries, although when he does, you know about it. Mrs Elias wears a faint but caustic smile when she hears Luke cry: you wait, my girl, her grin says – you'll rue the day you cast supercilious looks upon me and my boys. Luke's birth was brutal. Beatrice feared, then knew that she was dying; she tasted the bitterness of a double death, the baby being too large to move, or lying back to front, or upside down. The throes were abortive: she was a labouring grave. She began to tire and weaken. Requesting pen and paper, Beatrice scrawled a will. Everything to her sister. In your own right, darling. That and my love. I hope to see you in the next world. And forgive me my many faults. For Joss had made a settlement of Beatrice's property upon herself: it was hers to give.

Mrs Bunce however reassured her: all was likely to be well. She'd turn the baby with her hands. Done it a thousand times. She kneaded the mound like dough. Something in there began to give. A crumb of hope came. But then Dr Quarles appeared with Dr Palfrey of Salisbury and dismissed the midwife. Science had arrived.

Removing their jackets, the physicians rolled up their sleeves and washed their hands and forearms at the ewer. Though preoccupied with the business of dying, Beatrice in one corner of her mind was mortified at the threadbare towels Amy had laid out. At least they were clean. And Dr Palfrey was a practitioner of the latest sanitary doctrines learned in the Crimea.

Forceps and knife emerged from Dr Palfrey's black box. She thought of Mr Mussel the butcher and his cleaver. She started to pray. One moment you saw the two physicians; then their heads ducked down. They set to work on, no, *in*, the furnace of scalding pain that was Beatrice's lower body. They reached up and dragged out what was there, bloody and silent.

The baby was big and blue. She reached for it, corpse though it was. They mustn't take it from her. Let me see his face.

Alive! You have a son! My son, my son. She wept. The baby pumped out screams. The father came in, looking pale, and held his swaddled son, praying for a blessing on child and mother.

Christian Luke Jacob Jocelyn Pentecost Ritter has an elongated head like a turnip, from the forceps. Bald. Cross-eyed. Snub-nosed. A scatter of pearly pimples on his forehead and cheeks. Beautiful to Beatrice beyond all language.

Luke opens his eyes and milk floods in for him. The breast is rock-hard, the cloth that protects her clothes saturated. Hurry, hurry, relieve me. Luke, in her lap, gazes into Beatrice's eyes as she undoes her shift. He battens on and the jaws work to drain her life into his. The tender ache as he drinks is something Beatrice never wants to lose. If only life could remain at this suspended moment. Never be weaned. Always be mine. She has fallen in love, for only the second time in her life. No comparison though. Her love for Will whirled her in a vortex of desire and illusion and incipient disappointment; this passion is all goodness. It commands the heart through a singing network of veins and nerves. A wholly innocent love. Chaste and sensual. Nobody had let Beatrice into the secret of the sheer physical delight of nursing a child. Once the baby learned to latch, pleasure radiated in a delicious melt and she fed the child for both their sakes.

She knows what Anna would say: 'Don't tell anyone. If they discover the pleasure of it, they're sure to forbid it.'

Loveday makes no bones of her incredulity at Beatrice's

contentment, never having detected motherly qualities in her friend. But she sympathises too and is transported back in memory to the birth of her firstborn – that time of dreams when nature tricks one into not knowing that the beloved will grow into a creature that insists on being intransigently herself.

'To be honest, I had no notion of what to do with a baby when my Patience came along,' she admits. 'I knew they had something out of a bottle and that they're always getting something the matter with them and then they get over it. Best thing to do is not to fuss, especially with girls. Girls are tough. Boys are more fragile.'

Patience glares. At her mother, at Beatrice, at her two brothers, at the baby in his crib.

'Ugh', says Jack Elias when introduced to the newborn babe: 'It's like a slug.' Patience calls her brother a naughty boy and begs to be allowed to hold the darling little baby. 'Oh do look at his sweet little face.' Something in Patience's expression – a simpering irony – keeps Beatrice on her guard. Into her mind come the words of the Psalmist: *Happy shall he be that taketh and dasheth the brats of Babylon against a stone.*

'You must miss your dear sister so much,' says Loveday. 'And she hasn't seen her little nephew.'

'We hope they'll come home soon, if only for a visit.'

'How I envy her,' sighs Loveday, who doesn't, at all, but likes to pretend that Wales is her earthly paradise. It's funny, thinks Beatrice, how the Welsh can't wait to escape their poverty and narrowness but no sooner are they over the border than they're nostalgic for their native land.

'Don't bounce Luke up and down like that, please, Patience,' she says.

'Oh, but he likes it. Don't you, Lu-Lu? Why don't I take him

into the garden to look at the birds? Nice birdies, Luke!'
Bounce. 'Shall we see the nice birdies?' Bounce. The baby's
mouth squares up to cry.

'I'll have him back now.' Beatrice reads *brat of Babylon* in
the minx's eyes. Patience is only pretending to be a human
being. The razor intuition acquired with motherhood reveals
this to her. 'Now, this minute.'

Patience, complying, studies the red-faced mother with
interest, testing her tension, relishing it. She brings her face
too close to Beatrice's, garnering information for the future.

Later that glorious afternoon Beatrice carries the baby out
and sits him on a blanket beside a phalanx of daffodils facing
the long, low rays of the sun. No one can see them from the
house. Why shouldn't Luke's little body benefit from the fresh
air? At least let me loosen all this padding. Removing his cap
and opening the quilted barracoat she embroidered with such
care, Beatrice releases the child from his bodice, unwinds the
yard of flannel bellyband, leaving just his vest and the pilch
that guards the napkin. Free! Luke waves his bare arms in the
air, pointing here and there, cooing. She kisses the silken
shoulder and smiles into his face.

The baby bats at the daffodils, tugging them towards his
mouth. It's a sign of his curiosity and intelligence. But he
mustn't, of course, and Beatrice gently disengages Luke's hand
from the petals, making a game of it. His fingers are yellow
with pollen.

Sometimes it's as if her love is too great for the world to
hold. She has to sit back and take breath, in order to tolerate
the throb of tenderness that passes through her. This
revelation is all she needed in the world and might have
missed, had she continued as Miss Pentecost, living only for
herself. She has awakened to the knowledge that one can take
pleasure in being no more than a bridge for another life. What

I was born for. Thank you, my Maker. Is this what You feel when your children turn to You with praise and thanks? Only do not take my lamb from me.

A jealous God. Do not even think so. It may anger Him.

Now look. The golden trumpet. The stem that stands so tall. Pistil and stamens poking nearly out of its mouth, to attract the bee. Surely I have never seen a daffodil before. Beatrice lies down to share Luke's eyeline. The little boy-girl, for a boy is a girl until the age of five. Later they'll cut your hair and dress you as a manikin. They'll take you out of frocks and frills. Today you are your mother's child. Wispy, blond curls stand up on his head. She'll delay having him shorn for as long as she can.

Luke's head turns; he stares, with fixed enquiry, at her chest.

Why not?

Surrounded by greenery, Beatrice opens her shift and offers the breast. Who's going to see? How can mothers bear to hand over their children to wet nurses? Luke crams his fingers in his mouth, lurches forward. Milk pearls from the nipple; the drop falls; the breast floods. And the baby in a storm of wanting is upon her: lips latch on, dragging in the milk that's there to excess, always. She inserts her little finger between gums and nipple, to put him to the other breast. His first hunger slaked, the baby laps and pauses, gazing up, grinning around the nipple, tonguing, playing. Sun-warmth blesses their naked skin. Pleasure ripples through her veins, his veins.

Thrushes build in the nest robbed last year. The tabby slinks past, prowling for prey. The baby dreams its dreams. The mother dreams hers, one ear open. Sounds of horses clopping down the lane rouse her but the walls are high. Voices murmur from the direction of the house. She buttons herself back into her clothing. If this life could just continue

229

as it is, she'd ask of God nothing more. Thirsty herself, Beatrice dresses Luke in an approximate fashion and carries him back towards the house. His swaddling needs changing; the smell is rather ripe. Amy can do that.

Opening the back door, Beatrice knows immediately: the Anwyls are back.

'She was in the garden all along! Will went to look and couldn't find you. Oh, dearest, how are you? And look, here's my little nephew!'

Whatever sins and crimes Anna has held to Beatrice's account in the past, she seems to have forgiven in the joy of homecoming. Thank heaven. Anna looks bonny and thriving. And Will too: but Beatrice hardly dare meet his eyes. Later, when Beatrice's brother-in-law is left alone with herself and Luke in the parlour, it occurs to her that he'd been sent out to greet her and bring her indoors. Did he come up behind them; snatch a glance at the baby at her breast, her shift undone, her hair loose from its net, all down her back in the sun? He'll have slipped away, abashed. Beatrice flushes deeply. What he saw, if he did, will never be spoken between them. It will be buried with his other knowledge of his wife's sister.

But then it's piety to suckle one's child. So Luke teaches her, the best of preachers, mute and helpless as he is.

Will bends above the crib, studying Luke Ritter in a long unbroken silence.

His hair's longer and he has sprouted a scrubby apology for a moustache. She has seen Joss looking at it with amused pity. Beatrice remembers the feel of Will's hair between her fingers. So soft for a man; too soft maybe. Sleeping with her sister, does he register the likenesses and differences between their physiques? How could he help it? Perhaps he has banished those sensual memories from his mind. But Beatrice remembers that she dreamed last night; dreamed that Luke was her brother-in-law's son, as he would have been, had the enigmatic right words been spoken, at any moment during any one of a thousand days. As the silence lengthens, Beatrice casts her mind back and cannot pinpoint the moment at which she chose for Christian and against Will.

Providence chose for her and doubtless chose wisely. Had Will been hers, Beatrice would have burned with jealousy whenever he looked at a woman or a woman looked at him. However could she have trusted him?

'A beautiful, gracious child,' Will says. 'You are greatly blessed, Mrs Ritter.'

For a moment he speaks and even looks like a pastor. It was what she always desired and thought would never come, that gravity and grace.

*

She never expected to love her husband like this, to take his hand when no one's looking and stroke with her fingertips the thin skin of his wrist. Maybe, if it hadn't been for the visit to Wales, Anna would have been able to keep her neutral, friendly distance; to tolerate his capers and caprices; to nourish a genial contempt for him, as someone less intelligent and serious than herself – as many wives do. They go their own way, live their lives within the domestic sphere, outwardly toeing the line with an inferior mate. Lip-service. Standing at the door, she sees Will and Beatrice bending over Luke.

Beatrice is altered: motherhood absorbs her. She glows with her love of the boy and smiles quietly to herself as if nursing a secret. The lioness would kill for her cub. She'd maul the lion himself if necessary or die in the attempt. Anna, entering the room with a rustle of skirts, smiles radiantly and is allowed to hold Luke.

'Is this all right, love? Am I holding him right? Such a bonny boy. Our little nephew, Will.'

Beatrice comes over and kneels at Anna's feet. 'Look, Annie, he's smiling. He likes you.'

Such a little creature has no likes or dislikes, Anna knows. She recognises Beatrice's goodwill. The baby's hand grips her forefinger and drags it to his mouth; sucks hard. Blood floods the fingertip. Luke means to live. A robust lad.

'I was asking Beatrice who she feels Luke resembles,' Will says.

'In the early days his face seemed to change from day to day. At twenty-four hours old he looked so old and sage, I could see Papa. To the life. It was comical but it made me cry.'

'Oh Beattie, I wish I'd been there with you.'

'I do too. You'd have seen it. Though Joss of course pooh-poohed it. And then Mama appeared and Grandmama – they came and went – just fleeting resemblances, as if they visited for a moment. How I wish they'd lived to see him. And you, Annie, I can still see you now … his lips, the set of his jaw – can you see her, Will?'

'Yes, I do believe I can. How Anna cried when your letter came, Beatrice! She sobbed so much I thought I'd better join in. But I can see you yourself, Beatrice, quite clearly – about the eyes. Can't you see it, Annie?'

'And his dear Papa, of course,' Anna reminds everyone.

'His Papa is so proud. He has mighty plans for Luke. It's a shame he has to be away so often and miss the little daily changes. But of course I write and keep him informed of every detail. Mr Elias came in and read to me from Genesis. *And the Spirit of God moved upon the waters*. I thought, Yes, I've been there, I've seen that, God has shown that to me. But then this terror came over me – and I thought, My lamb is mortal. I've made someone live who's born to die. Which I have. He is. What have I done?'

Anna sees in her sister the child she once was, standing in her smock at the edge of the wilderness, holding up her wrist with a bee sting and a discovery: they give us honey and they wound us too.

'Not for many, many years, dear heart, I hope,' says Will. 'And even if our Father thought it best to take him before his time, dear Luke is a Christian child; you would sustain it, you'd only be waiting. He'd be safe with the Father. You would expect to see your darling's face again, in Jerusalem.'

'Yes, yes of course, Will. Thank you for reminding me. It's so silly of me. I hope to see him born again in conversion and be baptised. Christian has all but put his name down for Regent's Park College to train for the ministry – to which I say, *Festina lente*, hasten slowly. One of the few bits of Latin I know.'

Anna settles Beatrice's mortal boy back in his mother's arms. Luke roots with his mouth, hungry now, whimpering and peremptory. Rejecting the little finger his mother offers him to suck, he breaks into urgent shrieks. A hale, strong lad, nothing like poor Magdalena.

Glances of tenderness pass between Beatrice and Will. His sister-in-law has called out to him from her heart; her brother-in-law has ministered to her. She is eased and comforted. Good then, that the Anwyls are back. Anna feels some justification for coming between her husband and his calling in Wales, if there was a calling. For every choice there's a charge. A down-payment, followed by further drafts in the future, should a woman elect to follow her own will. Anna understands that Will and Beatrice have at last reached the point at which they could have married. Paradoxically – for they have had to lock themselves in cages first. And surely this love is something she ought to – and can – respect. It's family love, the sort of affection that can be accepted without danger to other loyalties. Especially if, as Anna trusts and vows, there's to be peace between herself and Beatrice.

# Chapter 17

Sabbath dawn; clement weather. Way up in the pear tree, the rambler roses at Sarum House are lemon-yellow. The corn fields are ripening; if the good weather holds, a fine harvest is due. Beatrice walks with her husband down Florian Street to the church, her arm in his, their son having been left in the care of his aunt. She dislikes leaving Luke but there are times when you're obliged to do so; she represses the thought that all time not spent with her son is time lost.

The saturated earth is already drying, releasing scented steam from the lavender hedge at Florian Street. The Kyffin congregation has risen at first light to rendezvous before the usurpers gather for Morning Service. A crowd stands outside the doors of Florian Street Church, where a blacksmith is making light work of chiselling out Mr Prynne's locks.

The Kyffinites are soon in at the side door; they unbolt and throw open the main doors. In pour womenfolk with baskets of flowers. Beatrice helps to adorn the interior of the church. Scandal has leaked beyond the local press to the national newspapers, exposing a factionalism that gives satisfaction to nobody but the Archbishop of Canterbury and Bradlaugh the atheist. A spirit of violent bigotry reigns at Florian Street, where Mr Prynne is overreaching himself. Since Mr Kyffin's martyrdom, he has caused his adversaries to be excommunicated. Setting himself up as the church's acting minister, the shoemaker preaches hellfire for the unbaptised and the apostacised. Cross him in trifles and you're damned. Prynne's faction has itself splintered and there have been secessions. Meanwhile he has appointed a new set of deacons, folk he can control, like the young match-manufacturer, Mr Carter, and Mr Short, the retired tanner.

The body of the church is packed, not only with the remnant of the Florian Street congregation but with dissenters from several sects looking for Revival. Beatrice watches her husband mount the dais after the deafening first hymn.

Christian's opening message is brief and crisp. He preaches full and free grace to all who confess their sins to Christ, repent and ask for mercy.

No one's excluded from Heaven – except the excluders.

And yet even the excluders' stony hearts must melt when they see the sacred fire of Awakening crossing continents, from America to Wales, from Wales to Wiltshire, and thence to London, Prague, St Petersburg, Peking.

The service is well into the second hymn when the Prynnites begin to appear. A mighty wall of sound stuns the latecomers as they stumble into a packed church. Absorbed into the body of the congregation, they seem to surrender the will to protest. There's no sign of Mr Prynne himself.

'Isaiah Minety of West Grimstead has agreed to speak to us about his experience of Revival on his recent visit to Wales.'

The lad has shot up into gangling young manhood. His voice, in the process of breaking, executes bagpipe skirls when least expected, lapses he accepts with remarkable equanimity.

Although Isaiah's sleeves are too short for his bony arms and acne flames on his face, he has grown in confidence, following in the steps of Mr Spurgeon and learning the lessons of that great man's meteoric rise, without the Calvinist theology that goes with it. Or any theology, as far as Beatrice can tell.

Isaiah takes as his text verses from the second Book of Kings, Chapter 2. Elijah, like Mr Kyffin, is taken up to God in a whirlwind. The prophet's mantle falls upon Elisha. Who shall be our Elisha? Who'll be Mr Kyffin's successor? He tells the story of how a rabble of youths mock Elisha in the street. Oh good, they think, here comes a funny-looking old geezer: *Go on up, thou bald-head; go on up, thou bald-head*! Elisha turns round and curses them in the name of the Lord.

'What happens then? A she-bear rampages out of the forest. She kills and eats forty-two boys.'

And Isaiah roars from the pulpit, an incensed bear with an appetite. Nobody titters, though it wouldn't take much to set them off and what a good thing Anna is absent. A baby cries.

'A scene of carnage – God's terrible judgment!' Isaiah leans forward, his gaze roaming the congregation. What next? More roaring and gnashing? Beatrice has heard of a Welsh preacher shredding a Bible in the pulpit and scattering the leaves, to indicate the pre-eminence of the Spirit over the letter. The pulpit is in danger of becoming a circus, a freak show.

But, with a precise sense of dramatic timing, turning from God's wrath to His Gospel mercy, Isaiah reaches out his arms to the congregation with an expression of yearning. In Pastor Pentecost's time sermons were classically composed, weighted with pithy matter, memorably expressed. And yet Beatrice finds herself fascinated. She too cranes forward to hear the prodigy's next revelation.

'But *our* Elisha, our saintly and tender Mr Kyffin, did not curse anybody. No bear came dashing out of the Chute Forest to munch you up alive, did it? The man you mocked died loving and forgiving all. He received his death-wound here where I'm standing. Like someone else we know. Who died for me and you on the Cross.'

Silence rings in the body of the church. The majority of the congregation of Florian Street knows already who its next minister is to be.

When the pale shoemaker appears and demands to speak, Isaiah courteously permits him to do so. But he does not descend from the pulpit.

Hat in hand, Mr Prynne raises his eyes to heaven and cries in a loud voice, 'Oh God, when we hear the shrieks of the damned ascending from the everlasting flames of the bottomless pit, give us grace to shout, *Halleluiah! Halleluiah!*'

There is no response.

*

The boy of West Grimstead has been tutored in Wales by Anna in the use of a napkin; the handling of cutlery; how to pick up peas without shooting them off the table. Now she signals a twofold message: do not saw your beef so urgently and keep your elbows to yourself. She indicates the presence of gravy on his chin. Red-faced, Isaiah demonstrates the use of the napkin, quite correctly.

'I saw an acquaintance of yours in Salisbury, Anna,' confides Mrs Elias, as they are placing steamed pudding and custard on the table.

'Oh yes, Loveday, who was that?'

'Mrs Sala, as she calls herself.'

'Why do you say *calls herself?*'

'You have not heard?'

'I do not listen to gossip, I never do; it's my rule.'

'Yes, Loveday,' Beatrice interrupts. 'We know all about that.

No need to discuss it any further.' She continues to pour water from the jug into glasses, shoulders high and tense.

Mrs Elias says no more, though she makes it clear that there's a great deal she could reveal if she chose. She ladles pudding into the young preacher's bowl: he must be hungry after his great work at Florian Street. Have more, do.

Jack and Tom glare at Isaiah's heaped plate, since his plenty means their dearth, and then begin to snipe.

'Why do you talk so funny anyway?'

Isaiah looks alarmed. During his younger days, preaching at the market cross, he just said whatever came into his head. But the advance of his ministry brings social anxieties – and no Mr Kyffin at hand to counsel him. Becoming aware that his speech is considered uncouth, somehow or other he has managed to add the ghost of a Welsh accent to his Wiltshire burr.

'Well now, Jack, I do not speak funny, far as I knows.'

'Knows! Ee knows, does ee? Ee do know, Tom, don't ee?'

'Ee talks as if ee got a pebble in ees mouth.'

'Or a pinecone,' Tom suggests.

'Or a hedgehog.'

'Or a whole duck. *Wack wack wack!*'

'That's quite enough of that.' Anna sees Beatrice come down on the Elias boys in quite her old peremptory spirit. The bowls are swept away. 'Besides,' Beatrice goes on, 'Isaiah is about to become a minister of the church now, like your Papa.'

'Yes, *Mr Minety* might curse us,' says Tom.

'Ooh, I'm so frightened! *Mr Minety! Mr Minety!* Don't throw an anathema at me!' Jack slides down his chair until only his head shows above the tablecloth. 'The baker's boy, the baker's boy,' he murmurs through his teeth.

Isaiah has evidently kept the best portion of his pudding, with a dollop of jam, till last. It cheers him to see it there in

the middle of his plate, with custard to go with it. He nudges
the last morsel onto his spoon with his thumb, bends his
head, sucks it in and swallows, setting down the spoon exactly
as Anna has taught him.

'*Disgusting* boys, those Eliases. So ill-bred!' observes Rose
Peck when the children have been taken home. Through the
open window Loveday can be heard whining at them and
threatening them with a telling-off by their father. 'Oh yes,
I'm sure Mr Elias will correct them,' Rose goes on. 'He'll play
the flute at them. Their hides need tanning. But it's too late
now. Spoiled. Tell us all about your honeymoon, Mrs Anwyl.'

'What do you want to know?'

'Well, what *apparel* did you wear for your wedding journey?
Start with the shoes.'

'Stout boots for mud and rain, Rose.'

'Oh dear, really? I've heard that Wales is *excessively* wet.
But it is said to have some picturesque views. I shall be
spending my honeymoon in Paris, shan't you, Lily?'

'Are you getting married, dear?' asks Anna.

'Well, some day, of course. I have nobody in mind *au
moment.*'

And besides, Rose's eyes seem to say, you've removed the
only man worth playing for: it's too tragic. I know Mr Anwyl
would have married me if you and your sister had not been
so forward. He used to take my hand when you weren't
looking. He tickled my neck with a feather. He taught me *amo
amas amat* behind the outbuildings after the tea meeting.

But the Pentecosts knew all about his fun and games. We
were never in the dark, thinks Anna. Nothing can happen in
Chauntsey that escapes the network of spies. What we didn't
see for ourselves we were sure to hear about, doubtless with
embroideries. Will's dallying and flirting and what Mr
Montagu called 'concupiscence', apparently incorrigible, was

the reason Beatrice couldn't allow herself to marry him. And why she wished him on me, Anna thinks. Her mind carries back over the patched items she has received over time from her elder sister: this used thing will do for Anna.

The human hand-me-down, just arrived from Fighelbourn, slips into his seat and grins across at his wife. And I'm beginning to love him, Anna thinks. So much. I never expected to and thought myself safe. But surely I am safe? He doesn't go off into corners with girls any longer. At least as far as Anna knows.

'*Prynhawn da,* Will.'

He likes it that she greets him in Welsh, the language of Paradise and of Heaven, according to him. '*Ti'n iawn, cariad?*'

Rose and Lily turn up their snub noses. You're welcome to his gibberish, their looks say. And besides your husband's hair is growing thin; he has no true distinction: we can do better.

'*Ydw, diolch, cariad. Beth wyt ti eisiau?*'

Will accepts bread and cheese and a glass of wine, since he's so late. He's always obliging like this: makes no fuss about his meals and is happy with simple food, which he enjoys wholeheartedly. Having seen where Will was raised, Anna understands this more readily. She has never experienced the least want. Even on the few occasions when Anna was sent to bed without supper, the servant would be sent upstairs with a portion of rice pudding or toast. Joss would fill his pockets with cake which they'd share together. What entitlement does Anna have? None. Will has taught her to relish dark bread, good butter. What could be more delicious? Will eats hungrily and never forgets where he came from. Anna is grateful to have seen his home and to feel that in some sense it is – at a suitable distance – hers too.

Last night: it's in Will's eyes now. His gaze reaches for hers and says, *Remember?* Anna smooths the tablecloth, brushing spilt salt into her hand. Yes, I remember. He is tenderness itself, his hands delicate on her skin as if softened with lanolin like the shepherd's after the shearing. She looks at Will's tapering fingers. The Ritters sleep only a wall away. How does Anna's sister feel when the Anwyls bid her goodnight and mount the stairs together? Beatrice speaks off-handedly: 'Oh, are you going up already, isn't it a bit early?' And they yawn and say how tired they feel. 'Very well, good night then.'

Only one thing is lacking with Will. There is none of that spiritual aftermath she shared with Lore, lying in one another's arms, tender as breath; the sadness and poetry of Lore, the strange bitter-sweetness of their encounters.

He slept, a sudden collapse. She lay awake. The candle had not been snuffed; the flame stood tall and still. Anna, slipping out of bed, padded over to her portable desk; opened the diary where Lore had adapted scraps of Sappho.

> *You burn me, she said, you burn me*
> *& she wept & said, Neither for me the honey – nor the*
> *honey bee*
> *She whispered, Of all stars the loveliest*
> *she lied when she said, Yet I am not one who takes joy*
> *in wounding. Mine is a quiet mind.*

No, there will never be such revelation again on this earth. Nothing as elusive as the poetry in Lore, for no child could spring from it. A kind of perfection is buried – but at least it is buried in *me*. And when I die I shall go to *her*. It makes Anna sad for Will. I was married before I married you, *cariad*. And I'll make sure you never know.

Her husband cuts another hunk of cheese. Anna offers to bring in more, since he's so famished. He declines. 'I'll get fat. Spherical. You'll be able to roll me down the street.'

'You'll have to eat the entire table to get fat – you whippet.'

Last night he said, 'This will make a baby.'

She's seen that he's mesmerised by their nephew, more attached than Luke's own father, that cold fish. Poor Christian Ritter: his mind's too lofty and he talks to his son as if he viewed him as a budding theologian. Christian, quaintly ill at ease in holding Luke, is grateful when he can restore his son to his mother – perhaps in case the baby possets on his saintly shoulder or sleeve. But Will likes nothing better than to cradle his nephew and ponder his face. He admires the babbling sounds the child makes, echoing them back to Luke. 'Hallo, little book: Uncle's come to read you.' Is it that Will has been thinking, 'This is the part of Beatrice I'm permitted to adore?'

Anna is not uneasy, no, not really. Not at all. Why should she be? She too has loved before. Why not be generous? A married couple can be like a living hearth, inviting outsiders to warm their hands at the fire. That's how it was with Mirrie and Baines. Both seemed to love Anna. And they do still love her, surely? Now more than ever, while the whole world censures them with blackened tongues, having sucked the licorice of *Schadenfreude*, the Salas need friends.

'Will, *cariad*,' she asks when everyone has gone into the garden to have tea and Will is polishing off a dish of strawberries, 'are you busy this afternoon?'

'Well, no, I don't think so. But I have to be back to assist Mr Elias by teatime. Why, love, what are you thinking?'

'My friends – our friends – are back at Toplady's. I've not seen them for so long. The Salas. Might we pay a visit this afternoon? – or, if you're too busy, could you drop me on your way to Cressington?'

There's a pause; he doesn't look up. Then, 'Oh, well, dearest, that's a painful question.'

'How come?'

'I don't think we *can* go.' Will puts out a hand; Anna doesn't take it. 'Or rather, you know, it may be unwise for me to go – and you, well, it's *impossible* for you.'

'Oh?' She waits. He offers no explanation. 'Why?'

'It would not be wise or sensible – and I am very sorry to have to say so.' Will is on his feet and pushing in the chair, patting his pockets for tobacco.

'Don't just get up and leave, Will. Did Beatrice tell you to say that?'

'It's just how things are, dear. I'm sorry. Let's not quarrel over this; there are just some people who are – out of our orbit. *Cariad*, don't take offence, now don't. Trust me.'

'You liked Mirrie, Will! You were fond of her. You said she was an original. You were glad enough to accept her hospitality in Cornwall. Capering all round the cottage, playing the fool. Presumably you're the same Will Anwyl everyone said eloped with me to St Ives and spoiled my reputation. But perhaps you're a different Will Anwyl – and if so, my mistake.'

'Perhaps I'm not quite the same, Annie.' He has the grace to look abashed. 'As for liking! I like Miriam and Baines well enough. It's not a question of dislike.'

'So what is it a question of?'

'Dear heart. I am a married minister and I see that many of the things I used to do, the way I acted, left me open to criticism. I am contrite. I cannot be that person any longer. And there's the Revival coming – one must not prejudice ...'

'Prejudice? *She* has got to you. And who is *she* and who are *you* to judge?'

Anna strides out in her riding dress, with hat and crop; saddles up for herself, since her husband refuses to take her. Will follows her out. Beatrice joins him and behind her ambles Amy holding the baby. Rose and Lily Peck look on, fascinated.

If Mr Anwyl had married either of them, they are sure there'd have been no tantrums. They'd never have left their beloved's side, impending baldness or not. They'd have managed him for his own good.

Anna's sister and husband stand like wren parents arguing with a cuckoo daughter; it's suffocating and ridiculous. They're threatening her now. *Social death*! Beatrice must have cautioned Will – for Will is easy-going and pliant. If Anna wanted something, he'd ensure she had it, if it were in his power, and never moved against her. Look at how he made no fuss when she said she couldn't live in Wales. He will ultimately settle for the easiest course of action. Until now. Condescending to me as if I were a child. Insulting, humiliating. '*Cariad*, let's talk it over together; come back in with me, dearest.' Anna won't listen. At the same time she's ashamed of herself and wishes she could go back without loss of face. I am being ridiculous. And less than intelligent.

Spirit, moody and uncooperative, makes everything worse by refusing to stand still; he circles as she tries to mount and Will won't help her as she struggles. Joss, cigar in hand, saunters out, hearing the altercation.

'Joss! – stop loafing around; do for goodness' sake give me a hand.'

Without a thought, Joss hands the cigar to Will and makes his hands into a stirrup; she mounts. 'There you are. What's all the to-do?'

Beatrice catches hold of the bridle. 'Annie, Annie, dearest!' Her upturned face is pleading. Annie, think about this. Your husband is a minister. We are wives now. Everything we do reflects on our husbands. You have obligations. This person – I know you were fond of her but she's a pariah. You cannot associate with her without compromising yourself. Please, darling, it will all come back on us, on the church. None of this is said aloud but all of it is heard.

'Come indoors, love, do, and have a cup of tea. We can discuss it.'

'I'm just going for a ride. Nothing more.'

'What would Papa say?'

Spirit is away. Anna waves without turning. She sees with her inner eye Beatrice, skirts spattered with mud, retreating to the house with Joss and Will, grumbling at her brother for aiding Anna's escape, certain that she could have talked her round.

Anna comes up behind Isaiah Minety in the lane. The gawky lad is whistling, one hand in his pocket, playing catch with a stone with the other. He has forgotten his high calling and impresses Anna, as she canters past, as having slipped the reins. He waves, grins, runs beside the horse for as long as he can keep up and is just a boy, acting naturally.

# Chapter 18

Toplady's: the white curved facade of the Salas' villa is brilliant in the sunlight. Pampas rustles; the cedar casts a green gloom of rocking shade. A gardener pruning a line of bay trees in terracotta urns helps Anna dismount and tether Spirit. A new servant answers the door, with a foreign accent, immaculate in a dark blue uniform: Madame is busy and seeing no visitors. 'But would you just mention to Mrs Sala that Mrs Anwyl – Anna – is here? I don't mind waiting.'

New portraits of Miriam and Baines dominate the dining room, majestic oils, framed in monumental gold. Hot and sticky, Anna stands to view them. I smell like a groom, she thinks, taking some deep breaths and holding her arms away from her body to let the perspiration dry. The painted Miriam, opulently dressed in jet-black silk, wears a little fur-edged cape; a diamond necklace winks and so does the bracelet at her wrist. The German artist has given the impression of catching the novelist unawares in a moment of concentration, still half-absorbed in her writing, not quite alert to the presence of an observer. At the same time it's clear that the sitter has been dressed theatrically for a public performance. She presents herself as the Author. Miriam's abundant hair falls loosely around her face, softening its ruggedness, but the chin juts in a characteristic expression, as if she were about to push her face through the frame.

The artist has made the most of her beautiful hands. Miriam's right, her writing hand, rests on the table in lamplight, holding a mother-of-pearl pen suspended above a cut-glass inkwell. A sheet of paper is half-covered with writing. Anna goes up close, and twists her head, to try and decipher it.

'My dear Anna.' Miriam, quite composed, extends both hands. 'I hardly imagined you would come.'

'How could I not come? But am I interrupting your work? I'll not stay long – but I had to see you.'

'Dear. Come through. Maria, would you bring *Kaffee und Kuchen*, *bitte*? And the delicious marzipan cakes? Have we any left? We've brought staff with us from Germany, Anna, having become so fond of them at Weimar – and we're making quite a cosmopolitan little household of it. They speak limited English, and that may be to the good.'

Though the Salas have always disdained the vulgarity of show or display, now Anna clearly sees evidence of the presence of money. Everything has been refurbished or replaced. An aura of luxury prevails, as if there were more money than Miriam and Baines knew what to do with. What should be said about the silence between herself and the Salas? She stops herself bursting out with, 'Your letters stopped telling me anything. They were like formal essays on morality and culture. You ceased to count me amongst your friends. I was hurt. Please explain. Can we ever go back?'

'I am very glad to see you, Anna. And you are a married woman now! You and Mr Gwilym Anwyl! Do you know, I never suspected for a moment, though it was obvious when you visited us at St Ives that you were close.'

'To be candid, neither did I. But, yes, Miriam, I am Mrs Anwyl now.' She shows her the ring. It seems the one thing in the room that doesn't sparkle.

And clearly Miriam is struck by the cheap tin alloy; she studies it, bringing Anna's hand to her eyes. 'What is its story, Anna? Such a precious – unique – object must surely have a history.'

Miriam has little difficulty in drawing Anna out about her bridal journey to Wales. Will the ring turn up as a pregnant detail in one of Miriam's novels on the hand of one of her friend's suffering heroines? Anna wonders disquietly whether she'll open a new novel to find a skewed version of her own face staring back at her. And yet wouldn't it be an honour, showing that she continued to have some importance to her friend?

Miriam lets go of Anna's hand. 'Dearest – when the scandal broke – I suppose you heard – ?'

'I didn't listen.'

'No. You are loyal. Nevertheless. I thanked my lucky stars that you had not accompanied us to Europe. You would have been tarred with the same brush.'

'And is that why – ?'

'Why – ?'

'Why you stopped writing to me.'

Miriam looks puzzled. 'Well, I did write, dear.'

'Yes. But not – to me as *me*, if you see what I mean. You wrote to Miss Pentecost, not to Anna. I expect you wrote in the same way to Miss Jackson and all your other' – she thinks 'courtiers' but says 'friends. Forgive me. It's not that I don't value any word you send me. They were wonderful letters. I treasure them. Just that – Mirrie – I missed you in them.'

Miriam sighs. She looks a little ashamed but not very. She's wearing an invisible veil. 'Oh dear, did I go all sermonical?'

'Please don't think I'm complaining. You will have had reasons. But in my heart – you know – I missed you. I had no idea how to reply.'

'Unfortunately I am a preacher *manqué*, you know. An evangelical minister without a church, without belief. And in a rather defrocked condition. On my high horse because of that. It was a painful time, Anna. Forgive me.'

'But you must have known – I would *never* abandon you.'

There's a nervous tic under Miriam's eye; the expression of strain makes her face tensely brooding. Lugubrious. The gaiety is gone and it's possible to understand why people disparage her as ugly – and why she believes herself to be so.

'On the Continent, of course, one is accepted on merit. Nobody turned a hair at my situation – but in England, I am an outcast. I didn't want my more vulnerable friends involved. I never thought, to be honest, that I'd ever come home – better to hunker down in Weimar or Geneva. I used to quote Milton: "My native land is wherever it is well with me". But we grew homesick, Baines and I. Besides, Baines needed to come back to transact business. And in the end, well, I prefer to live and die in England, on whatever terms.'

'I'm glad. It's so brave.'

Miriam's rueful look plainly says, You know nothing. You are as innocent as a child. 'Hardly. It's the sick dog, licking his wounds, cringing back to his lair. I don't intend to bring anyone I care about down into the gutter.' Drawing her green shawl more closely round her, Miriam shivers in the warm room. How to edge closer? Anna has no idea. All she can find to say seems to land short or to hit a transparent wall. Whenever Anna threatens to breach it, Miriam rebuilds.

'But your friends, your true friends, would want to gather round you, Miriam – Mirrie. Dear.'

'You cannot, my dear. If you wish to live in society. I am infectious.'

'I don't care.'

'You have to care. You lack my armour. Notorious as I am, I'm also revered as a writer – under my other name. You enjoy no such protection. Baines shields me from reviews, of course, bless him, and manages all our business affairs. I am making a great deal of money – do you need any money?'

'No – *no*. Don't push me away, Miriam. That's not what friends do. What about Miss Jackson? Is she also excluded? And Mrs Bodichon too?'

'Anna, don't.'

Anna is aware of being childishly petulant in her envy of those who, it seems, are still permitted access.

'Poor Eleanor would climb in at the window if I tried to exclude her. Or down the chimney. She has nothing to lose, being herself an outsider.'

'Then I'll get in the window too.'

'Well, you're here now, dear Anna, and I'm glad of it. You must realize that I never meant to offend people. I respect traditions – I genuinely do – perhaps more than you do. There's always a need for decencies and decorum. If Baines and I could legally marry, we would do so. I do not stand for women's rights, suffrage and so on, as you know. Not yet awhile, at least.' She brushes some speck of invisible dust from her lap. 'The majority of women are not yet fit for freedom. It may take centuries for them to be capable of enfranchisement. If you come again, you know, I shall not receive you. And one day you'll thank me.'

'No. I shall not.'

A door is closing. Anna is being nailed into the world of

Dorcas meetings, sewing meetings, prayer meetings, bazaars, piffle.

'Yes. You really will. Let me explain.'

\*

Dazed, Anna rides Spirit down the drive and onto the Chauntsey road through a web of drizzle. Slackening the reins, she allows him to settle to a swaying, dreamy rhythm: sinister-dexter, sinister-dexter, the rolling, circling gait of the walk. Despite the rain there's no hurry to get home, none in the world. Only by lingering in the gaps, inhabiting private spaces, will Anna be able to live her true life from now on. There'll still be books; there'll still be writing, she reminds herself. Is it so very far from a journal to a work of greater witness?

'You lack my armour,' Miriam Sala informed Anna, with some condescension. But how does Miriam know what Anna Pentecost is capable of? She's unsure herself. As a child Anna had the courage of her oddity – of her left-handedness. With great gentleness and meaning only the best, Papa corrected this tendency, teaching through praise, never condemnation.

But outward conformity masked sleight of hand. Covertly, Anna became ambidextrous.

Beatrice has always said that Miriam had something of the mesmerist about her, a power over weaker people. But no, Miriam is terribly afraid, Anna thinks: she is a prey animal that has broken cover and lives in dread of further exposure. Mirrie's hands, as the two of them talked, lay clasped in her dark lap. Her face angled forward, so earnest and meaningful and beseeching – as if she feared you might penetrate her defences. Patrolling her own boundaries, Miriam pushed them forward, a little here, a little there. Then came the confession.

'And besides ... there's something else, not generally known until now – but it has been in the newspapers; I'm surprised

252

you say you didn't know, Anna. The world knows. The world says I have abandoned a child. My son. I am accused of deserting him when I left his father's house. I have not seen my Johnnie for three years. It was not as they claim, not at all – anyone who knows the law as it relates to the custody of children knows that – but I shall not go into details, I am high-minded; it is a fault, but nevertheless it does not please me to cast aspersions on others, even those who have wronged me. My life, Anna, is rich in mistakes. Stupid mistakes; crass, grotesque mistakes. Baines is not one of them. No, don't speak. Don't. Please. It sears me, I've wished to die. I never speak of my boy, even with Baines.'

\*

The room's so quiet that Beatrice hears not only the nib scratching the paper but Anna's breathing.

The clock chimes the quarter and Beatrice lays aside the little coat she's embroidering for Luke. 'I'll just go and see to my boy,' she tells Anna's turned back. 'And Will was wondering if you would like to accompany him to the meeting?'

'Oh – no, not really.'

'But aren't you going with Will?'

'No, I've explained to him – I'm busy. Will doesn't mind.'

Beatrice is perhaps less taken aback than she ought to be. Anna, who has shown no further sign of wanting to visit the Salas, still goes her own way, simply ignoring the duties of a minister's wife – and Will tolerates this neglect perhaps as part of the bargain. Good people in Chauntsey and Fighelbourn will already be noticing this disdain for duties. But that's not my business, Beatrice reminds herself.

'May I bring Luke in to feed him here, Annie? It's pleasant sitting with you. So peaceful.'

'Fine. Do.' Anna vanishes again into herself.

Beatrice sits on the sofa with her feet up to feed Luke. His cheeks are pale, he fails to latch and feeds listlessly, allowing milk to dribble from the side of his mouth. Perhaps the teeth coming through are giving him pain. She can see needles sticking through the bottom gums. But he doesn't appear distressed and Beatrice is not perturbed. She knows him now. Knows him through and through: when he's tired, when his belly aches, when he wants to nuzzle and nestle.

I'm supposed to mother him but the fact is, he mothers me, she thinks. There's a wisdom born with infants that we lose along the way. Never was there such a comical baby: casting indiscriminate smiles, kicking up and down with his right leg when he's excited. Luke gazes into everyone's face with wonderment, trusting all, recoiling from none. But of course only those who love him come near him.

Her sister turns in her chair, resting her chin on her arm, observing them. She looks like someone emerging from sleep, surprised to find the world just where she left it. But Anna's according Beatrice and Luke a new attention, examining them closely, the way they are with one another.

'What are you thinking, Beattie? Now, this moment?'

'Oh – about – I'm not sure. Just being peaceful, with you and Luke. He's a bit slow this morning. Very slow. He doesn't look quite right, I'll maybe put him down for a longer rest. He was whimpering and restless in the night. Why do you ask?'

'Just wondering how one would describe your expression – faraway-eyed perhaps.'

'You're surely not writing about me?'

'Goodness, no.' Anna doesn't say what she is writing about or to whom. Beatrice lets it go. 'More to the point,' Anna continues, 'what is *he* thinking? Do they think at all, before they have language? Do you think he thinks?'

'Annie, they do have language! How can you say Luke has no language?' For a clever woman, her sister is wonderful at ignoring what's going on under her nose.

Anna puts down the pen and gets up; kneels at Beatrice's feet to study Luke, whose lids are closing. She passes her hand over the baby's forehead and looks from child to mother with a concerned eye.

'He's sweating a little. Is he all right?'

'Just tired. I'll put him down in a minute.'

'What does he say then, with his language?'

'Oh, the great simple things. I hunger, I thirst, I am weary, I feel pain. I love.'

'Yes, of course. I hadn't thought of it that way. And, really, what else is there in life worth saying?'

'Annie, there's ink all over your hands and there's even some at the corner of your mouth!' Beatrice indicates the place with her finger. 'And under your eye. Don't rub, you're making it worse. Honestly, look at you. You look no more than nine years old.'

'The age of reason,' says Anna. 'It's all downhill from there.'

'I've been thinking, dear. About the medical men. When I was having Luke – well, it wasn't easy.' She pauses. Anna gives a piercing look; fails to respond to the hint that she may freely ask intimate questions. And indeed the doctors and their forceps did only what was required to release the child. They performed their duty with courteous efficiency. Yet Beatrice felt tampered with. And perhaps if the doctor examined her sensitive sister in a way that embarrassed her, there may have been a sense of violation. Beatrice understands that now. There was no woman there to hold her hand and protect her dignity. 'What I mean to say is that I'll never call Dr Quarles against your wishes.'

'No. And it would always be against my wishes. I don't even like to see him in the street,' Anna says sharply.

'In future – I shall do nothing against your will, dear heart. I know I've … offended you in that way in the past but I never shall again. Knowing better. It's my besetting sin. One of them.'

'Well, that's true,' says Anna.

Beatrice stops herself from taking umbrage. It's one thing to confess one's self-righteousness; another to have it confirmed. 'The Germans have rather a good word for it,' she says. 'Christian told me. *Besserwisserin*. Know-all.'

'Anyway, dearest,' Anna goes on, responding in kind to Beatrice's generosity. 'You've *had* to know better, haven't you? – because the burden fell to you as the elder – and often you have known best. And I have not. So – there we are.'

She straightens up, touching Beatrice's hand lightly before returning to her desk. She's soon scribbling again, tongue between her lips.

From now on when Anna needs medical treatment, a Salisbury doctor will have to be called out, at greater expense and at the risk of offending the Quarles family.

Summer will soon be over. Beatrice takes St John's Gospel out to the summer house to enjoy the last rays of sun beneath the canopy of the chestnut tree, Luke in his crib, sound asleep, a blue shawl over the hood, to shield his eyes from the light. My own darling. When Beatrice looks up Luke is awake, wearing an expression of placid, open-mouthed amazement at the face the world presents: its stir and dazzle. What is he looking at? His eyes are fixed on something beyond her ken. Unblinking. They see, perhaps, the angels. Floating nearby on dragonfly wings. Why should that not be so? And as we age, our spiritual eyesight fails.

Beatrice thinks: I glean so much from Luke. He teaches me

everything: holds me down to the earth but directs my vision to the skies. She feels renewed in his presence and even the long nights of wakefulness after his birth have yielded gold. I hadn't anticipated that, isn't it strange, I thought I knew it all. But all I thought I knew unravels. I seem to be at the beginning again, with a second chance of life. Seeing it all afresh. Thank you, gracious Lord, for that. Beatrice hopes as her son grows up she will not forget but be able to take advantage of this second chance.

He dies without a sound. There in the garden under her gaze, God takes Luke from his mother and, in one fell swoop, orphans her.

# Chapter 19

The dray arrives with the milk. Her ears register the clop of hooves, the clash of cans. The light is not up yet. Another day is due to begin but so far there's just a line of red fire at the horizon. All the shutters of Sarum House are closed except hers. Amy's clearing ash from the hearth. Beatrice hears this too, the small sounds of a poker riddling, pan against grate, side door opening and closing as the ash is disposed of. The great machine of the world is going on with its business for it can do no other. And Joss is down there with the servant: Beatrice hears his rumbling laugh, cut off, as if he thought better of it. Anna helps her dress and supports her down the stairs.

'There will be other babies for your wife,' Dr Quarles has assured Christian. 'Let her weep for now. It's helpful to her and healthy. But don't let it go on for too long. That is unhealthy. She should get plenty of sleep: laudanum in the measure I have indicated here. And port wine to strengthen the blood. Does your wife like port wine? It is in the nature of things for babies to die and for mothers to feel it. No reason why Mrs Ritter should not bear a whole string of viable children. As soon as you feel inclined.'

'Her sister tells me she hasn't wept, Dr Quarles. It is a concern to me. Not a tear. I have even spoken to her in a manner calculated to draw tears but without result.'

'In her own good time. Nature is a great healer. And, you know, she is prodigal with her seeds.'

'But God is not prodigal,' Christian replies, with some energy. 'He numbers and names them all. He is concerned for the fall of a sparrow, though a sparrow has no soul. How much more then for a human child?'

'Indeed, of course.'

'But we have not lost our child; we relinquish only his mortal part.'

Beatrice hears them discuss her as if she were a fictional character, which it may be she is. They feed her broth and other slops. Her breasts have been bound tight. The milk still leaks, less in volume but copious enough. It erupts like a sneeze or burst of tears. Yes, I do cry: I weep milk.

Out there the servant drops the ashes in the can and shuts the lid. The bells of St Osmund's toll across the town. Crows go sailing up into the grey cloud above the limes in St Osmund's churchyard. Joss wants to say something. He fidgets in his chair, takes a breath, opens and closes his mouth. In the end he offers Beatrice snuff. She breathes tobacco dust and spice. It's an odd thing to offer. Beatrice shakes her head. As children she and Anna used to steal Grandpa Pentecost's enamelled wooden snuffbox, atchoo-ing over a pinch each. But that was then. Before she died.

The way they extracted him from her arms was by ambush. Beatrice would not give him up. The muscles of her arms burned with holding him. 'A little laudanum,' said Dr Quarles. 'It is the kindest thing to do, to give her sleep.' Beatrice snarled as they came for her. She gripped the angel to her. They tried to force the drink down her throat. Swallowing some, she spat more.

'Leave her alone, let her be, she will give Luke to me, get away from her,' Anna cried. She came up close and Beatrice let her. 'You shan't be forced, you shan't. But let me hold him a minute, *cariad.*'

'No. Don't touch.'

'I'll be gentle. If you'll let me.'

'Well, don't drop him then.'

For as long as she could, Beatrice watched Anna hold them all at bay with her calm, fierce look.

The baby's eyes had sunk back into its eye sockets like those of an old man. They were glazed and seemed to have turned their full attention to the inner world. It was less Luke than a waxwork effigy. As custom dictates, Beatrice and Anna dressed him in his most gorgeous gowns, all of them, and his two caps, till, frilled and ribboned and bound, he was a stiff, small pharaoh ready for his journey to the underworld. Beatrice drank the tea they gave her and fell asleep. When she awoke, Luke's aunt had surrendered him. Beatrice wasn't angry with Annie. What can a woman, any woman, do against a pack of wolves? Luke lay in a box made of blond beech wood. But it was sealed. Then open it please and let me see him. Just one look. Don't deny me this. People lie to you, she sees it now in all its enormity. They have sealed the pretty coffin, contrary to custom, to prevent her from taking him back.

'There will be other babies.' It's the sin against the Spirit to say so. Beatrice would have died for Luke, killed for him.

Her husband urges, 'Our children are only lent to us, we know this, my treasure, and we should not mourn to excess but instead be thankful for the love we shared with our darling – and we are grateful, are we not? And we know that God has rescued him to a fuller, deeper love.'

It is very chilling to hear these words. *Beattie hates*, *Beattie loathes*.

The crows mass over the garden to peck out Luke's eyes. This is what they do to the living lambs in the fields. The shepherd must be vigilant. He must never doze. Beatrice has lost the power to sleep – and then suddenly (when they have tricked her into swallowing a narcotic drug) she does plunge headlong into an unconsciousness so black it's like being buried alive. When she awakens, Anna's head is on the pillow face-to-face with her. They look into one another's eyes.

Where is he? Where? Anna's eyes are so puffy and red that they look half-closed.

What if he awakens underground and finds himself in the dark? Nobody there to comfort and reassure him.

He won't.

So they say. But they cannot be sure. It has been known for the dead not to be dead. They sit up and rub their eyes and yawn. They say, I've had such a funny dream. I flew down a dark tunnel and at the end there was a light and in the light stood my mother and father with open arms. I didn't want to wake up. But why are you people all in black?

It's the day of the funeral. Christian carries the box. Mr Montagu, Mr Jones, Mr Elias and Mr Anwyl gather round the open grave. Five black ministers: each lets fall his handful of soil. A mother of course may not attend; nor may an aunt. Why not? No point in asking. Beatrice used to understand but has forgotten the explanation. I brought him into this world. You take him away from me. From Beatrice's bedroom window she and Anna have a full view of the chapel yard.

A glass shatters in Beatrice's hand. The blood runs down.

She feels no pain. Look, you've cut your poor wrist, darling, let me bind it up.

'Don't fuss her, it was an accident,' says Anna to Amy. When Anna has dressed the wound, she sits and holds Beatrice's uninjured hand. For hours and hours. Both have lost weight: they're shadows of the original Pentecost girls. Loveday sends in Patience with a pot of nettle and spinach soup to build the sisters up – and some seed-bread. The soup tastes surprisingly good. There's not much you can do to spoil nettles, is there, Anna observes. Beatrice gives a weak smile. How come I can enjoy the taste of anything when he is in the earth? Inwardly lashing herself, she lays down her spoon. Gasping for air, Beatrice throws up the sash and hears Mr Elias over the road at the piano. The music's wordless sympathy steals into her spirit and calls forth the helpful tears.

She lies down. Doesn't think she slept but perhaps she did, since she never heard him come into the room – the only one who might be able to comfort her.

Will says, 'Dearest – I have picked these.' Wild flowers, jewel colours, particularly the speedwell blue. Where did he find them at the dark end of the year? He must have walked for miles around their old haunts. Will reminds her, 'He loved flowers, didn't he, our little Luke? I remember him with the daffodils. Would you like to take him these? I loved your boy as my own. You know I did. And so did Annie, even more so. I can only take comfort from the thought that Luke is with Jesus now.'

Her old affection for Will was not mistaken: there's something of God in him. Yes, she'll get up, Beatrice says, and come downstairs. Wait for me outside the door, I'll go down with you.

Will and Anna, one either side, accompany Beatrice to the graveyard. It seems a terribly long way, though it's only over the road. Her husband always treated their son as an infant theology student. Did he, though? Is that fair? She can't judge. Christian walks beside them, with his pale, beautiful face like that of a waxwork.

Luke was sweating, he couldn't take his food, he was dying and I didn't notice. How could I not notice? What kind of mother am I after all?

Will and Mr Elias sing together *'Iesu Mawr'*. Desolation dipped in honey.

'Our lamb is safe now,' Christian says. He speaks too loudly, as if to a mass meeting, offering rigid consolation by the book, not from the heart. 'My love, try to be consoled. We shall see him on the final day. And, oh, thank God for this mercy. It's just a matter of waiting.'

Mercy? Beatrice looks at her husband with disdain. Can't he do better than that? God's mercy? It's a crumb that wouldn't feed a sparrow. But she does not dissent. It's what Beatrice has been taught and always thought she believed. The words still mean something but seem to exist outside her hurt.

Will reads from St Matthew's Gospel: *Take heed that ye despise not one of these little ones, for I say unto you, that in heaven their angels do always behold the face of my Father which is in heaven.*

Beatrice sees many opportunities to join Luke. A rope, a knife, a shard of glass, rat poison, the River Avon. She sees a use for Salisbury Cathedral, if one could just reach the tower. But God has barricaded all doors. Should she take this route, the Almighty will never allow her near Luke again.

Damn Him. Damn God. How does He differ from Moloch, the child-murderer?

Beatrice falls to her knees to beg God's pardon. He will have overheard her blasphemy and the recording angel will have taken note. The universe is a vast collodion camera that captures every transgression and stores the record for eternity. The light that shone on every misdeed is caught and preserved as an authentic remnant. Do not let this stand against me in the sum of my sins. Which are great.

But human sin is nothing, surely, compared with the carnage the Creator has unleashed on the Creation. The secret voice of heresy persists inside her head. I'm becoming Anna, Beatrice thinks. Don't tell her, she'll gloat. And while it's all inside my head, it may perhaps count as temptation rather than as sin. God condemned and cursed Eve and Adam and every generation of their children: 'You've eaten forbidden fruit; get out of my garden; go and rot. The land you till will be full of thorns. Your offspring will be born in sorrow. And all creatures will fall with you.' Would I, a human mother, have punished *my* children's small fault of curiosity with a world of pain and death? And teased them by appearing in a burning bush or intervening in a whale's stomach? And now, to cap it all, the Creator may be preparing to annihilate me for thinking this thought.

'Will you come out for a walk with me?' asks her sister. Beatrice stands up and allows a cloak to be spread over her shoulders. 'You're so pale. The trees are glorious. Come and see.'

The chestnut has turned ginger and copper and the earth around it is stained with the same rustling colours. Conkers are glossy on the lawn. Over towards Fighelbourn the woods redden.

'Mrs Kyffin has written to say she'll visit tomorrow, dear. It will be good to see her.'

'Will it?'

'Her sister will bring her to visit Charlie and they'll come on from his lodgings. She says she has a message for you.'

*

'Great changes are taking place,' says Mrs Kyffin, setting down her teacup as Mrs Elias hands round scones. 'Did you bake them yourself, Loveday? They are an interesting shape – rustic. Ellen will enjoy one, I'm sure.' Ellen shakes her head, before accepting one with an expression of despair. 'Undreamt-of changes are afoot in the spirit world. But do not be apprehensive. We have promises.'

Gone is Antigone's attitude of perplexed defeat. Her bearing is upright and her figure has filled out; there's a new serenity in her expression.

'Previously existing relations between men and angels,' she goes on, 'appear to be in transition.'

'*Mother*,' begs Charlie. 'Don't.'

'Charles of course is much bound up in his chemistry studies – and various newfangled ideas of a not entirely savoury nature,' Antigone explains. 'But he will soon see the error of his ways. His employer is a follower of the monkey studies so popular amongst a certain section of the scientific community. I can see the look on your face, Charlie – well, I'm sure you can agree at least that yours is, in any case, a different *field* of science to ours. He hasn't *seen* what we in Bradford on Avon have seen. In the light of this vision, as my dear pastor says, this world dissolves to mist.'

A pause. 'That is a very poetical turn of phrase, Antigone,' observes Mrs Elias. 'What does it mean?'

'Mother and Aunt Sarah have joined a new church. And I am not pursuing *monkey studies*.'

Flushed, Charlie tugs at his collar as if choking. Catching Anna's eye, he gives a small shrug. Anna wonders how much time the filial boy is actually giving to his chemical studies, for she hears that not only does he associate himself with Mr Lee's evolutionary theories but he has taken to following Mr Prynne around Salisbury, saying not a word when challenged.

Prowling after Prynne, Charlie observes his every movement. Whenever Mr Prynne looks round, Charlie Kyffin is there, stock-still, like a child playing 'Freeze'.

We've all gone mad with grief, Anna thinks. The loss of Luke lodges in her like a swallowed stone. She shares her sister's desolation. One thing gives her hope: the wall of separation is down between the two of them. For this reason Anna is keeping a new secret. She cannot tell Beatrice that she thinks she herself may be expecting a child. She has said nothing to Will. And, after all, she may be wrong.

Antigone says, 'Yes, a new church, though we prefer to think of it as an old church, in the sense of the original, the primitive church – the Magnetic Church of Jesus.'

When Charlie opens his mouth, his mother raises her hand and passes on swiftly to define the church as a laboratory; revelation as a science. Let the soul be constituted of magnetic fluid. Let Divine influence be the magnet. Let the magnetic influence be passed on, its power drawing others to the chain.

'You of all people know how abject I was. Lost.' Antigone's body sags in her chair. 'All of you here saw me, a broken creature. But now – !' She sits upright. 'The healing galvanism passes through me. The wounded soul, through Christ's magnetic influence, becomes the healer. We are nothing. As female vessels we are less than nothing. He is everything.'

Ellen squirms. At school she has learned, along with piano, watercolours, use of the abacus and the rudiments of French, the manners acceptable in the polite world. To succeed as a governess when she grows up, she'll need to observe these scrupulously. Out of petticoats now, the fatherless girl is dressed as a miniature adult. She sits to attention as her corset dictates, shoulders tensely raised, nibbling fragments of dessicated scone.

Anna dollops raspberry jam onto the side of Ellen's plate

and winks. Too decorous to return the wink, the girl gratefully spreads the jam on the scone and makes better progress.

The baby's silence pervades Sarum House.

Luke was never a crying baby so this hardly marks a radical change. It's as if they're all on tenterhooks, waiting for him to awaken. How the silence must ring in the mother's ears. When Anna cannot attend Beatrice, Will often goes in and sits with his sister-in-law. Taking her hand, he speaks to her of the simple, ordinary things going on in the world outside the room. Through the gap between door and jamb, Anna sees her sister looking at him with burning eyes but whether she's registering Will's words is unclear. He says he feels as if Beatrice is always about to say something but gives up at the last minute. Christian's away in Ireland and Beatrice hardly seems to miss him. His letters are left lying on the table unread.

'Anna, dear, where is your sister?' asks Mrs Kyffin. 'I have a message for her.'

Anna knocks: no answer. She peeps round the door. Beatrice, sitting on her bed, hands in lap, looks up as if drugged: 'Yes?'

'Antigone is here to see you, dear.'

'Oh, is she? Do I have to see her?'

'Of course you don't *have* to, dearest.'

But Mrs Kyffin is already in the room and occupies a fair amount of its space with her crinoline. The acolytes of the Reverend Mr Rayne seem unexpectedly fashion-conscious. 'Now, how are you? Do you eat and drink properly? Does she, Anna? Nourishment is of the essence at these times of crisis – as I should know. And what a poor example I set with my whining and drooping. Now, dearest, tell me –' She takes Beatrice's hand in both of hers. 'Are you tempted?'

'Tempted?'

'To despair?'

Beatrice's expression as she turns away answers for her. A guilty, sardonic look that says, Do not look into my heart for you will find there a cesspool. I killed my son with my neglect. But God foreknew it and failed to intervene. He may have warned me but, if so, I didn't receive the telegraph. Faith? Oh yes, I have faith but faith in the divine mercy? Anna reads the stricken look and her heart goes out to Beatrice. She has been somewhere near the bad place where her sister now finds herself – but never in exactly the same abyss. One never is and that's why no one can reach through to heal another's grief.

'Despair is a sin,' says Antigone sternly. 'It's the sin against the Holy Spirit. We all know this.'

'Don't,' says Anna, registering her sister's flinch. 'How is this helpful?'

'Let me explain. After my husband's passing, I left Salisbury for my sister's house. I was shown my room. Under the eaves. A perfectly adequate room, formerly a servant's. But despite all Sarah's kindness, I found my position in the household demeaning. I looked out of the skylight – nothing to be seen but the leads. The thought came – I'm ashamed to say it – that I should hang myself. I threw myself on the bed, howling into the pillow. The door swung open. And what do you think? A kitten came padding through. She has saved my life. I do believe she was sent. And since then we've shared nearly every waking and sleeping hour together. Tilly is a tabby with one white paw; her brothers and sisters were all drowned.'

'I'm glad you have some comfort, dear Antigone,' Beatrice rouses herself to say. 'Yours is a heavy burden.'

'Ah, but Tilly was only the beginning. The following day I awoke early, dressed and looked round my shrunken world. I am a widow, I thought, looking in the mirror. That's all I am now. A relict. There came a sense of warmth – of presence. And *he* was there, at my shoulder. Our eyes met in the mirror. He spoke no words – aloud. I don't think so. He may have. But what I heard in my own mind was: *Woman, why weepest thou? Whom seekest thou?* The words of the risen Christ to Mary. I don't know how long this went on. But I knew – I know – it was my husband. In person.'

Ghost or hallucination, Anna thinks, it was a Second Coming of sorts for Mr Kyffin – and no less, after all, than the poor man had promised.

'Is this what you wanted to tell me, Antigone?' asks Beatrice.

'This was just the beginning, dear. For then, you see, my sister introduced me to Mr Rayne, our dear pastor. Have either of you attended a séance? No, dears, of course not – your Papa would never have approved and you may well look sceptical – there are so many charlatans about to exploit the credulous. But we place our faith in the scientific method and revelation both. There's a word for Mr Kyffin's manifestation in my mirror.'

Yes, thinks Anna. It's delusion.

'It is *crisis apparition*. At times a phantasm visits before a death; at others after it. The veil parts for a moment, our beloved slips through to comfort and advise. Beatrice, since then I've come to understand the Mind. The Mind is a great miracle. But no more than, say, the electric telegraph. Do we dismiss the telegraph or underground cable? Do we say, Oh dear no, this cannot happen, our senses are deceiving us? Such-and-such a message cannot have been transmitted from New Zealand or India? At our church we receive communications from the World Unseen. Many times Mr Kyffin has visited me through table-rappings, mind-readings, automatic writing, mesmeric trances. He came on Friday last, about seven in the evening, and this is why I am here. May I pass you his message?'

'Is it from Luke?' Beatrice asks.

'Oh yes.'

'But how could he possibly speak to you, Antigone? He had no – vocabulary.'

'Ah, but these messages come through *mediums*, dear. Otherwise we'd be at a loss to understand them. They are confided to the mediums by tutelary spirits in the Other World. The messages are at best translations. Besides, children grow up there far more rapidly than here. They're generally taken care of by their grandparents.'

'Then how do you know it was him? How do you know it's authentic? The voices could be demons deceiving us.'

'That could always be the case, Beatrice,' Mrs Kyffin gravely acknowledges. She explains that we're surrounded by evil angels as well as good – and the world is shifting in relation to its Creator. From what the Magnetic Church has gathered, the angels and demons are massing in vast armies ready to fight the final War. 'We have to sift all messages carefully.'

'Tell me then,' Beatrice says. Anna sees with misgiving the hunger and determination in her sister's face.

'Luke wants you to know that he is safe and well. He says Grandmama Pentecost is looking after him. He says he swam back where he came from across the river. God made it an easy journey for him. He just gave a big yawn, closed his eyes and fell asleep. At first he didn't realize that he'd died. He begs you not to cry, dear heart.'

Beatrice asks, trembling, 'But does he miss me?'

'No, dear, why should he? He is here.'

'Here?'

'With us now, as we speak.'

'Where?'

'In this room.'

'Let him tell us so himself. Let me see him.'

*

Christian would be dismayed. Probably. But Christian hasn't been told. He's in Ireland converting the Catholics. A job that could detain him indefinitely, Beatrice thinks cynically. What does he care anyway? Her sister has agreed to come, just for company and curiosity – and not because she believes in conjuring tricks.

They sit in a circle, blinds and curtains closed, the fifteen senior members of the Magnetic Church of Bradford on Avon, venerable and great-bearded gentlemen and several respectable-looking ladies. Beatrice is placed between Pastor Rayne and Antigone on a comfortable sofa, a hand held in each of theirs. The whole thing is conducted as a religious service and there's little to distinguish it from a prayer meeting. The nervous storm that all but prostrated Beatrice in the past week has waned. Once we arrive at the threshold, what's left to fear? The two Beatrices have fought like tigers and the mother won over the sceptic.

Shall I see you again and hear your voice?

Nothing whatever happens. The pastor emits a gentle purling of prayer. He's a handsome man with a silver wing of hair, softly spoken; pale blue eyes. The murmured prayer seems to go round in circles, calming one's breathing. By and by there's a shift: they all seem to be breathing as one organism. Between her lashes, Beatrice sees in the dim light Antigone Kyffin sitting like a sleeper propped in a chair, her head lolling forward. Antigone is vacating her fleshly house, opening it to the use of whatever spirit may wish to inhabit it. Through the closed blinds and curtains comes the dreamy song of the mistle thrush, with an echo to it. A dog barks in

271

the distance; the clock, at first unheard, ticks louder and slower. Beatrice begins to slide. Her head tips back on the sofa; her lips slacken; her hands in those of her neighbours relax.

'Gentle Saviour who dearly loved children,' Mr Rayne continues. 'Breathe consolation into our sister Beatrice. If it be Thy Will, bring her into communication with her beloved Luke, the soul who has gone before her.'

Beatrice slips further down into a pool of quiet. Warmth seeps into her hands. She has a sensation of well-being. Then it's as if her face is being blown upon.

'Mama!' A high, thin voice pipes from Antigone, whose head has fallen back in a swoon, face ashen.

Beatrice is on her feet, hands over her mouth. 'Luke! Is it really you?'

Lispings. Babblings. Sighs and shifting sounds just like those Luke used to make as he was waking up but before he was completely awake. Beatrice would bend over the crib and her face would be the first he saw as he opened his eyes.

Then a lisping voice is heard, speaking in sentences. She makes out, 'Mama! I am well. I'm over here with Jesus and Magdalena, Mama.'

Now Anna's on her feet, sobbing, and she cries out, 'Magdalena! Lore, are you there?'

Finger on lips, Mr Rayne gestures to Anna to sit down and be silent: this message is not for her. The quiet resumes. Beatrice can hardly breathe. She refrains from looking at her sister and closes her eyes. So it's true then: the graves are opening. The dead are coming amongst us. Mr Rayne squeezes Beatrice's hand. There's a scent of … something calming … lavender, lilac.

'Luke – dear heart – it's your mama – darling – '

No answer. Anna's outburst has driven the messenger away.

Mr Rayne resumes his prayer. He asks for the peace of God that passes all understanding.

The baby on the other side begins to babble. There's an enormous chuckle as if he were being tickled. Mrs Kyffin heaves with laughter. Beatrice dissolves in tears. Then an elderly voice quavers a lullaby and one has the feeling that the baby's being rocked, rocked to sleep, and Beatrice rocks too.

But now there's another voice, adult, speaking with the suspicion of a foreign accent. Lore? It's Lore to the life, terse, tinged with asperity.

'For whom in this room is your message? Please speak slowly and distinctly.'

'For. My. Sister. Is that slow and distinct enough for you?' Beatrice thinks: but Lore had no sister.

'From whom is your message?' asks Mrs Kyffin.

'From a child who is here.'

'What is the child's name?'

'You should know.'

'Boy or girl?'

'A mother's child.'

'Does the child wish to speak to its mother?'

'Why would that be necessary?'

'Lore!' cries Beatrice. 'I know it's you! For the love of God. Have some pity.'

Antigone begins to whistle. It's a high-pitched whistling between her teeth like a lad blowing on a grass blade between his thumbs; uncouth, unladylike. Antigone would, in the normal way, be ashamed to make such a rude noise. She'd be physically incapable of it. Over there in the Other World someone is mocking us. Beatrice claps her hands over her ears. The shrilling wakens Antigone herself. As she comes to with a jolt, the whistling stops. Drained of energy, the medium collapses. She is revived and offered a glass of water.

The pastor resumes his prayers. He asks the Lord for a blessing on the dear medium, peace of mind and a replenishment of her magnetic powers. He lays his hand on her head. Pastor and medium gaze into one another's eyes; Antigone's slowly close under the influence of his.

And Beatrice knows.

It's a theatre of illusion. Luke has gone forever. He no longer exists in any world that she can know. She understands that God has ordained this separation between herself and her beloved. She bends to the knowledge. What can there be but compliance? He ordered it at the beginning of time, before the Spirit moved on the face of the waters to create the world. He not only foresaw but ordained the arduous birth and painless death of Luke Ritter one thousand eight hundred and sixty-one years after the birth of Christ. He did this for reasons of his own, inscrutable and terrible and, in our human terms, arbitrary. Mr Spurgeon is right and Christian Ritter is wrong. There's no scaling God's high wall. It's just as her father told Beatrice. With our spectacles and telescopes, and standing on a mountain of books, we cannot even see to the top. All we can do is to kneel here in the dust and wait. Beatrice rises, puts on her gloves, picks up her bag and, without a word, leaves.

That was certainly Lore, she thinks, and shudders as she latches the door behind her. A demon got in.

\*

It was Lore, thinks Anna. To the life. Lore is over there but also in here perhaps, in the room with us now. She looks round fearfully. Lore's death was nothing but a sham – a trick. When the dying woman turned her face to the wall, Anna thought she saw the suspicion of a smirk on her lips and has always had this odd feeling that Lore went into hiding.

What is one to make of the apparition's claim to have a sister? Who is Lore's sister? She had no sister.

I am Lore's sister, Anna realises. *A garden enclosed is my sister, my spouse, a spring shut up, a fountain sealed.*

The phantom told not lies but riddles. Yes, she claimed a child was present. But Lore never named Luke. She withheld the gender. So it was not Luke then – perhaps – but Magdalena. And when she was asked if the child wished to address its mother, Lore answered, 'Why would that be necessary?' It wouldn't be necessary if mother and child were already united and together. Over there, beyond the invisible wall.

Yet reason revolts against all this. Anna has so often scoffed at reports of haunting zither music from a musical box strapped to a medium's leg; levitations out of windows; a ghostly banquet in which sugar plums were decanted from a medium's sleeves and skirts. She gathers herself together. There's a chill in the air of the panelled room; the gaslights burn low and Anna wraps her cloak tightly round her. She has been born into a world that believes that the dead survive. When she rose from baptism in the Avon, she did so as an immortal. She has been brought up to credit miracles – water into wine, Lazarus resurrected. It would be blasphemy to ask whether Jesus was a conjuror. Lore was always looking beyond, to some homeland across the border of death: *'Kennst du das Land, wo die Zitronen blühn?'* She'd recite Goethe's poem, haunted by the absent land of the lemon trees, so present in her mind. Turning her head to peer along Lore's eyeline, Anna saw nothing but the heavy furniture of the material world.

It all hinges on the authenticity of the medium. Antigone's no trickster. She is, to be frank, not intelligent enough.

'Did anyone come through?' Antigone asked, emerging from the trance.

Yes, Anna thought. The whistler came through. There you were, hands in your lap, eyes closed, whistling like an urchin. Without the least inhibition. Wherever could a woman as observant of proprieties as Mrs Kyffin have learned this unladylike art? It does take a lot of learning, Anna knows, for as children she and Joss would whistle to the birds imitations of their various songs. Joss could deceive the chaffinches with his flutings. Anna's songs were more miscellaneous – owl hoots, dove coos, thrush calls, a little of everything.

So what if it all comes somehow or other through or from me? Anna wonders.

Beatrice is overtaken walking back towards Chauntsey. Drawing level, they persuade her to enter the carriage, where she sits tight-lipped, veil lowered. On arrival she makes straight for her room. Later, Anna sees her slip over to the chapel where she remains for an hour and a half.

Sitting at her desk with a candle, Anna thinks it through. Perhaps, just as we all dream, our minds can somehow re-enact what they remember. Doubtless Mrs Kyffin well remembers Lore, having found the third Mrs Pentecost distasteful. Not that Antigone ever voiced her disapproval. She didn't have to.

So maybe all this was Antigone's unconscious performance. The other possibility, Anna thinks disquietly, is that it was somehow staged by me? And I threw Lore's voice like a ventriloquist?

Because I've never let Lore die. Not for a moment.

I've clung to her skirts and willed her back. Anna fingers the locket with Lore's miniature and a curl of her hair. She slips it off. The locket sits in the palm of her hand, warmed by her skin. Her thumbnail unclasps it. The hair has changed colour. Lore in life was fair, almost flaxen. The dingy hair is now a shabby red-brown. Anna shakes it into her palm, holding it to her eyes. As dead as horsehair, she thinks. No more than a relic, like the splinters of bone or skull venerated by the Papists. It's cheap as the trove of pilgrim artefacts dredged from the Avon – whistles and bells and a badge with a priest holding the devil in a boot.

Gazing at the tiny silhouette of Lore to try to tease out a living face, Anna sees with regret how out of date the sitter looks, with her topknot, her leg-o'-mutton sleeves – archaic even then. You do not see her face at all.

*

Beatrice is bent on drumming Lore Ritter out of Sarum House and Anna's heart for good and all.

'This was not of God, Anna,' she repeats, her face stony. 'The spirit was a demon sent from Hell. We should neither of us have gone. I have prayed and it has eased me. No blame attaches to Antigone but she's making a mistake and I shall tell her so. Whatever is she thinking of, opening herself to demonic possession? And yet it has done me good. I went to receive a message from Luke. And … yes … in a way I did. My son is gone, Anna. That's how it is. No, don't say anything. He will not come back. He has nothing to say to me. He has no tongue to say it. No lips, no hands, no heart, nothing. And I can weep and I can rave and I can pray but Luke is dead and I must leave him in the earth. Anna, you won't go again, will you?'

'I think – if it is quackery and delusion – which it may be – but not on Mrs Kyffin's part – she's as innocent as a child –'

Beatrice gives her a straight look. 'It *may* be?'

'Beattie, I did really think it was Lore. At first.'

'But, don't you see, the likeness proves that this was an unclean spirit. Horrible. Now do not allow yourself to be sucked in, Annie, don't. I've learned my lesson now. Let's be calm and try to forget it.'

Beatrice sees Anna shaking her head at talk of demons. But surely she's thought the same thing? The evil spirit somehow or other gained access to Anna's memories. The spirits detect hysteria and an unmade bed. An unmade bed? Beatrice has glanced into the Anwyls' bedroom several times to glimpse rumpled covers spilling off the bedstead. Is it possible that the living, when they allow themselves to be preyed upon by excessive grief and heretical questionings and sexual passion, even within marriage, can give space to spirits who then generate spectres? A kind of mating between the two parties, garbled and skewed. One's sacred inner world profaned and derided.

'Are you going to speak about it to Will?' she asks Anna.

'Oh yes. I tell him everything.'

*

In the night, Anna shivers under a mound of bedclothes, less with cold than with irrational fear. She hears Joss coming up to bed and velvet footsteps seem to tread in his wake. She's convinced there's someone with him. She catches the hint of a giggle, a rustling. Opening her door an inch, she peers into the corridor. Reassuringly, there's nothing but a powerful waft of tobacco and Joss's bedroom door just closing. Her brother is too solid and corporeal to attract spirits – whereas her own mind seems permeable; anyone may reach in who likes, ransacking the contents.

After a while Anna decides to knock on Joss's door and see whether he's awake. In his jolly, grumbling way he'll make space for her and plump a pillow so that they can sit and chat, as they used to do. Barefoot, Anna approaches his door and listens. A streak of candlelight seeps between door and jamb. She hears small shuffling sounds, a creak of floorboards.

He's awake. And again Anna has the peculiar sensation that he's not alone. Don't be silly. She taps lightly with her knuckles. Silence.

'Joss, it's Anna. May I come in?'

There's the sound of someone slowly lumbering out of bed. Her brother appears in his nightshirt, peering round the door, yawning.

'Oh, I'm so sorry, did I wake you?'

'What is it, Annie? Are you not well?'

'No, I just wanted to chat. Sorry to wake you. I thought I heard … something in here.'

He grins and holds the door wide. Looking past him, she sees Mr Elias's mangy old dog on the rumpled mass of bedclothes. She kisses her brother goodnight and apologises. What could she have told Joss anyhow that wouldn't have brought an amused smile to his lips? That's because the easy-going fellow has some sense. More sense than herself and Beatrice put together.

When Will joins Anna in bed, she clings to him, burrowing her head down into the space below his shoulder.

'What is it, *cariad*?'

He listens carefully to the account of the séance and tries to give a verdict. But Will's mind is now fixed on the Awakening and he judges everything in relation to it. 'Dearest, I don't disbelieve it. The Spirit cannot be limited. We've seen Revival in Wales – speaking with tongues, healing – this may, just *may* be the Spirit coming amongst us. But if it has upset you? Let me look at you. Light the candle. I want to see your face.'

In the candlelight he holds Anna's face between his hands, stroking it with his thumbs, reading the expression. 'I think it has distressed you,' he concludes. 'Rather badly. That may be the sign we need. Did the voice have a gospel ring?'

She can hardly say it did. As they lie close and warm in one another's arms, does the jealous spirit of Lore look down through the darkness?

No, she doesn't, Anna thinks. It's not Lore. She's at peace among the lemon trees. It's me. I'm throwing out illusions like a diorama.

Everything's in convulsion. Papa's Jesus is slowly perishing, his life's being drained. It's nearly run out. And in a hectic panic we start rushing to and fro with this extreme remedy and that. Spirit Guides, Awakenings. We deliver galvanic shocks to what remains of him and when we see the spasms and paroxysms we insist he's still alive and with us. Look! He moved! Mirrie saw all that – and has, sadly and reluctantly, let go and walked away, taking what she can salvage with her. Which may be the wiser way.

# Chapter 20

It's a matter of what you settle for, Beatrice thinks to herself as she awakens. In earlier life there was always the longing for something beyond this mundane round, dreamy and gleaming. So I've been made to chew a bitter cud. On my knees, I'm inching forward like a beast of the field: the fate of Nebuchadnezzar. And I should thank God that I've lived to discover my place in this world and its rigid obligations. She remembers that the pig-sticker is coming this morning for Lucy. The creature, knowing nothing of what is intended, has a life less harrowing than ours. Beatrice opens the curtains on the charmless earth. It's grey out there, a little soiled: a light has been extinguished. The pulse beats low. But this is the lacklustre universe to which she must accommodate herself.

> Who sweeps a room as for thy sake
> Makes that and the action fine.

The hymn enters her head with the force of a command. That's what I must do, then. Nobody in the house is stirring.

Beatrice lets herself out into the damp air. She takes a broom and begins to sweep, attempting to do this for her Maker's sake; to make, as the poet said, drudgery divine.

I am *not* a servant, she once told a visitor who mistook her for a skivvy. How dare he? I am Miss Pentecost.

No. For I am nobody in particular. I never was. The only comfort will be to acknowledge my low status on the scale of things. Amy is better than I am. I must be punished. The sweepings of Beatrice's broom disclose dust, ash, weeds and crumbling leaves, a feather, snail shells, seeds, one of the Elias children's lost jacks, which she slips into her pocket, to return to him. Sycamore seeds are falling all around, spinning on their wings. She picks one up and holds it to the light, looking through the veined transparency of its brown wing. Wind has floated the pea-sized seed a good fifty yards from the parent tree. She fingers the feather: grey, a gull's. The snail shell cracks between her fingers, its creature devoured. All these remains have been dropped here for me to clear, Beatrice thinks. Leavings and waste. Voidings. And this patch of paving is the boundary of my ministry. Here God has set me with this broom.

There are no tears to shed, only this tedious round of disciplined obedience.

God may grant you another child. The child may live. Once you have suffered this penance. It may take years. Not that you deserve such grace: no, but He does not torment his children beyond what they can bear. So the Bible promises. But that means I shall have another child to lose. How many will He take from me? Mrs Gartery in West Grimstead lost all but three of fifteen. And two of those three sailed to Tasmania.

In the barn a crossbar looks surprisingly like a gibbet. As she comes and goes during the day, between the chickens and geese and the kitchen, Beatrice spies it from the corner of her eye. The pig-sticker with his bulbous features arrives and does his work. Some of the blood that escaped the pail wastes itself in the soil, enriching it. The pig-sticker, aided by Amy, is dismembering Lucy.

Perhaps God will take Beatrice in her sleep. It will be an easy and acceptable journey. How grateful she'll be to see her son again on the other side and, gathering him to her breast, gather herself in too from this great scattering. Nevertheless (she warns herself) not my will but Thine be done. For what Beatrice has understood is that no prayer of ours can make a jot of difference to what Almighty God ordains. She cannot argue with Him as she can with her sister or even with Papa when he was alive. There's no gaining the upper hand. Occasionally she could plead with Papa sensibly enough to change his mind over a trifle and Anna could wheedle him out of this or that resolve. But no proposition or offered bargain moves the Maker to acquiescence. How could it? Everything has been decided; the book was written before time began. Everything was foreknown. All one can do is to pray for a submissive heart.

How can Christian, so highly educated, have come to dissent from the doctrine of Calvin? Even Mr Spurgeon has spoken on this subject in a lax way Papa could not have countenanced. It's a conundrum very hard to address: Christian preaches full and free salvation for all; nothing determined in advance. Impossible to argue him out of this – she has not the intellect, and besides it is not her place. Her husband would doubtless be quick to offer chapter and verse in Greek and Hebrew for his view. Nevertheless he would be wrong. It is a slippery slope. But what a curious paradox it is that Papa, so indulgent, preached an implacable God, whereas the authoritarian Christian's God is all-loving, all-forgiving.

'Are you well, dearest?' Anna seems to ask this question

from a distance. Her voice has had to travel furlongs to enter Beatrice's ears.

'Yes, I'm quite well.'

'You don't look it. Does she, Will?'

'I'm sure you'll say if there's anything troubling you that we can help with – won't you, Beatrice?'

'There's nothing. Nothing new. I'm giving Amy the afternoon off – and doing the baking myself.'

'Why, dear?' Anna tries to take her sister's hand but Beatrice shrinks from her touch. 'May I help you? We can do it together, as we used to do with our second Mama – do you remember? Mmm, the scent. And licking cake dough off our fingers. A hoard of currants in our pockets. She knew, of course.'

'No need. I can manage. Do you really want to help me?'

'I do. Of course I do. Anything.'

'The spirits. Annie, turn your mind away, don't dabble – if not for your sake, then for mine. The practice is anathema, it will damage our souls. I shall say the same to Mrs Kyffin. You agree, don't you, Will? You see the danger?'

His nods have a particle of 'no' in them; his shakes of the head leave latitude for 'yes'.

Anna replies, 'I do see the danger. It might not be the same danger you see, dear heart – I've been thinking –'

'Don't *think*,' Beatrice comes back. 'You think too much. Curiosity is so dangerous. Life is so short. At any moment one of us might be taken and then it would be too late.'

'For what, dearest? I can't promise not to think. You look so strange.'

Yes, I would look strange. But why are you surprised? I am the walking dead. You live in the world of fancy still, as if your wishes had some chance of altering your destiny. I'm a soul God in His infinite wisdom has singled out to flay alive.

And yet I feel no pain. And perhaps that comes of faith. The power to continue without a skin.

'Too much thinking,' Beatrice says. 'Altogether too much. You can't think against your Creator, Annie. He made the moon and stars. He made you. There's no point in thinking.'

She stops dead. Luke comes stealing into her mind. She recalls the pulsing of his skull, where the fontanelles hadn't fully closed – and Will said one afternoon while Luke was taking a nap, 'What is that called? – the open part of the skull? – we see it pulse – he's still close to Jesus, not sealed off.' How grateful she has been for her brother-in-law's consolation, taking his words as gold, hoarding them in her memory. Beatrice's heart pauses between one beat and the next.

'Doesn't she look strange, Will? Should she sit down?'

The next throb comes after all. Beatrice's heart will persist a while yet. For a moment it was as if the door to the other world opened a smidgeon. To let her out. Oh, may it be soon. The knife handles are made of discoloured bone. They offer themselves in a bunch, the blades buried in a wooden block.

'She does look pale and weary. Won't you rest now?' Will Anwyl, the only one capable of touching her heart, comes up close and his voice is too beautiful for words; it will unstring her. Beatrice daren't look into his dangerous eyes. 'Why don't Annie and I roll our sleeves up and bake the bread?'

'You, bake bread?' The faint gleam of a smile lightens her face but it seems to jeopardise her defence. Will is, after all, a slippery character. 'What do you know about baking bread?'

'Well, I know something, perhaps not much as things stand. But Annie will teach me. I'll be her apprentice. Or yours – perhaps you'd like us to do it together, just you and me? Then Annie can carry on with her writing. I know she's itching to.'

No need to ask Anna twice. But she lingers and says, 'Dear,

we shall come through all this. We shall. I won't do the least thing to worry you. I promise. Please don't look like that.'

'I'm not looking like anything.'

'Exactly.'

'Well, but let's not badger her, Annie,' Will advises.

'Am I badgering you, love? I'll stop. But what can I do to console you?' Anna's eyes swim with tears. 'Anything at all. Whatever it is, I'll do it, just ask me.'

Him, Beatrice thinks. Give me him. Give him back. My old love, my one love, who I now see is filled with the Holy Spirit, the Comforter.

'You deny me, Anna,' she cries. 'You *deny* me!'

'What do I deny you? Because I won't promise not to think my thoughts? I can't not think and still be me.'

'Then don't act on them,' says Beatrice.

'I will try.'

Anna puts her arms round her sister and kisses her cheek, imploring some return of emotion – but Beatrice can find none to give. The last milk has dried in her glands. A faint tingling: then the star goes out. This is all as God wills. And remember, she tells herself, Will is your sister's husband. You have no right to him. She scrubs the kitchen table. Everywhere seems to have been let to slide. Beatrice will not blame Amy for the state of Sarum House; it's her own lackadaisical self who bears responsibility for the housekeeping. Every corner betrays signs of neglect. Blade marks score the beech table, into whose wounds blood and fat have run over decades. Very hard to scour out, however you attack them; such deep and polluted scars.

S*he* knew the man who killed her, the dear old sow understood at once. Such intelligent beasts they are, swine; they recognise individual human faces. They look you in the eye and return your scrutiny. Pigs understand you perhaps through their noses. To me Lucy would come lolloping with that funny barking sound and snuffle at me and lie down at my feet to have her fat belly tickled. But at the sight of the pig-sticker she screamed like a baby. He is skilful, mind, very. He dispatched her as fast as it could be done and there she swung, upended, hooked. She'd ceased to be Lucy. Hams and flitch, blood for pudding. Her lifeblood poured into the bucket: plenty of salt to stop it congealing. The scream died fast in her throat. Singeing, scalding, scraping. The pig-sticker went at it, snorting. A reek arose, until her skin looked like a field of mushrooms. The guts flopped out cleanly, secured in the white transparent sheath of the bowel: no stench. Everyone present tasted the jellylike texture of the meat, succulent, still warm. And now Lucy is part of me, part of us all. Strange eucharistic sacrifice. And this is the world in which our Maker has set us, for our sins. Lucy was without sin. She suffered for Eve's mortal transgression, like the whole Creation.

Beatrice stands back to survey her work on the table, which is still unclean. How could she have let it get like this? It will have to do. *He* says it is spick and span. It isn't really. But they're ready to bake. Fetching an apron for Will, Beatrice ties it for him; he obediently washes his hands to the elbows. Dirt kills, she reminds him: Miss Nightingale has warned us. She scrubbed the filth out of the Crimea. But foetid airs arise from the earth and poison us. We breathe them in; they kill our babies. And our house is low-lying: so near to the river, the earth saturated. All this unhealthiness is Eve's gift to us.

They knead together, knuckles in the dough, flour whitening her companion's hair. He has a confession, Will says: this isn't the first time he's played the baker. He used to bake bread before, at home with his foster-mother. The dark *bara lawr*, laverbread, eaten with bacon and cockles. One day he'll prepare for Beatrice and Anna such a breakfast. But also they'd occasionally bake the good white bread. The scent as you took it out! Always it was a miracle of transformation. The way the loaf rose under the cloth. The way it goldens in the oven. The way the smell gets into your clothes and hair and beard, and haunts you on the stairs and strays into every corner of the house. The following day, even then, there's the ghost of the scent, reminding us perhaps of our duty to enjoy the God-made world.

'What is your view, Will,' she asks him, 'of the spirits? Am I wrong?'

'Hard for me to judge, dear – because of course I was not present. All I know is that anything is possible to God, anything at all. I will pray about it. Or shall we do so together? Shall we kneel? Here and now, what better time?'

Here on the rust-red tiles, dusted with flour, they fall to their knees, hand in hand – and Amy, entering with a clattering pail and a grumbling word on her lips, stops in her tracks, retreats and closes the door softly.

*

Can one listen in to other folk's conversations, even from a separate room? Or overhear when nobody's actually speaking? Her floor is their ceiling and shields the two of them from her gaze. But Anna is convinced that no sooner did she retreat than the two of them turned to one another. They were made for each other: simple as that. She imagines Will saying to his sister-in-law, 'God is infinitely merciful, Beatrice. Don't be tempted to imagine that His heart is hard. Or that He turns away from your grief. He has lost a son of his own, don't forget that. He knows, *bach,* he knows. How could He fail to know?' No need of salt in the bread: their tears savour the dough. Tears for a havoc larger than Luke. The chaos that made Will marry his beloved's sister.

Meanwhile in the chamber below the soles of Anna's feet,

her sister and husband reach out to clasp one another close. Perhaps not in body. But in their hearts they embrace. She cannot blame them. There in the kitchen with the flames from the range casting a red glow, they set aside the dough in the pantry for the yeast to raise. They turn to one another. Anna looks down at the floorboards and witnesses it as it happens, as if from above.

*Who giveth this woman?*

'I give her,' Anna thinks. 'Fully and freely. Against all law and custom. I give him too – because my love for him, like his for me, though real, turns out to be a kind of adultery.'

Anna takes the pen in her hand: Will's wedding present to her. The weight of its tortoiseshell body sits snugly on the join between her thumb and forefinger. Tendrils of inlaid flowers wander from the mosaic capstone along the shaft. Loading the pen, Anna touches it to the blotting paper, where a blossom of ink forms. Once it's bled out, she suspends it above the paper.

The glass water-jug on the desk casts a pale shadow on the page. The surface of the water trembles; light travelling through it traces a faint spangling ellipse, which sways from side to side. She sees the smudge of her lip-print on the rim, the trace of a living moment. The glass blower has trapped a bubble of air – his breath perhaps – in the vessel, creating an imperfection, the vestige of another moment, years ago. Something microscopic afloat in the water – perhaps a flake of human skin – casts the shadow of a speck. In the sunlight, the grain of the cherry wood desk has a depth of brown that is remarkable: what would a word for this colour be? The years have stained the wood with a dark luminosity of varnish and polish. Its grain is eventful, waylaying the eye with knots and whorls where once branches forked in the living tree.

In a world without spirit, Anna thinks, all you're left with is matter. Is that so very bad? All objects have a story. The world's a reliquary and here we are sifting about in the remains, turning up a shard here, a fragment there.

She fingers one of the fossilised sea urchins she and Lore loved to collect. You might find a cache of fifty in a shallow grave the plough unearths. Millennia ago a creature crawled in the mud of a warm sea. Its soft insides were consumed by other lives. Into the empty shell oozed a jelly that hardened to a flint cast. Ice and wind and water eroded it out of layers of chalk. Someone picked it up, someone human or nearly human, thousands of years before Anna came along; someone in mourning perhaps, who saw this blind stone eyeball as a sacred object and buried it with the tribe's dead. Thousands of years later a second wandering collector, Anna Pentecost, pocketed it and took it home and kept it for luck and inspiration.

A scent of baking bread arises from downstairs: delicious. There's laughter from the kitchen; Beatrice is laughing. Will's miracle, bless him. What to write? Miriam has made a profession of the pen, behind the mask of a male pseudonym: Calder North. The public lie has betrayed the private woman. So what should Anna call herself? Is she capable of writing anything that hangs together? I'm all odds and ends, she thinks. I know nothing systematically. My thoughts are all questions.

The metal box contains a trove of these thoughts that are only questions, going right back to childhood. Opening the lid, she's confronted with a sea of papers – wallpaper scraps, packing-case paper, flour bags full of jottings, leaves from notebooks, blanks torn from books for her scribbles. Paper in those days was expensive: it had to be conserved. Anna's tiny script was meant to have a printed effect and yet to be secret.

She holds to the mirror a tiny volume sewn together with

minute stitches, labeled 'The Tump Book by Anna Pentecost'. Inside there are minute illustrations: an earthworm with its segments carefully drawn, a stag beetle and a parade of ants.

*My bank or hillock or Tump or mound is a great Mystyry ... In my Tump are special tregures and on my Tump are special things going on.*

Grasses and dandelions, poppies and vetches are jostling one another, along with ants and earwigs, worms and bees and a dead blackbird mauled by a cat that wasn't hungry.

*And it is My Mamas Tump I have left her the tregures*

Anna begins to sort the scraps from the flour bag. The first thing to do is to decipher and transcribe all the scraps. And then begin to write her book, a work not of fiction but of observation. And I need to read, Anna realises. I need to buy books. I need a study. And I need time. I have a vocation. And I need to investigate the Tump. The name on the cover will be, quite plainly, Anna Pentecost.

*

Meeting Mrs Quarles in the street, Beatrice blurts in response to her polite enquiry, 'My sister tells me she is writing a book.'

'Oh dear!'

Mrs Quarles is onto it like a cat with a grasshopper. Her face brims with the riling sympathy that feasts on a neighbour's mortification. She remarks that dear Anna was always a highly sensitive young person. The brain can become inflamed in such cases. The doctor's wife has observed what she calls 'unusual ladies' going in and out of Sarum House. 'There was one lady who seemed to be carrying a whole pheasant on her head. Doubtless a city fashion.'

Mrs Quarles drops the subject and goes on to lament Dr Quarles's toothache and his refusal to visit the dentist. Dear oh dear: great men can often be fretful patients. How did the Bard put it: 'For there was never yet philosopher who could endure the tooth ache patiently.' A profound truth there. Shakespeare never lets you down. 'Do you read much Shakespeare, Beatrice?' she enquires. 'The Bard is a tonic. I could never manage without my Shakespeare.'

'Very little. Dr Quarles's tooth should come out,' Beatrice observes trenchantly. 'Without delay.'

The lady with the pheasant hat was a female bookseller from London. She and Anna sequestered themselves with a catalogue from which Anna selected works she 'needed' to read. 'It's my own money, Beatrice.' Two boxes duly arrived, which Anna carried up to the spare bedroom she has requisitioned for a 'study'. Locking the door, Anna pocketed both keys. No by-your-leave. But Anna's manner was and remains calm and gentle, even humorous. When Beatrice pointed out that the room was frequently required for a visiting minister, Anna apologized – 'I'm so sorry, love, if it puts you out'. But she said there were plenty of rooms for that; the ministers could double up – and anyone extra could be accommodated by the Eliases. Anna is affable, no trouble to anyone. Never quite here with us really, Beatrice thinks. Anna wears her inkstains like a badge of office. She wanders round the wilderness muttering to herself.

It's no longer Beatrice's place to assess her sister's reading: that duty falls to Will. All one can say is that there have been no further visits to or from Antigone Kyffin and Anna has assured her sister that she views the whole performance with irony. 'It's sheer legerdemain,' she says, evidently trying out a new word and feeling pleased with it. 'Only (and this is the interesting part) the poor deluded conjurer has no idea she's playing tricks. So it is not intelligent. Interesting though. As a phenomenon.' She would like to attend more of the séances to observe – but not if Beatrice objects.

And every day Anna seems, in a subtle way, to cede her

husband to her sister. There's to be an ecumenical meeting in Salisbury, to prepare for the Awakening. Will naturally assumes that Anna will accompany him.

'Oh no, Will, I'm so sorry, I can't go.' She says this sorrowfully, not as wishing to give offence but with an air of perplexity. 'Take Beatrice. You'll go, won't you, darling?'

'It will be a great pleasure to me if Beatrice accompanies us, Annie. But your presence will be looked for, dear. As my wife.'

'Surely not, Will? Beatrice will even enjoy it.' And so I would, Beatrice thinks; just sitting with Will is a comfort, even if he never looks at me or speaks to me. But he does look, he does speak, his whole person is aware of me. That will always be so. She knows that, in Anna's warped mind, every hour she's kept from her desk and books is an hour lost.

'Your absence will be commented on, dear. I'm constantly being asked where you are these days.' Will speaks lightly but there's a level of grave concern Beatrice never saw before his marriage.

'People will always talk though, won't they, *cariad?*' Anna responds, not in a cantankerous spirit but touching Will's arm, with a confident smile. 'Let them. You'll go for both of us, won't you, Beattie?'

'No, Annie. I'm afraid not. Not if you don't.' Beatrice won't make it easy for Anna to shirk her responsibilities. She can't make her out. It was so much easier in the days of her hysterical illnesses. Is this calm just another kind of insanity? Anna has crossed some line but Beatrice cannot make out how this happened. She's acting – yes, that's it – like a man. As if she had the right to dictate her way of life. And everyone else should recognise it. Yet she looks hale and happy. She's put on weight and eats like a horse.

'Bless you, you don't realize, *cariad,*' Anna says to Will.

'Realize what?'

'Oh, sweetheart, there's just so much work to get through.'

Will takes a deep breath; puts his hand through his hair. Softly Beatrice lays her hand on his back for just a moment.

'But what is it you're doing?' he asks. 'And why? You won't let anyone in. Why keep it secret?'

When you knock, Anna peers round the door. She doesn't invite you into the room she has usurped. She's behaving as if she were the head of household. It's risible. Risible too that she takes herself for a great authoress. What has she ever written worth keeping?

'Books are my *vocation*,' Anna says.

'I am a minister of the church, Anna. That is a vocation. And you – are my wife – and a Christian.' Will speaks with studied patience as if explaining to a child. There's also a note of pleading in his voice. Beatrice, who keeps quiet, sees how the pulse at his throat throbs.

'Well. But, dear heart,' replies Anna in the most rational way, 'not in any narrow sense.'

Will says nothing. He turns to the window, looks out through the slanting rain. Beatrice stands perfectly still. When he turns back to them, Will suggests that they all three pray together: 'Peace upon our house,' he begins. 'And fellowship one with the other.'

Anna, closing her eyes, seems to surrender to the prayer; she bows her head. She's just waiting to get back to her scribbling, Beatrice knows. And Will can never winkle her out. She appeals to Joss to talk their sister round.

'Poor Annie has temporarily mislaid her sense of humour,' is all Joss will say. He's expecting a visit from Mr Munby and cannot spare much attention, having let fall that he has something important to discuss with his friend. 'Annie will come round, won't she? Not to worry, Beattie, she'll soon recover. Just let her be. Always the best way.'

For once, Beatrice takes her brother's advice. And in any case she intuits that nature will soon clip Anna's wings. Routinely Beatrice trims the wings of the hens to stop them escaping, clipping the flight feathers of one wing so the bird's out of balance. Hens can't fly but could easily leap the fence. As long as you start above the shafts of the feathers where the blood vessels are, there's no pain. And every time the bird moults, you repeat the process. It's time. Beatrice will do this soon. She has deliberately ignored, could hardly bear to acknowledge, her sister's state. In point of fact all she has to do is ask, 'When do you expect your confinement, dear?' And Anna will fall to earth, her Icarus dreams of fame aborted.

In the night Beatrice is awoken by the sound of the Anwyls' door opening and closing. The door of Anna's so-called study also opens and closes. There are sounds of a whispered altercation. Anna has gone in there to sleep – is that it? – and refused her husband entrance? There's a long pause, then the sound of slow footsteps down the stairs. Beatrice waits for the click of the latch. Peering from her window, she sees her brother-in-law in the garden, walking slowly up and down, fingers at his temples.

There's no answer when Beatrice knocks. 'Anna! What on earth are you doing?'

Nothing.

'Come to the door, dear.'

Nothing.

If Anna won't go to Will, Beatrice must. She'll bring him into the kitchen; brew him tea; talk the whole thing through and work out what steps to take to rid their home of turmoil. *Vocation*, she thinks, *vocation!* The voice that's calling Anna to wall herself up like an anchoress in her cell must be either demented or demonic. She thinks of the voice of Lore speaking through poor Antigone. Whatever's going on in that room, in that wayward head of Anna's? Beatrice shivers: she doesn't really want to know. Wrapping her shawl around her, she follows Will out. The fragrance of night-scented stocks hits her with the shock of an archaic memory. She looks up to see if her sister is standing at a window. No – and the candles are all out. Anna can't be asleep?

Once upon a time I met Will at the end of the garden, she thinks. The barn owl was out hunting. Will's fingers brushed me – just here. I've not been touched since then; Christian has never touched me. It seems a world away and only yesterday. He asked me – again – and he kissed me – and I could have accepted him – and whyever did I refuse?

Will threatened: in that case I shall go to *her*.

And now we're both paying for our mistake. How can I ever have said no to darling Will when I wanted him so much? And still I melt every time I hear his voice. Now Anna is saying, too late: 'Here you are, have him back. The two of you are welcome to one another.'

Will has moved away from the house. She calls his name.

There's a churring as of a nightjar. They fly on silent wings around Chauntsey Woods and never sing by day or venture far beyond the woods. Beatrice moves into the voluptuous darkness and is enveloped.

# Chapter 21

The long prophesied Awakening is at hand. Florian Street has been praying and singing, soliciting a special outpouring of the Spirit. The faithful keep it up all night, attending in shifts. Dissenting and evangelical Anglican churches join forces: the bickering sects lay down their ancient quarrels and unite as one. The Call is out. Conversions are expected on a mass scale and the churches must be ready, for it's not just a matter of harvesting souls – in a sense the easy part – but of settling converts in stable congregations.

The Spirit is due to arrive on the London train in the persons of four ministers: Christian Ritter, home from his Irish mission; Idris Jones; John Clifford and – a singular coup – the famous Charles Haddon Spurgeon. Later a deputation from Wales is expected: five young evangelists, millenarian disciples of poor Humphrey Jones, who, having brought the flame of Revival from America to Aberystwyth, has wandered along strange paths leading to Carmarthen Mental Hospital.

Waiting with the Eliases on the platform at Salisbury Station, Beatrice is in a painful state of tremulous anticipation

– less perhaps at the prospect of the Awakening than at the expectation of having her husband home. Her dear husband, for he is dear. The head of her family, for he is master of her house. Surely she has never wished it otherwise, even in her most vagrant state? Whatever happens now, at least it will bring an end to the struggle in Sarum House. Christian must speak to Anna about her behaviour.

And surely Beatrice has nothing with which to reproach herself, beyond the general worthlessness of a common sinner. Whatever occurred in darkness between herself and Gwilym Anwyl may surely remain in darkness? She has tried and failed to feel guilty about it.

For after all, what did happen? Are words actions? Indeed, are silences actions? Are they events?

Yes, in all honesty, one must admit that they are. It cannot be said that the two of them uttered more than a handful of words. All was communicated in darkness, haunted by the vanilla perfume of unseen flowers. Love held them as close together as people can be who are scarcely touching. Every pore of Beatrice was open to Will in the darkness. But only their fingertips met, in parting.

Could it be said that they met and spoke as brother and sister – or soul with soul? Beatrice hopes that the love they expressed and lived might be as blameless as that. If that was not so, she asks God's forgiveness. Nothing was said that should injure Anna or Christian.

And Luke seemed there in the quiet, beside them, hushed in his cradle. For the first time she felt his presence in God. Not as a troubled spirit struggling to approach her from the Other World but in a vast repose. Safe, my boy, safe beyond suffering. In a region where there are no more tears, for God has wiped them from mortal eyes.

This knowledge Beatrice must close in her hand, a pearl

never to be shown, even to dear Christian. For he is dear. Let in the common light and the pearl will lose lustre. It has to last the rest of her life.

The following morning Anna appeared at the breakfast table with apprehensive eyes. But nothing was said. They ate together quietly. There were no questions or recriminations. Anna fell to wolfing eggs and toast.

And, oh yes, Beatrice thought once more, with scarcely a pang: you're with child. Anyone with eyes can see that.

It threw everything into a new light. These aberrations, apparently under the influence of the notorious Mrs Sala, may be nothing more than the freaks and foibles of pregnancy. Be patient, wait, and they'll be brushed aside by the imperatives of the coming baby. Beatrice, to her surprise, is conscious of no particular envy.

'Step back!'

The locomotive approaches, precisely to time, in a hissing welter of steam and smoke. Doors are thrown open and here they are, the four ministers. What a treat for their fellow-passengers to have overheard their conversation, perhaps the most inspired voices in England – and Beatrice's husband not the least of them for eloquence. Christian hurries ahead and takes his wife's gloved hand in his gloved hand. Their eyes meet with comical bashfulness. And here is young Mr Clifford, with his social passion. It occurs to Beatrice that it will be good for Anna to talk with him: he might do better than Christian. In the doubt-laden atmosphere of the times Mr Clifford is a shining beacon and may bring Anna round. Beatrice remembers how caught up with him her sister was when he preached at Chauntsey. The look on Anna's face was quietly focused. 'One loves the man, one venerates him,' she said then from her wheeled chair.

The pastors shake hands cordially with the welcoming

party. Idris Jones of Bedwellty scarcely seems his usual ebullient self, loquacity quenched maybe in the company of the matchless Mr Spurgeon.

No sooner has he alighted on the platform of Salisbury Station than Mr Spurgeon is recognized, perhaps by folk who've attended his services at the newly built and stupendous Metropolitan Tabernacle. The word goes round. Over there. Spurgeon! What, that little roly poly youth? The same. Railwaymen, doffing their caps, mill around him and Beatrice is aware of a lady passenger sidling up to touch his coat.

Mr Spurgeon, aware of the approach, wheels round. She takes a step back, flustered and apologetic.

'My dear lady,' he says. 'What can I do for you?'

'Oh – beg your pardon, sir, but my boy – he's sick. Over there with his Papa. We're going to the spa hoping for a cure, though the doctor says it's too late and we should give up our hope and save our money to bury him.'

'The golden-haired little chap?'

'I'm afraid he's red-haired, sir.'

'No, no, *golden*. Eighteen *carrot!* – ah ha! At least that's brought a smile to your lips, and what are pastors for? No earthly use in them if they can't do that. Bring the lad here and I will speak to him. But, you know, I'm no miracle-worker. Don't mistake me for my Master. Hope is a precious thing; there's no putting a price on hope; we have to hope – but let us place our hope in our Jesus. *He* will not let us down. Is your boy in pain?'

'No, I don't think so.'

'That's a blessing. And you must take it as such.'

The pale, freckled boy is carried across in his father's arms. Beatrice, close to the puny five-year-old, suffers a reeling blow. He's a collection of bones. The boy has never walked.

And now cannot eat, scarcely drinks. Beatrice looks up at her husband. His hand cups her elbow and squeezes.

'My dear little fellow – what is your name, darling?'

The boy stares from his pale green eyes. The mother asks for a blessing on Bertie and Mr Spurgeon places his hand on the child's forehead. He nods to the father to pass him the lad. He will hold the bag of bones and bless it. The child is transferred to his arms. No weight at all.

A hush spreads through the station. The mother and father fall to their knees on the platform amongst heaps of luggage and mail bags. It's a biblical scene. Mr Clifford and Mr Jones are down on their knees. Beatrice finds herself sinking down beside her husband, her mourning gown billowing into the dirt. The station master is down; porters and railwaymen follow. The impulse spreads amongst the passengers; first-class passengers kneel, removing their top hats. Ladies in crinolines stand, hands clasped, eyes closed.

Mr Spurgeon's voice is a rich instrument. Its trumpet-call penetrates every corner. The father and mother weep. The weeping spreads through the station. The child hangs limp and open-mouthed in Mr Spurgeon's arms. As he prays, Beatrice feels that Jesus stands beside him. It must have been like this in the Holy Land, she thinks, at Bethesda or Galilee in the time of miracles.

The minister finishes. Opening her eyes, Beatrice sees the unremarkable, thickset man with his large head, protruding teeth slightly crossed, his eyes which don't quite match, shorter in stature than Anna: transfigured.

The boy is restored to his father's arms. With stammering thanks that are waved away, the parents vanish into the crowd, more reconciled perhaps, quieter in themselves for the journey ahead.

Assembled in the carriage, the mood changes. Good cheer

prevails as Mr Spurgeon tells stories against himself and teases Mr Clifford about his appetite for education. 'So John is looking to study for his doctorate! Doctorate! I wouldn't give you tuppence for a bushel of 'em! I've all the doctorates I need here.' He slaps the wide pocket where he keeps his New Testament. 'I hear you've just graduated with a B.Sc. in Geology and Palaeontology. Did Jesus sit at the feet of the Pharisees and study for his Bachelor of Mouldy Rocks and Fossils? Fiddle-faddle! Jesus taught *them,* or would have, if they'd just pinned back their lugs.'

Mr Clifford, smiling, refuses to take the bait. We must all be educated, he insists: the poor as well the rich. As for his mouldy fossils, his optimism sees no antagonism between the competition of species for survival and the possible progress of the human race.

'Would you perhaps speak to my sister if you have a chance, Mr Clifford?' Beatrice asks as they enter the garden of Sarum House. 'Speak to her about your studies. I feel she would enjoy – benefit from – a conversation with you.'

'It will be a pleasure. I remember Miss Anna very well. A remarkable young woman.'

'She is in some turmoil of mind, I fear.' Beatrice says no more, leaving Mr Clifford to make his own assessment.

Amongst these distinguished gentlemen, Beatrice feels as she did in Papa's day, as if she's eating with angels, the greediest creatures in the universe. They can empty whole pantries at a sitting. It's not until after tea is served and before supper preparations begin that she can snatch half an hour with her husband while the house is temporarily quiet except for Amy's tramping up and downstairs with hot water for the beardless ones to shave.

Glancing out of the window, Beatrice is comforted to see her sister walking in the garden with Mr Clifford, deep in talk.

'What kind of married life is this for you?' asks Christian. She is tying his necktie for him, hands all of a tremble. 'I'm ashamed to leave you alone for such long periods. Do you ever regret marrying an evangelist?' He places his hands on her shoulders and bends to study her face. 'I have so much to occupy me of my Master's work while you –'

'I'm well occupied, dear. I knew from the beginning how it would be. But yes, I've missed your steadying hand.' Should she confide in him now? Or keep the question of his sister-in-law's waywardness until they have time and privacy? What a relief it will be to turn over the whole burden to Christian. He'll doubtless be shocked and perhaps critical of the way his wife has handled the situation.

'I believe our work is bearing fruit,' he says and begins to tell of a family in Bristol with whom he periodically lodges, the Leytons: Mrs Leyton is a widow who has felt a call of her own to the ministry but – *mirabile dictu!* – so has her twelve-year-old daughter, whom he personally baptized. Ruth is a promising child with whom Christian has sat many an evening in deep and earnest conversation. Unless her fire burns itself out, the name of Ruth Leyton will be heard in the future.

'But surely – a woman – a young girl – you cannot approve of female ministers?'

'There are precedents, Beatrice. The Quakers, the early Methodists. In America I met remarkable women preachers. There are Gospel precedents: in the Gospel of John, of course, we read of the preaching Woman of Samaria.'

Beatrice bursts in with, 'We are not Methodists and this is not America, Christian. Their ways are not ours.'

'Good things come from America, Beatrice, do they not? Not least amongst them is Revival – and the war against slavery. And who knows what women may be called to do in the next generation? The women who are children now will see a new world. Ruth Leyton, I find, understands these matters with a more than childlike grasp. And yet she is modest and biddable. You'd be impressed, dear. And, Beatrice, I hope we may welcome the Leytons to Sarum House so that you can get to know them.'

'Of course, Christian. If that is your wish.'

'I know you will find them delightful.'

'Very delightful, I'm sure.' The pastoral relationship is fraught with intimate temptations. Beatrice would never have thought Christian, towering above them all in his purity, would have been susceptible.

'I know what you're thinking,' he says.

You always do – or you think you do, she doesn't say.

'I am impervious to all charms but those of my dearest wife.'

Beatrice cannot help laughing aloud at the pompous formula. Christian suppresses a look of irritation or apprehension, she can't tell which. He begins to speak of a lady in Indianapolis who threw her lovely arms round Mr Beecher's neck and cried, 'Oh, Mr Beecher, save me!' Beecher's grave and correct reply was, 'You must look to a higher power.' The pastor removed her hands from his neck and fell on his knees: 'Let us pray.'

'Love, of course,' Christian says, 'is always good. I love many souls. I seek to love *all* souls. You would not limit that? But I stand as straight as a poplar for any sin of the flesh. At the same time, you cannot doubt me, Beatrice?'

'Of course not. But is it wise ...?'

'Come, darling, we have a few minutes,' he says, taking her hand. 'Let's talk, really talk. Sit on my knee by the fire as we always used to do, since you were ... so high.'

*Beattie hates, Beattie loathes.*

She sees in her mind's eye a twelve-year-old with hectic

eyes and flaming face in the lap of a grown man, being rocked, being sung and preached to. The name of the girl was Beatrice Pentecost and is now Ruth Leyton.

When her husband sits down and pats his lap, Beatrice makes no move to join him but stands beside her husband in the firelight, one hand on his shoulder. There's a moment's tense silence. Then Christian says, surprisingly, 'I dreamed of him, Beatrice. Our boy.' He turns aside and his voice chokes; he seems unable to trust himself to speak his son's name.

'What did you dream?'

'We were all three in the garden. Luke was in your arms. But he began to, I don't know, dissolve – slowly – until I could see right through him. But you still held him – cradled – he just melted – he melted back into you. Finally he couldn't be seen at all. I said to you, "Oh Beatrice, he has gone. Can't you see he's gone?" But I looked into your face, darling, and I saw.'

'What did you see?'

'He was in you. I see him now. He'll always be in you. But there was something about the dream – that left God out – that placed the human mother above the divine Father – or so I thought on waking – and I trembled. But then I thought, Might the Father be in the human mother?'

Never mind the Leytons. Never mind any of it. We have had a child together; we've lost a child together. Tears run down their faces and mingle. *For he is our peace who hath made both one and hath broken down the middle wall of partition.* Beatrice glimpses what she rarely has before: the father's likeness to the son.

Already Christian's drying his face and settling its expression. He reaches for his slouch hat.

*

Mr Clifford does not mock Anna as she leads him through the

305

wilderness to the mound. He listens with that unique sympathy of his. 'It was your sanctuary, Anna. Your refuge.'

'Warmth seemed to come up from it – a motherly kind of warmth. All sorts of little games I played here and I wrote books about them. Tiny books a few inches across. I could show you. Recently I opened the box I kept them in. Not just stories but descriptions of the creatures on the mound and the plants and what was happening to them – what I saw and observed – a sense of those lives entangled there, all struggling and entwined. And I'd dig. I'd excavate. Does that sound heathen?'

'It sounds human, Anna. It sounds – if I have caught your drift – filial.'

That sticks in Anna's mind when he's gone indoors. He saw that the beloved was down there in the earth, the beautiful and terrible earth. Anna finds a trowel and lays back the turf. Her fingers scrabble in the soil till she uncovers and lifts the lid of the earthenware pot she buried there so many years ago. Anna reaches in to pluck out her treasures one by one. A leaf-shaped arrowhead. A tiny silver bell. An amber bead. A bone comb. Green tesserae. Anna sits cross-legged with the hoard spread in her lap, weighing each object in her palm, turning it to the light.

The treasures return to their urn; the urn to the earth.

*

Isaiah Minety prepares to preach the sermon of his young life, making his mark on the great visitors from the capital. It was at a similar age that Mr Spurgeon's star began to rise from low origins: the oracular, button-nosed boy-preacher of the Fens attracted the scoffs of worldlings. He'd been ministering since he was a toddling child, perched on a hayrick to address an infant congregation.

Why not therefore the baker's boy of West Grimstead? Perhaps it's for Mr Spurgeon to single out Isaiah for a special prophecy?

But will he? There cannot be a surplus of prodigies in the Baptist fold. London does not possess enough Surrey Chapels or Exeter Halls to hold them. Mr Spurgeon, having outlived his reputation for extreme youth, will hardly be on the lookout for up-and-coming lads to ape his glory, Anna thinks as she arranges Isaiah's necktie and dusts down his lapels. And besides, Mr Spurgeon is surely likely to take exception to Isaiah's growing tendency to preach something that sounds like the doctrine of universal forgiveness.

Times have changed: it's the age of the show, the performer. Isaiah seems to intuit this. The theatrical turns for which he has become renowned in Wiltshire and Dorset have raised expectations of a service of surpassing power and originality. Passed round the chapels and churches like a box of surprises, Isaiah is permanently in demand. Traditionalists are alienated by his antics, as when he produced a concertina in a village pulpit and sang along to this squeezebox, an instrument more appropriate to a public house or a fair. Deacons complained. And then again, the lad's theology, if that's what you could call it, is what some call heterodox and others gibberish. Just as the Pharisees set traps for Our young Lord, so his enemies have tempted callow Pastor Minety.

And in his inexperience he has taken the bait. Isaiah, backed against the ropes, has been understood to state that God could not make a frog.

The Creator of all things not capable of making a frog?

No, Isaiah is alleged to have parried. God would be bound to begin with spawn. The spawn would become tadpoles, the tadpoles frogs.

'For shame!' the Alderbury deacons protested. Quarrels broke out at Fighelbourn and Cressington concerning the vexed issue of God's relation to the laws he had ordained. Mr Gosse's

*Omphalos* has been quoted by Plymouth Brethren in Cressington Market Place, on the related question of whether Adam possessed a navel. The Brethren, acknowledging that Adam, never born of woman, should logically have required no navel, nevertheless maintained that he was created as if he were a mature man of about twenty-five. Hence our great progenitor came into being complete with all manly parts. On the same principle the Adorable Workman created trees in Eden with growth rings that had never grown; He planted fossils in the earth representing the skeletons of animals that never existed. He created frogs according to the same principle.

An atheistical youngster from the Mechanics' Institute has spoken up for Mr Darwin and Mr Wallace and against the Creation as depicted in the Book of Genesis, claiming that Mr Gosse has made God into a liar and a fraud. The lad was knocked down by a fellow student in the name of the authority of the Book of Genesis. At the Mechanics' Institute a subsidiary row has broken out about male nipples. Were we once hermaphrodites or even, as Mr Darwin's book on barnacles might seem to imply, descendants of original females? The frogs have bred an avalanche of arguments on polyps and earthworms, spirogyra and animalcules undreamed of by Isaiah Minety.

But the pastor's conversions, especially amongst young people, are generally held to speak for themselves.

And besides, Mr Minety, somewhat concussed by it all, does not recall saying anything about frogs.

Much hangs on Isaiah's performance today. At breakfast Anna reads anxiety in his fiery cheeks; there's a mob of butterflies in his stomach. Isaiah closes his eyes and his lips move. He's praying for grace. She understands very well his blurtings about the frogs; it's on her conscience. The snatches of ill-digested zoological thought he has caught from her have set him thinking. And once that happens, Anna knows, the cork's out of the bottle.

Mr Spurgeon too is praying but in his case it is for his voice, having caught a cold on the train. Anna has been up and down to him in the night with hot drinks and eucalyptus balm. Oh, how he misses dear Wifey on these occasions, he confides. Susannah, his nurse and comforter, though far from well herself, never heeds her own sufferings when her husband's health is poor, for Mr Spurgeon's well-being is essential to Christ's church in this land. Anna asks if she should summon Mrs Spurgeon – or does he require a doctor? Unfortunately, she adds, the Pentecost doctor is not a Baptist or even a Dissenter.

'I shall pray instead,' Mr Spurgeon says, shuddering, perhaps at the thought of an unknown High Anglican physician. 'The Lord will heal me if it be His Will.'

He huddles in a limp and streaming state, unsure whether his voice will serve. He was minded, Mr Spurgeon says huskily, to speak on the Bible, telling the congregation that the Book has wrestled with him, smitten, comforted, smiled on him, clasped his hand, warmed and wept with him, sung with him, ministered to him. Why read anything else?

Anna bites her tongue. Her profane library is growing, locked away in her study. She has thought of chaining the books to prevent theft, as they did in mediaeval libraries. But she expects no further raids: Anna has made sure Beatrice knows that Mr Clifford himself approves of her collection and has promised a set of books on palaeontology and geology.

In the event, so many Christians attempt to crush into Florian Street that the service must be held in the open air and Mr Spurgeon, who daren't risk pneumonia, returns to Sarum House in a carriage.

A dais is erected from packing cases for the ministers;

benches are carried out for the old and sick. Isaiah, mounting the improvised platform to open the meeting, is joined by the visiting ministers, gazing out at the sea of faces, an immense flock standing in attitudes of prayerful waiting. Gradually the quiet settles – they might as well be at a Quaker meeting – into a silence that covers the whole green.

Anna finds herself breathing more slowly, dipping down into calm reaches. The baby in its hidden interior, making its acrobatic vaults and dives, informs her, Here I am. I'm coming. I'll soon be with you, wait for me. For the moment I am you and you are me; isn't it lovely? Anna smiles an inward smile. Drawing her cloak around herself, she lays her hand on the swell of her belly.

In her pocket is her leather-bound red notebook, with a little pouch for the pencil. The baby is not – or not yet – her be-all and end-all. The quality of the crowd's stillness fascinates Anna. It builds a sense of expectation and then, when nothing happens, the silence becomes a thing in itself, a solid substance like rock, though by and by tremors of agitation begin to ruffle its surface. What are we waiting for? Why doesn't the pastor start? Or someone start for him?

Isaiah opens his mouth. At last. Nothing comes out and he closes it again. You hear the crying of the gulls, the clopping of horses, the laughter of children bowling hoops on the road. The huddled ministers consult amongst themselves. Isaiah looks across the heads of the multitude with a tranquil smile. Perhaps he's praying.

Whereupon a dumpy, dark-haired woman clambers up to the dais and announces that she has been asked to speak.

Who is she? Who has invited her? Not Isaiah, apparently, but he nods and takes a step backwards. Not the ring of pastors, who appear baffled.

'Friends! My name is Phoebe Palmer the Evangelist and I

come to you all the way from New York!' She opens her arms wide. 'Via Huddersfield, England! Do not be startled that I raise my voice before all these folks! I'm not here to assert Women's Rights, so called. I believe Woman is happy in her legitimate sphere of influence. But – now I will say this,' and she wags her index finger at the congregation, a sparkle in her eye. 'Pious men have inflicted a wrong on pious women, in gagging their mouths. Oh yes! God calls forth a woman – he says to her, *Phoebe, will you speak?* How could I refuse? Will you hear Jesus's words – not my words – of comfort?'

It's a relief that someone is saying something. Mr Ritter shakes Mrs Palmer by the hand, introducing her as an evangelist with whom he's happy to be acquainted. This acknowledgment is enough. And presumably Christian staged this, Anna thinks.

Mrs Palmer pithily outlines the shorter way to Holiness and how we can be holy now, this very moment, resting on Christ.

And we can continue to be holy. Complete sanctification is ours with conversion.

Easy as that!

Mrs Palmer's voice is a powerful, carrying instrument. It reaches from end to end of the green. What is she, some kind of Methodist? Yes, a Methodist. Ah, that explains it. No proper sense of sin. No understanding of predestination. No sense of a woman's place. But she possesses all an entertainer's confidence in manipulating a crowd, acting on a stage, performing before an audience. Phoebe Palmer, whichever way you take her, is a sensation.

She's naturally timid, the voluble little woman explains – but when God taps you on the shoulder, what can you do? 'I'll give you my testimony and you will judge. Everything He did for me, He'll do for all of you, my dears.'

What impresses the crowd is Phoebe's account of how the

death of three of her four children brought her to this ministry. Alexander, Phoebe's firstborn, died aged nine months in 1829. Her second son died in 1830, seven weeks old. Her fourth child, Eliza, was burnt to death in a fire which caught the gauze curtain of her cradle.

'Can you conceive the grief of it?'

A murmur of assent rises from the women in the crowd.

'I know you can, I see you can.'

Phoebe's head is bent, her hands are clasped; she stands still as a statue.

'My Eliza is in heaven,' she says, pointing upwards. 'Doing an angel service. And now I have resolved that the time I would have devoted to her shall be spent in work for Jesus. And if I'm diligent in carrying out my resolve, this child's death may result in the rebirth of many.'

And as suddenly as she appeared, Mrs Palmer quits the platform, rejoins her husband in the crowd and becomes an anonymous little woman in brown.

The hymn, 'And Can It Be?', rises on the west side of the green. And spreads.

*And can it be that I should gain An interest in my Saviour's blood?*

The body of the crowd catches fire: *Died he for me, who caused his pain?*

As the chorus is reached, the entire green is alight.

*Amazing love, how can it be That thou, my God, shouldst die for me?*

They're weeping; they're on their knees. The scene in the wake of Mrs Palmer's speech resembles the vast camp meetings led by Wesley and Whitefield.

A ragged boy of no more than ten raises his voice, to the astonishment of all, and a pauper woman from Fighelbourn, a Methodist, presses forward and shouts 'O Jesus!' over and over again until she sinks from exhaustion. In the tumult around her, another woman, understood to be her next-door neighbour, stands over her and prays for her until she's hoarse. Both women have to be carried off, insensible.

Many hours pass in a delirium of ecstasy, or rather of competing raptures. One by one the preachers mount the dais to speak. But the Spirit is everywhere. Other lay preachers have arisen in different areas of the field and only those in direct proximity can hear their voices. In the eastern corner, the newly saved are gathered together in a flock, queuing to be interviewed by a group of lay preachers. For hours the crowd, growing rather than waning as news travels through the region, prays and weeps and sings. And faints, for there's nothing to eat or drink until enterprising pie-men appear.

As the twilit air thickens, Isaiah finds his voice and, with a few brief sentences, welcomes to Wiltshire the person of the risen Lord. He has witnessed Jesus walking amongst the people, dressed as a local shepherd and carrying over his shoulder a lamb. Isaiah has not imagined Him. He has seen Him – with his mortal eyes – in the flesh – as clearly as he stands here now. Jesus made his way barefoot and bleeding through the multitude, looking into each face, his hand raised in blessing.

Nothing will be the same now, Isaiah predicts. Inspiration will spread from town to town, the length and breadth of England. It will travel to the four corners of the earth. Peace on earth. The poor will be clothed, the hungry fed. Secularism will die, and the Anglican church will be disestablished. Science will bow to the Gospels. The world will be changed, you'll see.

# Chapter 22

## 1871

A girl is – disgracefully – turning cartwheels in the Close. The carved saints and bishops and kings on the cathedral front stare over her head, all save one stone bishop who bends his neck and angles his reproachful gaze down at the cartwheeler. Beatrice, who is to meet Mr and Mrs Quarles here, has arrived, as ever, early. It hasn't been something she particularly relished, the invitation to the world of the Established Church and its grand men. The mediaeval cathedral seems to her somewhere between museum and mausoleum – but how its towering splendour draws you. At first she's as interested in the warm and breathing presence of the lively little girl as in the architectural wonder. And yet: look at the blond and beautiful stone. Look at the grandeur both of concept and craft, a monument fashioned in the days before modern engineering. Beatrice cranes her neck.

With raised eyebrows, she pays up her entrance fee: sixpence towards the cathedral fabric. The edifice is still being restored, its soaring columns and exquisite fan vaulting strengthened and beautified. The heart is lifted and sails way above your head. Slender Purbeck marble pillars rise to support the intricate vaulting like a forest of heavenly trees. And yet, and yet: Beatrice deplores the odious Chantry built with the filthiest lucre, so that monks could pray to exempt the souls of the rich from thousands of years in Purgatory. She recoils from the warrior barons in chain mail on their tombstones and from the bishops, condemned as 'bite-sheeps' by her Puritan ancestors.

And yet, and yet.

As she walks into the echoing nave, Beatrice again spots the girl. This scrap of dauntless mischief has somehow or other found her way into the cathedral – doubtless eluding the entrance fee. She skips and whirls, flinging arms and legs about, giddy skirts spinning. Yes, go on, dance, you little warm moment in the cathedral's ancient chill. Several men in black cassocks are already striding towards her.

And the child is gone, racing down the nave and out into the brightness.

Beatrice's heart squeezes at the painful resemblance to Magdalena. She lingers at the aristocratic tombs. You can't help but notice, at the feet of the effigies, the touching little dogs and horses eternally watchful at the corners of the great warriors' stone beds.

She's glad when the Quarleses arrive with General Fox the antiquary: not the kind of company Beatrice could ever have expected to keep but Christian is a great and celebrated man now. Doors open to you and there's some obligation to go through them, according to her husband. You might prefer it on occasion if they remained closed.

At the dinner they are consuming the Great Bustard.

The last Great Bustard in England. An exclusive treat! The bird, a member of the turkey family, was once so common, General Fox is saying, that every mediaeval family in England could enjoy a roasted bird for its Christmas dinner. And the creature has been extinct in our land for forty years.

'So, if they are extinct,' says Beatrice, 'how come we are eating this?' The scent of the meat as it's carved is delicious. Her mouth waters and she swallows hard. Her pregnancy has reached the stage which succeeds the nausea, when you feel elated – and hungry. Always ravenous and always eating. Forever pregnant and never your own. And years of the same to come. She feels as if she could consume the whole thirty-pound bird herself.

'Ah, well, it must have blown in from the Continent. From France, I assume,' explains their host, Mr Stevens, the director of the Museum. 'This hen bird was sighted in a group of four above the Downs at Shrewton by, of all people, a bird scarer. The lad saw it was a big bird and took aim. With a marble. Quite a feat – to shoot a hen bird from 132 yards with a marble! He duly passed it on to the farmer. Who sent it on to me.'

'A thoroughly honest bird scarer,' comments Mrs Quarles.

Maybe, thinks Beatrice, there's another bustard the enterprising lad kept for his own table. The plates are set before them. The ten guests taste the novel flesh – oh, luscious, the most succulent Beatrice has tasted. The meat melts in her mouth.

Anna turns her head, looks into Beatrice's eyes. The last of these creatures on your earth and you are devouring it. You are just a stomach on legs. All of you. What are you doing cheek by jowl with these Tories of the shires? Beatrice lays down her knife and fork. She can't swallow. Come on, chew. The meat wedges in her throat. Beatrice takes a drink of water; coughs the morsel into her handkerchief without drawing attention to herself.

'The taxidermist has stuffed the very bird we're eating,' Mr

Stevens goes on. 'And we have displayed it behind glass, to honour the last Great Bustard – and immortalize, so to speak, our meal. Some memorable facts about the bird for you. Its wings can stretch to seven feet. Its flesh was prized by the Ancient Greeks. Aristotle calls it flavoursome. It appears from General Fox's investigations that the Great Bustard was relished in the Stone Age.'

Mrs Stevens, proud of her cook's prowess, tells the guests of a recipe in the book of a French chef, Grimod de la Reynière. 'It begins, Stuff an olive with capers and anchovies and put it in a garden warbler. Put the warbler in an ortolan – I'm not familiar with an ortolan, doubtless a French bird. Then put the ortolan in a (was it, Mr Stevens?) lark, the lark in a thrush ... and so on and so on, a quail ... in a partridge ... a teal ... a duck ... put the duck in the turkey and, finally, the turkey in a bustard. I forget all the avians in the recipe – sixteen in all. You cook it for a whole day.'

'Now that I should like to have tasted,' says Dr Quarles.

'Does it not seem sad to you, Dr Quarles,' Beatrice hears herself say. 'To rejoice in the extinction of one of God's creatures?'

'Well, yes indeed, dear Mrs Ritter. A signal loss to modern sportsmen. And to modern eaters. Game birds require careful management.'

'I didn't quite mean that.'

Beatrice is looked at with some condescension. It's just the sort of priggish thing a Baptist lady might be expected to say. A Baptist lady, moreover, who has just consumed her portion of the last of the species with gusto and perhaps exhibiting less than perfect table manners. Nobody likes to remind Mrs Ritter that the animals were created by the Almighty for our use. Or to pour scorn on the current fad for subsisting on vegetables and objecting to vivisection.

'Extinction of species is indeed a lamentable fact,' says Mr Stevens. 'But a fact nevertheless. Here at the Museum we've done our best to record the local flora and fauna that have been, in the course of things, sadly (as you say) lost. Natural selection, if you take that view, is the law that creatures who cannot adapt must die.'

'Oh no,' says Beatrice, blushing deeply. 'I don't take that view.' She says no more.

Christian does take that view, of course, and sees no discrepancy between Genesis and Mr Darwin's revelations. So much of what ten years ago was regarded as atheistic has lost its sting and been assimilated into an idea of progress. When the ladies retire for coffee, Beatrice, feeling queasy, eyes the Great Bustard she has just devoured in its glass case. A beautiful piece of work, as the ladies agree.

*

Magdalena is out playing in the wilderness. Again. She has given Beatrice the slip. She's always doing it. And of course she has taken Florence with her – Florence who'd never have gone of her own volition and really doesn't like to dirty her pinafore but who can rarely say no to her strong-minded cousin. She cannot say no to her mother either, or Papa, or anyone in the world, which places her in a constant dilemma. A premature frown mark has imprinted itself between Florence's eyebrows. Sitting with her eldest daughter, Beatrice often finds herself trying to smooth the frown mark away with her finger tips. Florence wants to please, to defer, but will do it promiscuously, without regard to the structure of the hierarchy.

All this changes when Florence's Papa is at home. A model household greets Christian, dreading his awe-inspiring silences, the straight blue looks from his handsome all-seeing eyes. Christian never raises his voice; never has to. Sitting each child in turn on his knee, he enquires after their little deeds and offers them loving counsel, as once he did to Beatrice as a youngster. A great man in the church, known on five continents, a powerful speaker and a tireless fund-raiser, Christian has founded an orphanage and an almshouse. Mr Beecher, the subject of sexual scandal in his New York church, is no longer Christian's watchword. His gaze is bent on the momentous business in which God has engaged him. We all creep on tiptoe, Beatrice thinks, around the aura of perfection Christian carries. Those tender moments when their firstborn died seem like dreams.

And of course we have to welcome his protégées. Ruth Leyton has given place to Esther, the daughter of the missionary Herbert Thoms. Esther, who is being educated in London, spends her vacations at Sarum House. She's a pious child rather too eager to declare herself a backsliding daughter before any and every congregation where personal testimony is sought. Beatrice has given up attempting to warn her high-minded husband. She locks herself into the room Anna used as her study when she can stand it no more.

Florence appears as if on cue and looks at her mother with melting eyes. She holds up her hand, dripping with blood where a blade of crabgrass has pierced the webbing between thumb and forefinger. Making no complaint, she brings her hand to her mouth and sucks it, then takes another look. To her dismay beads of blood seep out. It's bleeding rather freely and must be smarting. Florence seldom acknowledges pain in front of the spartan Magdalena, who now appears beside her, skirt hitched up in her belt, and says, 'Flossie's cut her hand, I'm afraid. A little bit.'

'I can see that. We'll bind it up for her now. And where's her hat? Pull down your skirt, Magdalena, do. I've told you before about that. Haven't I?' She binds the cut, which is tiny.

'Hundreds of times. You're a young lady now and must behave like one. I saw a little girl in the cathedral close turning cartwheels. And she reminded me of you, darling. You are nearly a young woman now and cannot afford to behave in this way. It will be thought immodest.'

Obligingly Magdalena drags down her wayward skirt. Beatrice, who has indulged her niece more than any of her own, is concerned for Magdalena. Have I spoilt her? No, but I've come close to it. She's so original – and along with this goes such a blitheness of disposition. She'll achieve something in the world, the child has recently announced, something *tre-men-jous!* Isn't that pride, Magdalena dear? Yes! Good pride, proper pride! Hopping from foot to foot, she spun like a top until she tumbled in a heap. With every minute Magdalena draws nearer to obstacles that will floor her or force her to fight. The leaking of blood, the griping of pain, sensations of shame, tight corsets. Beatrice winces at the premonition of what is about to thwart agile, intelligent, never-say-die, affectionate Magdalena, who now comes up close to say, 'Sorry, Auntie *cariad*. It's up the tree, her hat.'

'For goodness' sake! I hope you've not been luring Florence up trees. It's so dangerous and it's not ladylike. Is it?'

'Not really.'

'Not at all. Which tree?'

'Oh no, I wouldn't let her climb. I was the one who threw it. We were playing catch; it skims really well. The beech tree.'

The straw boater is resting on the cross-bough. Beatrice hoists Magdalena so that she can grab for it. As she brings the child down, the scallywag's dark, sparkling eyes arrest Beatrice's and although Maggie is flaxen-haired where her mother was dark, they're Annie's eyes and also the eyes of Will. Beatrice's heart squeezes, a double pang. She holds Magdalena's lithe, light body up against her own for a moment and feels the drumming heart under the layers of cotton. In her mind's eye a dead sister is whirling round the Pentecost lawn, face brown as a labourer's, around and around until you're dizzy watching her. Papa is egging her on, her stepmother's asking, 'Who'll have dear Anna if she grows up like this?'

'Don't lead Florence on, Maggie my sweetheart. Now don't. She's only a little person, isn't she? And small for her age. She could hurt herself badly and you wouldn't want to have caused that.'

'All right, Auntie Bee. I won't.'

'Don't just promise, do it – or rather don't do it. Florence would follow you anywhere, you know that. It gives you a special responsibility. Do you understand that?'

'Yes.'

A small hand with grime under the fingernails, stained with juice from stolen berries, is placed on Beatrice's own. The raspberry mouth comes close and offers a kiss. Anna's daughter waits to be absolutely sure she is forgiven. There's that urgent look on her face: she cannot *live* if she is not certain of forgiveness. Beatrice can't help but smile. There's purple juice round Florence's mouth too.

'Ah, Maggie, whatever shall we do with you?'

Magdalena's promises don't mean a thing, when it comes down to it. I really should speak to Will about this, she thinks, when he and Jane visit. But I might not.

Mr Moody the revivalist and Mr Sankey the singing evangelist have been staying with the Anwyls in Manchester. This is where the future lies, according to Will, in mass meetings staged at the Free Trade Hall, witnessing tens of thousands of conversions. Powerful forces are required in this day and age to defend against the tides of atheism and secularity. Beside Moody and Sankey the Welsh Revival seemed a sideshow. The Chauntsey Awakening could only be accounted a brief prelude. For the Holy Boy of West Grimstead, the great hope of Wiltshire Dissent, burnt out. Occasionally you see Isaiah Minety at the back of his father's shop, taking batches of loaves from the oven or pummelling the dough. And what to make of this Beatrice has no idea. Isaiah stretched himself too far, is Mrs Elias's view: the odd lad had no background, no education and perhaps in the end no calling. Her own sons have avoided the ministry. Piano tuners and music teachers, they have quit the nest for Huddersfield and Sheffield. Of the new generation not one has entered the ministry.

Will uses such horrible slangy language; he has caught the modern idiom. The American missions to Britain leave Beatrice cold. To her the old ways still seem best: what she has received from her father and her father's father stand her in good stead. Will's mind at the best of times resembled the feather they used to blow round the drawing room in those games that seem so long ago.

'Businesslike evangelists!' Will has said. 'That's what we want. Modern professional men, oh, and ladies, of course, like my wife, who know how to stage events. Conversions by the thousand – tens of thousands – hundreds of thousands. The Florian Steet Awakening was less a precursor than an echo. Using up-to-date methods, if you add up the figures, you'll have the whole population of our islands Christian within twenty years. That's the modern way! How else could we stem the rot of freethinking and scepticism? Ah, Beatrice, you should have heard seventeen thousand people singing "There is a fountain filled with blood!" It nearly took the roof off! Music you'd normally hear in a tavern or music hall is now captured for God! And then we were all asked to bow our heads in silent prayer. As we did so, a whisper began, the organ sighed. And then, oh so softly, Mr Sankey was singing a solo – "Come home, come home, o prodigal child". And the massed choir took up the chorus, with the organ bursting out in majesty. Come home, come home. Knocks poor old Spurgeon into a cocked hat. We were all in tears.'

Oh yes, she thought, God's circus in a big top.

How thankful Beatrice feels to be resident in a backwater where, after that unprecedented convulsion, talk centres on church redecoration and the next bazaar. Can it really be eight years since Anna went? And Mrs Sala insisted, against all protocol and decency, not only on attending the funeral but on speaking too. Well, don't think of that.

What she said, of course, was beautiful. Allegedly. There was no gainsaying that. Apparently. Mrs Sala – who had no business there on any grounds, as being a female, a notorious adulteress, an infidel and hardly a true friend to Anna – arose and insisted on speaking. She described Anna Pentecost, so Beatrice was told. She'd prepared a text from which she had the effrontery to read. But what did she say, Christian? Beatrice asked, dry-mouthed. What exactly? He couldn't reproduce the message, he said, for the effect depended not only on the words but on that exquisite contralto voice. It seemed to them all that Anna rose up there in the midst of them, to the life, in all her loveliness. At first Christian had been taken aback; he could not approve of Mrs Sala's behaviour, what he knew of it. But when she spoke ... it was necessary to listen. It was not long, he said. Or it did not seem so. When she had spoken, Mrs Sala left. And when Beatrice asked Will, he said more or less the same.

I'll never forgive her, Beatrice thought. The harpy. Snatching my sister from me at the last moment. The bitterness of it, the fury. And, even worse, Mrs Sala seems to be outliving her shame. Her writings soar above it. Crowds of worshippers, so Mrs Elias has reported, gather at her At-Homes, where the authoress gives readings from her works, dressed in black evening dress hung with diamonds. That great ugly horse-face. That almost-not-a-woman at all.

Forget all that. With time the fury settles; only at night Mrs Sala will keep appearing in Beatrice's dreams, veiled sometimes; when the veil's removed the pockmarked face of Lore Ritter is disclosed.

When Will left Chauntsey for a church in Manchester, he seized the chance to change his reputation. Will has charmed his way into powerful circles; he speaks a different language. Beatrice shelters his child in her garden and puts off the day when Magdalena must be yielded up to her father and her evangelising stepmother. Perhaps that day will not come. At least do not let it come soon. Annie's daughter with her harum-scarum ways and her ravishing smile tugs at Beatrice's heartstrings more than any of her own brood, nearly as much as Luke did in that other world when her wound was fresh.

God has chastised Mrs Ritter. She has bent, chastened, to the lash. But then, it appeared, He withdrew his wrath. The torture became less. Beatrice lay where she had fallen until the sense came that the angel of death might have passed over. For now. She ventured into the garden, bareheaded, under the fine rain and found calm. Anna's pony was led riderless from the stable, hooves clopping in the quiet. Anna's robust daughter slept soundly in her cot, her face flushed in sleep.

One by one her own children arrived, and lived. Then Beatrice knew that God's wrath was appeased.

Gradually she began to flag under the endless childbearing. I am a broodmare, Beatrice sometimes thinks: my body is not my own.

Amy Pentecost comes rushing out, calling that Mr and Mrs

Anwyl are here. No change has been as strange as the embarrassed adjustment forced on Beatrice by the transformation of a servant into a sister-in-law. Mr and Mrs Jocelyn Pentecost had been secretly married, it appeared, for a year. Married, not even in a church but in a London register office, their union witnessed by Mr and Mrs Munby. Good that Mama and Papa never lived to see their one son descend to this breach of protocol.

Not that Amy isn't one's spiritual equal – of course she is. Equality before God is at the foundation of Christian belief and Beatrice scorns anyone who questions it. Oh, but our social equal? – no, never. Joss is not without wry enjoyment of the general consternation. Sometimes, he confesses, to a burst of hilarity from his wife, it was a near thing. For instance, when you came into my room to clear or clean, many a time my Amy was hiding *under the bed!* – ha! – with her lord and master perched on it in case you decided to look for dust and smoke her out. Yes! Really! What a joke! He couldn't bring himself to look particularly shamefaced. Rather the reverse. Beatrice, stunned, senses that Joss positively relished the conspiracy and will hanker after his secret and forbidden world now that things are out in the open.

What does he see in Amy? Plump and waddling in gait. Hair rather thin and mousy brown. No sense of how to drink a cup of tea, though you'd think she'd have learned in the years of studying Pentecost manners. Her Wiltshire burr, raucous, snorting laughter, muscular arms and broad hands. And worst of all is Amy's indifference to the things of the spirit. Will Joss ever be baptized? Probably not now. To treat Amy as an equal is out of the question and Joss sees and resents the slight. 'My wife has more reality in her little finger than some of us have in our whole bodies – and a jolly sight less pretension,' he has rebuked his sister. Did Anna have any inkling? Or perhaps she was party to the secret? Joss has never said. The one fly in his ointment is Amy's growing jealousy of the two servants who've replaced her, Tabitha and Jenny.

The children harbour no such prejudice. They flock around Amy for the barley sugar she carries in her pocket. Her solid, comfortable body is as pleasing to them as it is to her husband.

Magdalena hugs Beatrice. 'Is it my Papa, Auntie Amy? Oh lovely, lovely! Is *she* with him though?'

'Try to be courteous to Jane, dear,' Beatrice advises. 'And call her Mama without being asked. Your father wishes it. She is a good woman and fond of you.'

Magdalena's face is expressive on that subject but she says nothing, allowing Beatrice to tidy her hair and stoop to pull off the sticky catchweed from her skirts.

'Smile nicely at Jane when you see her, dear, and let her kiss you and don't scowl.'

Magdalena gives a wriggle and a squirm. She pouts, scuffing the toe of her shoe against the paving stone. Florence does the same, without knowing why, her underlip over her upper one, tears coming to her eyes although she has no idea of feeling sad. Harry, coming into this scene of woe in the nurse's arms, howls, arches his back and hurls his body backwards. Beatrice removes him from the nurse and pacifies him.

She understands. Magdalena is worried that, if her behaviour is too accommodating, Jane will want to take her back with them. Magdalena is bright and intuitive. Beatrice will not remonstrate with her. You know I'm on your side, heart's darling, don't you? she says silently to her niece. You are mine. I shall never willingly give you up but one must be canny and proceed by indirection: you understand that. With you I shall not fail, I never shall. She straightens the ribbon in Magdalena's hair and, with Harry morose and snivelling against her shoulder, takes her niece's hand.

Amy is entertaining the Anwyls in the parlour. You can hear it from the kitchen door, her loud, crude patois. Better relieve them.

What a shock: Will's hair has gone completely white. The face still young beneath the abundant silver curls is piquant and arresting. He has put on weight and has a small paunch. He affects dandy clothes, doubtless selected for him by the second Mrs Anwyl. Bounding in, Magdalena flings herself into her father's arms. He scoops her up and spins her round. Begins to romp. Throws her in the air. Catches and clasps her tight against him. 'My, how you've grown! Are you sure it's really you? Are you Maggie Anwyl or a very tall fairy?'

One can read on Jane's face, through the mask of propriety, how little she wishes to be at Sarum House. But you knew what you were getting, Beatrice thinks, when you married Will. She shakes the resolute smiler's mauve-gloved hand and asks the usual questions. You've netted a widower nineteen years your junior, with a daughter and old ties you will never break – so of course you're bound to think of me as a rival. Jane is one of the lady evangelists who've sprung up in the wake of Mrs Palmer and have no hesitation in preaching alongside the menfolk on public platforms.

Jane pats the sofa beside her; Will sets Magdalena down. He cannot take his eyes off his child; is mesmerised and saddened, at once famished and fed. No doubt it's the mirror of the beloved face he sees – and wants to see – and can't bear to see, which may be one reason why he visits rather rarely.

'Come and greet your dear stepmama, Maggie,' he encourages her. 'She has brought you something nice, haven't you, dear?'

Jane's smile pleads. It says to the child, 'You are strong and I am weak. Give me a chance to please you.'

Magdalena's composed, sharp features reply, 'I'm sorry to have to disappoint you but you're wasting your time and money. I do not like you. I cannot be bought.'

Jane takes from her bag a parcel wrapped in a piece of lace. 'Just a little something for you, dear. And how are your lessons going, Magdalena? Does the dear one attend church and Sunday school regularly, Beatrice? I always did at your age, you know, three times a day on the Sabbath ... Ah, the little angel! Has the angel hurt its wing? Do come to Auntie Jane!'

Florence, all pale curls and smiles, reaches out with her unbandaged hand for Jane's parcel.

'You have it, Flossie.' Magdalena is altogether too eager to relinquish the gift. 'I don't want it. Go on, take it.'

'Magdalena!' says Beatrice.

'It's all right.' Jane is still smiling. 'I understand. I'm not offended, Magdalena, not in the least; I expect you're a teeny bit nervous. And you don't like to have nice gifts when your cousin has nothing.'

Florence has the parcel torn open in a trice. 'Oh, it's, what is it? Some sewing? Handkerchiefs to embroider?' she says. 'That's nice, Auntie Jane. You have them, Maggie.'

'I've got plenty. Nice *plain* ones. Big proper ones for the snot.'

Jane feigns deafness; Beatrice gives up; Florence perches on a low stool with her doll; Will stifles his amusement. Magdalena goes up to her father, leans forward so that he can see nothing but her face and gazes into his eyes. Soon she's seated on Will's lap, sharing toasted teacake with him, butter running down her chin. I shall not let you take her, thinks Beatrice, staring at her sister-in-law through viper eyes. She includes the father in her pledge.

When Annie went, she and Will could not go near one another. Every time he entered a room, Beatrice departed, carrying the baby. She'd leave the house altogether if possible. The pain each carried was a knife in the other's heart.

They had to stop this senseless dance because the baby, against all expectations, appeared determined to thrive. It was robust. Magdalena soon smiled, made jolly spitty, chortling noises, waved chubby arms and legs and generally insisted that the world take notice, for she was here to stay. Maggie was not to know that she had killed her mother.

After a difficult birth, Anna's fever climbed. She was scalding hot to the touch. Beatrice ordered in ice to bring down her temperature. She sat with her sister day and night. You are not leaving me. I will not permit it. By and by, Anna perceived through bouts of delirium that she was unlikely to survive. Her sister and husband stayed at either side of the bed.

'Yes, *cariad*,' Will said. 'Your mother and father will be there. And our Magdalena will come to you. And Lore will be there, tenderly waiting. All the people you've loved. Shining. And Beatrice and I will come to you.'

'Love is God,' said Anna.

Strictly speaking she'd got it the wrong way round but Beatrice didn't wrangle. She accepted what Anna was able to offer. 'Yes,' she said. 'That's right, Love is God.'

Anna agreed to take communion from Will's hands, more perhaps for her husband's sake than her own. She begged pardon of all those she had offended.

'You'll look after Magdalena for me?'

'I will.'

'You'll be a true mother to her?'

'Annie, I will. She will be as my own child. Are you in pain, darling?'

'I can't honestly say I am,' replied Anna, and slept.

Mrs Sala was detected mooning under the windows at dusk. I let her down, she moaned. Did she mention me? Had she no message for me? Nothing at all? Please do not turn me away. I loved her. I let her down. Will went out to speak to the woman. Beatrice watched her walk away on Mr Sala's arm, into her fame and notoriety. Good. Go and be damned.

And then, a couple of years later, Mrs Sala returned. It was a chilly, misty morning, the red beads of rosehips suddenly gleaming at you as beams of sun pierced the mist. She appeared at the front door in a rust-coloured fur-trimmed cloak. By her side was a boy of perhaps nine or ten years of age – her son, very obviously, though in him all that made his mother unattractive produced a harmonious impression. The son had been restored to his mother at the death of her legitimate husband.

Now that she'd legally married Baines Sala, their relatives clamoured to receive and visit her and to bask in her celebrity. Miriam Sala had been rehabilitated; the intelligentsia of Europe were at her feet. Mrs Sala's works had been translated into sundry languages. A collection of her *Wise, Witty and Tender Sayings* had been selected and published by a Miss Jackson, one of her disciples. Mrs Sala's fictions were works with a high moral tone, apparently; their heroines made mistakes for noble reasons, in a world unfitted to value or understand them. Beatrice knew this, though she'd never read a word. The change in Mrs Sala's circumstances and status made no difference to her feeling. It was sheer hypocrisy to allow a sinner to profit from the death of the man she had wronged.

What Mrs Sala wanted, it appeared, was the correspondence she'd shared with Anna. She came straight to the point, without prelude or prevarication. The woman's eyes were powerful, a pale colour, intense, arresting, burning in the plain face, which might have been that of an agricultural labourer clothed in a lady's finery.

All Beatrice said was, 'I cannot oblige.'

'But are there letters of mine? If so, I hope you will return them to me, Mrs Ritter. This is my dear son, Johnnie.'

The introduction meant: for Johnnie's innocent sake, return my letters which might perhaps cause scandal for him at some later date.

'How do you do, Johnnie,' said Beatrice. 'But you are mistaken, Mrs Sala, there are no letters extant.'

'Nothing whatever?'

'Nothing whatsoever.'

Beatrice spoke in an even tone, without animus. She perceived her visitor's flinching vulnerability to insult. But after all, the woman should be relieved to know that no record survived to distress either herself or her heir in years to come. Mrs Sala however seemed heartbroken. Nothing was left, nothing whatever. There was no echo, no trace. She had to leave with empty hands. Her son opened the gate onto the road; she turned, an autumnal figure, and looked back for a moment. The mist rolled in and took her away with it.

*

Entering the room Anna had called her study, Beatrice seated herself at the desk and turned the key in the lock of the metal box. It was brimming with papers. Scraps and shreds. Blank pages torn from old books. Wrapping paper. Wallpaper. Anna's childish writing, crabbed, backward-leaning, crawled everywhere. Some of it was written backwards. Often there were no spaces between words; punctuation was absent. Anna had been transcribing the fragments and linking them up into a sequence of observations or stories.

As Beatrice dipped her hand in the sea of papers, she came

up with a flour bag crammed with letters. Letters from Miriam Sala. Letters from Lore.

She began to read. The children romped with Amy in the garden. The baby screamed. She ignored it. She read on. The grandfather clock struck the hour. Someone was knocking on the door. Beatrice read on. She closed the lid of the chest. She let herself out. The rest of that day was a blank.

Beatrice wandered – vainly – around the wilderness in search of the tump. She came upstairs with scissors and began to cut out and glue. She locked herself in. It went on for weeks, the deciphering and the sorting and the separation. Beatrice was inside Anna's locked mind. Fascinated, enthralled. And yet judging, censoring. Saying, This may be kept but this must be discarded. She had pledged herself to preserve a picture of Anna that would represent her best qualities for those who came after. And later she would transcribe it in her own handwriting and destroy everything else.

One has a duty to one's children.

Was it the following week that Beatrice lit the fire?

'What are you burning?' Joss strolled out to ask.

'Just some old papers.' I am burning our shame, your shame, Papa's shame, Beatrice didn't say. I'm burning a stigma. It will be completely forgotten and erased.

'What in God's name are you doing, Beatrice?' Joss demanded. 'These are my sister's papers. They don't belong to you.'

Joss was angry and cursed. She was shocked at his gutter language. But I'm doing this in God's name, Beatrice thought. You should thank me. It's my clear duty. Whatever that was with Lore, it was – what can one say? – unnatural. A sin against Papa, against the sacred bonds of family, against God's law. Beatrice's face flamed in the scalding fire. It's impossible to unknow something one knows but nevertheless let me try. Draw the veil, decently. The fault was in Lore, not my sister. Christian can never have had the slightest suspicion. Will cannot have known. It's over now, Beatrice thought, thank Heaven, over, and Joss, down on his knees and raging, was unable to salvage more than a few scraps, which he took into the house as if they were sacred scriptures. Finally Beatrice fed the odious books to the flames. *Freedom Seeks Her* was the last to burn.

*

Within a generation all trace of Anna's waywardness will have vanished. And already Beatrice's own memory of her sister has softened. The price is a sense of having somehow mislaid something. She's forever casting around for something she can't quite name. Whatever is it? Beatrice occasionally finds herself standing in the wilderness not quite sure what she came out here for. Doubtless pregnancy does strange things to the memory. This endless fruitfulness of hers.

Where have you gone, Annie? Beatrice can't help asking in the still reaches of the night. Her sister's faith was, at best, intermittent and anomalous. Heresy was a magnet. She'd go out of her way to make provocative assertions, which perhaps she didn't mean. Where a line was drawn – thus far and no further – you could be sure that Anna would be tempted. And yet wasn't it also the case that whenever she did cross the line, she'd keep fairly close to it, in case she wanted to skip back? And, oh, if Anna *had* gone too far, surely our kind Lord would have gone the extra distance, made up the difference for her. Curious how much easier it is to believe in the possibility of mercy for others than for oneself. People have had to remind Beatrice that theirs is the God of love who died for all of us, including herself.

But my shortcomings, Beatrice would lament. My failings.

One day, not long before he left for his ministry in Manchester, Will caught her unawares. He stood with her beneath the larch at the edge of the wilderness and ministered to her. He said, 'Shortcomings? You have no shortcomings. None. The anchor has gone. The winds blow. The earth spins. But not because of your shortcomings. Do believe me. I would know, wouldn't I, if you had? Annie and I agreed, we two were both much of a muchness and God makes do with that, if we have loved – or tried to love. Annie understood that very well.' He explained that he, like Christian, no longer believed in Calvinism or hellfire. It had all been superceded.

Beatrice stands by the hearth, rocking to and fro, with Harry quiet in her arms. Although he has been cross and irksome all day, the teeth piercing the lower gums making him drool and whimper, Beatrice doesn't feel inclined to lose his company. Everyone is in bed. The only light comes from the hearth. She lays the baby on her lap and they look at one another. Quite steadily. The fire rustles and flaps.

She thinks of Will and he comes. One moment he was in her mind, the next he's in the room. He hesitates, explaining that he came down to smoke a pipe. He's sorry if he's disturbing her.

'No, you're not. Of course not.' She relaxes and smiles. 'Come and sit with me for a moment.'

'There's something I need to ask you, Beatrice.'

'Yes?'

'About Magdalena.'

'No, don't ask me.'

'Dearest – I know you love her – but, think, I love her too. And my wife is eager to take care of her. We cannot have children of our own and it makes sense –'

'I can't lose Magdalena, Will, and she can't lose me. No. I

promised Annie. No. Don't – please – ever – even speak of taking her away from her home. You will kill me.'

'But I'm her father.'

'I'd rather give you Florence. Take Florence. Take her. Go on. Tell your wife I am giving you Florence. By far the easier child. I mean it. And your wife – with the best will in the world – which I know Jane has – forgive me, Will – your wife cannot love the daughter of your first marriage.'

And when he's gone, Beatrice, faint with relief, clutches at Will's promise. It's all he can do for her now and he has done it.

Magdalena is nowhere to be found. She hasn't said goodbye. Perhaps she couldn't bear it. Or maybe she feared that, at the last moment, her father and stepmother would bundle her up and force her to go to Manchester with them: she'd never see her home again.

There are hiding places. Beatrice knows them all: how could she not? Niches and alcoves. The cellar. The store cupboard. She pauses at every point in Sarum House to listen. Mice stir in the wainscots. She sees the black crumbs of their droppings. She listens for the sound of sobbing. Nothing. The clock chime skirls the half hour. Lunchtime soon. No healthy girl of eight can ignore hunger pangs for long. Magdalena may not be in the house at all – but as it's pouring with rain; she's unlikely to be in the garden. Beatrice ticks off all the secret places where the Pentecost girls used to hide and tries them all.

She thinks of one more possibility indoors before she tries the outhouses. Instinct leads her to the broom cupboard under the stairs, with its triangular door.

How is that you know there's someone behind a door even when that person is making no noise at all? But you do.

She pulls open the stiff door and there are the grubby pinafore and scuffed shoes of a foetal girl making herself as inconspicuous as possible as she huddles beside the buckets and mops. Beatrice kneels down. She speaks Magdalena's name softly. Trapped smells of carbolic, lavender polish and menthol flow out. Maggie won't answer. She won't come out. Rather than try to coerce her, Beatrice gets down on her knees and crawls in.

*

# Afterword

A writer of historical fiction, imagining within the gaps of the historical record, plays host to the voices of extraordinary strangers. My story originated in diaries, memoirs, essays and sermons of the nineteenth century: in, for instance, Darwin's notebooks; Emily Brontë's diary papers and the French essays she wrote in Belgium; Edith Simcox's amorous journal; the writings of Mary Benson, the extraordinary lesbian wife of the Archbishop of Canterbury; the personal testaments of the Thomas sisters, the Pountneys and the Winkworths. I followed Philip Gosse to Tenby, G.H. Lewes to Ilfracombe and George Eliot to Swansea.

Such Victorian dissidents, arguing vociferously amongst themselves in my head, contributed to my story's invented composite figures. In Sarah Thomas's wonderful Fairford diary (The Secret Diary of Sarah Thomas: A Victorian Lady, 1860-1865) I found two Baptist sisters and a circle of very human pastors; in George Eliot's journals and letters a narrative of the freethinking female author. Some of my sources invited themselves into my pages to make cameo

337

appearances: Charles Haddon Spurgeon, the Baptist luminary, and his wife Susanna; the lovable John Clifford; Philip and Edmund Gosse; the American revivalist, Phoebe Palmer; Arthur and Hannah Munby; feminists Barbara Bodichon and Bessie Parkes.

I decided to open the story in 1860, the year following both the publication of Darwin's *On the Origin of Species by Means of Natural Selection* and the outbreak in Wales of a spectacular religious Awakening. Anna's 'tump' sprang in part from Darwin's famous 'entangled bank' in the last paragraph of his great work, exemplifying the connection of biodiversity with the laws underlying the 'war of nature'. The setting is an invented village near Salisbury, my mother's home town, where Dissenters and free-thinkers alike were overshadowed by one of the world's most beautiful cathedral spires and where the great plain was the scene of crucial Victorian archaeological discoveries. My people are Baptists partly because my own path led through this branch of Dissent into humanistic agnosticism. The surname Pentecost was the maiden name of a Wiltshire great-aunt, Florence – a rather blessed inheritance, since at Pentecost the Holy Spirit descended on the Apostles, endowing them with the gift of voice.

Locked in sororicidal struggle, the Pentecost sisters test the limits of what was permissible to women in a world of politicised medicine and misogynist law and custom. *Awakening* is a story of virtuous transgressors and transgressive virtue, in which some characters, like the renegade minister, Mr Kyffin, dance on the edge of madness; others turn to the séances of Spiritualism; Dissenters look to Revival or Awakening to deliver them from the age's perceived infidelities. When Awakening comes, it happens darkly and in singular ways: as sexual discovery or as motherhood, as the finding or hearing of a voice in a fractured modern world.

'Christianity is fissiparous,' as Anna remarks, to Beatrice's disgust: the Church splinters into sects and then the sects splinter and the splinters splinter, until each man's hand is against his neighbour's.

Many years ago Alan Shelston of Manchester University introduced me to the study of Victorian literature: I am grateful to Alan for passing on his passion and knowledge. Over the years I have received invaluable help from the staff of the Brontë Parsonage Museum, Haworth. I am grateful to the Revd. Stephen Copson, Honorary Secretary to the Baptist Historical Society, for generously furnishing me with documents relating to nineteenth century Baptist ministers. I thank Dr Lyndall Gordon for our ongoing conversation about our Victorian foremothers. Of course, any errors and eccentricities are the sole responsibility of the author.

I should like to thank friends of many years for their encouragement and support – especially Helen Williams, Rosalie Wilkins, Barbara Prys-Williams and Andrew Howdle. Andrew will recognise some words of comfort memorialised in the text. I am grateful to M. Wynn Thomas, Neil Reeve and Glyn Pursglove of Swansea University, most learned and kind of colleagues; also to my fellow writers at Swansea, Anne Lauppe-Dunbar, Nigel Jenkins, David Britton, Fflur Dafydd, Alan Bilton, Jon Gower and Jasmine Donahaye. I owe a considerable debt to the staff at Parthian, Richard Davies, Claire Houguez and especially my wise and thoughtful editor, Francesca Rhydderch. I'm endlessly grateful to my children, Emily, Grace and Robin, for their tender support.

I have listed below some of the books that fed the writing, in case readers would like to track me in their snow:

Benson, Mary, journals and letters, in Bolt, Rodney, *As Good as God, as Clever as the Devil: The Impossible Life of Mary Benson*, London: Atlantic Books, 2011.

Brontë, Anne and Emily Jane, *Diary Papers*, as transcribed in Juliet Barker, *The Brontës*, London: Weidenfeld & Nicolson, 1994.

Brontë, Charlotte, *The Letters of Charlotte Brontë*, 2 vols., ed. Margaret Smith, Oxford: Clarendon Press, 1995-2000.

Brontë, Emily, *'Le Chat'* ('The Cat') and *'Le Papillon'* ('The Butterfly'), in Charlotte and Emily Brontë, *The Belgian Essays: A Critical Edition*, ed. & tr. Sue Lonoff, New Haven & London: Yale University Press, 1996.

Clifford, John, 'On the Social Gospel' [together with sermons and writings by other Dissenting preachers], in *Protestant Nonconformist Texts: The Nineteenth Century*, Vol. 3, ed. David Bebbington, with Kenneth Dix & Alan Ruston, Aldershot: Ashgate Publishing, 2006.

Darwin, Charles, *The M and N Notebooks*, in Howard E. Gruber, in *Darwin on Man: Darwin's Early and Unpublished Notebooks,* transcribed and annotated by Paul N. Barrett, London: Wildwood House, 1974.

— *On the Origin of Species, or The Preservation of Favoured Races in the Struggle for Life*. London: John Murray, 1859.

*Eliot, George*, letters and journals, in *The George Eliot Letters*, ed. Gordon S. Haight, 9 vols., New Haven: Yale University Press, 1954-78.

Gosse, Edmund, *Father and Son: A Study of Two Temperaments*, ed. Michael Newton, Oxford University Press: Oxford, 2004.

Gosse, Philip Henry, *Omphalos: An Attempt to Untie the Geological Knot*, London: John van Voorst, 1857.

— *Tenby: A Sea-side Holiday*, London: John van Voorst, 1856.

Holland, William, *Paupers & Pig Killers: The Diary of William Holland, A Somerset Parson, 1799-1818*, ed. Jack Ayres, Stroud: Sutton Publishing, 2003 edn.

Lewes, George Henry, *Sea-side Studies at Ilfracombe, Tenby, the Scilly Isles, and Jersey*, Edinburgh & London: William Blackwood & Sons, 1860.

Lister, Anne, *The Diaries of Anne Lister, 1791-1840*, in *I Know my Own Heart*, ed. Helena Whitbread, New York & London: New York University Press, 1988.

Munby, Arthur, diaries, as transcribed in Derek, Hudson, *Munby, Man of Two Worlds: The Life and Diaries of Arthur J. Munby, 1828-1910*, London: Abacus, 1974.

340

Parkes, Bessie, letters and documents in Emma Lowndes, *Turning Victorian Ladies into Women: The Life of Bessie Rayner Parkes, 1829-1925*, Palo Alto: Academica Press, 2011.

Palmer, Phoebe, *The Way of Holiness*, New York: Palmer & Hughes, 1845.

Pountney, Adelaide, *The Diary of a Victorian Lady: Scenes from her Daily Life, 1864-1865*, illustrated by Adelaide Pountney, foreword by Rachel Sillett, Ludlow: Excellent Press, 1998.

Simcox, Edith, *Autobiography of a Shirtmaker*, in *A Monument to the Memory of George Eliot,* ed. Constance M. Fulmer and Margaret E. Barfield, New York & London: Garland Publishing, 1998.

Smith, Margaret, *From Victorian Wessex: The Diaries of Emily Smith, 1838, 1841, 1852*, Norwich: Solen Press, 2003.

Spurgeon, Charles Haddon, *The Letters of C.H. Spurgeon, The Spurgeon Archive, Daily Devotions, A Defence of Calvinism*, also writings by Susanna Spurgeon, http://www.spurgeon.org/mainpage.htm.

Thomas, Sarah, *The Secret Diary of Sarah Thomas: Life in a Cotswold Market Town, 1860-1865*, ed. June Lewis-Jones, Stroud: Nonsuch Publishing, 1994.

White, William Hale, writing as Mark Rutherford, *The Autobiography of Mark Rutherford, Dissenting Minister*, London: Trubner & Co, 1881.

Winkworth, Catherine and Susanna, *Memorials of Two Sisters: Susanna and Catherine Winkworth*, ed. M.J. Shaen, London: Longman, 1908.